MW01125361

just in time

just in time

escape to new zealand, book eight

rosalind james

Copyright 2015
Rosalind James

All Rights Reserved

Cover design by Robin Ludwig Design Inc.,
http://www.gobookcoverdesign.com/

Formatting by Dallas Hodge, Everything But The Book

synopsis

What happens in Vegas…

Will Tawera doesn't do commitment, except on the rugby field. Moving to Las Vegas to become a kicker for the NFL would be a big change from New Zealand rugby, but then, he's ready for a change. And when he's asked to do a little modeling on the side? Thousands of dollars to hold a beautiful blonde while looking dark, dangerous, tattooed, and Maori? He could do that.

Faith Goodwin doesn't do dark, dangerous men. Especially not when they make her laugh, take her miniature golfing with four-year-olds, and are far too sexy and sweet for comfort. But when Will finds himself in hot water back in New Zealand, who's he going to call? And who would be able to resist answering?

author's note

The Blues and the All Blacks are actual rugby teams. However, this is a work of fiction. Names, characters, places, and incidents are products of the author's imagination or are used fictitiously and are not to be construed as real. Any resemblance to actual events or persons, living or dead, is entirely coincidental.

other books from rosalind james

The Escape to New Zealand series

Reka and Hemi's story: JUST FOR YOU
Hannah and Drew's story: JUST THIS ONCE
Kate and Koti's story: JUST GOOD FRIENDS
Jenna and Finn's story: JUST FOR NOW
Emma and Nic's story: JUST FOR FUN
Ally and Nate's/Kristen and Liam's stories: JUST MY LUCK
Josie and Hugh's story: JUST NOT MINE
Hannah & Drew's story again/Reunion: JUST ONCE MORE
Faith & Will's story: JUST IN TIME

The Not Quite a Billionaire series

Hope and Hemi's story: FIERCE

The Paradise, Idaho series (Montlake Romance)

Zoe & Cal's story: CARRY ME HOME
Kayla & Luke's story: HOLD ME CLOSE (December 2015)

The Kincaids series

Mira and Gabe's story: WELCOME TO PARADISE
Desiree and Alec's story: NOTHING PERSONAL
Alyssa and Joe's story: ASKING FOR TROUBLE

Cover design by Robin Ludwig Design
Inc., http://www.gobookcoverdesign.com

table of contents

new zealand map

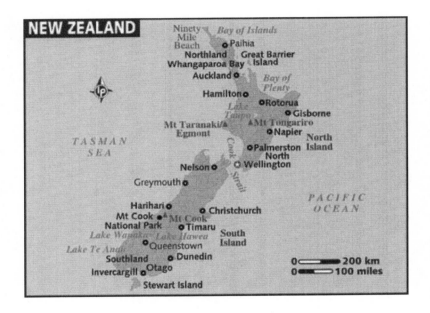

NOTE: A New Zealand glossary appears at the end of this book.

dream date

♡

It all started with Mrs. Johnson's toilet.

Faith Goodwin wielded the blue plastic plunger with everything she had. She was late, and every plunge was making her later. The accordion pleats compressed with a *whoosh,* then released with a sucking sound that...never mind.

"Three"—*whoosh*—"hundred"—*suck*—"dollars," she chanted in her mind. The amount of rent she paid in exchange for managing the six-unit apartment building. It was a good deal, even though she was wearing rubber boots and rubber gloves, and this wasn't the first time she'd unclogged Mrs. Johnson's toilet. Or any toilet.

"It's the colitis." The quavering voice came from a nice, clean, dry spot behind her. "I have to use extra paper. And you know, dear, these toilets could stand to be replaced."

Faith closed her eyes and counted to ten. "You need to start flushing more in...in between, Mrs. Johnson. This makes twice this month."

"Maybe a plumber..." the old lady suggested.

"He'd charge me a hundred dollars to do the exact same thing," Faith said, doing her level best to detach from her surroundings.

1

"So, please. Flush."

She plunged a few more times, then gave the lever a push, crossed her fingers in the yellow gloves, and held her breath. The toilet thought about it for a minute, and then reluctantly decided to resume normal service, the water gurgling its way down the bowl. Yay.

"All right," Faith said. "Good. If you'll hand me the mop and the bleach, I'll clean up."

Yet another job they didn't tell you about during Career Day. She was late for work already, she was going to be later, and she couldn't stay in this spot for another moment. So as usual, she took her mind somewhere else.

She was jogging down the hard-packed sand of the beach in a pink—no, a *black* bikini, which looked great on her, because...well, because this was a fantasy, and she'd obviously put in some gym time before it started. The gentle crescents of blue lapped up onto the shore, delicate scallops edged with cream, and her feet were getting wet, but that was all right, because she was running barefoot, as she did every morning. Past the group of guys throwing a football, and she could see their heads turning out of the corner of her eye. She pretended to ignore them, but she could tell they were watching.

And then one of them streaked past her as if she were standing still, turned and waved an arm, and Faith looked, too. Which was lucky, because the ball was headed towards her like a missile.

She shrieked a little and threw an arm across her face to block it, but even as she did, the man planted a foot, swiveled in mid-step, and was leaping, stretching sideways to intercept the ball. His arms were across her body, the ball was smacking into his palms, and his feet were tangling with hers. She went down on the sand, flat onto her back, the breath knocked out of her by the fall—and by him falling on top of her.

He shoved himself off her where she lay gasping, sprang to his feet in one quick motion, and reached a hand down. "All right?" he asked a little breathlessly. "Bloody hell, I'm sorry. Tell me I haven't hurt you."

Ooh. Her fantasy man had an accent. And the sweetest smile as he hauled her to her feet, looking so relieved at the sight of her smiling back. He started to laugh, white teeth flashing in his tanned face, and she laughed, too.

"Yes, dear?" Mrs. Johnson asked. Because Faith wasn't actually lying on a beach beneath a half-naked man with muscles that required their own ZIP code. She was wringing out a mop into a toilet in an eighty-five-year-old woman's apartment in Las Vegas, and it was January.

"Nothing," Faith said. "Just something I thought of. Or the general ridiculousness of life, I suppose." She gathered her bleach solution and her plunger. Onward and upward.

"Laugh or cry, that's the choice." Mrs. Johnson's smile launched a spiderweb of tiny wrinkles across her face, and her blue eyes twinkled behind her glasses. "Getting old isn't for sissies, and sometimes the rest of life isn't either, is it?"

"Nope. It's not. But, please, next time? Flush more."

After that, she headed back to her apartment again for a shower she didn't have time for, because there was no way she was showing up smelling like Mrs. Johnson's bathroom. No time to dry her hair, either, so she shoved it into a messy bun instead. She was more than twenty minutes late by now, and it was raining. And she still had to pick up the coffee.

sacrifices
♡

"Not exactly Hollywood," Will Tawera said dubiously when his mate Solomon Salesa pulled into the strip mall parking lot on West Charleston Boulevard and stopped in front of a blank storefront with *Calvin Quisp Photography* painted on the single glass door. "You sure this is legit? Because if anything ever looked like a porn studio, it's this."

"And if it is," Solomon said cheerfully, "that's your job. Drag me away before I get myself into trouble."

"Yeh, right. How about if I get carried away myself?"

"Then all bets are off," Solomon said. "I'm not going to promise to drag you away, whatever Lelei thinks. Such a thing as living vicariously."

Will had agreed to come along on this adventure a couple days earlier, when Solomon had invited him to dinner in true hospitable Pacific Islander fashion. Will had turned up at the modest tract home in the Vegas suburbs to eat roast pork and sweet potatoes with Solomon, his pregnant wife Lelei, and their two kids, and it had been one of his better nights in the States.

"Cuz," Will had told Solomon after his first reverential bite, "you know how to make a Maori boy homesick."

"Aw, had to do it," Solomon said with a grin. "Lelei says you're too skinny."

Will laughed out loud, Solomon joining him, as Lelei stammered out her own laughing protest. And that was another thing he missed. Laughing. Pakeha—white people—didn't laugh enough, especially here in the States.

"But I should probably be on the two-grapes diet," Solomon said. "For the audition I've got coming up."

"Oh, no," Lelei said comfortably. "You're perfect as you are."

"Well, it's not going to be you doing the judging," Solomon told his wife. "Or I'd be in, wouldn't I?"

"Really." Will accepted another serving of pork. "You going to be on the big screen? Thought you were all about the football."

He'd met the other man when they were both running through drills for the Las Vegas Outlaws, the NFL's new expansion team. Will's agent had got him the tryout, which was why he was here— that, and to do some offseason training during the break from Southern Hemisphere rugby. Will still wasn't sure how he felt about it, but he hadn't felt like he had anything to lose, either. He was feeling reckless just now, and that was the truth. If the Outlaws wanted a rugby-style kicker and were willing to pay millions to get one, why shouldn't he at least entertain the idea? The States hadn't been in his life plan, but that didn't mean they couldn't be.

For Solomon, though, the tryouts meant more. They meant the difference between working construction and a continued career in the NFL for the big Samoan free agent, who'd spent the last few seasons bouncing on and off various teams' practice squads. Solomon had seemed fit to Will, and he'd have said the other man would be in with a good chance at the linebacker spot. Of course, what he knew about gridiron would have fit on the head of a pin, so he might not be the best judge. But Solomon was going after an acting career as well?

"Not the big screen," Solomon said. "The small one, more like. If I get lucky and they choose me."

5

"Or unlucky," Lelei said. "I still don't like it."

"It's four thousand dollars," Solomon reminded her. "Which would pay a lot of rent. For a few weeks of work—a few days, more like—and I'm laid off anyway."

"Still," Lelei said. "What if the kids find out?"

Solomon cast a glance at four-year-old Sefina, but she was poking her little brother in the side and giggling, not listening to the adults' conversation. "They're not going to find out. I probably won't get it anyway, and if I do?" He shrugged a huge shoulder. "It'd be ten years before any of them cared enough to look at something like this, and by that time, it'd be long buried."

"Something like what?" Will asked. "Or should I ask?"

Solomon sighed. "Nothing that bad. And no, it isn't," he told his wife, who had opened her mouth again. "It's a few photo shoots over three weeks. Five or six times, maybe. They're looking for a brown brother with a tribal tattoo and a set of muscles, willing to strip down to his jeans—and all right, *maybe* his undershorts, and pose with a pretty girl in some...compromising positions."

"Uh-*huh.*" Will tried to keep the smile from showing. "Sounds like you ought to be paying *them.*"

"See," Lelei burst out. "That's what I'm saying."

"Aw, baby," Solomon said. "You know I don't want anybody but you. I'm not interested in some skinny blonde with no..." He coughed. "Curvy parts. But a man's got to work, and for what they're paying? You bet I'll do it. I'd do just about anything for you and the kids, you know that. I'd dig ditches if it came to that. And if I get this? I'll be happy to have it. You want to come with me and check it out?"

"No," she sighed. "Of course not. I trust you. I don't like it, but I trust you."

"Tell you what," Solomon said. "We'll get Will here to come along with me. He can check it out for you. Be my chaperone."

"Will?" Lelei laughed, her mood changing in an instant, back to cheerfulness, and that was another thing Will had missed, that cheerfulness. "I doubt he's had much experience at that."

"Well, no," Will admitted with a grin of his own. "But this is an audition? Just for the blokes, or…"

"Oh," Solomon said, "both. That's what they said. Both."

"And there's going to be some stripping down involved?" Will asked.

"Well, I don't imagine you'd be invited to watch that part," Solomon said. "I'm guessing it's going to be a lot of sitting around and waiting. But with some pretty girls in the room."

"With nothing to do," Will said. "Nervous, like. Needing a bit of a chat-up to distract them while they wait to see if they're, what? Blonde enough? Sexy enough?"

"Both things." Solomon pulled his phone out of a pocket, punched a few buttons, and handed it over. "Here's the ad."

"One male," Will read. "Pacific Islander, tattooed, muscular, minimum height 6'0", max age 32. One female, petite build, delicate, blonde, angel look, under 5'6", max age 25. Erotic imagery, no full nudity. Model release required."

He handed the phone back to Solomon. "Sounds like a big ask. But…" He sighed. "I've eaten at your table, haven't I. I'm obligated."

mr. muffin
♡

Faith hopped out of the truck, juggling her purse, her laptop case, the drink tray, and the bag of muffins. To add to everything else, it was raining, and the drive-through window at Starbucks had been closed. She'd had to run inside, and now she was wet as well as late, and a little flustered, too, because she didn't do late.

She dashed across the glistening asphalt, through the pelting rain, trying and failing to avoid the puddles, arriving at the front door of the studio at the same time as two guys. One of them noticed her, pulled the door open for her, and motioned her in.

She nearly dropped the tray. He was tall, at least six-two, and...and *built*. Nearly-black hair cut sharp and close to his head, his skin a velvety bronze, his eyes dark under strong black brows, with just enough black beard going on to spell "danger." To spell "testosterone." With a capital *T*.

Model, she thought, getting herself under control with an effort. *Pretty person.*

"Thanks," she said, preparing to duck under one muscular arm. Which featured a swirling deep-blue tattoo, the intricate pattern twining up from his forearm and disappearing into the sleeve of his white T-shirt, which was a little damp now. And clinging to a whole lot of chest. Oh, boy.

That was when the bag broke, the brown paper weakened by the rain. She grabbed for it, but she couldn't get it, not with the drink tray in one hand.

He could, though. Somehow, he'd let go of the door, snatched two muffins out of midair, and come up laughing.

"Half of them," he said. "That's something, isn't it." Because, indeed, there were two more muffins lying in a puddle, getting soggier by the second. His friend bent down and grabbed them, handed them to her with a kind smile, but nobody was going to be eating those.

"This was mine," she told them, juggling the tray to stick the ruined muffins onto it. She held up the carrot one, or what was left of it. "Which I didn't need anyway. But thanks. You may have just saved my job. My boss hates it when he misses his muffin."

The bigger man was holding the door for her now. Another massive arm decorated with a tattoo, but somehow, she wasn't looking at him. She shut her mouth, because she was standing here in the rain, babbling—worse, babbling about why she shouldn't be eating muffins—just because one of them was her fantasy come to life, accent and all. Time to shut up, go inside, and get to work, so she did.

"What d'you want me to do with these?" her rescuer asked, holding up the muffins.

"Oh." She pulled herself back into some poise. "I've got no hands. Bring them back for me, will you?"

He followed her through the door at one end of the outer office—which was already half-full, because nobody else seemed to be late—and into the studio proper. She led the way into the little kitchen at one end and set her burdens down gratefully, ignoring Calvin's fulminating gaze. Time enough for that.

Her rescuer set his two lonely muffins down on the butcher-block counter as she dumped her own into the trash.

"Thanks," she said. "If you'll just…"

9

"Yeh," he said with a smile that was—that was her guy. Her guy who had tackled her, in her bikini. All right, her guy had been blond, and this one was anything but—but he was her guy all the same.

In your stupid daydream, girlfriend. He's not your guy.

"I'll go back out there," he said.

"You here for the shoot?" she asked, then snapped her mouth shut. Why else would he be here?

"Nah. Just an interested observer." One dancing brown eye closed, and yes, her dream man was winking at her. "See ya."

He walked away. More of a lope, really. All fluid motion, like his joints were better-oiled than other people's. An interested observer? Yeah, right.

"Nice of you to show up," Calvin said as her helper disappeared into the anteroom, leaving the studio charged with a few extra attraction molecules.

Faith pulled two coffees out of the cardboard tray and took one to Calvin. He was in a temper, clearly. Well, he was nervous. He had a lot riding on this.

"Want to hear the story of Mrs. Johnson's toilet?" she asked him. "It's all to do with her colitis, you see. She has to use extra paper."

He paused with his cup halfway to his lips. "No," he enunciated. "I do not. I think you're fired."

"I am not fired. You need me too much." Her anxiety was settling now that she was in control again. She hated being late, but she was here now. It was all good. She went back and grabbed the folders out of her bag, then handed a couple to Calvin. Portfolios, with the photos attached, one folder for the men, and the other for the women. "I put them in order. Of who looked best to me, but you tell me, of course." She handed him another list. Alphabetical. Six men, six women, here for an audition in front of the cameras, because you never knew which one would be right until you actually got them into the studio. "You tell me," she repeated.

"You think I haven't gone through them?" he growled, fixing

her with a pale-blue stare. "I've gone through them."

"Right. So give me a number, boss. One to six."

"Who was that one just now?" he asked absently, scanning the list, flipping through the portfolios, because he'd have looked at them, sure. But he wouldn't have put them in order, not like she did. It always amazed her, how other people did things.

"Which one?" She sat down opposite him on a stool with her own list, poised to take notes.

"Mr. Muffin," he said, and she had to choke back a laugh.

"Oh." Her poise faltered for a minute, because she didn't know which one he was. She flipped through her own copy of the portfolios. "Uh...unless he's a Master of Disguise, he's not in here. A drop-in?"

"I don't allow drop-ins."

"No. Want me to tell him to go away?"

"What are you, stupid? No, I don't want you to tell him to go away. I want you to get his portfolio."

"Right. So...order?"

"Him first. And then..." He flipped a little more, gave her the rundown. All he needed was the nudge, and she was a champion nudger.

"One and one," he told her as he finished up. "One boy and one girl at a time."

"Of course." She took her folders to the door, opened it, and went on out there.

He was there. Sitting beside his friend, totally relaxed, unlike most of the rest of them. His head back, laughing. Next to a pretty, petite blonde. Well, they were all pretty, petite blondes.

Gretchen Galveston, she thought automatically. Number One on her girl-list. Her Fantasy Man had good taste.

"Hi, everybody." She cast a smile around the room. "Thanks for coming. We're going to get through this just as quickly as we can. Any questions before we start?"

She did her best to be respectful, because she'd hate to be the one auditioning, the one hoping for the callback that meant the auditioning could stop. The one depending on somebody else's approval to say that she was acceptable. Calvin didn't normally do this kind of project. He usually had his models pre-selected by the client's art director, and Faith was glad, because she didn't have a thick enough skin for auditions. Even being on the other end of them.

"This isn't porn, right?" one of the girls asked. A nervy, anxious look to her, too tightly wound. She wouldn't be picked, Faith knew, and her heart went out a little bit to her.

"No," Faith said. "But if you're uncomfortable being in some pretty skimpy underwear, or being in one of these guys' laps…" She paused, got a little laughter out of that one. "Maybe a good time to re-think. Anybody else?"

Nothing, and she looked at her folder again. "Gretchen?" she asked, and yes, the perky little blonde next to Fantasy Man bobbed right up. "And…" Faith looked at her muffin-rescuer. "I don't have you on the list. Do you have a portfolio?"

"Me?" He pointed to his broad chest, widened those spectacular eyes at her, the liquid whites setting off the most delicious dark chocolate centers, and laughed. "Nah. I'm just along for the ride, aren't I. I'm the chaperone. Looking after Solomon here, making sure he doesn't get excited."

"Dude," the big man with him said, looking pained. "No." But he smiled all the same.

"Right," Faith said. Not here for the shoot? She looked down at her list. "All right, then, Solomon. Come on back."

Calvin didn't mess around when they got there. "I didn't ask for him first." He jerked his chin at Solomon.

"Don't mind him," Faith told Solomon, who looked a bit taken aback. "He's grumpy because his coffee was late."

Calvin snorted. "Excuse me? Who's in charge here?"

"You are," she said equably. "Go on."

"*Thank* you. Where's the other guy?" Calvin demanded.

"Ah…" Solomon scratched his nose. "You saw Will," he said with resignation.

"Yeah. I want him." Calvin cast a dismissive eye over Solomon. "You're too big."

Solomon grinned. "Not what my—" He stopped, shot a look toward Faith and Gretchen, and clearly re-thought his words. "Never mind. I'm done, then?"

"Yeah," Calvin said. "I want your friend. Send him on back here."

Solomon shrugged. "Good enough."

"Have a seat," Faith told the young woman hastily. "Gretchen, right? We'll be right with you."

"I'm not worried," the girl said. "It's exciting." She sat down and actually bounced a little. Perky was the word, all right. "When you get my guy, I'm ready."

Faith gave Solomon an apologetic look as she led the way to the doorway again. "Thanks for coming. Calvin can be a little abrupt."

"No problem. My wife will be relieved, tell you the truth. I'm destined for better things." He laughed, a rumbling sound, and Faith found herself laughing back. "Yo, bro," he called out, entering the anteroom again. "They want you. Story of my life." He heaved a gusty sigh from somewhere in the depths of his six-foot-five frame. "You're going to have to find your own way back to your place, because I'm not hanging around."

"What?" Mr. Muffin looked startled, off-balance for the first time.

"If you have a few minutes," Faith said, trying her best for brisk, "Calvin's interested in taking a look at you."

Some of the other guys looked disgruntled, and no wonder.

"Dunno." He sounded bemused. "I'm not a model."

"Would you come back here and talk to him anyway? Just for a minute," she coaxed. She could see why Calvin wanted him, because he was perfect. Absolutely perfect. For Calvin.

model behavior
♡

Will followed her into the studio again. So far, this wasn't going anything like he'd expected. He'd just been along for the ride.

She was bloody pretty, the coffee girl. He'd been enjoying taking in the scenery in the outer room, but Solomon had a point about the...curvy parts, he decided as he walked along behind her. Her waist was small, and her hips weren't, and that long-sleeved T-shirt was working pretty hard, too. Her jeans were nothing but practical, her hair was brown, wet, and tied into some sort of deliberately messed-up knot with the ends sticking out, and if she were wearing any lipstick on that luscious pink mouth, he'd just say it looked natural. But she had a tiny mole just above the outer edge of her perfectly carved upper lip that any man would long to kiss, right before he got down to business on that mouth. Her eyes were blue, wide-set, and clear, and her smile was something special.

He got a bit distracted by the sight of Gretchen, whom he'd met in the outer room, doing a few unselfconscious stretches. Leaning back with her arms overhead, hands clasped, so her tiny T-shirt rode up over some very nice flat little belly. Yeh, there was heaps to look at in Vegas.

14

"Hi!" she said with her sunny smile.

"Hi." He gave her a smile in return, then turned to the older fella, sitting and frowning over a folder in his lap.

"Morning," Will said. "What can I do for you?"

The older man looked up, still frowning. "Who are you?"

Will had to laugh. Well, *that* was dead rude. "I'm the Designated Driver, you could say. Will…Will Taniwha." He didn't know why he hadn't given his real name. Well, because he wasn't sure what this was about. "Who're *you?*"

"Calvin Quisp. Photographer. Looking for a model, which hopefully you know."

"I'm not looking for a modeling job, actually," Will said. "I'm just here on holiday for a few weeks."

"It'll only take a few weeks. Six days' work. If I want you."

"Well, if you don't want me, there's no point, is there?" Will was getting a bit narky now.

If the other man noticed the narkiness, he didn't show it. "Take off your shirt," he said, "and we'll talk."

"You know," Will said, "when I try saying that to somebody, it almost never works."

The coffee girl was trying not to laugh, he could tell. Those blue eyes were sparkling at him, the pink mouth curving, even though she was fighting it hard. "He wants to see your chest," she told Will. "That's all."

"And I don't have all day," Calvin said. "So take it off, or leave. Shoes, too."

What the hell. Will stripped his still-damp T-shirt off in one quick motion and tossed it onto a chair, then kicked off his jandals. "There you go. Those are the goods."

Calvin stood up. "Come on. Over here." He pointed Will to a spot against the bare wall, painted a dull black like the rest of the studio space, went to a camera mounted on a stand, and looked through the lens.

"Get those softboxes in there," he told the coffee girl, and she moved to oblige, carrying a couple of rectangular lights on stands and positioning them in some way that must have made sense to the photographer, because he grunted at her, turned back to the camera, and took a couple of snaps.

"Fold your arms across your chest," he told Will, "tattooed arm on top." Will did it, then moved some more at the other man's direction, feeling like a bit of a fool in just his jeans, his bare feet cold against the engineered flooring.

"You," the photographer told the blonde, who'd been sitting and watching. "Got a bra on under there?"

"Yes," she said, and giggled.

"Then take off your shirt, too," he said, "and your shoes, and go stand over there with him. Your back against his front."

She did it, and this was getting interesting at last, because she was tiny, pale-skinned and big-eyed, and her breasts were a pair of pretty little cupcakes in the light-blue bra.

"Don't mind me," she said, and snuggled up. She was wearing jeans too, low-slung, tight ones that hugged her equally tight little bottom, which she was pressing into the tops of his thighs.

"Hold her," Calvin told him. "One arm across her chest, just above the bra. The other hand right down at the top of her jeans, like you're about to reach inside both places. Like a second later, your hands would be there." He was behind the camera, shooting as he spoke. "Oh, yeah. That's it. Spread your fingers a little on that lower one. Show us how big that hand is. You're just about to touch her real good."

Gretchen had jumped a bit, though, and Will pulled his hands hastily off her. "Sorry. I'll…"

"It's just that your hands were cold. Don't worry. I'm good." He couldn't see her expression, but she didn't sound the least bit affected. "Go on," she urged him. "Do it right. I need this job." Which was about the biggest turn-off he'd ever heard.

"Sorry." He rubbed his hands together briskly to warm them before taking hold of her again. "This isn't the real thing, right?" he asked the photographer. "Because I haven't agreed to anything yet."

"This is just the audition," the coffee girl said. She said it soothingly, like he was nervous, and he scowled at her a little.

"Oh, that's good." Calvin was sounding excited behind his camera. "Bad Boy all the way. Hold that thought. And keep reaching down there. Look down her bra now. Just that mad. Just that bad. Hold that. And you...Gertrude."

"Gretchen," the coffee girl reminded him.

"Whatever. No smile. You're so turned on, and just a little bit scared, maybe. He's got you, and you don't know what he's going to do with you. Put an arm up over your head, reach around for his neck, behind you. You're pulling him into you, because you can't help it. Arch that back, because his hands feel so good. Yeah, that's it. That's beautiful."

Knowing that he was about to dive down a woman's jeans would have been good. It would have been brilliant, if Will had had the least bit of confidence that she was enjoying it. As it was, it was about as sexy as a rugby scrum.

"That's got to be enough," he said after Calvin had snapped away some more. "And you're not using it unless I say so."

Calvin stepped away from the camera, popped out the memory card, and took it over to the computer. "I couldn't anyway. Don't have the lighting right. Sit down, shut up, and hang on."

Will's mouth opened a little. Bloody hell, Americans were rude. He should walk out the door. Why wasn't he walking out the door?

Because he was curious. He shouldn't care what this arrogant bastard thought, but his pride was on the line now. He wanted to see if he'd passed.

"Yeah...yeah," Calvin was muttering, scrolling through image after image. Will glanced over his shoulder. He looked like himself, maybe a bit narky, but then, he had been. But Gretchen *did* look sexy. Her mouth was soft, her head thrown back, her eyes half-closed, her back arching under his hands. She looked like a woman who was two-thirds of the way there already. Like she'd been a whole lot more into it than she actually had been.

"Pretty good," Calvin said. "All right. You two wait outside

17

while I get through the rest of them, and we'll see."

"I don't think so," Will said. Enough was enough. "Talk to me. Tell me what the job is, because I know bugger all about it. How much I'd be…putting my hands on somebody, if I did it. Let alone anything else, because I'm not doing anything else." He could see why Lelei hadn't wanted Solomon to get the job. There wasn't a single one of Will's own sisters or cousins who'd have let her man sign up for this, no matter how many babies had been on the way.

The girl with the coffee spoke up. Soothing him again. "Mostly standing up. Well, not entirely. But mostly. Mainly wearing just your pants, or with your shirt open, because men look better wearing a few clothes, for some odd reason. Whereas women look better without them. Why is that?" She grinned at him, and he had to laugh, because she was right, at least as far as he was concerned. And because he liked her smile.

"Because women are prettier, maybe?" he suggested. "All smooth and soft? And you know what they say. The circle is Nature's perfect shape."

She choked back a laugh, then went on hastily at another glare from Calvin. "Ahem. There'll be some shots lying down on a bed, too, of course, tangled up in her, with your hand in her hair. Like that. You won't be kissing her, because kissing doesn't photograph well. You'll be looking dark and dominant and broody, that's all. Here." She reached for a clipboard, came and stood next to him, flipped a page. "This is a partial shot list, just sketched out, but it should give you an idea."

Her hair smelled good. Like flowers. She was leaning into him a little, holding out the clipboard. Wearing all her clothes, and not pretending anything at all. Somehow, it was so much sexier than holding a half-naked Gretchen, and he was getting distracted. Because she was so…curvy. So soft and pretty and warm there beside him.

He made himself focus, ran a finger down the list, and came to a screaming stop near the bottom. "Bondage Shots? Shower shots? *Spanking* shots? Hang on."

"It's not real," she said. "It's all just suggestion. Very tasteful. You won't even be in all of them, especially the bondage shots. It's all about the girl, for those. Some shots of you holding her, at most, with her hands behind her back. You know the kind of thing. And as for the shower shots, you can wear a...a Speedo or something. And I won't peek." She was laughing at him again, he could tell. Or trying not to. Like he was funny. Clearly, standing close to him wasn't doing nearly as much to her as it was to him.

"So what's this all about?" he asked.

Calvin sighed. "Time's a-wasting," he said pointedly.

"And I can leave right now. Or you—I'm sorry," Will told the assistant-girl. "I don't know your name."

"Faith," she said.

Calvin sighed again. "Faith Goodwin. Which I still say is a *perfect* name for our girl. Innocence sullied. Oh, I love it. I want it."

"Well, you can't have it. You are not using my name. We've had this discussion. Forget it." She turned back to Will and said, "We're doing sexy pictures for a new website, a subscription-based thing. The site won't just be about the pictures, it's going to have stories, too, because it's also a writing contest. That's the big idea. That's the new angle."

"A writing contest," Will said slowly.

"Yes. Where people can submit their episodes of their own unfolding story every week, as new pictures go up. Erotica, or erotic romance. Whichever." She was smiling at him encouragingly again, like she was talking about some kind of kids' writing contest, describing their Best Christmas Ever. "We give the two characters names, and people write stories about them. They write about what's going on in the pictures, do you see? And the viewers get to vote on which stories they like best. The most popular stories show up on the site first. Fun times reading, and looking at pictures of sexy people being...well, sexy. Win-win for everyone."

"Isn't there a basic flaw in that idea?" Will asked.

"What's that?" She looked startled. She hadn't thought of it? Seemed doomed to fail to him, although what did he care?

19

"Why would somebody pay for this?" he asked. "Isn't there porn online for free? I mean," he added hastily, "I've heard."

Her eyes danced with merriment. "Yeah, I'll bet you have. But there's nothing like this. It's surprising, I know, with all the free stuff out there, but erotica's about the most profitable genre people can write in these days. I did the research. The new idea is the...full-service aspect. You get the pictures, and the stories to go with them, and you get to vote. Interactive. Nothing too dirty either way, don't worry. There'll be rules."

"Well, not that many rules," Calvin said, and she made a shushing gesture at him that Will didn't miss. Who was running this show, anyway?

"Well, you think there's money in it, anyway," Will said, although he still doubted it. "Or you wouldn't be paying people to pose for it."

"And I wouldn't be sitting around yapping to somebody about it, either," Calvin grumbled. "Instead of getting on with it."

"I can leave," Will reminded him. He crossed his arms again, realizing he hadn't put his shirt back on, which Gretchen had already done, quick and businesslike. "How much does it pay?"

"Four thousand," Calvin said. "Full model release." Whatever that meant.

"Wait a minute." Faith held up a hand. "You're on vacation, right? From...somewhere?"

"Yeh. From New Zealand." He thought about explaining why he was here, about the football, and the rugby, and abandoned the idea fast. Who knew what kind of extra visibility they could get out of that? That would be the last thing he needed.

She sighed. "Never mind, then. We're wasting our time. No work visa."

"Hang on," Calvin said. "I didn't hear that. Payment in cash, is what I meant to say. Of course," he added smoothly, "in cash, it's thirty-three-fifty, because I can't deduct it."

"Wait." Gretchen spoke up. "You said four thousand."

"For you," Faith said, "four thousand. And Calvin—No."

20

"Oh, yes," Calvin said. "Yes. You say yes now," he told Will, "and you're in."

"Me too?" Gretchen asked.

"No," Calvin said. "Not until I test the other girls. But I want him. Yes or no?" he demanded.

"Uh..." He shouldn't, but what the hell. If he'd been worried that he'd get too aroused, embarrass himself, he'd just been put shockingly right on that one. He was in limbo just now, and a person could only train for so many hours a day. Meanwhile, he could pose in his jeans a few times, holding a pretty girl, which wasn't exactly hardship duty. And hang out with Faith. That wouldn't be bad, either. That wouldn't be bad at all.

Why not? He wasn't in New Zealand, not in the relentless scrutiny of a harsh public eye. He didn't have to behave himself here, and if his photo appeared on some pay-per-view website in the States that didn't have a hope anyway, who was going to know—or care?

What happened in Vegas stayed in Vegas. He was in Vegas, and he needed something to happen. Perfect.

"Right," he decided. "I'll do it. What the hell. One for the memoirs."

the hurtin' kind
♡

Will had surprised her. And excited her, which wasn't going to do her any good at all. Standing next to all that bronzed flesh, all those delicious muscles and the amazing tattoo that covered the slab of one broad pectoral muscle, ran over the bulge of his shoulder and then all the way down to his forearm, the faint, deliciously spicy scent of him filling her head while she tried not to look at the narrow trail of hair leading down into his jeans…it had all been a little rough. The only other choice had been to look at his face, and that hadn't helped matters one bit. A few minutes was all it had taken, and here she was with a hopeless, thoroughly embarrassing crush. Pathetic.

It wasn't getting one bit better, either, because she was sitting across from him now in the Turkish restaurant next to the UNLV campus, running through her list. Calvin had been impatient to keep looking at the girls that morning, and Will had said that he had to get on, that he had a workout to do. And while Faith had been distracted imagining Will working out, Calvin had muttered something caustic about models who came to auditions without being prepared to stay a while. Will had answered cheerfully that he

22

hadn't come there to audition and wasn't going to sit around now, and Faith had delegated herself to handle the details. Because that was her *job*.

"So who's the lucky girl chosen to be my victim?" Will asked now. He'd insisted on buying Faith's lunch, too, which had been nice of him. It was almost like a…date. *Stop it. It's not a date.*

"Oh, pardon," he said when she looked up in surprise, "my partner in almost-nearly consensual yet decidedly dirty acts of love."

"Darn it," she said, fighting a smile. Did he have to be smart and funny, too? "Nobody's even written anything yet, and you've already got the plot. And it's Gretchen."

"Ah. Gretchen." She couldn't tell if he was pleased or not. "I saw the list, remember? I'm guessing here that I'm meant to be the hard warrior. Got some dark tribal desires, maybe. I'm a wee bit…savage." He leaned closer and whispered the word, those liquid brown eyes widening a little, and she very nearly choked before he sat back and continued in a normal tone of voice. "Of course, I'm painfully jaded by my past experience with women, too."

"You are?" She took another bite of salad and tried not to laugh.

"Yeh." He sighed pitifully. "They've hurt me, and now I take what I want—which is a bit nasty, by the way—and don't let them get close. So we start in on it, because she can't resist me. I tend to have that effect. I'm all broody, like I've lost every game, and yet she melts whenever she sees me, because apparently she likes blokes like that. Must be an odd girl."

"You've lost every game," she repeated. "Huh? What game?"

"Sorry. Best metaphor I've got. I'm cranky, like, the way you are when you lose. But in a totally manly way. How am I doing so far?"

Faith had lost the battle not to laugh. "Don't make me snort out my drink. You sound like you're ready to enter the contest yourself. You got a secret reading habit?"

"Just an ordinary amount of attention to the popular culture.

One of my sisters was reading one of those books at Christmas. Pretty shocking, I thought, when I had a wee look. In fact, I'm a pretty ordinary fella, sad to say, in that department. Don't tell. I mostly just want to have fun, and to make sure she's having fun, too. I'll do my best to be Dark and Dangerous instead, though, especially if you keep me as narky as you did today."

To make sure she's having fun, too. She'd bet. All she'd have to do was to see him naked. That would be fun all by itself. And to touch all…that. To look into those eyes while he was over her, moving slowly at first, because he wouldn't rush a woman. And then getting a little…decisive. A little commanding, even.

She couldn't help it. Her mind went right there. She hadn't had sex in way too long.

Focus. "Me?" she asked. "What did *I* do? And what's narky?"

"Annoyed."

"I am *never* annoying. I am helpful. I am kind."

"Smiling at me, being all encouraging? Soothing my fragile male ego?"

"That's my job, though."

"Well, keep doing it. Because it's bloody annoying. That worked."

She was laughing again. "All right," she said, attempting to compose herself, to get back to her normal efficient self. "Moving on. You signed the release. Next steps…we start shooting day after tomorrow, so please go get a really good wax."

"Uh…exactly what am I meant to wax? Maybe I *am* going to be broody at that, if you make this hurt enough."

"Well, chest, obviously." She was still trying for businesslike, but he was making it much too difficult. "Belly, all the way down to…as low as you could go without actually getting into Happyville, I imagine. Beyond that, do what you want, and don't tell me, because I don't want to know. Except, of course, any extra trimming you may need. Think about that very tiny Speedo you'll be wearing in the shower scene. Think no…no foliage."

"Happyville?" Now he was the one laughing. "Foliage? Who

knew this modeling business had so many uncomfortable rules? I thought the girl was the one meant to be doing the hurts-so-good business. Ouch."

"Count yourself lucky," she said, registering the fact that he really hadn't done any modeling before. Which was interesting, wasn't it, with a body like that? "Gretchen will be waxing a whole lot more."

"That'll surprise Gretchen, that she's the one."

"Why? She was the most angelic, no question about it, and that's what we're going for."

"We're not compatible," Will told her, his expression serious. "She's an Aries, and I'm a Virgo."

"Tell me you did not just say that."

"Well..." He forked up another bite of beef. "I wouldn't say it had occurred to me as a stumbling block, but she seemed concerned about it. Apparently I'm likely to be too shy and modest. Repressed, you could say. Whereas she'll be taking charge. So you see..." He paused and sighed. "Exactly wrong for the job, aren't I. Why are you laughing?"

"I'm not sure what a Virgo is or isn't. But let's just say that I'm pretty sure somebody forged your birth certificate. And Gretchen seemed like she'd be able to fake it. I saw those pictures. I'd have sworn she was about to..."

"Yeh. Looked that way, didn't it? I'm having a serious re-think of my actual effect on the opposite sex, because I don't think she's going to fall asleep dreaming about me tonight."

Well, *Gretchen* might not be. "As long as the two of you can make other people dream, or at least daydream," Faith said, deciding that the issue of his effect on the opposite sex was going to stay right off the table, "we're all good. Anyway, we aren't actually giving out a storyline. If somebody wants to make up a plot where she turns the tables on you, you being the shy, retiring Virgo you are, I guess they can. Not sure how well that'll sell, but that's not really my problem. But on that note, Calvin and I wanted to know...what are you? I mean, what ethnic background? And would anybody be able to tell? We thought we'd offer a little bio on each of you. Fictional, of course."

"Maori. Some people would be able to tell, if it matters. And fictional would be good."

She set that one aside to think about later. "Maori—that's something New Zealandish? Because that'd be good. New Zealand is sexy." And New Zealanders were sexier.

"It is, eh. Didn't realize that. And, yeh, Maori's about as New Zealandish as you can get."

She got out her notebook. She'd do some research. "What would be a good Maori name for you? Something fierce. Something strong."

"How about 'Hemi?'" There was a smile trying to work its way onto his lips now, lighting up his eyes. Some mischief, clearly. She'd better double-check the name. "Means 'James' in Maori. Not too hard for Pakeha—white people—to pronounce, either."

"Ooh!" She tried not to bounce with it. "Hemi…and Hope. Oh, yes." She started scribbling again. "I'm so good."

He laughed out loud. "Yes. I'm beginning to think you are."

"And here's the shooting schedule we've worked out." She handed it over. Time to get things back on track, even though the frivolous part of her desperately wanted to keep—well, flirting. Indulging her ridiculous crush. "Six days, as advertised."

"OK. I'll be there. Waxed and all. And if we've got all that sorted, I'd better get out of here. I need to go look at a couple places to live, or I really *am* going to be dark and dangerous, because that hotel's about to drive me mad."

"I thought you were on vacation," she said, her guard instantly up again. Had he been lying about just passing through? She didn't like the paying-under-the-table thing, whatever Calvin said. She'd argued with him about it earlier, to no effect. But this guy could be anybody, however much he turned her on and made her laugh. Whatever he said about not being dangerous, he had "dangerous for her peace of mind" written right in the tattoo.

"I am," he said. "I need a place to live while I'm here, that's all.

Those bloody ching-chinging machines in the lobby are getting on my nerves a bit. I'd like to have a cooker, too, make my own breakfast. Not rapt about my choices so far, but..." He shrugged. "It's just a few weeks."

"If you're really looking..." she said slowly, then stopped.

"What? You know someplace?"

"I manage an apartment building. And I've got a place that's open."

"Has to be furnished. I don't have anything. Nothing but a couple suitcases."

"Oh," she said, and couldn't suppress her smile. "It's furnished. And three weeks? That'd be perfect."

Or incredibly stupid. One or the other.

♡♡♡

"It's...uh..." he said a half-hour later, groping for a word that wouldn't insult her. "Comfortable, I guess."

"It was Mrs. Ferguson's apartment." She moved briskly inside and set her ever-present laptop case down on the coffee table. "After she died last month, her son came and got a few things, and told me to get rid of the rest. Which isn't ideal, because it means I have to sell everything, or dump it, before I can paint and rent it out again. I took care of her clothes and emptied the bathroom cabinets and the refrigerator and so forth, and it's clean, but I haven't had a chance to do the rest of it. I was actually thinking about seeing if it would work for a short-term rental, since I've got the furniture already. You could be my guinea pig."

"May work better for girls," he said.

That was the understatement of the year, because if he'd ever seen an old-lady apartment, this was it. The couch was flowered. The chair was flowered—with different flowers. It was like a bloody garden in here, though a fairly musty-smelling one. There were cushions everywhere, most of them with little tufts or big, hard buttons, looking like nothing he'd want to lean his head against. Framed prints on the wall, the most loathsome one, over the couch, featuring a cottage in the middle of a garden, with brightly lit windows glowing cozily in the twilight. A painting he was already placing on his personal Most-Hated list, and he'd only been looking at it for a minute. Every little table, and there were heaps of little tables, was wearing a skirt, like God hated a naked table. And there were flowers on the skirted tables, because apparently you could never have too many flowers. He fingered a petal. Silk flowers, he guessed. And ceramic statues of cats. Even the dining-room table had a skirt, with a glass top over it. And fake flowers on it, with some cats posed around the vase in a circle. Crouching cats. Stretching cats. Cats curled in sleep. Cats with kittens. Many, many too many cats.

"Her son didn't want the cats?" he asked. "Or the flowers?"

"Ah...no. But I'll get rid of them," she promised. "And anything else you don't want around, if you decide to take the place. I should've donated them already. But let me show you the kitchen."

She led the way into it, and as always, he enjoyed following her. There weren't flowers in here, at least. Looked like a kitchen. Except for the canisters, which were in the shape of cats. He lifted the head off a Siamese and peered inside. Tea.

"Still some basic staples in here," she said encouragingly. "So you wouldn't have to do so much shopping. As long as you like, you know, tea and cookies."

"I'm from New Zealand. I have to like tea and bikkies. It's required."

The bedroom was more of the same, and he eyed the pink-canopied bed with a jaundiced eye. Canopied? This lady had clearly been the last of the true romantics. But the worst was the bathroom. Painted pink. "Why is there a Barbie on the toilet?" he asked. "Case I get bored?"

"Not a Barbie." Faith lifted the plastic doll, revealing what was under the flounced white crocheted skirt. "Look at this! Your new apartment comes equipped with an extra roll of toilet paper!"

"Brilliant. Well, it's got a bathroom and a kitchen, anyway. Bigger than one of those extended-stay places by the airport, and the price is better, too. One thing you can say about this—it isn't sterile." He spent enough of his life in hotel rooms. He didn't need to spend his holiday in another one. If he'd been in New Zealand, he'd have been in a bach, somebody's holiday home, with all their bits and bobs about. It was comfier that way, even if you didn't much care for their bits and bobs. And it was an excuse to get closer to Faith. That, most of all. "But if it's all right with you, I'll bung that doll into a drawer somewhere, along with a few other things. That thing is going to give me nightmares, staring at me while I'm on the loo."

"I'll take it." No smile this time, and she tucked it into her arm a bit protectively.

"Sorry. No accounting for my bad taste, I guess."

"No, it's terrible, you're right, and so are the cats. It's just...I liked Mrs. Ferguson. I wouldn't use this, but I'll...I don't know." She fingered the doll's flounced skirt. "She'd crocheted me an afghan for Christmas. I opened it after she was gone. Her arthritis was bad, but she still did it, just because she needed to do things for people. She was that sort of person." Her voice wasn't quite steady now. "I miss her."

He waited for her to say more, but she didn't. He knew about missing people, though. About the ache that settled low in your chest, the tears that would come up behind your eyelids, always at the most inconvenient time, when a snatch of song, a joke, even a truly hideous doll reminded you. When you thought of something you wanted to tell the person, and realized that he wasn't there to tell anymore.

It wasn't that she liked the cats. She'd kept them, and the horrible doll, and the awful paintings, because she hadn't been able to get rid of them yet. And since Will was wearing his grandfather's watch right now, which didn't even keep perfect time, he could understand that.

"I'm sorry," he said gently, and she nodded once, quick and

29

short. "Are all my neighbors old, then?" he asked, trying to help her move on.

"Well, depending what you think of me," she said, clearly rallying her forces.

"You? You live here?" Better and better.

"Right next door. I told you, I manage the building. So what do you think? Cats, dolls, flowers, and all—which could all be gone, I promise, in fifteen minutes—do you want it?"

"Yeh. I want it. Especially if you're living next door."

She crossed her arms across the front of that T-shirt, which was a nice look for her, because she had some curves and no mistake. Unfortunately, it was also nowhere close to the body language of a woman who was saying, "Come and get it, boy."

"I'm sure I don't need to say this," she said, and no, she didn't. "Because I'm also sure that I'm nothing close to your type. But I'm not interested."

"Not?" He made a joke of it, even as he felt a jolt of...surprise? Disappointment? Something. "Convenient as it would be to have your very own Maori warrior right next door? Bit of a winter fling? I'd never tell."

"No. I don't fling. And I'm very busy."

"Ah. Very busy."

"And," she added hastily, "not interested."

Well, that was a little too much protesting. "Not even if I promised to be dark and dangerous?"

She laughed out loud, and he grinned back, because he liked the way she laughed. She had a little gap between her front teeth that was just...absolutely adorable. She really *was* the girl next door. She'd be *his* girl next door, and he needed...he needed something.

Looking at the shape of her, the warmth of her, he found himself filled with a yearning for that sweet oblivion he somehow knew she'd be.

He was close enough to taste it. That perfect moment when he'd slide inside her for the first time, would feel her opening to take him in. That instant when the world would shrink to only this

30

woman, only this body. He looked at her leaning back like that, smiling at him, and he could feel the way her hands would grab for his shoulders. He could hear the way she would sigh, the way she would moan. He could very nearly taste her, warm and sweet and salty as the sea, and he wanted to. He *needed* to.

"Well, since you already revealed your dirty secret, that you're not actually dangerous…" she said, not seeing it in him at all. "I'm afraid the magic is gone. I'll have to hold out for the hurtin' kind."

"Right." He kept the smile on his face, shoving the thoughts back where they belonged. He held out a hand instead. "Friends?"

She hesitated a moment longer, then took it, and her hand felt good in his. Warm, and firm, and just soft enough. Exactly like her.

"Sure," she said. "Friends."

hemi te mana

♡

Will turned up at the studio at nine o'clock two days later as promised, his hair still a bit damp from the shower, grateful for the trainer he'd found to help him out during his stay. It might be called his holiday, but nothing was a holiday, not if you wanted to be the best.

Now, he was awake, alert, and relaxed the way you could only be when you'd been doing twenty-meter sprints, quick turns, and up-downs, one after another, on a rugby field. When you'd been running with the heavy bag across your shoulders, fifty meters each way, then, without much pause at all, quick-stepping through a network of orange cones, knees high.

His latest session at the Outlaws' brand-new field the day before had been much the same, and nothing like the same. The same kind of running drills, but he'd felt like an...an accessory.

What they had really wanted to see was his kicking. He'd showed them that, but afterwards, he'd mostly been relegated to watching. He hadn't even been invited to join the tackling practice, because it seemed that kickers in gridiron, the American version of football, almost never tackled. Where was the fun in that? Or in

32

kicking, if you hadn't even been on the field beforehand? It was so much better when the kick came after you'd sprinted to intercept a fleet-footed winger, made the tackle, then switched effortlessly to offense when one of the forwards forced the turnover. When you were shouting to your backline, getting them into position, watching for the chance.

Subtle as a chess match, direct as a punch to the gut. When somebody dove across the tryline at last for those hard-earned five points, and you pounded him on the back for doing it, then had to settle your galloping heart, breathe deep, and find the stillness at your center before you took that toughest of kicks all the way from the side. When you'd sent the ball between the posts for the two points that could determine the outcome of the game, and you didn't even have to look, because you knew it had gone through. When you were pulling your mouthguard out of your sock, shoving it into your mouth, and trotting back out to await the other team's kickoff so you could do it all again.

Eighty minutes' worth of busting a gut, even as you were keeping your head. Eighty minutes straight of keeping your composure, because that helped everyone else keep theirs, and a team couldn't win without composure. And because a winning team was a team working as one.

Instead, there he'd be, putting on enough padding to stop a tram and a helmet he could barely see out of, just to kick the ball from nearly dead center and run off again to wait a half-hour for the next time? At least ten times as much money, and that mattered, but all the same…how much challenge would there be in that?

Well, today would be a challenge, anyway, he had a feeling. He came through the glass door of the studio to find Gretchen, Calvin, and an older woman he didn't know sitting around the table accepting coffees from Faith.

It was good to see her, and all at once, he wasn't second-guessing the decision to do this quite so much. He was living next door to her, but he'd only really seen her once since he'd moved in.

He'd spotted her the day before starting to haul out the rubbish bins, and had sprinted down to help her. Which might have earned him a few points in the "friends" department, but wasn't exactly wine and candlelight territory.

"Good," Calvin grunted when Will walked over to join the others. "You're here."

"Morning." Will decided to take that as a greeting. He sat down and accepted the coffee Faith handed him. She'd asked him the last time what he liked, and she'd remembered, too. "Beautiful day out there."

"It's always a beautiful day," Calvin said gloomily. "It's Las Vegas."

Faith laughed. "Never mind him. He's always a little nervous before he starts a big job."

"I beg your pardon," Calvin said. "When I need you to apologize for me, I'll tell you."

"You constantly need me to apologize for you," she said calmly. "That's why I do it."

"Why I put up with you..."

"Well, never mind," she said. "You can fire me when this is over. I'll hold my breath, shall I?"

"Cheeky," Will said.

"Isn't she, though?" Calvin said. "Thinks she's cute."

"Well, she is, a bit." Will grinned at her, and she smiled back. Her hair was in that messy almost-bun again, and she was wearing a T-shirt and jeans again, and she still didn't have much makeup on. And she still looked good.

"This is Charlotte, our stylist," Faith said, and Will shook hands with the older woman.

"And while we're doing introductions..." Faith did a drumroll on the glass tabletop with her hands. "Hope Sinclair, meet Hemi Te Mana, your new employer."

"Oh," Gretchen said. "Hope. I like that. Hi, Hemi!"

Will didn't answer her, just stared at Faith, and her confident smile faded. "What?" she asked. "Is it a dirty word? I thought it

34

sounded good, and mana is power or something like that, right? Perfect."

"No." If he sounded a little grim, it was because he felt that way. "It means prestige. Honor, the kind you earn for the person you are. That man, that woman who walks through the world upright—that's what it means. It's an important word."

"Well, then, even more perfect," Calvin said, impatient as always. "I agree, sounds good. Let's go."

Faith didn't move. "If it's offensive, though..."

"It's an actual name, right?" Calvin demanded of Will. "Te...Te Mana?"

"Yeh. It is." How could he say that he didn't want his heritage treated like some Vegas show? He was the one who'd agreed to do this. They didn't want him for his fine rugby brain, or for the content of his character. They wanted him for his color, his size, his muscles, and his tattoo. He couldn't very well complain that they were objectifying him. He was doing it to himself. And he'd agreed to this. "Right," he said in resignation. "Hemi Te Mana it is."

"Well, then, Hemi," Calvin said, "let's get on with it. Charlotte's got some wardrobe for you. Get yourself into it."

fact and fiction
♡

Faith moved lights and softboxes, set up cameras, checked angles. All the while watching Will being prepped by Charlotte, who handled him with the matter-of-fact briskness she brought to every shoot. The older woman rubbed oil into his chest and fussed with the waistband of his trousers with all the emotion she'd showed when she'd been braiding hair on a six-year-old for a book on Making Your Own Paper Fairies. Less, actually, because Charlotte liked kids. And if Will was uncomfortable, he didn't show it either.

The first shots were of him alone. A white shirt unbuttoned over his broad chest, his sleeves rolled up to show bulky, sinewy forearms and the start of his tattoo. A thumb hooked into the waistband of dark dress pants, the woolen fabric stretching tight over muscular thighs, a black tie loosened around his neck. His gaze lowered, his stare dark and a little menacing.

He posed, and Calvin shot, and Faith's mind responded in spite of herself, going off on its own volition even as she shifted equipment and crawled along the floor and tweaked.

She had the story. It was right there in front of her. She could hear Hemi's voice in her head.

I did a lot of things differently before that day. Or rather, I did them the same way. I did them my way. I kept my personal life in shadow, for one thing, partly because mystique was good, but mostly because my personal life didn't bear scrutinizing.

My physical presence was a different story. I'd seen the articles saying that I was a walking advertisement for my products, but that wasn't the reason. Vanity is a weakness and a delusion, like love. I knew that my appearance, like my intelligence, was nothing more than a gift bequeathed by my ancestors, a gift it was my responsibility to hone. I'd built up a naturally strong body the same way I'd built up my company, and for the same reasons. If we were both powerhouses, that was because winning was the only option. Close didn't count, and second place was for losers. You could call it my philosophy.

I didn't get photographed for my ads, of course. I left that to the models, which was why I was there that day for the kickoff shoot for my new underwear line. I always came to the first day to make sure they did it right. I knew some people called me controlling. Arrogant. Obsessive. As if any of that were a bad thing.

Now, I stood in one corner of the spacious studio and kept an eye on the slow progress before me. They'd be shooting outdoors tomorrow, with Central Park in the background, but I wouldn't be around for that. No need. Anyway, I could see Central Park anytime from the windows of my Manhattan penthouse.

My fingers flew, checking and responding to the messages on my phone as I waited for the crew to finish their endless fiddling. I indulged one brief flash of annoyance at Galway not being ready for the ten o'clock shooting schedule I'd specified, then let it go and concentrated instead on the task at hand. Annoyance wouldn't help right now, and I never indulged in unnecessary or unhelpful emotion. My assistant would be reaming him out after I left. That was what he was there for. Instead, I typed out a quick answer to my VP of Finance about the upcoming bond issue, then moved on to a question from Martine in Publicity about the Paris show. She thought she was short-staffed, but everybody always thought that, when the reality was that they didn't want to do what it took to get the work done. So I texted back,

Make it happen anyway.

and moved on.

My attention kept straying, though, and that was completely unlike me. It was the girl setting up the camera who was doing it. She seemed too small for the task of hauling those tripods and umbrellas around, and I had to restrain myself from going over to help her. She was as fragile as a flower, her pale-blonde hair falling in a soft cloud to just below her narrow shoulders, her little face a perfect heart dominated by enormous blue-green eyes.

And then there was that mouth. Surely, that mouth had been created for a man to use. I remembered the way her lips had parted when I'd touched her. The way I'd been able to feel her heart fluttering, even when I wasn't touching her at all, and the kick of pure lust it had given me, a shot straight to the groin. When I'd licked my fingers, and she'd watched me do it—the connection had been as strong and sharp as a lightning bolt.

And when she was on her hands and knees, crawling to plug in the cords...I lost my train of thought entirely, my fingers and mind both stilling as they never did, taken over by one thought.

I want that.

"Hope!" Vincent Galway, the prima donna behind the camera, was barking again now. When I'd first met him, I'd appreciated his brusqueness, his cold insistence on perfection. I'd been accused of possessing exactly those same qualities often enough. Now, it was making the hot rage rise, and I couldn't afford that.

"Hurry up with those lights," Galway ordered. "Mr. Te Mana is waiting."

She bit her lower lip, and it trembled a little as the delicate color rose in her porcelain cheeks. "Sorry," she said. "One moment." Her fingers were fumbling, and I somehow knew that she needed this job. That she couldn't afford to fail.

Nobody should be treating her like that. Nobody should be doing anything to her. Nobody but me.

♡♡♡

"Faith!"

She jerked herself back to awareness, stepped hastily forward again and pulled the memory card out of the camera, went to plug it into Calvin's computer and load up the photos.

"Get his shirt and tie off," Calvin told Charlotte. "We'll get a few in just the pants. Or maybe keep the tie," he said consideringly. "Faith? What do you think?"

"Oh, yes. Just the tie. Loose, like that." She grinned at Will. "The better to lead you around by."

"Really?" He gave her one of those slow, devilish smiles, more mischief than danger. "That wasn't how I was planning on using it."

"You'll get your chance," she said. "But not until Day Four. I'm sure Hope will be begging for it by then."

"Right. Hope." Another meaningful look, and he had her heart fluttering despite herself. "And you said it, I didn't. A gentleman never tells."

"Oh, and you're a gentleman?"

"Always," he said softly. "Except when I'm…not."

"Ooh." She opened her eyes wide at him. "I'm oddly intrigued. Please. Tell me more."

"OK, enough chit-chat," Calvin said. "Fifteen minutes," he told Will. "Take a break."

A break. Yeah. She needed a break. And all right, she might have interjected herself just a little into her story. Too bad. That was why they called it fiction. Because you could make up whatever you wanted, including being tiny, delicate, lovely, and fiercely, completely, utterly desired by Will. Uh, by Hemi.

chocolate cheesecake
♡

Will opened the door to his ridiculous granny flat, dropped his duffel, and headed for the shower. He was a greasy mess, and that was the truth. Posing for these kinds of photos, he was finding, took heaps more effort than training. Too much standing around. His least favorite thing. And all that pretending to be broody, deep, and dark—it was exhausting. He wasn't deep, and that was that. He liked being shallow. So much easier.

Faith had seemed to notice every time he'd been flagging, had talked to him encouragingly, and when he'd scowled at her, she'd laughed, because she'd known that he'd known what she was doing. She hadn't seemed the least bit bothered that he'd been holding Gretchen, either. Well, neither had Gretchen, but that didn't matter. Faith was friendly. She was cheerful. And that was all. But maybe that would change. Maybe tonight.

He got out of the shower feeling better, saw a text from Solomon, and rang the other man back.

"Lelei wondered if you wanted to come for dinner again tonight," his mate said. "I think she's worried that you'll develop a cocaine habit, now that you're a model."

Will smiled. "Thanks, but I've got plans. And tell her no worries. I don't think the model life's for me. I'll stick with footy."

"Good idea. How's the new place working out?"

"Well...I'd invite you round, but you'd expire from estrogen overload."

"I've got a wife and one-and-a-half daughters," Solomon reminded him. "Is it that bad?"

"Not if you like flowers."

He heard the deep chuckle. "Sounds like a much safer spot for you. Well, not necessarily to me. But Lelei also thought you'd fall into bad company at the hotel. Lelei thinks about you too much, in fact, if you ask me. Hmm. Maybe it's good that you can't come to dinner."

"Bad company's my favorite kind, though." Will cradled the phone between shoulder and ear as he pulled on black boxer briefs, then a clean pair of jeans.

"Yeah. I just barely remember about that. That model looked like she could work out to be some bad company of the very best kind, especially if you're getting naked with her every day."

"I'm not getting naked, remember? I haven't even got down to my undies yet, although she has, because life's unfair to women in the stripping-down department, I guess. I think she's going to be able to resist me, too. And I may even be able to resist her, undies or no." Which was quite the surprise, wasn't it? Gretchen *was* pretty. She was very pretty. But she wasn't the one his eyes had kept straying to today.

"She know who you are?"

"Nah. Nobody does, because I didn't sign my real name to the release."

"Makes it not legal, then."

"Who cares? And, all right, one person knows. Faith knows. Because she's a bloody stickler, isn't she. I handed over the money to rent the apartment for three weeks up front, no fuss, no muss, and what does she do but ask for my passport all the same? Told me I could be running from the law, for all she knew. Me."

"Imagine that."

"And I wouldn't put it past her to do her research, because she's just that way."

"She could be publicizing you, then, for that site. Her very own New Zealand rugby star. Step right up and see him up close and personal, girls!"

"Not exactly a star in the States, though, am I. I don't think anybody here even knows what rugby is. They probably think it's a type of carpet or something. Anyway, I won't be a rugby star at all if this deal works out, and who'll care what I do then? It's a whole new, free world. Anyway, Faith's not like that. She's…she's straight. She's—she's good, I guess." He got a little embarrassed, and went on hastily, "But yeh, it's a gamble. When in Vegas, eh. Besides, I love to live dangerously."

"So you're working with her, *and* living in her place? That's some fast moving, brother. How long did that take, a day?"

"Well, she *is* my dinner date tonight. Her and her mum, because her mum owns the building. So she can vet her new tenant. I'm not moving that fast at all, but I got dinner all the same, and I'll be working on the rest of it, no worries."

"You're meeting the mom? Sorry to tell you this, but that doesn't usually translate to, 'Hey, baby. Let's do it quick and dirty and move on.'"

"Don't remind me."

♡♡♡

When Faith had come back over to Mrs. Ferguson's apartment with the rental agreement and the keys that first day, it had been a real struggle not to betray the anxiety attack she'd had in her bathroom in the interim. What had she been thinking, suggesting that he live next door to her, after looking at him half-naked in the studio? Especially after that little scene in his own bathroom. He was looking for some easy companionship during his holiday, it was clear, and what could be more convenient than getting it from his next-door neighbor?

She knew all that. She did. And she wasn't stupid. She knew what he was offering, and that it wouldn't be enough for her. She'd only end up feeling used, because she couldn't do casual sex. She just wasn't built that way. And she especially couldn't do it with Will. The exact thing that made it so hard to say no—that was the reason she had to say it. Because he didn't just make her heart beat faster, he made her laugh, too. Because he'd been so sweet about Mrs. Ferguson. Because his hand had felt so good around hers, and when he'd asked her to be his friend, had smiled at her like that, she'd melted a little.

She'd checked him out online that same evening, of course, once she'd seen his passport and found out his real name. She didn't know anything about rugby. She didn't even know anybody who knew anything about rugby. But it was easy to see that he was a star—and not just in New Zealand. He was, in fact, the brand-new starting "Number 10" for a New Zealand rugby team, and before that, he'd been the starter on a top Australian team. A little more research had told her that the 10 was the director of the offense. The quarterback, in other words, although not the captain.

Will Tawera—because that was his real name—was, in fact, a very big deal back home, and in some other parts of the world, too. And for some odd reason, he was modeling for what must be peanuts to him, and living in Mrs. Ferguson's apartment. She'd love to think that had something to do with her, but it seemed awfully unlikely. And anyway, she wasn't going to be some incognito star athlete's Part-Time Good Time. She had more self-respect than that.

Well, once he met her mother, she probably wouldn't have to worry about him trying again, because Bella Goodwin had a tendency to come on strong.

"I want to meet him," her mother had said when Faith had called her with the news that she'd rented the apartment, and her mom, of course, had pried out all the details. "A hot model? From New Zealand? Bring him over."

"Mom," Faith had sighed. "He isn't going to want to come to dinner with my mother. I've known him for one day."

"You could be in over your head," her mother had insisted. "I'm getting a vibe, and you know I trust my vibes. If I'm wrong, he'll say no to the invitation, and I'll be satisfied. If I'm right—and honey, if he's renting Mrs. Ferguson's apartment, he's doing it for a reason—I think he'll say yes. And then, we'll see."

And her mother had been right. He'd said yes.

♡♡♡

It didn't take long for things to get out of hand. In fact, it took about five seconds.

Her mother came to the door of the modest ranch house at Faith's knock, preceded by a cascade of yapping—Montclair, her little poodle, on the job.

"Hi, Mom." Faith gave her mother a hug that was returned with interest. "This is Will."

"Bella Goodwin." Her mother held out a hand to Will, looking as neat and pretty as always in a pale-blue sweater and cream pants, both of which showed off her still-excellent figure. She cocked her head of neatly bobbed platinum hair at an angle and smiled up at him. "Now, aren't you just the nicest surprise?"

Which sounded pleasant enough, but Faith wasn't relaxing. Her mother's ways were devious.

Will laughed, the easy, rich sound filling the little hallway, an influx of testosterone into Bella's feminine surroundings. The half-circle of mahogany table was set with a vase of calla lilies tonight, the crystal chandelier sparkled overhead, and Will stood, big and brown, in the center of it all, flashing a smile that competed with any chandelier.

"Didn't think I was a surprise, but we'll hope it's nice. I'll do my best. And who's this wee fella?" He crouched on the oriental hallway rug to give Montclair's fluffy gray head a rub, sending the little dog into a frenzy of tail-wagging ecstasy.

"That's Montclair. Oh, my, the accent," Bella said. "That's just the cherry on top of the ice-cream sundae. I do like some decoration at my dinner table."

"Mom," Faith said, "you'll embarrass Will."

"Oh, I don't think Will's easily embarrassed," Bella said. "I think Will's heard it all before." And there she went, X-ray vision at work.

"Now, that'd be telling." He rose to stand with another grin. "And I'm thinking you've heard it all before yourself, because if I'm decorative, I'm not the only one here. I've been trying to get Faith out with me for days, and now I get a double dose of Goodwin girls? My mum always did say I was born under a lucky star."

"You have not been trying to get me out with you for days," Faith said, feeling the treacherous color rise in her cheeks. Her mother never blushed, and Faith never failed to.

"No?" he asked. "Who asked you out for coffee yesterday? And who said no?"

"Ah...I had work to do."

His smile was all for her now, those eyes gleaming. "Yeh. I remember. Work. But I'm here now, because I *am* a lucky man."

"Oh, boy," Bella said. "Come have dinner. It's getting too warm in here for me."

A break, then, that Faith sorely needed, while she helped her mother dish up, and then they were sitting around her round oak dining table, set with pretty lace placemats, having dinner. Dinner, and that was it.

"You know, I can't believe it," Bella said, taking a dainty forkful of, yes, eggplant casserole. Which Will was eating, too, because he was polite. "Here's Calvin getting back into the skin trade again, after going respectable for so many years, just like me. Makes me think that I should see if I've still got it." She gave her hair a little pat. "Nah. I know I've still got it. But maybe not with my clothes off."

Faith concentrated on her chicken medallions. "My mother was

45

a showgirl," she told Will with resignation. How long had that taken? Fifteen minutes?

"Seriously?" Will asked. "Awesome. With the…" He gestured towards his own head. "The feathers on your head and all?"

"That was me. And those headdresses weighed a ton, I'll tell you. Calvin started out as a photographer for the casinos himself. That's how we met. He's known Faith since she was a little girl. And the two of us—we had a good time together, back in the day." She sighed. "We both had our share of adventures, but we were each others' go-to, when we needed a friend. He's never been a smooth talker, but that's overrated. Always good for a nice, comforting—"

"Too much information, Mom," Faith put in hurriedly. "Will does not need to know that."

"Well, it's all a good twenty years ago anyway." Bella shrugged and took another ladylike bite. "And if I've shocked Will, let's say I'm surprised. He's a model himself. He's been around the block."

"Well, I'm not quite a model," Will said. "But I'm not too shocked, no."

"Mm-hmm." Bella nodded. "Just breaking into the business, are you?"

Will seemed to be having trouble keeping a straight face. "You could say that."

"Then you should know that Faith's the one who really gave you your big break," Bella said. "And that she's got more power there than you probably realize. Assistant? Maybe so and maybe not."

"Mom—" Faith said again.

"Oh, shush, honey. I'm proud of you. Calvin was just thinking about taking some stock photos," she explained to Will. "Dime a dozen. The rest of it—that was all Faith."

"Ah," he said. "The website. And the writing contest."

"Well, yes." Faith needed to change the subject. She'd known bringing him to dinner would be a bad idea. If her mother pulled out the album with her publicity photos, Faith didn't care, she was hauling Will off pronto. Bella was trying to get a rise out of Will, or expose him, or warn him off, or something. Faith couldn't tell *what* she was trying to do, but it was making her more than a little nervous. "I thought, if Calvin was going to be taking pictures for stock photo sites anyway, we'd try something new with it, hopefully something more lucrative. Especially for me, since I'll be managing it. If it works, I could get a full-time job out of it. That's the point. And it's not the skin trade. Really, Mom. The skin trade?"

"I'm beginning to see what you meant about being very busy," Will said. "What with the erotica management and all. Nightmare, thinking all that up, eh."

"Would you stop—" she began, and broke off.

"What? Teasing you? Nah. Sorry. Can't. Too easy." His smile was slow, and now she was nervous for more reasons than one, because that smile was sending tingles down her spine. And more than her spine.

"Oh, honey, the whole thing was her idea," Bella assured him. "My hard-working, proper daughter. My naughty side is coming out in her at last, but in a whole lot smarter kind of way. She'll never let it get the better of her. The erotica contest, the special website, even the idea of the big Polynesian warrior and the little blonde girl? Beauty and the Beast, because she knows that never gets old. That was all Faith. You're just part of the plan."

Will was still looking at Faith. "Beauty and the Beast."

"Of course not." Faith tried to ignore the warmth that she could feel creeping up from the all-too-wide boat neck of her sweater. Her chest was heating, and her cheeks were glowing, too, and he was watching it happen. "That sounds terrible. I was just trying to think of something more interesting, something that would make it…work. Which, yes, was out of self-interest. My job with Calvin's only half-time, but if this takes off, with me handling the marketing end, I could drop my other job."

"Oh, no," Will said. "And me getting so attached to my apartment manager. What if I have a power failure in the night? Who am I going to call?"

"I told you." She was trying not to smile, but she couldn't help it. She knew he was just being smooth, just flirting, but he was so...so tempting. "I'm very busy. I wasn't talking about the apartment management. I also work in marketing communications for the Roundup. The casino. Very, very busy."

"Well, then," Will said, "I'd better do my bit, I guess, to help you on your way. Be the very best Beast I can be, inspire as many dirty stories as I possibly can. As it's for such a good cause."

♡♡♡

He sat, watched the tide of pink creep up the porcelain skin of her chest, her throat, into her cheeks, and felt the heat rising in himself right along with it. Even as she tried to be matter-of-fact, tried to pretend that all those dirty thoughts, that entire shot list hadn't been hers, when he knew they had been. He was looking at her, and she was looking straight back at him, her blue eyes caught in his gaze, and she seemed to have forgotten that she was holding her fork. He was ready to lay her right down on this table, and she could see it. Never mind what he'd told Solomon. Never mind what he'd told Faith. He couldn't help himself.

"You know," Bella said after a minute, "I'm the last to be prejudiced because somebody's in the business. How could I be?"

"Looks like you still could be in that business, too, whatever you say." Will tore his gaze from Faith and concentrated on Bella. "Easy to see where Faith gets her good looks. Although," he added with his best smile, "I won't go any further with that. Such a thing as dinner table conversation, at least that's what my own mum tells me."

Faith passed him a dish. "More green beans?"

"What, nobody's ever told you that you're as pretty as your mum?" He took it from her and served himself up a few more vegetables. At least it wasn't eggplant—which had sounded terrible, and turned out to be aubergine. But then, he didn't care for aubergine, either. "Hard to believe."

48

Bella laughed. "You are so good. You've really got the gift, haven't you?"

"I have?" Not quite the reaction he'd expected, because there was a cynical gleam in her eye.

"In fact, you've got more than that. You weren't standing behind the door when anything was handed out, that's obvious. Good thing you brought him over tonight, honey," Bella told Faith. "Because this one..." She shook her head. "I could have given you a run for your money, back in the day. But Faith? No. She's not up to your weight."

"Mom." Faith's color was even higher now. "Please. We talked about this."

"Men like you..." Bella sighed. "You're like that chocolate cheesecake going around and around in the display case at the diner. It looks so good, you just can't help yourself. It tastes just that good, too. You're taking that first bite, and you're thinking, oh, yeah, this is delicious, and I'm not sorry. And then it's gone, and, yep, you're just that sorry."

"Uh..." Will sat, at a loss for once.

"Thanks for the tip, Mom," Faith said. "Please stop."

"Hope I'm—" Will began, then broke off. "Hope I'm a bit more than that," he managed. "More than...ah....chocolate cheesecake."

"You're thinking I'm racist," Bella said calmly. "But I'm not. Chocolate cheesecake's delicious. So is regular old white cheesecake. So is...lemon cheesecake. But it's all the same in the end. A real nice moment on the lips, and a lifetime of regret on the hips."

"All right," Faith said. "We get it." The color was all the way there now. Will didn't think he'd ever seen a woman blush as much as she did, and he was embarrassed himself, and a little offended, and turned on as hell by her all the same. But however embarrassed he was, she was more so.

"So I'm not specially bad for her because I'm Maori," he said. "Just because I'm..."

"Yeah. Because you're that," Bella said. "Too good-looking. Too used to getting it easy. And, honey," she told her daughter, "if you have to take a number, take a pass. I'm just telling you for your own good," she said as Faith uttered a choked little sound of protest. "We can all see it. Not like he's hiding it. I'm just putting it out there."

It was out there, all right. It was right out there. And whatever his chances had been, they were that much less now.

♡♡♡

"I'm sorry," Faith said when they were in her truck again, driving back to her place. Their place. "I didn't know that would happen. But she's protective."

"I managed to suss that out, yeh. Reeled me in, didn't she. And then she got me straight through the gills." He didn't think he'd ever been so thoroughly dismissed.

"Sorry about that," she said again.

"No worries." He did his best to pretend that he hadn't cared. "She can think what she likes, though I hope I'm not as bad as all that."

"I can tell you're offended. And I'm sure you're thinking, what right does she have to say anything? When she talks about the skin trade, and what she used to do, and all that. But it's because she's a mom. A *great* mom. She's trying to make sure I don't make the same mistakes she did, just like she always has. She taught me that, and everything else, too. How to stand up for myself, and how to stand on my own two feet, not to depend on anybody else. That you can't count on anyone but yourself, and how not to get sucked into thinking you can."

"Well, that's a bit harsh. I'd like to think you can count on some people."

"Well, her," Faith amended. "I can count on her. Because she's still a mom. She wants me to be independent, but she has me manage her apartment complex, when she could get somebody with real handyman skills to do it, and then she pretends I'm doing her a favor. She does it because that's what she can do for me. She couldn't send me to college, but she's helping me pay off the loans all the same. She does what she can do. Everything she can do. And she's taught me how to do the rest for myself, so I can survive."

It sounded like such a lonely life. Such a hard life. The two of them against the world? "I wouldn't have said that she wasn't a good mum," he said cautiously, because she sounded a bit defensive, and why was that?

"She was," Faith said again. "She went to every parent-teacher conference, even if she'd just gotten home from doing two shows a night. On her feet for hours every night in spike heels, with that smile plastered on her face. Once she got the showgirl job, that is, because before that, yeah, she was an exotic dancer, and she wouldn't be ashamed to tell you so. So if she seems a little jaded about men, a little cynical? She's got reasons. But she'd trade shifts so she could go to Back-to-School night, even when the other parents didn't talk to her. That's the kind of person she is. She's always held her head high."

"But it's Vegas."

"Doesn't mean people don't still look down on women who take their clothes off for money. And she wasn't a hooker, if that's what you're thinking." She was driving a bit faster now, speeding down Tropicana Boulevard, her hands clenching on the wheel. "In fact, that's the one time I got in trouble in school. Fourth grade. A boy said my mother was a hooker. He didn't even know quite what it meant, I'm sure. He'd heard it from his parents. I didn't know, either. But I knew it was bad."

"What did you do?"

She laughed, but it wasn't her usual Faith-laugh. It was short. Dry. "I punched him. Gave him a bloody nose. Then I kicked him in the balls. Man, I'll tell you, he went down like a *rock*. My mom had to come get me at school, because I got suspended. I'm a dangerous enemy, just so you know."

"I'll keep that in mind. But I suspect your mum is, too. What did she say?"

"She told me not to fight her battles. I asked her what a hooker was, and she said, 'That's a woman who has to have sex for money.' You notice that? *Has to.* She said, and I still remember this, 'So you know? No, I'm not a hooker. But I'm not going to look down on women who do what they have to do to take care of themselves, or to take care of their kids. We're all just doing what we have to do to get by.'"

He didn't know quite what to say to that, so he didn't say anything.

"She was a good mom," she repeated after a minute. "She had fun, sure she did. You just heard her tell you so, because she's honest. But she told me I was smart, and that being smart mattered. She made sure I wouldn't have to use my body to survive. She pushed me in school. She was proud of me."

"I can see that."

"And you know, men want women to be sexy. Then they look down on them for being sexy. Like if they're sexy, that's all they are. My mom's more than that." She shook her head, pulled onto Torrey Pines at the light, and slowed to twenty-five. "I'm not making sense, I suppose."

"No. You are. So where was your dad?"

"Married."

"Ah."

"Yeah." She sighed, pulled into the little parking lot of the apartment complex, and turned the engine off, but kept sitting there, so he did too. "She didn't know, of course. Because men are good at lying. Some men, anyway," she went on hastily, as if that would be a shock to him. "She didn't tell him about me, because she didn't want to wreck his wife's marriage. She told me the truth, though, when I was old enough to hear it. She didn't sugarcoat it, because life's hard, and facing the truth is the only way through. My mom's a decent lady, although I don't expect you to see that."

"I see it. And my dad buggered off himself, didn't he," he

found himself admitting. "Worse than that, I guess you'd say. After five kids, when I was eighteen. So I know about strong mums who do what they have to do. And I know about looking after your mum, too. About wanting to protect her. Don't worry about me. She was keeping you safe. That's a mum's job, keeping her kids safe."

She was still sitting there in the dark, and she didn't look like she was moving. Normally, that would have been his signal that a woman wanted him to kiss her. Normally.

"You know," she said, looking at him at last, "you're just way too confusing."

That startled a laugh out of him. "Me? How?"

"Would you just be one way? Let me make up my mind? At first I think you're a player, and my mom's completely right. And then you're so *sweet*. Stop that. It's messing me up."

He wanted to kiss her. He'd never wanted to do anything more. If he was sweet...she was that, too, and so much else besides. Sweet, and warm, and curvy, and so bloody sexy. Her embarrassment, and her passion, defending her mother. The way she'd blushed, the way he'd seen her breath coming a bit faster, there at dinner, when he'd looked at her. He'd known that if he'd put his palm on her chest, just above that wide vee of neckline, he'd have felt her heart galloping, and the need to do it had pulled at him. Was still pulling at him.

So, yes, he wanted to kiss her. But he didn't. "Your mum's right," he said instead, and felt the wrench of it, the twist in his gut. "I'm a player. I'm chocolate cheesecake. And I'm leaving in less than three weeks."

"Yes. You are."

He looked at her there in the dark. She wasn't looking at him, was staring out through the windshield, her hands still on the wheel despite the fact that they weren't going anywhere at all, and her expression was so...so troubled. So sad, and it was making him sad, too.

"I'm never noble," he said, "and I wouldn't have said I had a clue how to be. I'm doing my best, though. I'm leaving, and I don't stick anyway. So I'm going to get out of this truck, and I'm not even going to kiss you goodnight, because I like you too much. And I don't want to muck that up."

She turned her head at that. "All right." It was just a breath. Had he been wrong? Did she want him to kiss her?

He couldn't help it. His hand went out like it belonged to somebody else and tucked a wisp of hair that had fallen down from its knot back behind her ear, then brushed her cheek. Her skin was soft, and her eyes were, too, that gorgeous mouth had parted, and she was leaning into him a bit, surely.

And then she pulled away like it was an effort and got out of the truck, and he followed her, and said goodnight, and *didn't* kiss her.

And why was it, he wondered as he walked down the hall to his empty apartment, that doing the right thing had to feel so wrong?

true confessions
♡

Cold Days, Hot Nights at the Roundup

Faith sat at her little dining-room table, typed the headline, then stared at it for a minute, her fingers hovering over the keys. *The weather outside might be frightful,* she wrote. Well, it had rained that one day. *But the entertainment at the Roundup is always smoking-hot.*

She inserted an image of Sheila, one of the casino's dancers, riding the mechanical bull in a pair of chaps, a G-string, and nothing else, with Robert, the principal boy dancer, up behind her, looking like he was ready to take over.

What was she thinking? She'd get fired. Too many sexy pictures, too much looking at a half-naked Will. Too much *fantasizing* about a half-naked Will. She substituted the PG version, the one where Sheila was wearing a sparkly vest.

As a valued VIP, you and your guest will have a front-row seat on opening night of our brand-new show, Lassoed. *Afterwards, you're invited to an exclusive backstage meet-and-greet with our talented dancers.*

And you're not invited to feel up Sheila, she didn't write. Last time, the dancers had complained.

"Tell them not to hug me!" Sheila had said, storming into the

Marketing Department during what had become the most
entertaining meeting Faith had ever attended. "I don't get paid
enough for that, and the next nasty old guy that tries it? He gets a
knee."

Faith sighed, now, and looked out the window at a slightly
unkempt palm. She needed to do some pruning. She should clean
the gutters, too.

Inspiration really wasn't coming today, if cleaning the gutters
sounded better than writing the February copy for the Winners'
Circle. She stared at the palm a minute longer without really seeing
it, then opened a new document. Maybe just for five minutes. Just
to clear her head.

The problem was, it wasn't Sheila and Robert taking up all her
available brain-space, or the dirty-old-man members of the high
rollers' club, either. It was Gretchen and Will, from the day before.

Not really, though. It was Hope and Hemi.

Hope in a pale-pink bra and a filmy white shirt that was falling
open, because Hemi's hands were unbuttoning it from behind, his
mouth just grazing her neck, his jaw dark with the barest hint of
stubble. Faith had had to set up a box for Gretchen in order for
Will to reach her, had had to keep adjusting angles so Calvin could
get the shot, with Charlotte in there redoing Gretchen's makeup,
spraying Will down again to keep his skin glistening while Faith
crawled on the floor.

It didn't matter that she knew what was really happening behind
the scenes. The images were still there, exactly as if they were real.
The two of them kneeling, Hemi's arm, bare now, around Hope,
his hand on the zipper of her unbuttoned jeans, his other hand
pulling her blond hair back, his mouth near her ear.

Faith's fingers were moving despite herself, despite every better
intention.

*The elevator stopped on the 43rd floor, and my heart slammed against my
chest. Because it was Hemi Te Mana himself getting in, his glance flicking over
me just as it had the week before.* A predatory glance, *my wild imagination
provided. Or a dismissive one, more likely. A little smile on his beautiful lips.*

He'd probably noticed my shoe. Rumor had it he noticed everything.

"You're here," he said, pushing the button for 51. "Looking forward to your interview?"

Oh, God. I was staring. At his shirt, open at the neck to reveal a triangle of smooth brown skin, glimpsed for a single glorious instant before he turned to stand beside me. Which gave me a great view of the perfectly tailored black suit jacket that clung to his broad shoulders and narrowed to his trim waist.

It took me a moment to register what he'd said, and not just because I was stunned to be standing beside him. It was the accent. I'd heard it in interviews as well as at the shoot, but all the same, the clipped tones and New Zealand vowels fell strangely on my ear. But there was nothing a bit strange about the low voice. As creamy as chocolate, as deep and rich as his skin. As hot as a New Zealand summer. Well, what I imagined a New Zealand summer would be.

"How did you know?" I asked, struggling to focus on what he'd said.

"I make it my business to know everything. Because it is *my business."*

The elevator came to a stop, the doors glided open, and he put a hand out to hold them. "Here you are."

"Thanks," I said. "Wish me luck." Then I could have kicked myself. Why was I talking to him like that? Like he was...anybody?

A faint smile warmed his brown eyes for just a moment, lightening his expression so he wasn't the cold, forbidding figure he'd seemed at the shoot, and then the mask had slipped back into place, and my heart was fluttering, beating out a fierce tattoo.

"I don't think you'll need luck," he told me. "I have a feeling you're going to knock them dead."

♡♡♡

Shoot, Faith thought. *Shoot, shoot, shoot.* This wasn't paying her own bills. And she was fresh out of inspiration for the Roundup. She just couldn't get excited about simulated sex on the mechanical bull, not when she had simulated sex of her own to write about.

Because hers had a *story,* that was why, and it was a story that was itching to be told. Who was Hemi, underneath? And who knew that Hope was desperate for this job? Faith did, that was who.

An hour later, she'd given up on the Roundup, but at least she was working on something practical again. And she was sweating.

"Don't you have somebody to do that?" she heard from behind her. That same dark-chocolate voice, and too bad she wasn't in an elevator, and that he wasn't about to make all her financial worries go away.

"I do." She continued to saw, because she needed to finish this, now that she'd started. She still had one more tree to go. "Me."

"You do the gardening? That's pretty heavy work."

The thin-bladed, long-handled wooden saw bit through the final bit of tough, spiky stem, and she leaned back. "Watch it," she warned. "Sharp edges."

The heavy frond fell to the ground to join its fellows, the wicked teeth along its edges missing him as he jumped back.

"I don't do all the gardening," she said, turning on her stepladder to look at him. He was in a T-shirt, shorts, and running shoes, a damp vee of sweat darkening the light-gray fabric down his broad chest, but she wasn't looking at that. Well, hardly at all. "I have a service to do the grass and the basic stuff. But this is too expensive. And, hey. It's a whole lot worse when it's 110 out."

"So..." He kicked at the pile of fronds at the base of the tree, looked around at the two others she'd already pruned. "Need a hand?"

"No, thanks. Besides, you already worked out today."

"Do me a favor." He sounded pained. "I think I could manage that without straining myself."

"I don't have gloves that would fit you," she said, eyeing his hands. Which, as Calvin had already noted, were big. *The better to touch you with.* "And my insurance won't cover it if you get hurt. No."

He sighed in obvious exasperation. "What d'you do with all these? The fronds?"

"Put them in my truck," she said reluctantly. "Take them to the dump. There you go. My afternoon plan, at least part of it, before I get back to my real job."

"We aren't shooting until tomorrow."

"Marketing for a casino, remember? My other job, I guess I should say."

"Then let me help you," he said. "Let me just run up and change, and then I'll bung these things into the truck, how's that? And I'll go with you, too."

"You do not want to go to the dump. Plus, I have another errand afterwards."

He shrugged. "Why don't I want to go to the dump? I don't have anything else to do."

Which was why he was sitting next to her in the truck at the Waste Management site on West Sahara an hour later, having just grabbed the gloves from her despite her protests, wrestled them as far onto his hands as he'd been able to manage, and tossed the wickedly sharp palm fronds onto the trash pile in the concrete bay.

"All I can say is," she said when he'd hopped in to join her again, "star athletes must live differently in New Zealand."

"Not too differently from anybody else." He pulled off the leather gloves and setting them on the dash. "Because we don't make nearly as much money as they do here, probably. Maybe a tenth, if we're lucky. Makes it harder to set yourself up as some rich boofhead."

"What's a boofhead?" *That* was a new one. And a *tenth?* Wow.

He grinned. "Dickhead, more or less. I was being polite."

That startled a laugh out of her, but she quickly sobered as the thought struck her. "You didn't—"

"Didn't what? What have you dreamed up now?"

She couldn't believe she hadn't thought of it before. "You took the modeling job because you needed to," she realized. "And living in Mrs. Ferguson's place— You're not—"

"Oh, bloody hell," he sighed. "What am I not? Go on and finish a sentence. Are we back to the felon idea?"

She wasn't sure how to ask. "That you came to Las Vegas. Do

you have a...a problem? You're not...broke?" Good thing she'd gotten the rent up front.

She cast a hasty glance across at him, saw him looking chagrined, and her heart sank. He was in trouble. She'd known it.

Silence reigned for a few pregnant moments before he spoke. "I'm sorry," he said. "I didn't want you to know. I do have a problem. I need to get it sorted, I know it. I kept thinking I could keep it under control, that I could stop. But when I bet my house..." He looked away, staring at nothing, at blank concrete. "Afterwards, it was like a...like it had been some kind of bad dream. I ducked out of the hotel that day without paying, too. I didn't want you to know, but it's on my conscience." He swung around to her again, his dark gaze earnest. "I'm planning to pay it back, though," he assured her, "soon as I get the next payment from Calvin. That's why I agreed to it, the modeling, even though it's..." He swallowed. "Degrading. But it's what your mum said. You do what you have to do."

"You—" she began. The sweetness she'd seen in him, the rare flashes of vulnerability. This was why? She'd forgotten she was still sitting in the trash bay, backed up to a mountain of junk, because he was staring sightlessly out into the yard now, watching a garbage truck roll slowly by. As she watched, he swallowed, the Adam's apple moving in his strong brown throat.

And then she saw the telltale twitch at the corner of his mouth. "You're messing with me," she realized. "You are totally—" He lost the battle, started to laugh, and she slugged him hard in his solid upper arm. "You *jerk.*"

He grabbed her hand in a flash, tugged her towards him. "I'm a jerk?" he asked, smiling into her eyes. "Me? I'm not the one slagging off somebody's character."

His hand was hard and warm around hers, and she couldn't have said if she was leaning into him, or if he was doing the leaning, but her eyes were fluttering closed, and his lips were brushing over hers, his other hand coming up to cup her cheek.

It was all warm, and sweet, and soft. Then he was kissing her again, his lips a little firmer now, and every single nerve in her body was springing to life. She heard herself making a little whimpering sound that didn't even sound like her, and his hand was behind her head, his other arm going around her, pulling her close.

"Oh, *hell*, no." The voice was rough. Pained. "That's just sad."

Her eyes sprang open, and she was jerking back from Will, because a burly man in stained coveralls and a goatee was bent over, peering into the truck's window beside her.

"I'd say get a room, but damn, man," he told Will, "that's desperate. At the fu— the friggin' *dump?* We got people waiting, dude. Get out of here."

dress rehearsal

♡

He'd just kissed a woman in a rubbish tip. Worse, he'd kissed *Faith* there. What was next? He was going to make his big move at the cemetery?

She cleared her throat, shoved the truck into gear, and started off with a jolt. A little rough on the clutch, but he couldn't blame her. He was still shaken. Her soft, responsive mouth, her sweet, warm body...at the *dump*.

"So..." he said as she made a right onto Sahara, then moved on over through the late-afternoon traffic into the left lane. "Not my smoothest moment."

She laughed in surprise, and he grinned at her, and she laughed some more, and then they were both laughing, because they couldn't help it.

"I am *so* tempted," she told him, pulling to a stop at a light and raising a hand to swipe at her eyes, "to tell my mom."

He leaned his head back and groaned. "The worst. That would be the worst. Could we start again? I do a pretty fair line in dark, dangerous grabbing, I'm told, if you give me a bit of rehearsal and some coaching."

"No," she said, that smile trying to peep through. "Probably my fault, though," she added generously, because that was how Faith was. "I mean, with your gambling addiction and all."

"And losing all my money," he reminded her. "Don't forget that. I don't gamble, actually. I may have put a quarter or two into one of those pokies machines, can't promise I haven't, but a sportsman can't afford to be a gambler."

"One of those *what?*"

"Pokies. You know." He made the motion. "Ching-ching-ching?"

"Ah. Slot machines. Boy, you talk funny."

The light had turned green, and she was headed south on Valley View. "But I kiss all right," he said, and grinned at her again. "At least that's what they say." And then he could have kicked himself. He wasn't meant to be doing casual. He should have been romantic or something. He'd *felt* romantic, back there. When she'd been melting against him, he'd wanted to lay her down, touch her, kiss her everywhere, and murmur…things. When she'd made that little whimpering noise into his mouth…he'd been *gone*. But he'd said he wouldn't push it, and he had the feeling that no matter what he said or how he said it, she wasn't going to be playing.

"Yeah," she said. "I'll bet they do. And no. We're taking that right off the table." Which made him sigh again.

"Right. Friends, eh. And not with benefits."

"You want benefits," she said, sounding a little more sure of herself again, "go find some other girl. But…this is awkward."

"What?"

"I'm trying to be all businesslike about this whole thing. The photography, I mean. I thought, people do this all the time, right? The sexy pictures? No big deal. But I wasn't expecting it to be…you. I thought it'd just be some model, and I've worked with a lot of models."

"But?" he prompted.

"Maybe it's because you're not really a model. Who knows?"

"Well, I do. I know. Because I feel the same way. Not sure how anybody does it. Not because it's so sexy," he went on hastily. "Because it's not, is it. It's just…a bit weird. Especially doing it in front of you."

"And it's about to get weirder. Because my next errand? It's to the Adult Megastore."

"Which would be…"

"Yeah." She sighed. "The adult store. Not for me," she added, as if he couldn't have guessed that. "For supplies."

"Don't tell me," he said, all the humor gone. "You said nothing too dirty. I'm not posing with some…some kind of toys, or gear. No. Absolutely not."

"It's not that bad. You won't even be in the shots. Well, maybe a few of them," she admitted, "like we said. So maybe it's a good thing you're coming after all. I can show you, and then you won't pitch a fit, and make Calvin pitch one. But it's embarrassing, all right? Because I've never been in one of those stores," she confessed, and the color was rising in her cheeks again. "I researched online, of course," she added hastily, like the conscientious student she'd probably been, "but I don't know what to expect, and going there with you…maybe I need to ask you to wait in the truck."

"Oh, no. Not possible." The laughter was bubbling up again from deep in his chest despite his fairly serious disappointment. "I'm sure I shouldn't say this, but I'm guessing I can find my way around. Consider me your guide."

♡♡♡

Except that they had a guide. An older lady, wearing a tunic over stretch pants, a bright, beaded necklace, glasses, and a smile, guaranteed to take all the sexyfeels straight out of his dream date with Faith.

"Can I help you?" she asked as the two of them walked through the pneumatic doors into the store, which sat in a strip mall next to a swimming-pool supply and a pet-food shop. All in a day's work for Vegas, Will supposed.

"Ah..." Faith said, looking around her wildly. Ahead of them sat a huge display of condoms, while the racks to the right were filled with DVDs whose covers left nothing to the imagination.

"First time shopping with us?" the saleswoman asked.

"Yes," Faith said, and there was that blush again, creeping up her chest, into her throat, up her cheeks. "I mean, it's not for us. Well, it's for us, but—"

"Aw, darling," Will said, putting an arm around her and hauling her up to him. "She's a little nervous," he told the saleswoman. "It's my birthday, you see. Bit of a present. The kind I buy." He felt Faith stiffening beside him, and looked down at her. "Where did you want to start, sweetheart?" he asked her tenderly. "I'm all yours. Or do you want me to take charge?"

She cleared her throat. "I'd like to look at your scarves," she told the woman. "And various sorts of ties. Something in that general area."

"Ah," the clerk said. "The Restraint section. In the back, right down here. Follow me."

She led the way, her soft-soled shoes making no sound against the tile floor.

"Let go of me," Faith hissed at Will, and he dropped his arm and grinned at her.

"I'm paid back for that gambling addiction," he told her. "Not sure we've quite got past losing my house and all my money, but you're definitely working on it."

"Here we are," their guide announced, turning around in the back aisle. "You've got your ties here," she said with a gesture. "Handcuffs, lined and unlined. The lined ones are much more comfortable," she assured Faith. "Of course, it depends what you prefer, but we find that most couples like to start at the low end of the spectrum, at the fantasy level, then move up as their preferences dictate."

She pulled out a good-sized square box from the bottom shelf. "This is particularly popular, if you don't have a bed with posts.

The Under-Bed Restraint System. It fits between your mattress and box spring, and tucks away when you're not using it. Nothing for the kids to find."

"Very…sensible," Faith managed. Will would have answered, but he'd got a bit distracted by the cover of the box, at the woman spread-eagled on that white bed. He'd never run much that way, but he could definitely feature it. With the right woman. With *this* woman.

"Such a good idea, darling," he said, taking the box from the clerk. "I know you were after something a bit more extreme, but for your first time…"

She was still blushing, but she had a glint in her eye, and she'd grabbed the box from him, was looking it over critically. She opened one end and pulled out a tangle of black straps, testing the hook-and-loop fastening on one circular restraint. "You said you'd always wanted to wear real handcuffs, though. Now you're chickening out? How am I going to be a cop using this thing? Pretty tame. And I want you to have a really *good* birthday."

She closed the box again and handed it back to the clerk. "Actually," she told the woman in her usual businesslike tones while Will was still grappling for an answer, "I want something more scarf-like, like I said. Or maybe some really soft ropes. Pink, red. Those sorts of colors."

"I understand." The woman led the way down the aisle. "Here you are." She picked up a plastic bag. "Scarves, feather tickler, and blindfold. Very popular starter set. All pink."

"Fine," Faith said. "Can you just leave us here? We can manage now."

"Of course. I'll be up front, if you need anything else. Take your time, and please feel free to browse."

Faith put back the plastic bag and didn't look at Will. He waited until the saleswoman had moved away, and then said, "A cop, eh."

"Serves you right." Her hand was going out to touch various bits of tackle, testing, stroking, then moving on. She was still going for severe, but she wasn't quite managing it. "You are *wretched.*"

"I am, am I? You could have just done this online, you know. Not that I'm not enjoying it heaps," he hastened to add. "And I'd like to point out, as a comparison shopper, that this is a seriously well-equipped place, and I'm putting my hand up here and now to explore it with you. But if you're embarrassed, that's why they invented plain brown packaging and mail order, eh."

"I need to see the fabric," she explained, her cheeks still tinged with pink. "I need to feel it. It needs to look silky, and sensual, and not cheap. We're after some shots that are mostly black and white, just the one splash of color on her wrists. And maybe a blindfold, too. Just in case. But it's got to look pretty, not nasty or tacky, and I have to see it to make sure."

"Tasteful," he remembered, watching her caress a length of wide, heavy red silk ribbon. She pulled it off its hook, ran it between her fingers, held it up and tested its length.

"Like I said." She sounded distracted. "What do you think?"

"Mmm…" He took the ribbon from her, put a hand on her shoulder, and turned her around. "This the idea? Hands behind the back?"

"Yes." Her voice came out a little husky, because he was wrapping the ribbon around her wrists and tying it in a bow.

"I'd say," he said, stepping back and admiring the effect, "that it's brilliant."

"On Hope?" She turned her head to look at him over her shoulder, with her wrists side by side behind her back. Her hands tied with that red ribbon, against the swell of her rounded bum.

"Who?" He wasn't paying attention. He was busy.

"Gretchen. Hope. Your co-star. How is she going to look in it, in her bra and underwear?"

Who cared? He'd lost the plot, because he had an entirely different scenario in mind.

"Well?" she demanded. "Good? Not good?" She wandered over to the mirror on the wall and turned so she could see herself. "Oh, yeah," she sighed. "Good on her. Don't you think?"

"Yeh." Will cleared his throat, which had gone dry. She was

coming back over to him now, and her hair had fallen down from its bun a little more from the exertions of the day—and from his hand in it earlier. A few unruly strands framed her oval face, and a few hairs were stuck to her cheek, next to that mole over her lip. Having her hands tied like that was thrusting her breasts out towards him, and he reached out despite himself and brushed the hair back. His thumb traced the little mole, because he was only human, and what man would have been able to resist that?

"Good," he said. "And I really, really want to kiss you again. Could you remind me again why we can't?"

Her eyes had widened, and her lips had parted, and he didn't have to look down to know that her nipples had hardened under the T-shirt, because he could see it out of the corner of his eye, and if this kept on much longer, he was going to be embarrassing himself.

"Because…" She swallowed hard, and he saw it. "Because you're leaving. And you don't stick anyway."

"Oh, yeh," he sighed. "That. Honesty's a bugger, eh."

She laughed a little, just a breath out, swallowed again, then turned her back to him. "Untie me. Please."

He put a hand on her shoulder, felt her tremble a bit under his touch, and, with a Herculean effort, pulled the end of the red ribbon, untwisted it from around her wrists, and handed it back to her. "Changed my mind," he told her. "I'm not exploring this shop with you, because one little ribbon, and you're killing me. I get you in the vibrator section, and…no."

"Really?" She looked surprised, and pleased, he could've sworn, and then she hurried on. "Well, I just need to grab a couple more things, and we can go. And no, there's no way I'm going to be looking at vibrators with you. I don't even know what they look like, to tell you the truth, and I don't think today's the day to find out."

"You've never…" He stopped, then tried again. "You've never owned a vibrator? Don't most women?"

She closed her eyes for a moment, opened them again, and said,

"I cannot believe I'm having this conversation. I don't know. It's not something I generally discuss with my friends."

"You don't—" he began, then stopped.

She crossed her arms. "I don't what? Now you're the one who can't finish a sentence. And I can't figure out what kind of person you think I am."

"Because I can't figure it out myself," he found himself confessing. "You've had me on the back foot since the day I met you, and no mistake. I think I'm ahead, and then there I am, rocking back again. Sucker-punched."

She didn't answer that, and he never did find out why she'd never owned a vibrator, or even *seen* one. Seriously? Because she was repressed, or because she could get there without help? He was getting an idea which it was, but he wanted to know for sure. No, he wanted to *learn*. For himself.

He wanted it, and he wanted it bad. He wanted to buy that box, tie her to his bed, take off her clothes so slowly, and find out just how much he could make her scream by the time he was done. And he wouldn't be using any vibrator.

He could see her there. He could very nearly *feel* her there, and he was dying.

But he didn't get any of it. Instead, they checked out a few minutes later with her red ribbon, a couple pink scarves just to be on the safe side, black and red satin blindfolds, and the worst case of sexual frustration he'd experienced since he was fourteen.

He leaned his head against the seat of her truck with a groan when they were on their way back to the apartment building at last. "Next time you go to the naughty shop?" he told her. "Leave me at home."

The smile was playing around her pretty mouth, trying to escape. "I can't say that was the most comfortable experience of my life, either. And we haven't even gotten to the tying-up scenes yet."

"Trust me. Holding Gretchen when she's tied up? That'll be a doddle compared to what you and I just did. They say the dress rehearsal's the hardest bit, and I reckon they're right. If I'm going to be rehearsing with you."

hole in one
♡

Hope and Hemi were in Paris, for some reason, and things were heating up. The sexual tension was getting out of control, in fact.

Hemi sighed. "Going to have to do something about you, aren't I? Where did all this sauciness come from?"

"I can't imagine." It actually was a surprise. I was keyed up, yes, but in a good way. Feeling reckless and free so far from home, light years away from my real life. I was teetering on the edge, my wings spread, ready to take off and soar, and I was scared, but I couldn't wait. And teasing Hemi? That, I was discovering, was a pure pleasure. "Maybe you made me feel too powerful, with my suite and all," I suggested. "Maybe you're being too nice to me."

"Hmm. Maybe I am. I can do something about that, too. Eventually." He gave me another of those looks he specialized in, dark and intense, like he had a secret he wasn't sharing, and the tingle of awareness went straight down my body. "And meanwhile," he went on, forcing me to come back to myself with a jerk, "we're in Paris, so what would you think about the Musee d'Orsay? The Impressionist museum." He must have seen my eyes light up. "Yeh. Thought that might work for you. We could do the Louvre, of course, but..."

"No!" I burst out, and he smiled a little. "Please," I added more quietly, even though I had to laugh. "I'd love that."

"We'll walk through the Tuileries, shall we?" he asked.
"Oh, let's."

♡♡♡

Faith lifted her hands from the keyboard, let out a groan, lowered her head to the desk, and banged it a couple times. "Stop," she told herself. "Stop it now."

She'd written the Roundup copy, finally, the day before. After her day out with Will, and the next day, when they'd gone into the studio and used the supplies she'd bought. When Will had stood, bare-chested, acres of smooth brown skin on display, and held Gretchen.

Calvin had image after image now of Gretchen's tiny frame, viewed from the back, in a bra and a pair of the very lowest, tightest, darkest jeans. With her wrists wrapped in red ribbon, Will's hands all over her, and Will's dark head bent to hers.

Will, who wasn't Hemi. Who was Will, funny and sexy and sweet. Will, who *would* take no for an answer, because he wasn't a ruthless multimillionaire CEO. He was something so much better; a reasonable man living in the real world. And all the same, Faith had stood there in the Adult Megastore with him and battled to keep herself under control, because, like Hope, she had a hard time saying no to him.

Her copy, after all that, had apparently dripped sex, because Steve, her manager at the Roundup, had had a funny look on his face when she'd gone in today for their weekly meeting.

"Excuse me? Faith?" he'd said. "What have you been drinking? And where can I get some of it?"

"Oh," she'd said, and wished she could cure herself of the habit of blushing. "Inspired, I guess."

"Well, sprinkle a little more of that pixie dust, then, because you've just earned yourself the Ali Baba campaign," he'd said, referring to one of the company's sister casinos. "They've got a new show, too, featuring belly dancers. You ought to be able to do plenty with that. Think Arabian Nights."

"Scheherazade."

"What?"

"The Arabian Nights. That's who...Never mind," Faith had said hastily. "Thanks. Great."

Which was what she was supposed to be doing now. Thinking sexy Middle Eastern thoughts, not Maori millionaire thoughts, because one paid the bills, and one didn't. She turned back to the computer and closed the document on Hemi even as he walked down a the corridor of a luxury hotel in her seriously dirty mind with a couple of red ribbons in the pocket of his suit coat, about to show Hope how he liked his women. Which was restrained. And underneath him.

No. Work. She began to type something that would actually pay those bills, got a paragraph down at last, and swore when the knock came.

The knuckles banged again. *Hot desert night,* she typed hastily, then got up and went to the door.

Thursday afternoon. Maintenance request, she hoped. Not a medical emergency, please, because she hated those. She got attached to her old people. She couldn't help it.

It *was* a medical emergency, but only for her heart, because it was Will on the other side of the door. Will in shorts, a T-shirt, and a hoodie, his feet bare.

"Don't you ever get cold?" she asked him, trying to get some control over herself. "Most people wear pants in the winter."

"What? Nah, course not. It's not cold here. Besides, Kiwis wear shorts. Probably because we have such good legs." He grinned at her snort. "Although not waxed," he pointed out. "That would be a hill too far."

"What can I do for you? Besides admire your legs, of course." Which, all right, she was doing, but then, he had *major* thighs. A person would have had to be blind not to notice, and she wasn't blind.

"Thought we needed some family-friendly entertainment," he

said. "Something more wholesome than rubbish and bondage."

"We?"

"Yeh. You and me. We. Us. As we're friends and all. Because here I am, got nothing to do but think nasty rich-bloke thoughts, and I've got to tie Gretchen to the bed tomorrow. Need something to take my mind off that, eh. I've got some friends besides you in Las Vegas, if you can believe it, and I'm taking them miniature-golfing on Saturday."

"Miniature...golfing." It couldn't have been further from Hemi in the Hôtel du Louvre with his red ribbon and his powerful stare. She'd lost the battle, and she was laughing.

He grinned and scratched his nose. "Yeh. Well. They've got a couple little kids, and they've been looking after me a bit while I've been here, had me to dinner and such, so I wanted to do something for them, and that's what they suggested. Thought you could come along, be my date. And it's a Family Fun Center. Got racecars and bumper boats and pizza and all. Good times. Want to bump my boat?"

"No," she said, aiming for severe and failing completely. "But I want to beat you through the windmill. Five bucks says I do it."

♡♡♡

Which was why she was wearing a UNLV sweatshirt and holding a golf club two days later while the wind blew through the palms surrounding the Family Fun Center, watching Will crouch beside a four-year-old girl and work his magic.

"You just give it a good whack, sweetheart," he told Sefina. "Send it straight up that ramp, because our team's going to win."

The little girl duly swung, and her club missed the ball entirely, the force of her swing carrying her around in a circle.

Will laughed. "Once more," he urged her. "You've got this."

She didn't, of course, and Will ended up putting his hands around hers and helping her, then cheering and doing a little dance when the ball went up and through the hole at the top of the ramp.

"Pound it." He held out his big fist and bumped it gently against her tiny one. "We are the champions," he told her solemnly.

"The champions!" she echoed happily.

Lelei sighed beside Faith, one hand on her belly. "Such a good guy. Wish he was staying." She cast a glance at Faith. "Bet you do, too."

"Oh, no," Faith said hurriedly. "We're just friends. And I'm his...well, my mother's his landlady."

"Yeah. We heard."

Faith didn't answer, because Will was looking at her, a light in his eyes, a smile on his face that had her looking back.

"Breathe," Lelei told her helpfully, and Faith jumped and laughed. And breathed.

♡♡♡

"So how has this dude been in the clinches?" Solomon asked Faith. He had one big arm around the back of his wife's chair while they all ate pizza in the cavernous din of the café.

"Oh, you know," Faith said. "He's managing, although dark and dangerous doesn't come easily." Which wasn't one bit true. It came through loud and clear.

"You're glad you didn't do it, cuz," Will said. "Don't think Lelei would've gone for the bit we did yesterday. Had that girl tied to the bed in her undies." He'd lowered his voice out of deference to the kids. "I had to close my eyes and think of England to do it myself. And next time, we're in the shower."

"Nightmare," Solomon said.

"Yeh. That's what I said."

"Definitely not," Lelei said with a shudder. "Definitely, definitely not. Besides, something better is going to come along for you," she told her husband. "I know it."

"Well, you know," he said, "you're my good-luck charm, so it's bound to."

"Mommy!" Sefina announced. "We're all done! We want to

whack-a-mole!"

Lelei began to rise, but Solomon heaved his big frame up from the bench. "Stay there. I'll go."

"So what's the deal with these pictures?" Lelei asked when the kids were safely out of earshot. "I didn't realize it'd be that graphic."

"Oh, it really isn't," Faith said.

"Here we go," Will said. "Faith's specialty, explaining the purely family-friendly nature of the entertainment to you."

"Quiet," Faith said, trying not to laugh. "It *isn't*. It's not that nasty, and you know it."

"Hmm," Lelei said after Faith had finished. "So is this erotica for men, or erotica for women? Because in my experience, they're two different things."

Will stared at her. "And you know this how?"

"How do you think? You think mothers never have dirty thoughts? Or fathers, for that matter?"

He groaned. "I did not need to hear that. I think Whack-a-Mole is calling my name."

Faith smiled, but answered Lelei. "For women, is my plan. That's the bigger audience for real stories, for a storyline. We're doing the website all in softer colors, softer focus, keeping the shots more suggestive than graphic. I'm hoping we'll get more erotic romance than erotica, but it's all an experiment. The pictures are turning out great, though. Right along those lines. I think we'll get some good stories."

Will snorted. "Good stories. Right. Is that really what women want? Some fella to tie them up and whip them?"

"Nobody is whipping anybody," Faith said. "I told you."

"Of course not," Lelei said at the same time. "It's fantasy, not reality. Do you think women can't tell the difference?"

Will looked at her in surprise. "You read it? It doesn't bother you, how unrealistic it is?"

"How wonderful is realism, though?" Lelei asked. "Real life is hard. Maybe it isn't in New Zealand, but here where I live, real life is bad bosses and car trouble and wondering whether your baby can wear those shoes for another month, because your January gas bill is going to be way too high. What's wrong with wanting to escape for a little while?"

"Doesn't it set unrealistic expectations, though," he asked, "of what your average bloke actually is?"

Faith answered that one. "Well, let's see. What does a man think, if he reads some thriller about a guy who's six-five and 250 pounds, going around the country righting wrongs and beating up six guys with one hand tied behind his back? Sleeping with the best-looking woman in town, who happens to be single, and just happens to be looking for a quick, no-strings hookup with a mysterious drifter? Does he imagine he's that guy? No," she answered for him as Lelei nodded emphatically across from her. "He knows he works in an office, and he really should hit the gym more often, and if one guy punched him *once*, he'd probably be in the hospital. But he enjoys reading about it anyway, doesn't he? And somehow, because he's not a total *idiot*, he's able to discern that it isn't his reality."

"Although," Lelei put in judiciously, "maybe if more men actually read those books, they might get some ideas, make a little more effort, and their ladies wouldn't have to escape quite so much. Not speaking from personal experience," she added hurriedly. "I'm all good there."

"I'm not touching that," Will said. "But is that what women actually want? Somebody to…hurt them? Push them? I've been going about this all wrong, then."

"Of course not," Lelei said, sounding a little exasperated now. "But the fantasy? Sure, it's a filthy-rich dude who's absolutely crazy about you, who can't imagine anything better than spending all Saturday morning in bed making delicious love to you, no matter who's playing in the bowl game. He might even come on pretty strong, because he's so overwhelmed by how much he wants you. He can afford to make all your problems go away, and show you a really good time, too, and what's wrong with that?"

"Nothing, I guess," Will said. "I agree with you, if I think about it. I'm a sportsman, after all. That's why I have a job, to provide men with their fantasy escape. So they can watch me get bashed on the paddock, and live vicariously for a couple hours."

"That's what they do," Faith said. "Isn't it? They imagine that's them, put themselves in your place."

"Maybe," he said. "But they don't see what it's really like to do it, all the grunt that goes into it. It's a fantasy, like you said. But I have to laugh, you know, about the photos, about the fantasy. Can't think about it too seriously, because if I did…" He ran a hand over his jaw and grimaced. "It's harder than I thought it would be," he admitted. "I don't fancy having somebody else's girlfriend on her hands and knees in front of me, or tied to my bed. I need to laugh about it, or I can't do it."

"Gretchen's really pretty, though," Faith said. "I'd think you'd enjoy that no matter what."

"What, knowing that she's thinking about somebody else to get through it? That she's off with Quint in her mind? Nah, not so much."

"Quentin," she said reprovingly.

"Whatever. And is it just me, or does Quentin look a bit like a Labrador?"

Faith laughed, and Lelei was laughing, too, the brief tense moment forgotten. "She loves him," Faith said. "And bite your tongue. That's a Marine you're talking about. She showed us a picture of her boyfriend at lunch yesterday," she told Lelei. "And yes, he might be a little bit homely. But he's a sergeant!"

"She told me he was the jealous type, too," Will said. "That it was a good thing he didn't know about the photos, or he'd probably shoot me. Good to know."

"Maybe it's a good thing you're going back to New Zealand, then," Lelei said. "Or are you?"

Solomon came back with the kids then, and they clambered up on the benches and drank thirstily, worn out from their enthusiastic whacking.

78

"Good talk?" Solomon asked.

"Tell you later," Lelei said. "You'll be interested. Call it pillow talk."

"Oh?" He was looking interested right now.

"I am never, ever going out with the two of you again," Will pronounced. "Geez. I'm embarrassed."

"Really? By us? Man, baby, we're doin' good," Solomon told his wife. "Embarrassing the porn star and all."

"What's a porn star, Daddy?" Sefina asked brightly.

"Never mind," Solomon said hastily. "New subject."

"I was just asking Will," Lelei said, fighting a smile, "about going back to New Zealand. About if he was. About whether he'd heard."

"I didn't realize that was a question," Faith managed to say. He wasn't going back? Here he'd acted like he wanted to pursue something with her, but he couldn't, because he was leaving. But he wasn't leaving? Was it all a story, then?

Will glanced at her and seemed to read something in her face, because his hand came out to cover hers. "I wasn't lying," he told her gently. "I'm leaving."

She nodded once, feeling dangerously close to tears, just like that.

Lelei was looking at her, but Solomon was frowning at Will. "You didn't get an offer? I could've sworn—"

"Nah. I did. Least my agent did. And I said no. Part of the reason I've been here," he told Faith. "To have a break, and to work out. But also to try out for the Outlaws, the new NFL franchise. For a kicking spot."

"Oh." She swallowed. "And they offered you one, but you said no?"

"I did. Call me a prima donna, but I have to matter more than that. My position, in rugby—I'm a first-five. A Number 10."

"I know," she said. "I looked it up." And then could have kicked herself.

"I've spent my whole life directing the game," he said. "And I found out, when it came down to it…" He ran a hand over his close-cut hair, looking a little sheepish. "That I can't stand the idea of being a part-time actor, waiting on the sidelines for my chance to come on and do my bit. Sounds bad, I know, but there it is."

"Why does it sound bad?" Faith asked.

"Tall poppy?" he suggested. "A bit stuck on myself?"

"That's stuck on yourself? I don't think so."

"Multi-million-dollar choice," Solomon pointed out.

"Yeh," Will said. "And that matters, and even so…the only choice for me. Besides…" He shrugged. "I just got back to En Zed, didn't I. Spent a few years in Aussie," he explained again to Faith. "And I wanted to go home. Must've been mad to think about leaving again, but then, at the time, I *was* a bit mad. I've come to my senses again, maybe. And I'm going home."

Which was what he'd said all along. So why did she feel…bereft?

"Well," Lelei said briskly, standing up with some difficulty and beginning to collect paper plates and cups. "Now that everybody's ready to get good and sick, who wants to go on some bumper boats?"

"I do," Will said. "Got to celebrate winning that five dollars from Faith, don't I. Because who got a hole in one on the windmill? Me, that's who. Me."

easy-peasy

♡

It wasn't so bad after all, doing the spanking shots. It was much, much worse.

You can do this, Will told himself, standing in the toilet in Calvin's studio a few days later. *Easy-peasy.*

He was meant to be changing into the charcoal-gray suit again, but instead, he was gripping the edges of the sink, staring himself in the eye, and having a serious attack of stage fright. Or an attack of rational thought, maybe.

He'd balked at the idea of spanking Gretchen from the beginning, but somehow, he'd let things get to this point, because he'd let Faith talk him into it.

She always sounded so reasonable, that was the problem. And he liked her too much. That might be the *real* problem.

"There's no limit to the mad things a man will do for a woman's sake," his grandfather had always said, and Will had always thought, *Not me.* Well, he'd used to think that, before he'd met Faith. Now, he knew that as always, his grandfather had been right.

He'd taken her home after their miniature golf date. One of the silliest days he'd spent in a fair while, and one of the best. But one of the worst, too. He'd walked inside the building with her, said hello to Mrs. Johnson and waited while Faith chatted. And then he'd walked with her to her door, where the words, "Want to come over to my place for a bit?" had hovered on his lips.

"Thanks," she'd said. "Fun day. See you Monday, at the shoot. Last week, huh?"

That had been the "worst" part. *Last week.* Because on Friday, he was leaving.

"Yeh." He'd leaned down and kissed her cheek, his hand coming up to push her hair, loosened as always by the wind, back from her face. Had felt her lean into him, and had wanted so badly to keep kissing her.

"Still no? Or yes?" he'd murmured, his lips brushing over her forehead, his hand moving over her soft skin with a will of its own, tracing the curve of her cheek.

The sigh had been a warm breath against him. "Still no. Because…last week."

"Yeh. Right." He'd forced himself to step back, to say "See you then," and to walk away. Knowing it was the right thing, even though, as always, it felt so completely wrong.

Now, he looked at the face in the mirror. *In or out?* This was the last episode. Time to choose.

He'd done a shower scene already this week, after all, wearing the tiniest Speedo, with Gretchen in a microscopic flesh-toned thong and nothing more.

"Of course, we won't show bare breasts in any of the shots," Calvin had assured the pair of them, although Gretchen hadn't seemed fussed. "But we need to see all of her back. Arm bra works, too."

Which wasn't something Will had heard of, but he found out what it was. Hands—Gretchen's own hands, fortunately. And then an arm, which was Will's. The tattooed one, of course, his heavy forearm doing a perfectly adequate job of covering both of Gretchen's pretty little breasts, his bicep flexed to the max as he'd hauled her up against him. He'd been desperately careful all the same not to crush her, after the first time, when she'd winced.

He'd done all that, so having her over his lap in a pair of pink cotton undies wouldn't be so bad, would it?

Yes. It would be just that bad. But he'd agreed to it, mad or not, so he slung the black tie around his neck and began to knot it, although he still thought it was stupid.

"Who would wear a tie to spank a woman?" he'd objected when Charlotte had handed him his wardrobe.

"Hemi would." Faith had answered for her. "He's very, very rich."

"That doesn't even make sense," Will had said. "And I thought nothing was written yet."

"Trust me," Faith had said. "You can bet he'll be rich. Which is why you're wearing the tie."

It was as if their cozy family time with Solomon and Lelei had never happened, because she'd been all business again ever since. He sighed. *In for a penny, in for a pound.* He got busy tying, and that was when he heard the unmistakable sound of somebody spewing.

His hands stilled as the retching went on, and then, when silence fell, he finished up, pulled the suit jacket off the hanger and shrugged into it. Maybe he'd be saved by the bug.

He went on out into the studio and submitted to some readjustment by Charlotte. She clucked over the dog's breakfast he'd apparently made of the tie, unfastened it and re-did it, and was going over his jacket with a lint roller when the other toilet door opened and Gretchen came out in her robe. Her face was paler than ever, her eyes huge in her little heart-shaped face, and she looked fragile to the point of transparency.

Will stepped out of Charlotte's grasp with a "Sorry. One minute," and went across to Gretchen, putting a hand onto her arm to steady her, because she looked like she was about to pass out. "You OK?" he asked.

"Shh," she hissed, casting a wary glance at Calvin, but he was mucking about with his camera setup with Faith at the other end of the extensive room.

"We don't have to do this," Will told her, keeping his voice low. "If you're ill. We can reschedule for tomorrow, maybe."

"It won't be better tomorrow. I'm fine. Forget it, OK?"

The idea was dawning in Will's brain in all its horror, because he had sisters, and he had cousins. "You're pregnant," he realized.

"*Shh,*" she hissed frantically. "Not even a couple months," she whispered.

"What, they don't know?" Will jerked his head at Calvin and Faith. "They should know. Make sure we're careful enough not to hurt you."

She sighed in obvious exasperation. "You're not going to hurt me. Calvin doesn't know, because he wouldn't have picked me, and who knows what he'd do now? I need this job, and men are so weird about women being..." She looked around again. "That. And I need to save up for me and Quentin, and the...you know. Anyway, Faith knows. And don't worry," she added. "I brushed my teeth."

Will seized on the one thing he could grab hold of. "Faith knows? She *knows?*"

"She heard me being...sick." Gretchen was whispering again. "Like I guess you did. But she won't tell. Faith isn't like that."

"I need you over here, Gretchen," Charlotte called. "Right away, please."

Will had heard enough anyway. He left her there and stalked across the studio, grateful after all that he was wearing the suit. He was meant to be intimidating? It could start right now.

"I need to talk to you," he told Faith. "Outside." He jerked his head towards the carpark.

She started to say something, but he didn't wait around to hear what it was. She'd better be following him, or...Well, he didn't know what "or" was, but she'd better be following him.

He hit the glass door hard, then turned and held it for her, because, yes, she'd followed him. Wearing jeans and a blue Henley today, most of the tiny buttons undone, and wrapping her arms around herself against the brisk January wind. Even as he fumed, he noticed the way it pushed up her breasts. She was showing a fair bit of cleavage now. *Focus,* he told himself sternly.

"What?" she asked. "It's freezing out here."

He slipped impatiently out of the jacket and draped it over her shoulders, and she hugged it around herself, though it didn't hide the cleavage, and he needed to stop looking.

"Why the hell," he said, his voice rising, not that he was trying too hard to keep it under control, "didn't you tell me Gretchen was bloody *pregnant?"*

"Shh," she said, exactly as Gretchen had. "Because Calvin would have pitched a fit, just like you are, because men are ridiculous."

"Ridiculous?" he demanded. *"Ridiculous?* I've had my hands all over a pregnant woman. I've had her tied to the *bed."*

"Well, you didn't actually do anything to her," Faith pointed out. "She's just fine. And she signed up for this. It isn't *real,* Will. You've got nothing to be upset about. Nobody will know she was pregnant, and you haven't done anything wrong."

"Do. Not," Will said, gritting out the words, "give me that bloody soothing thing. *I* know she's pregnant. *I* know what I did. And I cannot—I can *not*—spank a pregnant woman."

"You don't have to spank her." Faith was still so maddeningly calm he could—he could hit something. "You just have to pretend that you're *going* to spank her. You don't like soothing? I won't be soothing. I'll point out that you're being patriarchal and patronizing. Gretchen's perfectly willing to do it. She doesn't need your protection. She's waiting in there for you to fulfill your contract. We all are. And don't tell me you can't even pretend to think about spanking a woman, because I won't believe it."

"How d'you know what I do or don't think about?"

She snorted. "I was born in the dark, but it wasn't last night. I saw how you looked when we were in that store, and that was just *me.* Besides, that's one of the most common male fantasies. I did the research."

"Of course you did," he muttered. What did she mean, "that

was just me?" She didn't know nearly as much as she thought she did. "Google must have a pretty interesting profile on you. I've thought about heaps of things I haven't done. When you're big and…"

"Strong," she guessed. "Powerful." Which would have been nice to hear, under other circumstances.

"Well, when you are, you take care that you don't scare a woman, and you bloody well take care that you don't hurt her. I don't have to hurt women. I hurt men. That's my job. If I've got any excess testosterone, I've got an outlet for it, haven't I."

"All very reasonable," she said. "All very noble, but it doesn't matter, because you won't be hurting Gretchen. You'll be doing a little fantasy fulfillment of your own. Here's your big chance to do something exciting without actually having to worry about scaring a woman, or hurting her. Everybody's happy, and we're done."

"Let's make this dead clear," he told her. "There's not one bit of fantasy fulfillment in my spanking Gretchen, because there's nothing I want to do less. I can think of one woman I wouldn't mind spanking, but that's not on offer, is it?"

Her eyes widened, then she seemed to catch herself and laughed, hugging his jacket a little closer. "Well, then, take yourself to your Happy Place. Whatever floats your boat. We done talking?"

"I've got an even better idea," he said. "If it's such an insignificant wee thing, how about if *you* do it? Hemi's got a threesome going, maybe. That seems like the kind of bloke he is. And I'd be rapt about having *you* over my knee. I could look dark and dangerous as you like."

She wasn't looking one bit comfortable now. He should care about that, but he didn't.

"Trust me," she said, "nobody's going to pay to look at naked pictures of me, especially not of my butt. And that isn't the kind of threesome that sells stories to women."

"No?" He took a step towards her, and she backed up, then seemed to catch herself. "I'd pay for that. And I'd do that shoot for free."

"You hold that thought." She was the one struggling for composure now, and he was enjoying watching it. "You're looking just exactly right."

"Dark and dangerous?" he asked softly, closing the distance, putting his hands on her shoulders. She leaned into him, and he took the jacket from around her shoulders and put it on again. "Then let's go." He saw her looking off-balance, and smiled. "You just keep looking at me while I'm doing it. You can know what I'm really thinking about. That way, we both get at least a taste of what we want."

over you
♡

For all his protesting, Will looked as cool and remote as an iceberg during the shoot that followed. He certainly didn't seem to mind having Gretchen stretched across his lap.

"All right there?" he asked her when they first got into position in the black leather chair. "You get the blood rushing to your head, you need a break, you just say the word, and I'll help you up."

"Not your job," Calvin growled. "I say when she gets a break."

"No," Will said, his expression hard for once. "You don't. She does. And if you'll get on with it, she won't have to be down there so long. Let's go."

Calvin looked like he wanted to explode, but the pictures were gold, and he knew it, and for once, he held himself back. "I'm not the one sitting around here yapping. All right. Arm in the air. Other hand on her back."

Will raised his arm, elbow high, and looked straight at Faith as Charlotte got in there, pinning his jacket back so it fell perfectly, then tweaking his tie.

"How am I doing?" he asked Faith softly. "This what you want?"

She stared back at him in shock. At what he'd said, at the fact that he'd said it here, in front of everyone. And he didn't smile.

"Hold that expression," Calvin said. "But look at Gretchen. You're mad, bad, and dangerous to know, and she's just about to find that out. More shadow on that arm," he snapped at Faith. "Quick."

Faith adjusted the light, calming her racing heart, until Calvin said, "Good. There."

She watched the shoot, moved, followed orders, but her mind wasn't on it. Nowhere close to on it.

He looked down at me, his expression impossible to read. "You're a pretty demanding girl. That's not what our arrangement is, is it? Didn't I tell you that the spider decides?"

"Not if you're never going to do it," I muttered. "And I told you. I don't do arrangements."

He tried to hide it, but I saw the twitch at the corner of his mouth. "Something else you said as well," he mused. "What was that? Hmm. I thought there was something wrong with it at the time. Can't think what now, though."

"What?" I asked. Something wrong?

We'd made it back to the hotel at last, and he didn't answer until we were in the elevator again, and he'd pushed the button for the fourth floor. I reached over to punch 3, but he shot a hand out and grabbed my wrist.

"Oh, yeh," he said. "I remember now. You wanted a lesson, thought you might go get it from somebody else. And that's not part of our arrange— er, relationship. Think I may have to remind you of that. And to give you that lesson, too."

My legs wanted to get a little wobbly at that, but the doors had opened, and he stood back and let me walk out first, then walked by my side to the end of the corridor, pulled out his keycard, and held the door for me.

Another suite, in rich blues this time, but I wasn't looking at the décor.

Hemi set the bag containing my lingerie down on the table near the door, took my purse off my shoulder, and added it as well.

"Take off your coat," he told me, and when I did, he took it from me and hung it in the closet together with his own suit coat while I tried not to shift

from foot to foot.

He looked at me and sighed, unbuttoned his shirt cuffs, and began to roll up his sleeves a few turns. "Rough, eh."

"Rough?" I asked, startled. He'd seemed to understand that I didn't want pain. Now he was talking about it being rough? No.

"Deciding which to do first," he said, and I relaxed a tiny bit. "So many lessons you need today. But you're still sore, I know, which makes it a bit fraught. I think I'm getting an idea, though." He walked to the couch that sat against one wall, pulled the coffee table out a couple of feet, then sat down while I stood and watched him. "I think you'd better come over here."

I swallowed hard, the nerves and the arousal fluttering low in my belly, and moved toward him, but when I got there, he didn't let me sit. Instead, he said, "Saucy girls who tease and don't do what they're told? Girls who go out without their undies? What do you think happens to them?"

Surely there wasn't enough air in here. "Um…" I said. "I don't know."

"Why don't you lie down across my lap," he said, "and I'll show you."

♡♡♡

She'd been writing more of the story down every night, just for herself, just for fun. And just because she couldn't help it. This last week, though, as she'd been working with the designer on the website, had been going through the images with Calvin, choosing the best ones, she'd been toying with the idea of submitting her own story to the site. The same way the images were going up, one episode at a time, starting with Hope and Hemi's meeting.

If none of the viewers knew it was her, it might be all right. And having an example chapter up there could set the tone for the entire site, couldn't it? That and the title, because she'd already convinced Calvin that *His Every Desire* had the erotic romance ring to it that would bring women to the site, that and the marketing campaign she'd already kicked off. Women would come to look at Will, and they'd come back for more of him. Gretchen was good. She was pretty, and she looked sweet. She worked, but Will *killed*.

It wouldn't be wrong, surely, to put her own submissions up

there with the others. She wouldn't be manipulating their rank, after all. Even if she'd known how to add votes for her chapters behind the scenes, the web developer would know she'd done it. Anyway, she wouldn't, because that wasn't the point. She just wanted to see if anybody wanted to read her story. She wanted to know what happened, how Hope and Hemi could ever find happiness. And she wanted to know if anybody else would want to know, too.

♡♡♡

Will had apparently decided to forgive her for the pregnancy thing, because he approached her again while she was cleaning up after the shoot. Gretchen had already left, getting a hug and a kiss on the cheek from Will that were nothing but brotherly, Charlotte had taken herself off as well, and their three weeks of shooting were over.

"Bit of a celebration tonight?" he asked her.

She looked up from the fridge, where she was dumping leftovers into the trash. "Finished with this?" he asked, and at her nod, began to pull the bag out and knot it as he'd done every week since the first one. This was the last time Will would take out her trash.

"Sorry?" She realized he'd spoken to her.

"I was thinking that you might want to go for dinner." He hefted the bag out of the can, and she couldn't help watching the bulge of triceps as he did it.

He glanced down at himself. "You're right, I'm not dressed for it. How about if we both glammed up, pretended we were Hope and Hemi?" He grinned. "So to speak. Minus any scenes you didn't care to reenact."

"Oh." She was blushing again, she could tell, because for one horrible, heart-stopping moment, she'd thought he knew. But he couldn't know. "Sorry. No, I can't. I have plans."

"Dinner with your mum again? You're right, she probably

doesn't want me. Maybe a drink first?"

Did he really think her only possible evening entertainment was with her *mother?* "No." She didn't try to disguise the edge to her voice, "I actually have a date."

She hadn't been wrong, because he looked startled. She was steaming up a little now, and not from his tattoo. "With a fella, you mean."

"Yes, this would be with an actual man."

He looked like he wanted to say something else, but he stopped himself. "I'll dump this and let you get to it, then."

"I'll come talk to you tomorrow, about keys and all."

"Course," he said. "Text me."

She wondered all the same, while she was dressing to go out, what it would have been like if she'd said yes.

A mistake, that was what. She was getting on with her life, pursuing a relationship that might actually have a chance, because Will was leaving in two days. He was leaving forever, and New Zealand was six thousand miles across the Pacific. She'd done the research.

the moon upside down
♡

Will set his duffel and suitcase by the front door for the morning. For when he'd leave the apartment, and leave Vegas.

He'd had one final dinner with Solomon and his family, had made an early night of it because of the kids, as usual. He could have gone out again afterwards, found himself the female companionship he hadn't had since he'd got here. But he hadn't, and not because he needed the time to pack. After nine years in professional rugby, he'd packed so many times that he could have done it in fifteen minutes.

He could still go out, though. He could go out right this minute. It had barely gone nine, and he had a whole long day of flying tomorrow to sleep. Vegas to LA, then LA all the way to Auckland, and home. And he was restless. He sat on the couch, picked up the remote, and switched the TV on. He started flipping channels, settled on basketball, then muted the sound and watched the action with half his brain, the other divided between thinking about the day before and the time ahead. About whether he was sorry to be leaving Vegas, happy to be going home, or both. And about when Faith had come in last night. He hated to admit that he'd fallen asleep listening for the sound of her door closing, the soft little noises that meant she was in her bedroom, on the other side of the wall from his own. He'd gone to sleep without hearing them, and that wasn't good at all.

He picked up the remote again and turned the sound up to drown out the thoughts. His hand stilled when he heard the bump, and then the footsteps. Directly outside. Not in the corridor, on the roof that covered the carpark.

Somebody breaking in? His blood stirred a little at the thought. That would be the perfect way to end his American odyssey, and the perfect cure for his restless doldrums, too. And then he realized that it might not be his apartment they were breaking into. It might be Faith's.

He was moving on the thought. He flipped the light switch on the wall, then edged to the window, slid it open as quietly as he could manage, and peered cautiously out.

At first, he couldn't see anybody. But he hadn't imagined that noise. He got his head out there a bit more, and that's when he saw her, sitting against the wall, wearing a jacket over her jeans, her arms wrapped around her knees. Her face shining in the light of the moon, nearly full tonight, while the glow of the Strip competed for attention to the east. Faith, on the roof.

He grabbed his jacket, shoved the window open the rest of the way, got a leg up there, and swung up and out. "This a private party?" he asked, keeping his voice low. "Or can anybody play?"

She turned her head, her cheek on her knees. "You still here? Not out…saying goodbye?"

"Nah." He decided to take her answer as a 'yes,' went over and sank onto a bit of the blanket she'd brought out to sit on. "There's nobody I want to say goodbye to more than you."

She laughed, sounding startled, and he realized what he'd said. "Aw, geez," he groaned. "I didn't mean that. I meant…I'll be sorry to go. In one way. In *that* one way."

"Mmm. Still. Funny." She reached for something beside her, held up a wine glass. "Want some? Got the bottle right here. I can

94

grab you another glass."

"Mind sharing?"

"No." She handed the glass to him.

She wasn't touching him. Not quite. Or he wasn't touching her. Not quite. But she was right there all the same.

He took the glass from her, sipped, and handed it back. She took a drink of her own, not bothering to turn the glass. Her lips were where his had been, and for some reason, even that...

Her eyes caught his over the rim for one arrested moment before she looked away and set the glass down again.

"So how was your date?" he asked, and then could have kicked himself. He didn't want to know.

"Well..." She sighed. "He was a back-door guy."

"Sorry?" he managed to ask through a mouth that had gone dry. *What?*

"No! Not...not that," she stammered, then laughed. "Well, probably, but only if he'd bought you a really expensive dinner. The hundred-dollar bottle of wine, which he'd have made sure you saw the price of, and if you didn't, he'd have told you. He'd have had a whole conversation with the wine steward about it, too. Then he'd have thought you owed it to him. Oh, man. I never thought of that, but he would totally have been that guy. But, no. Not what I meant. I've never said that to a man, obviously. All right. Rephrasing. He was a *leave*-by-the-back-door guy."

"Oh. Good. Brilliant." His heart settled down again. "Explain."

"When it's so bad that you excuse yourself to go to the ladies' room, and then you leave by the back door?"

"Women do that?"

"Well, not to you, obviously. And I didn't either, actually. These days, I try to be a little more up-front."

"So tell me."

"You really want to know? You want me to describe my *date* to you?"

"Well, now that I know it was bad, I do, because I know you'll make me laugh." He smiled into the eyes that looked up at his own.

"Before, when it was the back-door thing? Not so much, then."

"You're not…" she began, then stopped.

"Not what?"

"Not…jealous, are you?" She laughed a little. "Of course you aren't. Forget it."

"Yeh," he found himself saying. "Yeh, I am. Last night? I was jealous."

"Oh." She looked nothing but startled.

"Can't help myself, it seems. Surprised myself all over the shop with you, haven't I. I'm not used to being friends with women, and you don't make it easy." She wasn't coming up with an answer to that, so he went on. "So…date?"

"Oh." She seemed to pull herself back under control. "Well, you know. He works in one of the casinos, and I met him at a work party. I guess he did better in a crowd, because it turned into one of those interview dates, and I kept flunking. What I did for a living, where I went to school. Apparently I'm not impressive."

"Yeh, you are."

"You might think so," she said solemnly. "But you don't have an MBA, and he does. I went to UNLV for my undergraduate degree, and he went to Harvard. Know how I know?"

He laughed. "Because he told you?"

"Yeah. Sneakily, the way people who go to Harvard *always* tell you. They say 'Cambridge.' It's like a little code, because Harvard is in Cambridge. 'I played lacrosse for a while, back in Cambridge. Of course, you're competing with all the kids who grew up playing it at their prep schools, because lacrosse is big on the East Coast, but I managed to acquit myself pretty well.'"

"Sounds like a dickhead."

She laughed out loud, and he could see the little gap between her teeth in the moonlight, and the tiny, perfect spot of her mole, too. "He was. I was already planning on an early end to my evening when he asked me what my five-year plan was. Can you believe that? My five-year plan?"

"Well, I've never asked a girl that, put it that way. What did you say?"

"I told him I was working on getting my criminal record expunged so I could pass the employment checks and get a more prestigious job."

Will's bark of laughter rang out in the night. "And then what?"

"He sat there with his mouth open, looking like a very expensive fish, and I said, 'But when it's a violent crime, it's so hard to get them to even consider it. Even though the guy *totally* deserved it, because don't you think all pimps deserve to roast slowly to death?' She grinned happily at Will. "I could see him writing the memo to my boss at the Roundup in his head even as we spoke. Luckily, my boss has a great sense of humor. I'll be livening up our next meeting for sure. And then I stood up and said, 'But you know what? I'm getting that same vibe off of you, and I'm working on my anger-management issues. So I think we'll call this a night.' And I walked out."

He liked her. He liked her so much. "So tonight, you're up on the roof instead."

"I am. Much better date. One of my favorites."

"Come here often? And, yeh," he said with a smile. "I meant to do that."

"Sometimes. Especially if the moon is full. I look at the lights, and pretend…'" She laughed again, sounding a bit embarrassed.

"What?"

"That they're…stars. I always wanted to see a whole sky full of stars. You know?"

"Yeh. I do. That's why I'm going home. So I can see a whole sky full of stars. So I can see the Milky Way, and the Southern Cross, too. So I can see the moon the way it's meant to be."

"What? The moon's different there?"

"Upside-down here. Or we're upside-down Down Under. Something like that. Didn't you know?"

"No. I didn't. So you've missed it a lot? But still, you came here. You thought about staying, too. I guess you didn't know that you'd miss it."

Why was she living in Las Vegas, if she wanted to see a sky full of stars? He'd ask her about it, he decided. Later.

"I didn't know what I'd want, when I came," he said. "I was looking to get away. But I got away from all the good, too. And I brought all the bad with me."

Her cheek was on her knees again, and she was looking at him, her eyes soft in the moonlight, and the mood had shifted completely. The traffic noise was there, a constant, dull hum in the background, the neon lights of the Strip glowing harsh to the east, and the asphalt of the roof cold beneath him. And Faith beside him, the opposite of all those things. She didn't say anything, so he took another sip of her wine, and after a minute, he continued.

"My grandfather died," he found himself telling her. "In December. Just before Christmas. Sounds like a normal thing, doesn't it? Not like a thing that should knock you sideways."

"I suppose," she said, "it depends how much you loved him."

"Yeh," he said. "Yeh," he repeated after a moment. "And what happened. Because I was there. Because of...what he said. What I did. We were on a boat, on the lake. On Lake Rotorua. We were fishing."

♡♡♡

"Come fishing," his Koro had said that day, as he would so often summon one of his mokopuna. You didn't say no, because it meant the old man had something to say, and you were meant to listen, like it or not.

Koro waited until they had motored across to the mouth of the Waiteti Stream, where the trout would be biting in early summer. He waited until they had their rods out and were casting into the deep pool in the center of the stream, just downstream of the big rock. The spot where the big trout spent their days, fins beating lazily to hold them steady in the cool water of the pool.

"Glad you're home at last," Koro finally said. Taking the long way round, as always. "Been away too long, haven't you."

"Yeh." Will shot a glance the old man's way before flicking his arm back and casting again, letting his line settle as the day settled into his bones. Surrounded by the bowl of blue sky, the gentle breeze, the reflections of mountains and fern trees and the mighty giants of the forest shimmering in the blue of the huge volcanic lake. The young land, the old legends, both of them so alive here, as if you could touch Ranginui, the Sky Father, and Papatuanuku, the Earth Mother. As if they were still touching, still kissing each other, here at the heart of the world.

"And you're glad to be here, I can tell," Koro went on after another long minute. "Makes me wonder, though."

"Wonder what?" Will asked despite himself, because he still cared. He'd always care. There was nobody whose opinion mattered more.

"You play rugby hard," Koro said. "You play with heart. I see it more and more in you. You give it everything. You play with mana."

"But?" Will cast again, his heart thudding despite the serenity of their surroundings. At the praise, and at what lay behind it.

"So when are you planning to take the rest of your life that seriously? You play like it's work, like it matters. And you treat your life like it's play."

"Oh." Will laughed a bit. "Is that all? You scared me."

Koro was frowning at him. His hair might be gray now, but his face was still carved out of the hardest teak, and Will sobered fast.

"Sorry," Will said. "Tell me."

"Life isn't a game," Koro said. "But the game's the only part you really care about, seems to me. And that hurts my heart to see."

"I care about more than that," Will protested. "It's why I'm back here, back in En Zed."

"Because you want to be an All Black."

"Yeh. But I care about all of you, too. What else is there? I'm too young to think about the mokopuna." Will laughed a little, tried for something lighter. "Got to have kids before you can have grandkids, eh."

"Twenty-eight last birthday," Koro said, because you'd never stir him from his course, not once he'd decided on it. "Not too young at all. Getting too old not to think about them, aren't you. I want to know that you'll be sitting in a boat right here someday, long after I'm gone. I want to know that you'll be passing it all along to them, teaching them how to cast a line. And more, too. Teaching them everything they need to know. And I don't see you getting there."

"I'll get there."

"Yeh, you'll have grandchildren. One way or another. We can all see that. But will you be sitting with them? Or will they be something you found out about, just like you found out about their mum, or their dad? That boy, that girl you paid the maintenance for, and barely knew? Somebody whose dad you never were?"

Will had forgotten about his line, was holding his rod slack in his hand. "I'm not...I don't...I'm careful. I don't have any kids." As far as he knew.

Koro swung his arm back, cast his own line again, the transparent filament singing through the summer air, landing with a delicate kiss in the center of the pool. "And that's a good thing?" he asked, not looking at Will. "That what you want your life to be about? That you're careful, and there are no kids running around looking like you? Nobody running to you, asking for a ride on your shoulders when you come back from one of those overseas tours? No woman whose eyes are lighting up because you're home, and this is the day she's had circled on her calendar?"

"I'm twenty-eight," Will repeated. He was a failure because he didn't have a woman? Because he didn't have *one* woman?

"What are you afraid of?" Koro asked. "That if somebody sees you, really sees you, she won't be impressed? Your dad left, yeh. That doesn't mean you will. You can stay. You can stick. Your choice. Your life. You can run away from it. Or you can run towards it."

Will was getting angry now. It *was* his life. It *was* his choice. He wanted to say it, and he couldn't. He yanked his own line in with a jerk of his arm, and the line went wild, the fly swinging straight for Koro. He saw it happen, and he couldn't stop it. The fly flew straight into the top of his grandfather's chest, the barbed hook catching hold in the collar of his T-shirt, just above the life jacket, startling an exclamation from the old man.

"Sorry." Will set his rod down hastily as Koro looked down, began to reel in his own line, then stopped, grabbing at his chest with one gnarled hand. "I'll get it out. Hang on."

Koro began to answer, but he was gasping, the rod falling from his other hand and going over the side of the little boat with a splash that Will barely heard. Because both his grandfather's hands were at his chest now, and his face was twisted, agonized. His mouth opened, but only a grunt came out.

"Koro!" Will was reaching for him even as he toppled, laying him down across both seats, then scrambling over him. He fumbled desperately with the straps of the life jacket, then lifted his grandfather's heavy body to pull the thing off and shove it under the old man's head.

The fly was still caught in his grandfather's shirt, the rod dragging at it, and Will pulled it loose with force, ripping the cotton fabric, sending Will's rod, too, tumbling over the side.

Heart, he thought, because that was where Koro's hands were. On his chest, grabbing, clawing.

"Koro," Will said again, and the word sounded like it was coming from far away, from somebody else.

CPR, he thought wildly. But should he get him to shore first? He didn't even have his mobile, had come out on the water without it, because Koro hated texting, had always forbidden the intrusion of technology into family time.

No choice. Will had to do this, and he had to do it now. Because Koro's hands had stopped clutching at his chest, had fallen away. His face was gray, and his chest…his chest was still.

No other boats close enough, nobody visible on the shore. And a person couldn't live without oxygen.

CPR. Now.

He could never have said, afterwards, how long he'd tried. How many times he'd pressed on his grandfather's chest, his own ragged breath the only sound, before the other boat came close, the motor cut out, and the voice floated across the water.

"All right there?"

"No," Will said without stopping. "No. Get us to shore. Ring 111."

He kept on while the other fellas got the tow rope on, while they hauled his boat to the marina at the holiday park. While he heard the siren approaching, and even when the ambos were running towards him. All the way until they were putting Koro onto the gurney, and Will's hands fell away, and Will was scrambling into the ambulance after them.

The defibrillator, then, and the tears were streaming down Will's cheeks as he watched Koro's broad brown chest, the chest that held a heart that was surely too big just to stop. Too strong just to quit. Watching it jerk into the air under the paddles, then fall back onto the gurney again.

Stopped. Still. Gone.

♡♡♡

"He died?" Faith asked.

Will sighed and ran a hand over the back of his head. "Yeh. He died. Then and there. Dead, I guess, all the way back there in the boat. From the minute he stopped breathing. And I couldn't bring him back."

"That's horrible. I'm so sorry."

He made a hopeless gesture with one hand, then picked up the glass of wine again and drained it. "I wondered for ages afterwards," he admitted, "if it was the fly. Sounds mad, I know, but...the shock. Or just...being upset with me. That was the worst. That I didn't save him, and wondering if I caused it."

"Oh, no. Surely not."

"No. They said not. But still. When he went, he left a...he left a hole in our family. In our life."

He looked out at the moon and thought about Koro up there somewhere. Up there being proud of him, and disappointed in him. He wished he could have said things differently that day. Done things differently. He wished so many things.

"*Kua hinga te totara i te wao nui a Tane,*" he told Faith. "Means, 'A totara has fallen in the forest of Tane.' A mighty tree. When it falls...it's not replaceable."

"So you came here. Away from your family. Which seems exactly..."

"Wrong," he finished for her. "Yeh. Wrong. But then, that was the point of what he said that day, that I was doing wrong. Or at least not doing right." He hadn't shared the details with her, because she didn't need to hear that. And because he didn't want her to know that. "So I came away, to have a change. To have a think, was the idea. At least that's what I told myself. Probably just to run away from it, from all the bad thoughts."

"I can see that," she said. "I want to get away...oh, all the time. And after what happened? Of course I can see it."

"You can? Seems like exactly the wrong choice now. But Christmas was too sad, with that hole bang in the center of things. Nothing to stay for, I thought. But now, I need it more than ever. The feel of it. The sky, the sea, the lake, the hot pools. The mountains, and the hills. All the greens, because there's no green like it. I can't live in the desert."

He broke off with a laugh. "I sound like a travelogue for En Zed, eh. It's just that he's there, still. The ancestors are there, that's the idea. That's why a Maori is always buried in New Zealand. Why they still bring the soldiers back, if there's any way they can. So their spirits can go where they belong."

"It sounds like a good place." She poured a bit more wine into the glass. "A peaceful place."

"A slower place," he agreed. "A happier place. I mean, nothing slow about rugby, not while you're playing it. But when you're not,

103

you're joking around a bit with the boys, having a laugh. All of that. I miss it. I'm ready to go home. But sad, too." He looked at her, there beside him. The warmth of her radiated to his side, because he was almost touching her, and he wanted to touch her more. "Sad to leave you," he said softly.

She looked down, took a sip of wine, and handed him the glass, but he didn't drink. He set it down beside him and took her hand, lacing his fingers through hers.

It wasn't small, and it wasn't delicate. It was a strong hand, a capable hand, and it felt good in his.

"I'll miss you," he said again.

She was looking at him, her eyes huge in the moonlight, her mouth a little parted. She started to say something, stopped again, and Will leaned forward, put his other hand on her shoulder, and brushed his lips over hers.

He felt the shiver of it, the shock of contact. In her, and in himself. Her lips had all the softness her hand didn't, and he had to kiss them again, then touch his tongue to that tiny mole for just a moment before he returned to her mouth, because he needed that mouth.

She'd moved into his arms now, her own hands coming up to clasp his shoulders. She was against the wall, and he was kissing her harder, his hand behind her head, cushioning it, his fingers lacing through the hair that tumbled below her shoulders tonight. The blood was pounding in his ears, and everywhere else, too, and he wanted to keep going. He wanted to take her inside and make love to her. He wanted to do it *now*.

She moved first. He realized that she had a hand on his chest, but it wasn't to pull him closer. She was pushing him away.

"Will," she said. "Stop. Stop."

He sat back, tried to get himself together. The distress was there, plain to see on her face. What had he done, here at the end? This wasn't a joke. This wasn't for fun. This was Faith, and it mattered.

"Sorry." It came out a little shaky. "Got carried away, I guess.

Again. Because I...I like you."

"Yeah." She laughed, although it didn't sound like she thought it was funny. "I like you, too. But, no. Bad idea. You're leaving tomorrow."

"I am." Bad idea, she was right, however much he wanted to do it. "I'll just...say goodbye, then."

She picked up her glass, her bottle, and shivered a little, because the night had grown colder. "I'm glad you're going home." She shook her hair back and looked him in the eye, her gaze steady. "For yourself. And for me. Go home and...be happy."

"Thanks." He watched her go, saw her slide back through her window, back into her apartment. He looked at the moon. The next time he saw it, it would be right side up, and that was what he wanted. He needed to remember that.

leaving las vegas
♡

Will hated goodbyes. He usually avoided even saying them. He just…left. He'd said goodbye this time, though, and it had been as bad as he'd feared. Saying it to Faith had been the worst. But even saying it to Solomon and his family had been rough.

"When does the construction work start up again?" he'd asked the other man when he'd walked him out to his car after dinner the night before.

"Next week. Still waiting to hear on the Outlaws deal. But if not—" Solomon shrugged a big shoulder. "I'll work construction through the spring, and then my agent says there might be a chance with the Vikings. Minnesota," he explained at Will's blank look.

"Don't know where that is."

"Think cold. Think very cold."

"Bit hard, hauling around to all those different cities, isn't it? Seems like that's what players here do, though."

"You don't do that?"

"Nah. We mostly stay where we are. One team. We tend to stick, stay home." Except Will, of course, but then, he'd had his reasons, and he'd always had restless feet anyway.

"Yeah, well. Home. I barely remember what that is. Vegas is where our families are, but mostly—home is wherever I am. Or more like where Lelei and the kids are. Home is where she is."

Will sat back two hours later in the leather seat of the first-class cabin of the Air New Zealand Dreamliner and thought about that. *Home is where she is.* He wondered what that would be like, and knew that he didn't have a clue.

He did know something about home, though, and he was glad to be going there. He was rapt to be going there, in fact, just as he'd been rapt to leave Aussie in the first place, to come home to the land of the silver fern. And the land of the All Blacks. But all the same…

"Another beer?" the flight attendant asked on her way by, her accent falling on his ear with all the comfort of home.

"Please."

She brought it a minute later, poured it into a glass, and set it on his tray table. "Going home where you can see the stars, eh," she said, and Will glanced at her, startled.

She caught the look and laughed. "That's what I always think, when I'm making the return journey with a few days off. That I'll be able to get home where I can see the stars."

"Yeh." Will smiled at her. Nothing but a coincidence. Everybody liked to look at the stars. He raised his glass. "Cheers for this."

She swayed up the aisle as the big jet rocked a little in the airstream, and Will took a sip and realized that he never had got around, the night before, to asking Faith why she didn't move someplace where she could see the stars. Why she had to look at the city lights instead. Why she had to pretend.

♡♡♡

Faith's feet negotiated the rocky trail, her steps quick and light as she pushed a little more speed out of her body on the way up the steep slope towards Pine Creek. The winter quiet of the stark desert landscape surrounded her, Red Rocks' namesake formations glowing in the weak late afternoon sunlight, and her soul found a little peace, because this was her favorite spot in Las Vegas. Her escape, her beauty and solitude and space.

She focused on breathing into the sadness. Made herself examine each regret, holding it like a butterfly in her hand, its wings beating against her skin, then opening her fingers and letting it go.

If she'd slept with Will, she would have been missing him even more now, and probably feeling used, too. Feeling abandoned. The risk had been too great, and she didn't take those kinds of risks. Or any risks, if she were honest.

She'd wondered all along why Will had agreed to model, since he hadn't seemed to relish the idea. If it hadn't been for the money, why? Now, she thought she understood. He'd wanted some risk. He'd wanted something new. He'd wanted to feel alive, and who was she to judge that? She was living in her mother's apartment building, doing two jobs she didn't care about to pay off her student loans, dreaming of living by the ocean, of living a different life, but so frightened to take the leap, to leave everything she knew. So afraid to try, because if she tried, she might fail.

Enough regrets. They would get her nowhere. Time to escape into another world, another story, one she could control.

She could take Hope and Hemi to the ocean, or better yet…maybe Hemi flew Hope to New Zealand.

They'd travel on the corporate jet, of course, would eat five-star cuisine and join the Mile-High Club in the teak-paneled cabin…

Once she had them walking down the steps onto the tarmac, though, Faith's mind blanked. She could take Hope to Paris, because she'd seen enough pictures and read enough books for that. But she couldn't take her to New Zealand. Will was on his way back there right now, headed across the Pacific, and Faith had no clue what the view would be like on his way from the airport to his house, or what his house would look like when he got there. She knew he lived in Auckland and was going to be playing for the Blues, and that was all she knew, because she hadn't asked him any more than that. Because she'd held back, so afraid to care.

But she'd said she was letting it go, so she took Hope and Hemi to the Pacific coast instead. To her own dream, the sea stacks and crashing surf of Northern California, where they would walk on the bluffs above the beach, watch pelicans gliding overhead in a perfect V formation, their wings barely needing to flap. They would see the majestic birds diving down between cliff and sea, plunging into the water, and Hemi's hand would be strong around Hope's. Both of them savoring the moment, and that they were sharing it, Hemi's pleasure all the greater because Hope was loving it.

The two of them, walking into the wind, drinking in the sights and sounds and smells of the sea. Perfectly at peace. Perfectly happy, because they were together.

may surprise
♡

Four months later

Will walked out of the locker-room showers with his towel wrapped around his waist. "Shove over," he told Koti James, because the big centre was, as usual, taking up more than his share of the bench.

"Bugger off," Koti said lazily. "Some of us need space."

Will snorted, feinted, and threw a punch that Koti caught in a hand, and they stayed like that, palm to palm, doing some impromptu arm-wrestling. A few seconds of stalemate, and then Will was pushing Koti's arm slowly back until his elbow bent too far and his hand banged against the wooden cubicle.

"And some of us need more space," Will said. "Shove over."

"Try it when we're both sitting down next time, cuz, and I'll show you who's boss. That was me with one hand tied behind my back. Still almost won, didn't I." But Koti shoved over.

Will grinned, toweled off, and pulled on his warmups. Messing around like that was stupid, maybe. It was juvenile. But it was fun.

He grabbed his mobile out of his duffel to shove it into his

110

pocket, but paused at the sight of a text from his agent showing green on his home screen.

WTH have you been doing. Call me ASAP.

Will blinked. What the hell *had* he been doing? Nothing, that was what. Well, nothing that could have got Ian in a lather. He'd been training and playing rugby, just like always. Not doing too badly at it, either. He'd been head down, bum up all season long, ever since he'd come back from the States. He'd come back fit, he was in form, and he'd just been told that he'd been selected for the All Blacks' June series against England. He was going to be an All Black at last. What more was there?

He thumbed his mobile, shoved down to the end of the bench, turned his back on the banter and male laughter surrounding him, and rang Ian.

"Will." The exasperated sigh came clearly down the line. "Why? Were you *born* stupid?"

"What?"

"I'd say you got pissed and forgot yourself," Ian said, "but there are too many of them for that. You can't have done it all in a day. What could possibly have possessed you to pose for nudie pics, and then to let them be posted to some porn site? A brainless moment posting a selfie, that I could see. Don't get me wrong, I'd still tell you that you were a bloody fool. But this? What were you *thinking?*"

"Wait. Wait." Will was having a bit of trouble breathing. "I didn't use my name. And it isn't porn. It's just...suggestive. But it's got out?"

A snort was the response to that. "Too right it's got out. And I know what it is, because I saw it. Everybody saw it. You didn't have to use your name. You're a public person with a very public face. Can't believe I'm having to explain that to you. One person finds out, tells somebody else? You're a red-hot sensation, and not the kind anybody wants. What's the first thing I said to you when you signed with me? The first thing I say to everybody? Nothing is private online. We'd better get your story ready, because this has 'disgracing the jersey' written all over it."

Will tried to focus. "What story could there possibly be that would explain it? Other than that I had my head up my arse?" When he'd thought about it since arriving back in the goldfish bowl that was the life of a rugby star in New Zealand, the whole thing had seemed like a dream, one he'd tried to forget. It had been stupid and irresponsible. He'd known it even at the time, he'd done it anyway, and here it was, back to bite him.

"Well," Ian said, "I have a couple ideas. And meanwhile, no comment. I shouldn't have to tell you that either, but who knows? Absolutely no bloody comment."

$$\heartsuit\heartsuit\heartsuit$$

Three hours later, Will was holding the phone to his ear and counting the seconds until the ringing finally began. Three rings. Four. He calculated times. Ten P.M. in Vegas. He should have waited, but he couldn't stand to wait. He needed to know.

"Hello?"

"Faith? It's Will."

"Will?"

"Yeh. Will. Your model." She didn't even *remember* him? He'd ruined his life with her, and she'd already forgotten?

"What—where are you?"

"Wellington."

"Um...Oh. New Zealand." She took an audible breath. "The capital. Why are you there?"

"Because I've got a match tomorrow." What did that matter? "What I need to know is, did you do it?" He was trying to control his temper, but it was getting away from him again at the idea of it.

"Did I do what?"

"Did you leak it?" he demanded. "Did you tell somebody it was me on that site?"

"Of course I didn't tell anybody. Who would I tell? Who would even care?"

"All of En Zed and half of Aussie, that's who. It's blown up over here." He'd thought the site hadn't had a hope. It was still hard for him to believe it had gone global enough for somebody in a nation as small and remote as New Zealand to see it. But judging from the number of stories that had been uploaded, the number of votes for those stories, and most of all, the subscriber count—*something* had happened. It had gone viral, and, yes, it had gone global.

"Oh, my gosh." She did sound genuinely surprised, but he wished he could see her face so he'd know for sure. He thought of her that last night on the roof, of him spilling his guts to her, and of how soft her eyes had been as she'd listened. Surely she wouldn't have done this. Surely not.

"That's why the uptick in subscriptions," she was saying. "It's been doing pretty well, with the contest and all, but the past day or so…That's *you?* And, what? That's really a big deal? Why? We haven't even showed that much yet. Hardly any of the special stuff."

He groaned. "Oh, bugger. The special stuff. What's up there already, the writing—it's nasty. Thought you said it was going to be romance."

"*Erotic* romance. Which means sex."

He passed that one by, because she didn't have to tell him. All he'd say was, women were so much dirtier than he'd ever imagined. If those authors actually *were* women. He had his doubts. "And you didn't tell anybody else it was me?" he pressed. "Not your mum? Not Calvin? Because Calvin would've sold me out in a heartbeat."

He could hear the testiness in her voice. "Of course I didn't. I told you I wouldn't. What do you think I am?"

"I didn't really think so, but I had to know."

"Well, now you know. It wasn't me. I'm sorry if it's a problem, but, Will…"

"I know." He sighed. "You don't have to say it. My own bloody fault. And I signed a release."

"Well, yes. I wouldn't have put it quite like that, but, yes."

113

"There it is, then, and I have to do something about it. Could I pay Calvin not to put any more up, d'you reckon? Or better yet, to take the whole thing down?"

"No. I'm sorry, but no. I really doubt it. He's got visions of a million dollars, now more than ever. Not possible, unless you *have* a million dollars."

"Well, not right to hand, I don't. The damage is done already anyway. So it's Plan B." And he started to tell her what that was, doing his very best to convince her that she wanted to be part of it.

It had sounded like out of the frying pan and into the fire to him, but Ian had been convinced that it was the only way, and the consequences were too dire.

"You need to give a reason for it," his agent had said. "*Some* reason. It only has to be for a couple weeks, and then it's over. A few photos, a few strategic mentions in the press, and you've weathered it. Otherwise, you could be looking at playing overseas, and I'm not joking."

"It can't be that bad," Will had managed to say over the pounding of his heart. What had he been thinking? He hadn't been thinking, that was what. He'd lost his focus, lost his discipline, and look where it had landed him.

"It's going to be just that bad. You haven't spent enough time in En Zed, if you don't know that. In Aussie, maybe it wouldn't have been. *Maybe.* In the States, obviously not. They don't much care what their sportsmen do over there, long as they can play and aren't actually in prison. You want that kicking job, I can ring them again. Go back over there, and you can pose for all the dirty photos you like. But New Zealand rugby? The All Blacks, especially? Think they'll want this? Think your selection's going to stand for the June series? I'll tell you, mate. It's not, not without some damage control, not with the reputation you've already got. You want to take care of that family of yours? Either I start looking into an overseas club, or we come up with a reason, and a plan."

"That's a stupid reason, though. And a stupid plan."

"Well, then, that's perfect. Because it was a bloody stupid thing to do."

an unexpected journey
♡

"You're *what?*" Bella demanded.

It seemed like that was all anybody was saying these days. Even Montclair had gotten excited. He was turning in circles, yapping at the tone in Bella's voice.

Faith picked the little dog up, snuggled him into her lap on her mother's cream-colored couch, and stroked his whisper-soft fur. Snuggling with Montclair looked like all the comfort she was going to get tonight. "I'm taking an unexpected vacation to New Zealand," she repeated.

"You don't take unexpected vacations. This is about Will, isn't it? Wasn't he from New Zealand?"

"Yes. To both. Yes, he's from New Zealand, and yes, it's about him."

"But you said you hadn't slept with him, so why on earth would you go visit him?" Bella fixed Faith with her gimlet eye. "Don't you go chasing after that man," she warned. "That's the very last way you'd ever get him."

"I'm not actually an idiot." Faith was flushing a little now. "I'm not chasing after him. He's chasing after *me*. In a way. Although

116

not that way."

Her mother continued to stare at her suspiciously. "In exactly what way? Don't you dare lie to me, because I'll know. I want the whole story, and I want it now."

"You know," Faith couldn't help pointing out, "I'm twenty-seven years old."

"And I'm forty-nine, and I've known more men than you'll ever be able to shake a stick at. Your point?"

"All right. I'm sharing. Not because I have to, but because I'd rather you heard it from me. I'm going to New Zealand for two weeks to pretend to be Will's girlfriend."

Her mother, for once, seemed lost for words, so Faith continued. "Because of the modeling. He's in trouble. I didn't tell you this before, because he asked me not to, and there was no reason to break his confidence. He's a rugby player, and apparently he's supposed to behave himself. And he didn't."

"He's a pro athlete," Bella said slowly. "And it matters that he *modeled?* Or did he do something else? Is he gay?"

"Gay? No. Don't be ridiculous. Will?"

"Only thing that makes sense," her mother said with a shrug. "I didn't get that off him. I'd have said the complete opposite, but who knows? Sure what it sounds like to me. Why would anybody care about a few pictures?"

"It's different there," Faith tried to explain. "That's what he says. And the site—the pictures aren't so bad, but the stories—some of them are pretty risqué. And I guess the press is having a field day, and it means he might not be selected for the All Blacks—the all-star team. The international team. Which is a very big deal, money-wise and…everything-wise."

"And in what possible way does it help that you go over there?"

"Because then he can say that he did the modeling as a favor to me, because he was going out with me. I'm there two weeks, then I go home again, and everyone finds out we broke up, because that's the kind of heartless witch I am. I used him for the pictures, and I'm going to dump him. I'm American, of course—from Vegas, even—so that helps with the heartless part."

Bella snorted. "That is the dumbest thing I've ever heard."

"Well," Faith admitted, "I thought so, too. But…" She took a breath, and said it. "He's paying me. About five thousand dollars' worth, by the time you count the plane fare, and I can use it. This is my change-my-life move," she hurried on, seeing her mother's mouth opening. "I can see the light at the end of the tunnel. It's my big break, and I want to take it. I can still do the Roundup work while I'm there, and I can do the marketing for Calvin's site, too, even though he'll have to use another assistant. And I get to go to New Zealand, and I really want to go to New Zealand. I *really* want to. I want to see the ocean, and…and everything."

She knew that her mother wouldn't understand the yearning for space, for the ocean, for peace. For what Will had talked about, that night on the roof. For a lake, and mountains, and a sky full of stars. "I want to go somewhere and *do* something," she tried to explain, "and this is my chance. It's perfect, don't you see? As long as you can cover the apartments."

"*Paying* you?" her mother said in alarm, as if she hadn't heard anything else. "No. There's a word for that, and you're not doing it. If you need money, I'll give you money."

"It's not your choice, Mom," Faith said with a sigh. "And there's no sex involved. He told me so. It's acting, that's all."

Which hadn't been the greatest thing she'd ever heard, Will hastening to assure her that it would only be for show. But it was that much more reinforcement, too, would keep her from wishing for more, or, worse, trying for something he wasn't willing or able to give. It would be two weeks with him, and then she'd be going home. With an unbroken heart, because she wasn't stupid. But being cast as the villain? Could she really do that?

Yes. She could. Sure, she liked Will too much for any of it to be completely comfortable. But she'd lived next door to him for weeks already and had kept her head. She could do it again. For three thousand dollars and a trip to New Zealand? You bet she could. She could take Hope and Hemi there after all, because she would have seen it for herself, and what she'd told her mother was true. She wanted to go.

"Why didn't he ask the girl he modeled with?" her mother wanted to know. "Sounds like a much better cover story to me. He was in love with one girl, so he took dirty pictures with another girl? If a man told me that, it wouldn't fly for a minute."

"That would have been a little awkward, seeing as Gretchen's about six months pregnant."

"No. Really?"

"Yeah. I'm sure if she hadn't been, Will would have asked her. But she is, and he didn't."

"All right. If you're going to go, you're going to go. But I still think," Bella said, looking shrewdly at Faith, "that you've got more feelings about that man than you're letting on. So if you go, you're going armed."

"*Armed?*" Faith laughed. "What, I'm going to have to shoot him to keep him off of me? I don't think so."

"That's not the kind of armor I mean. You're halfway there already, but…when do you go?"

"Next week." The butterflies fluttered low in Faith's belly at the thought. "Eight days."

"Eight days," Bella said with satisfaction. "Plenty."

family party
♡

Will's grandmother eyed the straggle of weary arrivals coming through the big pneumatic doors. "I think they're starting to come out," she told her family. "At least those look like Yanks to me. Talia, go over and get your brother."

Will's fifteen-year-old sister looked up reluctantly from her ever-present mobile. "What?"

"Go get Malachai," Will's mother said. "Your Kuia's asking you."

Will's sigh was lost in the echoes of the Auckland Airport arrivals hall. He hadn't counted on a welcoming party for Faith, but here they were all the same. His mother, brother, and sister were varying degrees of reluctant, but his grandmother, as always, had carried the day.

Malachai slouched towards them behind his sister, who was already on her phone again. His flat-brimmed hat sat askew on his head, at some angle that was meant to be gangster, and to hide that he was well and truly hung over. As if Will wouldn't have noticed the bottles in the bin of the front hall when they'd stopped to collect him along the way, or the general state of the flat his brother shared with mates near Auckland University. There'd been a party last night, and last night had been Sunday.

Pity his mum wasn't hung over. She had her arms crossed against her chest, spelling nothing like welcome.

When he'd rung her the previous week to explain about the photos, he'd faced a deafening silence, and when he'd told her about Faith, it had stretched out for so long, he'd had to say, "Mum? You there?" He wasn't doing too well with the women in his life, and that was the truth.

"You're telling me," she said slowly, "that you're in love with some Yank girl you knew for a few weeks, who got you to pose for dirty photos."

"Aw, see," he said, trying to laugh, "when you say it like that, it sounds bad. She didn't ask me to. It wasn't her fault. It was my idea. Her job depended on it, you could say. And it wasn't so bad. All pretty tame, really."

"I saw them. They're not that tame. Not tame enough to keep you out of the naughty chair. What were you *thinking?*"

A question for the ages. "I guess it's just love," he tried. "Which is why she's coming out."

The frost down the line was so clear, he could swear his phone was turning cold in his hand. "She may be coming out," his mother said, "but don't think we're going to come running to meet her with open arms, because she sounds like nothing but trouble."

And yet here she was. Here they *all* were, but that was her own mother's doing, of course.

"It's not necessary," Will had told his grandmother when she'd rung the day before to tell him they were all on their way to Auckland and would be joining him to meet Faith. Including his sister, who was meant to be in school today.

"Too right it's necessary," she'd answered. "Showing that your family's supporting you, that we understand? We'll be there. Pity we can't get Caro and Hine and the rest over from Aussie for it, but they say they can't, not with the kids and all."

That would have been all he needed—his two other sisters,

their partners, and their four kids, an entire Troupe of Traveling Taweras turning up to stage Will's rehabilitation with the New Zealand public. Fortunately, it was only four of them here, but four was more than enough.

It was only for the day, though. They'd all be gone tomorrow. He'd hold that thought.

"Who are we looking for?" his grandmother asked now. Her dark eyes, still eagle-sharp at seventy-five, searched the monitor overhead, scanning the passengers straggling out one at a time pushing luggage carts piled high after the twelve-hour journey from LA.

"Blonde," Mals said laconically from under his hat, leaning against the barrier and looking like he needed to lie down. "Hot. Bound to be. That her?" he asked as a—yes, a fairly hot blonde came into view on the monitor, all hair and long, slim legs, and totally Will's type.

"She's not blonde," Will said. "She's not exactly hot, either, not the way you're thinking. I mean, she is, but not made up or anything. She's attractive," he added hastily. "Obviously, I think so. But not like that, eh. It's more of an…emotional connection."

He sounded like a bloody greeting card, and he was sweating a little now. He'd known this was a horrible idea. They were going to see straight through him, and so was everybody else.

"You're joking." Mals looked interested for the first time, although Talia didn't even look up. "You went for a girl who wasn't hot? Since when? Bro, you could get *anybody*. If I could hook up like that—"

"You'd what?" his mother demanded.

"What? Not like Will doesn't," Mals said. "Not like everybody doesn't know it. Course, he didn't always have a photographer recording it."

"It wasn't real," Will said in exasperation. "It was modeling. Why can't anybody get that through their head? And I didn't say she wasn't hot, exactly. And whatever I did before, I'm not doing it anymore, because I've got somebody special at last, haven't I."

122

There he went with the greeting card again.

Then he got distracted, because there was another pretty girl on the monitor. Head down, pushing a cart, her hair swinging around her face, wearing a short skirt and jersey that, even on the fuzzy black-and-white monitor, were showing off a figure that was keeping him looking.

Then she rounded the corner and was there in person, and it was Faith, and Will was standing there, gobsmacked.

She saw the group behind the barrier, and her hand came up in a tentative wave and fell again.

"That's her?" Mals asked. "That's not hot? You're joking. A bit old, maybe, but that girl is a stone *fox."*

"Yeh," Will said absently through a mouth that had gone dry. He was still just standing there, but so was she, her cart not quite out of the egress lane, the other passengers diverting around her.

He'd forgotten how she looked, maybe, but he could swear that she'd never looked quite like this. Her hair fell in wispy strands around her face, then to her shoulders, with a sexy fringe that fell below her eyebrows. That hair was glowing under the fluorescent lights, too, because there was some blonde in it now.

It was makeup, he realized, that made her eyes appear even larger, her mouth even lusher. She didn't need any makeup, though, for that tiny little mole above her lip, and he remembered with a jolt of recognition how much he'd always longed to kiss that mole. And as for that body—he remembered that, too, although surely it looked even better now. She was hot. Yeh. Or he was. He was, for sure.

"What are you waiting for?" his grandmother said. "Go get her." She thrust the flowers she'd insisted on stopping to buy into his hands and shooed him on. "Go."

Will stepped forward, because Faith still wasn't moving. He was conscious of the eyes on him, and not just his family's. He'd been recognized.

Faith seemed to realize she'd stopped and began shoving her cart again, coming to meet him. She reached a hand up and pushed her hair back as if she still wasn't used to having it around her face. Or as if she didn't know what to do with her hands.

"Hi," she said, and she wasn't smiling, but then, neither was he.

"Hi," he managed. "You changed your hair." Well, *that* was lame. He realized he was still holding the bouquet of lilies and shoved it hastily at her. "Here. Flowers."

"That's how you say hello?" his grandmother demanded from behind him. "The poor girl doesn't even get a kiss?"

Faith's eyes widened and flew to his. "Sorry," he said softly. "That's my family. Got to be convincing." He put his hands on her shoulders, felt the tension in her, and knew that, however different she looked, she was still the same Faith. Still not taking it lightly.

He'd meant it to be quick, just a peck. But as soon as he felt those soft lips under his own, the current was leaping between them again, and her eyes were opening wide, then fluttering closed. Her body softened, swayed into him a little, her hands had come up to his own shoulders, the tissue-paper wrapping for the flowers brushing against his back, and he was holding her more tightly, pulling her into him. His mouth was moving over hers, and he was kissing her harder, because it seemed he had no choice. Just like the last time, on the roof.

He stepped back at last, a little shaken, and she didn't look any steadier than he felt. "Hi," he said again. He reached for her cart, because he needed to do something, or he was going to kiss her again. "My family's here." The phones were being held up now, the cameras clicking away. Well, that was the point, wasn't it?

They had reached his family, and Talia was looking up at last from her ever-present phone. "Kuia," Will said, "this is Faith. Faith…" He stopped, horror-stricken, because he was so rattled, he'd forgotten her surname.

"Faith Goodwin." She put out a hand to his grandmother. "It's…Kuia? Or…Mrs.?"

"Miriama Johnson," she said. "Will's mum's mum. 'Kuia' means 'grandmother.' But you can call me Miriama."

Faith blinked a little. "Johnson?"

Miriama laughed. "You're thinking it doesn't sound too Maori. That's all right. Emere's always telling me I'm not Maori enough."

"Mum," her daughter protested. "That's not what I say."

"And *I* say," Miriama went on, "what's the point of being alive if you never color outside the lines? Where's the fun in that? But I guess that skips a generation, doesn't it, because here Will is, doing it his own way as well."

Will's mum wasn't looking too rapt about that line of chat. "And how's that working out for him?"

"Well," Miriama said serenely, "that's why Faith's here, isn't it?"

Will's heart stopped for a moment. Could she know? She went on, though. "It hasn't worked out so badly for him, all in all, seems to me. And nobody's welcomed you yet, Faith, though Will didn't do so badly once he got over his stage fright. *Haere mai.* Welcome to Aotearoa." She reached out for Faith and gave her a kiss on the cheek.

"New Zealand," Will murmured. "Aotearoa."

"Thank you," Faith said to his grandmother.

"And my mum," Will said hastily. "Emere Tawera."

His mother, to his non-surprise, didn't kiss Faith. She held out a hand, shook Faith's briefly and released it, and said, without a smile, "Will's brother and sister. Malachai and Talia."

And that was it. Photo opportunity taken, family introduced. "Time to go," Will said. "Breakfast, and a walk round the Domain, I thought. Sound all right?" he belatedly thought to ask Faith. "Did you sleep on the flight?"

"Uh...sure," she said. "Whatever the Domain is. And yes, some."

"Drop me at the Uni," Mals said. "I've got a lecture this afternoon. And I don't want breakfast."

Will fixed him with a stare. "You want breakfast. In your state? Breakfast."

close quarters
♡

Five hours later, Faith was drooping with fatigue. Of course, it hadn't helped that she'd barely slept on the flight over, however comfortable a seat—or bed, rather—Will's Business Select ticket had bought her. She'd been too nervous. But when he'd seen her, stopped, and stared, she'd felt a little better. The time spent fixing her hair and doing her makeup in the cramped toilet cubicle that morning had definitely been worth it. And when he'd kissed her, she'd *really* felt better, because, oh, could he kiss. And, oh, had his body felt good against hers, big and hard and strong. His arms wrapping her up, pulling her into him, his mouth moving over hers…

Oh, dear. She was in so much trouble. And that had been before she'd met his family.

They'd brought two cars, so at least Faith hadn't had to ride with Will's mother, although there'd been a little skirmish about who was going with whom all the same.

"Kuia and I should ride with Faith," Malachai had piped up when they'd been standing beside Will's car, which was, no surprise, red and sporty, exactly as Faith would have imagined.

Will had favored his brother with another dark frown. "No," he'd said flatly.

Could he actually have been jealous that Faith would have been sharing the cramped back seat with his brother? That had been a cheering thought. But no, he probably just hadn't wanted her to notice the alcoholic fumes that were coming off Malachai. Too late. That was hard to miss, if you'd ever worked in a casino.

They'd taken Will's sister, in the end, who had sat in the back and said nothing, but had been an effective deterrent to conversation all the same. The three of them had ridden into the City in constrained near-silence, Will asking her about her mother and her flight as if they were strangers. He'd pointed out the communities they were passing, the green hills that were actually the remnants of volcanoes, until they had reached the Domain, which turned out to be a big park situated in another volcanic crater. They'd eaten breakfast sitting on the patio of a little café, watching ducks paddling peacefully in a pond straight out of a fairy tale, lined by trees and ferns so lush, she'd half-expected to see magical creatures peeping out from beneath the greenery. Will's grandmother had been chatty, Will had looked relaxed and hadn't been, and nobody else had even pretended. And then they had piled into the cars again minus Malachai, who had headed off after breakfast to walk back to the University, and driven across a harbor that was so picturesque it hurt.

Ferryboats passing busily to and fro against a backdrop of a long peninsula, green hills dotted with houses, and behind them, when Faith turned in her seat, the bridge sweeping across the water to the skyline of the central city, with the spire of the Sky Tower taking center stage, as iconic as a postcard. Clouds scudded across a crystal-blue sky, and the sun shone, then was blotted out by a sudden downpour that passed as quickly as it had arrived. Then it was sunny again, and Will had taken a turn, and they were driving down a street lined with palms and majestic leafy trees, with big houses on either side. Some of her fatigue was lifting, because beyond the houses—that was the ocean she was seeing, those flashes of blue. Will pulled into a driveway on the ocean side, then into the garage of a white house that was all modern lines and glass. Which had, it turned out when Will had led her upstairs, only three bedrooms.

"Oh, no," she said when she was standing next to a king-sized bed that looked out over a wide balcony, past green lawn edged by palms, and straight out to the beach. Her dream location, but not her dream situation. "Absolutely not. Not part of the deal."

Will heaved her suitcase onto a low dresser and sighed. "Tell me you're not going to be passing out in three hours max. Believe it or not, I very rarely make moves on unconscious girls. Besides, it's just for tonight. And there's no way my family is going to believe that my girlfriend, the woman I'm madly in love with, is making me sleep on the couch the first night."

As she continued to stare at him, her hands on her hips, he sighed again. "Right," he said, then moved to the bed, threw the comforter back, and took the pillows out. "Barrier." He laid three of them lengthwise down the middle of the bed. "You have your side, I have mine, and never the twain shall meet. Even though you're beautiful."

Really? She almost said it, but caught herself. Instead, she just looked at him and said, "Good."

Her mother had been so right. "The better you look over there, the stronger you'll feel," she'd promised. "Take it from somebody who worked mostly-naked and faked a smile for almost twenty years. Knowing you look good is about a woman's best ammunition."

"I like to think that's my mind," Faith had said.

"And your mind's just wonderful," her mother had assured her. "But your mind doesn't always help if a camera's on you, or when you're trying to remember that you've got the upper hand over a good-looking man."

Especially a man who had had his picture taken all day long, nodded politely at calls of, "Oi! Will!" from people he clearly didn't know, stopped to sign autographs for a couple of kids on the way out of the airport, and signed them again over breakfast.

"I mean," her resident star was saying hastily now, "not that you weren't beautiful before. Just that you're *more* beautiful, or I'm noticing it more, because you're dressed differently, or maybe it's your hair, or..." He stopped. "I'm stuffing up," he said helplessly as Faith started to laugh, and he was the Will she remembered again, not the polite stranger she'd spent the day with.

"Yes," she said, "you are. But it's pretty cute. This is boot camp you're looking at."

"What? You joined the army? Then...why are you here?" He looked totally confused, and she had to laugh again.

"Of course I didn't join the army. Boot camp is fitness classes. I decided it was time to change some things in my life, and this was part of it. Six o'clock every morning, for six long weeks. So if I look better? Well, thanks. Boot camp, hair, makeup, and some new clothes, that's all." Which she'd had the money to buy because of everything else she'd changed about her life, but he definitely didn't need to know that. "And the same me underneath," she added. "A me who thinks it would be a *great* idea if you explained why your mother hates me before I go downstairs and she tries to kill me with her withering glare again."

He sat down on the end of the bed, so she sat down, too, the pillow-wall between them, and waited for his answer. "Same reason your mum hates me. You're chocolate cheesecake. Well," he amended, "you're *vanilla* cheesecake. And, yes, you are. Although I'll just say, I love cheesecake." He stopped and cleared his throat. "Off the point," he muttered. "Yeh. My mum. You're the brazen hussy who lured her innocent boy into a life of pornography. And the more beautiful you look, the more she's going to think so, so I'm afraid you're stuck."

"Wow. Me?" She actually felt pretty happy about that. "I tempted the player, huh? With my wicked ways?"

He smiled at her, and her heart did a funny little flip.

"You did," he said, "and you know it."

tempting the player
♡

Faith woke to blackness. She pulled her phone off the bedside table and blinked at it. Four o'clock. She set the phone down, rolled onto her side, and tried to fall asleep again.

It wasn't working. She could hear Will's breathing in the quiet, could sense his warmth across their pillow-barrier, and that was way too distracting.

He'd fixed her a sandwich the day before after she'd taken a shower and somehow managed to unpack, and then she'd gone upstairs to take a nap at four o'clock and hadn't woken again, just as he'd predicted. She hadn't even known when he'd gotten into bed beside her, which was kind of a disappointment. She'd slept with Will Tawera, and she hadn't even remembered it. And now it was a whole twelve hours later, she was awake, and she couldn't sleep any longer.

She stole quietly out of bed and felt her way across the room in the dark towards the closet. She'd just reach in there and grab her robe.

Instead, she let out a squeak of surprise and pain as she stubbed her toe, then lost her balance and fell forward, her hands coming out to catch herself against something low and hard.

"Faith?" The voice came from behind her. The light went on, and she shoved off what turned out to be Will's dresser. She hadn't even been close to the closet. She turned to find him sitting up in bed, a white T-shirt stretching across his chest, his jaw dark with stubble. His hair wasn't even mussed. It was cut too short and sharp to be mussed. In fact, he looked absolutely terrific, and she probably looked...

His gaze flew hastily back to her face, and she realized he'd been staring, too. "Nice jammies," he said.

"I wasn't planning to be sharing my bed," she managed, "or I'd have worn a muumuu." She'd thought the pinstriped pink shirt and shorts with their black piping were cute, and that they'd be lightweight for packing. But the V-necked collar plunged deep into her cleavage, the shorts were short, and they were riding low, she realized with a hasty glance downward, sitting inches below her navel, their black ribbon untied and dangling down her thighs. She grabbed for it and tied it hastily into a bow, and he watched her do it.

"Did I mention," he said a little huskily, "that you looked good?"

"Go back to sleep. It's four."

He lay back against the pillows, crossed his arms behind his head—which was just way too much bicep for her peace of mind——and grinned at her. "I'm used to odd hours. And I need to keep the light on if you're going to get out of here without bodily injury. But if you're going to be changing, I'll close my eyes. How's that?"

"Humph. I don't trust you."

He sighed. "Wounding. But probably wise. I'd *want* to be virtuous, don't get me wrong, but it would be so bloody tempting to peek just a wee bit." He sighed again. "I'm weak. I'd probably succumb."

She opened the closet door, grabbed her clothes from their hangers, then got her underwear, bra, and tights out of their drawer, trying to be inconspicuous about it. And then, of course, dropped her underwear and had to bend to pick them up.

"Your undies have a hole in them," he said.

"Will you stop looking at my underwear?" she said crossly.

"Another of those weakness things. Seems I just can't help it. Come on. Show me. Give me something to think about, if I'm going to have to lie here the rest of the night without you."

"Not part of the deal." She could feel herself beginning to blush. "Giving you something to think about."

"But how am I going to hold your hand and kiss your cheek when I take you out today, otherwise, so we can get our photo snapped?" he complained. "I need to get in the mood."

"You? You were *born* in the mood."

He laughed, strong white teeth flashing, and she couldn't help smiling. "Too true," he said. "You going to show me or not?"

She heaved a sigh. *The better you look, the stronger you'll feel,* she reminded herself. She would put herself in the power seat, that was all. She sat on her side of the bed, crossed her bare legs, dumped her clothes into her lap, and held her pale purple lace underwear up, draped over one finger.

"Bow in the back," she told him, then slowly reached for them with the other hand, held them up, and showed him. "With this little diamond-shaped cutout underneath it. It's supposed to be sexy."

She could see his Adam's apple moving in the muscular column of his throat as he swallowed. "It works, too. Work even better on, eh. You want to *really* inspire me…"

"Ha." She uncrossed her legs, scooted off the bed, scooped up her clothes, and wiggled just a little bit extra as she flounced—yes, flounced—towards the bathroom. "You're going to have to work with what you have," she tossed back at him over her shoulder, "because that's all you're getting."

♡♡♡

After that, and after she'd come out of the bathroom again to find him still awake, still watching her, it wasn't very hard at all to write her next chapter.

She'd stolen downstairs and curled up on one of the black leather couches that stood before the fireplace in the soaring space of the living room—the lounge, she remembered. And had begun to work. If you could call it that.

I sat up and stretched, satisfaction running like warm liquid through my veins. I'd never been as aware of my body as I'd become these past few months, or as happy in it. I felt Hemi's hands and mouth on me even when he wasn't touching me, and all he had to do was look at me to set me quivering.

He wasn't looking at me now, though. He was lying on his back, the white sheet pushed all the way down to his waist, one muscular arm flung over his head, still sound asleep.

I loved to look at him, at the powerful sculpture that was his body, the fierce, proud lines of his warrior's face. And now, for once, I could look my fill, because he was sleeping. Because he was helpless.

The happiness rose in me like bubbles in a glass of champagne, and I got out of bed, stole around to his side of it, and picked up the silk ties he'd used the night before. I'd been moaning then, straining against them, begging him to finish, to put me out of the delicious misery he'd kept me in for what had felt like hours, until every nerve in my body had been stimulated to its aching maximum, until I'd been shaking with need, panting with frustrated desire.

But that had been last night, and this was a whole new day, the first morning of the rest of my life, and I was a strong woman who needed to see just how far she could push a strong man.

I paused all the same when I'd laid the tie gently over his outflung wrist. Could I really do this? Could I take the consequences?

Yes. I could. I could take anything he gave me.

♡♡♡

"Working already?"

Faith jumped a full two inches and slammed the laptop shut. "Don't sneak up on me like that." She twisted on the couch to see Will coming down the spare open treads of the staircase, light-stained planks against stark white walls broken by one tall rectangular window, glowing pink now with sunrise.

He looked so athletic loping down the stairs in navy-blue shorts and a gray T-shirt. He looked like Hemi, but he wasn't. He was Will, and he was grinning at her. Her life was so confusing.

"What?" he asked. "Writing down all your naughty thoughts?" And she very nearly jumped again.

"Just doing a little work." It was the truth. It was just that some of her work, these days, was downright...pleasurable. If you couldn't do it, you could at least think about it, and she was spending a *lot* of time thinking about it. And writing about it.

"Operation Restore Will's off to a flying start, by the way," he said, "if you haven't checked it out yet."

"Huh?"

"We made the papers, if you want to see."

He sat beside her, and at his direction, she found the article, complete with a picture of Will kissing her at the airport. Her head back, his arms wrapped around her, her hand clutching his flowers in their pink-tissue cone, looking so incongruous against his broad shoulders.

She looked like a woman abandoning restraint, a woman being passionately kissed by somebody who knew how. Which was exactly how it had felt. For those few treacherous moments, she'd forgotten why he was doing it, why she was there, and had wanted nothing more than to keep kissing him, to keep feeling that hard mouth on her, those big hands exploring her. Until she'd remembered.

"We pretended pretty well there," she managed to say. "That looks real, doesn't it?"

"Yeh. Good job."

She read the headline, then. *The Player Meets his Match.* If she'd needed a reminder, here it was.

Rugby heartthrob Will Tawera has always been a player—in both senses of the word. It's no secret that the star No. 10 has left a trail of broken hearts on either side of the Tasman for nearly a decade. The hottie playboy's latest antics, though, looked like having serious consequences after he was found to have posed for some very naughty photos during his recent holiday break in the States.

Another picture, this time from the site. Gretchen on her hands and knees in bra and low, tight jeans, with a shirtless Will on his knees behind her, one big hand on the back of her neck.

"Whoa," Faith said. "Family newspaper?"

"Yeh. Surprised they put it in there, but hard to resist, I guess. That won't have helped."

Turns out, though, she read on, *that there was a reason behind our Will's apparent fit of Stateside madness. A curvy brunette reason named Faith Goodwin, to be exact, the femme fatale for whose sake, agent Ian Foster says, Will did his spot of erotic modeling. Faith was spotted yesterday arriving at Auckland Airport to keep her man company during his one-week suspension from the All Blacks' June tests against England. The stunning photographer's assistant looks like enough to make any rugby boy lose his head. It seems that Will's enforced holiday is off to a smashing start. Could the legendary player have finally met his match?*

"Well, that was the idea," Faith said, closing her laptop again and doing her best to ignore the sinking feeling in the pit of her stomach. "I guess it worked. It's good to be stunning, too, I suppose. Did your agent leak those pictures?"

"Yeh. He will have done. And you *are* stunning, although I'm not nearly as much of a heartthrob as they're making out, or as much of a player, either. Let alone a playboy. Makes me sound like I've got silk sheets on the bed. But then, I make it a point never to believe my press." He stood up. "And meanwhile, here in the real world, I'm off for a run. Want to join me? Keep you fit, since you don't have that boot camp anymore? I could give you some physical training myself, come to think of it. If you gave me a bit of time to think about it, that is."

His slow smile was pure sin, all teasing heat and wicked implications, and she was responding despite every better intention. The tingles she was feeling weren't coming from reason, because her body answered to a more ancient call.

But if she liked him, even if she just liked looking at him, well, that just made this easy money, didn't it? As long as she kept her head and enjoyed it for what it was. Flirting with a sweet, sexy man who made her laugh, and being in New Zealand. What could be bad about that? So she picked up her laptop, stood up, and said, "Sure. Let me put this away and go get my shorts on. I'm not fast, though, I warn you."

"No worries. I like to go nice and slow, too. Long as I've got company."

She put a hand on her hip and gave him her best glare, feeling a little better. "If you're going to make everything you say a cheesy innuendo, this deal's off right now."

He laughed. "Can't help it. Too easy. Go put on another pair of tiny little shorts, and we'll see if I can help it then. I'm guessing not, but here's hoping, eh."

change of plan
♡

When he'd switched on the light that morning and seen her bent over his dresser in those tiny pink shorts, Will's heart had just about stopped, and every moment after that had made it worse. Or better, depending on how you looked at it.

Worse, it turned out, because it had taken him almost as long to fall asleep again as it had the night before, after he'd tugged the duvet up a bit higher over Faith, and she'd murmured in her sleep and snuggled down a little deeper in the bed. She'd looked so soft and sweet, with her hair falling over her cheek. And when he'd climbed into bed beside her, separated by those bloody pillows, and thought about living with her...

At least they wouldn't be sharing a bed anymore, which was good, because surely this much sexual frustration wasn't healthy. He was going to rupture something. Ever since Faith had arrived, his agent's clever plan hadn't looked so clever after all.

Now, he was running down the hard-packed sand of Narrow Neck Beach behind her in the pink-tinged dawn light, and she was wearing shorts again, and he was beginning to doubt his aerobic conditioning, because he was having serious heart trouble.

She turned around to smile at him, and he jogged up to join her. "Told you I was slow," she said.

"And I told you that I like slow." Slow and easy, or fast and hard. Either way. Both ways. All ways.

She laughed, spun in a circle, then faced forward again. "It's pretty awesome, isn't it? How far can we go?"

"Far as you like. The tide's out. You won't see much, heaps of sand and sea, some trees and houses. About like the view from my deck."

"Mmm. And some ships." She eyed the behemoth that was making its ponderous way up the shipping channel towards the Hauraki Gulf. "What's that?"

"Car carrier. They come in almost every day. Everything has to be shipped to En Zed, remember. We're a long, long way from anywhere, down here at the bottom of the world."

"And what's *that?*" she asked, pointing at the immense low cone that dominated the horizon to seaward. "The mountain, or island, or whatever?"

"Ah. That would be Rangitoto."

"Let me guess. It's a volcano."

"Got it in one. Fifty volcanoes in Auckland. But just about that many beaches, too."

"You know what's funny?" she asked after a minute.

"No, what?"

"The day I met you, I was having a…well, a bad morning. And having this daydream of running on the beach. In a bikini."

He pivoted in an instant, and she turned with him. "What?" she asked in alarm.

"Dreams come true. Going back for it."

She pulled at his arm, tugged him around with her, and he came with her, and she was laughing again. "Too uncomfortable. I need a little more support, here in the real world."

"You had to burst my bubble, didn't you?"

"Better than bursting mine."

This time, he was the one laughing. "Well, yeh. When you put it like that—we'd better take care of yours, eh. Can't have my girlfriend suffering. So what else happened in this fantasy? Anything I can help with?"

She was smiling again. "Now, did I say it was a fantasy?"

"Well, I'm hoping."

"Too embarrassing," she decided.

"And now you have to tell me. What happened?"

"I guess, since you're my boyfriend…" He could tell that she was loving being able to tease him, and he was more than willing to keep her loving it. "The short story is, I sort of got…tackled by a guy."

He sighed happily. "I knew I could help."

"What, you're volunteering to tackle me? I thought you didn't hurt women."

"Don't have to hurt you to tackle you. I'm a highly skilled athlete. Or I could tackle you onto the bed, maybe, if you were worried about it. Yeh, that'd work. Just a venue shift."

"Remember you telling me that you didn't have to do everything you thought about? Anyway, you tackle? I thought you kicked."

He stared at her. "You really don't know anything about rugby, do you?"

"Nope. Not a thing. Except it's sort of like football."

"Not that much like it. Everybody kicks in rugby, though I kick the most. Everybody passes. Everybody runs. And everybody tackles. So you see, I'm clearly the man for the job."

She was still running. Not asking to be tackled one bit. "And again. Daydream. Not real."

♡♡♡

And all that was fun, and sexy, and sweet, until it wasn't.

A couple hours later, he was eating breakfast along with his family and Faith, who was looking proper and demure in her purple dress and black leggings, and not in the least like a man-

139

eater, no matter what his mum thought. Unfortunately. And his grandmother was making him an offer he was most definitely going to refuse.

"No. Sorry. Can't," he told her.

"And why can't you?" Kuia asked, her head on an angle, the feathers of gray hair framing the sculpted bones of her face. A hard face to say no to. "You're stood down anyway."

"Yeh, thanks. I remember."

"What's stood down?" Faith asked, taking a bite of toast.

"Suspended for a week," he said, the wrench in his gut exactly the same one he'd felt when Callum had told him.

The All Blacks' head coach had been blunt about it. "Do the crime, do the time," he'd said, and Will hadn't argued. He would pay the penalty, would go back to work afterwards and put his head down, fight to get his starting position back for the final game of the June test matches, and it would be behind him.

"Oh." Faith looked stricken, as if she really were the wicked temptress who'd lured him into this mess. "I read that, didn't I? I'm sorry, Will. I didn't realize…"

She needed to stop talking, because Kuia was looking curious again. Faith should have known that already. If she really *had* been his girlfriend.

"He'll get over it," Kuia said. "He's got over worse. Nothing but a tempest in a teapot anyway. He hasn't hurt anybody, hasn't done anybody over outside a pub or beat his partner or cheated on his girlfriend. Hasn't done anything at all but given a few women something to dream about when their own partners don't measure up, and what could be wrong with that? God gave you that body for a reason," she told her grandson.

"If He did," Will's mum said, "it wasn't to give randy girls something to dream about."

"How do you know?" Kuia asked. "Have God on a private line, do you? Who do you think gave women imaginations? And why? To get them through the bad times, that's why. Or the boring times. If our Will's helped them out a bit, well, maybe that's part of

His plan, too. Got to be a reason Will did that."

"I'd love to think the reason was God whispering in my ear." Will couldn't help it, he was laughing at the idea. He caught Faith's eye, and she put her napkin hastily to her lips and succumbed to what she was trying to pass off as a coughing fit. "I'm afraid that wasn't an angel on my shoulder that day, though."

"Well," Faith said, the smile escaping despite all her efforts, "not the way I saw it, no."

"Except that mostly, I did it for Faith," he remembered to say, and realized that it wasn't actually so far from the truth. He thought of her dropping the muffins, of following her from the anteroom into the studio and looking at the back of her jeans. "And she's pretty much an angel, so—"

"Oh, really? An angel's what you want? Huh," she said, and his grandmother was watching the two of them, her brown eyes alight.

"But then," Will said, "sometimes that little devil on your shoulder is exactly what you need." He watched the color rise into her cheeks, regular as clockwork, and smiled at her. "We all have dreams," he said softly. "Even if they're just daydreams. Making them come true—that can't always happen. But we can try." And the color rose some more.

"Anyway, you're stood down," Kuia said briskly. "Which means you can't train with the team anyway. So why can't you bring Faith down to Rotorua with us, work out at the gym there like you normally do? Haven't been home at all, have you, since the season started. And what were you planning to do with her next week once you're off with the All Blacks again? Leave her here all alone?"

"I'm fine," Faith put in hastily with a glance at Will's stone-faced mum. "I have a lot of work to do, and doing it in a house at the beach *is* pretty much my best dream come true."

"See," Will said, "she's fine. Besides, could be we want some privacy. We haven't seen each other for more than four months, and I only have this one week to spend with her."

"You have a bedroom in Rotorua," his grandmother said. "A

bathroom, too. Those should do you pretty well."

"Mum!" Will's mother exploded. "Talia's right here."

"Either Talia doesn't understand, or she does," Kuia said. "Either way, we're all good."

"Talia understands." It was almost the first time Will's sister had spoken this morning. "Talia's sitting right here. Talia is fifteen, and she isn't an idiot."

"Talia needs to remember who she's talking to," Will's mum said. "And we need to get back, because she's missed two days of school already."

"Which wasn't my idea," she muttered.

"Wasn't mine either," Will said. "Much as I appreciated all of you turning up to welcome Faith," he added with only a bit of sardonic intent.

"No," Kuia said calmly. "It was mine, and it's my idea that you drive down today with Faith. You can have all the privacy you want in the car, show her a bit of the country as well. She's flown all this way, and she's only going to see Auckland? That's not New Zealand."

"Privacy in the car isn't exactly what I was talking about," Will said.

"It was when I was young," Kuia said, and his mother was spluttering again, and he was laughing again, and that was just about that.

new challenges

♡

"What's going on with your sister?" Faith asked later that day, shifting in her seat to look at Will. He drove absolutely competently, no surprise there, but not fast, which *was* a surprise. But then, the roads here weren't wide, and they did some fairly serious winding. They'd even had to stop once for a herd of sheep being moved down the highway by a man on an ATV and a couple of very agile dogs, which Faith had already chalked up as one of the highlights of her life, and this was only her second day in New Zealand.

"Who? Talia?"

"No, I mean some other sister that I haven't met yet."

"Bit testy, aren't you?"

"Jet lag," she admitted. "I guess you fly a lot, huh?"

"You could say that. Or you could say that it's only every other week, and only about a quarter of those journeys are halfway across the world, so, nah. Not so much."

"So talk to me." She tucked one foot up under the other leg and wriggled around to get comfortable in the leather seat. "Because I *am* jet-lagged, and I'm nervous about hanging out with your family.

143

Besides, I don't want to fall asleep and be up at four again tomorrow."

"Nah, we don't want that. Having to watch you drop things and bend over to pick them up? Bloody nightmare. Just imagine, tomorrow I get to watch you get up at seven. In the light. Unless you want to stay in bed, of course. I'd be good with that, too."

"I'm not happy," she warned him. "You said one night, and it's going to be, what? Seven? You'd better have enough pillows, because that wall stays up."

He shot a look across the car at her. "*You're* not happy? You're not the one who had somebody holding up her lacy undies at him this morning. I wore a T-shirt and shorts to bed. I had some consideration."

"Aren't you making a pretty big assumption? That I'd find your naked self irresistible?"

"What, you wouldn't? Here I thought I was God's gift and all."

"To your *grandmother.*"

He laughed. "And the knife goes straight in again. Cut to the bone, aren't I."

She smiled with satisfaction. Yes, he was doing a pretty good job of keeping her awake and entertained, which was necessary, because the landscape spooling by outside the car was too pretty, too pastoral, and too storybook to do more than lull her to sleep. Rolling emerald-green hills dotted with sheep as white and fluffy as the clouds that floated serenely overhead, with the occasional teardrop of a serene blue lake to add its grace note, and a higher ridge fading to blue beyond.

"Your sister," she remembered. "Talia. What's the story?"

He shrugged. "She's a teenager."

"Really? Because it seems like more than that to me. She's the only one still at home?"

"Yeh. Two sisters in Aussie, and Mals at Uni, doing an engineering course."

"Engineering. Huh." He hadn't exactly looked like a serious student to her, but then, Will knew him and she didn't, and she didn't need to be butting into Will's family life. She was here for two weeks, and then she was leaving.

"So when you talk to her," she pressed anyway, "what does she say?"

"Talia? You're assuming she talks to me. I'm not that interesting to her, am I."

"Really? A celebrity like you?"

"Not a celebrity to her. Just her brother, who she barely knows, because I left home when she was six, and I've been playing rugby ever since, gone all the time. Four years of that in Aussie as well, remember."

"Why's that? Why'd you go to Australia? Seems like you like New Zealand, from what you've said, and your family's here. So why?"

"Money."

She waited for him to go on, but he didn't, and something in the set of his jaw made her decide not to pursue it. She wanted to ask about the tension she'd sensed in his mother and Talia. She wanted to ask about his grandfather, and why his grandmother, who had lost her husband only six months earlier, was the only person in the family besides Will who seemed remotely happy, but maybe today wasn't the time.

It wasn't her business anyway, because it wasn't her family, and she wasn't really his girlfriend. She was just pretending. So she lapsed into silence, looked out the window at grass and hills and sheep, and went somewhere else.

"So..." I asked tentatively. "You don't see much of your dad?"

I trembled a little as I waited for his answer. I knew he had a soft side hidden beneath the disciplined exterior. As fierce and demanding as he was when we made love—when he was holding me afterwards, I could feel all the emotion he had so much trouble expressing. The gentle touch of his hand stroking down my back. A kiss on my forehead when he thought I was asleep.

I knew his feelings ran deep, but when we'd met his cousin the night before, and Tane had mentioned Hemi's father, it was as if a steel curtain had come down. Hemi's face had been so forbidding, even Tane had dropped the subject.

145

"No," Hemi said tersely now, his knuckles showing white on the leather-wrapped steering wheel of the big sedan.

"Was your father not around, then? Like mine?"

"Hope," he warned, his lips barely moving, his face carved from teak. "This isn't a subject I discuss."

"You've helped me so much, though. With Karen, especially. Couldn't we…"

"No." His voice was so harsh, it sliced straight through me. "You couldn't."

It was the smell that brought her out of it. Sulphur, strong as a gas leak.

"What *is* that?" she asked.

"That," Will said, "is the smell of home. That's Rotorua."

The rolling fields of green had turned to higher, more rugged hills. They came around a corner, and there was the lake, a huge expanse of blue bordered by forested slopes stretching away on both sides.

"I thought it was a city," she said.

"It is. At the bottom of the lake. But it's ten more kilometers around it to get there. The smell is the geothermal features—all the hot pools. They're everywhere—back gardens and all. Rotorua's all about the hot pools. Geothermal areas all around here that are tapu—sacred. To Te Arawa, that is. My iwi. I'll take you to see one, if you like."

"Your iwi. That's your tribe? Te…Te Arawa?"

"You did the research. Of course you did. You researched the Maori? Should I be flattered?"

"It was for a project. You know, the site."

"Of course. The site. How could I forget."

"Oh, good. You're here," Will's grandmother said when they walked through an oversized front door and into the soaring great room of another big modern house set in a tree-shaded garden on another quiet, upscale residential street. No ocean this time, but the lake, Will had told her, was only a couple of kilometers away. "Show Faith around, Will, and then I'm taking her to three o'clock yoga."

"I don't actually know how to do yoga," Faith said.

"Course you do. You just don't know you do," Miriama answered, and there really wasn't a good answer to that.

Will sighed. "Remember that privacy we talked about? Maybe we want it."

"And you can have it," his grandmother said. "Tonight. Because don't tell me you're not headed straight to the gym anyway."

"Well, yeh," he said. "But it didn't have to be this minute."

"Wasting time," she said. "Go get Faith settled. She and I are going to yoga."

"Yoga sounds nice," Faith said, partly because it did, and partly because Miriama didn't hate her yet, and Faith wanted to keep it that way. "Nice and relaxing."

"Hmm," Miriama said. "We'll see."

That sounded ominous, but how could it be ominous? It was just yoga.

Except that it wasn't. It was *hot* yoga.

Fifty minutes into the class, she was dying, she was fairly sure of it. And what was worse, she was being shown up by a seventy-five-year-old. Or rather, she was continuing to be shown up.

She'd been sweating from the moment they'd walked into the studio, which was Vegas-hot, stickily humid, and by now, frankly disgusting, filled with the sweat from twenty straining bodies, with no way for it to dissipate in the stagnant air. Each pose was more grueling than the last, and this one was the worst, because Miriama was flat on her back beside her, her feet lying neatly beneath her hips, while Faith was only halfway down, the only upright person in the room. She must have lost at least five pounds in perspiration alone by now, and her mind, instead of being calmed, was a roiling mess of resentment. She'd tried more than once to take a break, but the instructor had called her out.

"Stopping isn't an option," the soothing-voiced woman, whom Faith was rapidly growing to loathe, had said. "Breathe into the discomfort."

Discomfort, hell. This was pain. This was torture. This was being pounded by iron hammers under the glare of the equatorial sun, and human beings weren't meant to twist this far. She hated the bully of an instructor, she hated the other students, all serenely twisting and bending away, and she was starting to hate Will's grandmother, too.

When she was finally allowed to stagger to her feet again and hang up her mat, which was probably going to have to be burned, she could barely bring herself to speak to Miriama. Luckily, Will's grandmother was busy exchanging cheerful goodbyes and hugs that couldn't have been sanitary with the other participants, all of whom looked equally, and loathsomely, refreshed after their punishment by the Hell-born.

Miriama was introducing her now, though, and Faith rearranged her features hastily into what she hoped was some semblance of good humor, although she probably looked more like a melting wax mask of tragedy, especially with her mascara and eyeliner running down her face.

"Will's partner," Miriama was saying. "You will have read about her, maybe. She's got the Kiwis up in arms, hasn't she, about losing another All Black to the Yank girls, but you can see why, can't you? Will's brought her down for a wee visit this week, seeing as he's been stood down anyway." Which was so forthright, Faith blinked. She'd thought *her* mother was honest.

"Well, we did notice that," one of the women said. "Noticed Will, too. Lovely photos, I have to say, and some *very* naughty stories. Stood down or not, I've been enjoying them, and I don't mind admitting it." She seemed to catch herself. "But I shouldn't say that to you," she told Faith. "How are you enjoying New Zealand so far?"

"I just got here yesterday." Faith wished they would move outside, because if she didn't get some air soon, she was going to keel over. "But so far, it's very...pretty," she finished lamely.

"First time doing hot yoga, eh," the woman said with a smile.

Faith laughed, then decided it had been a bad idea, because laughing took too much oxygen. "It shows, huh?"

"It does, a bit," the woman said, and they all laughed. "Never mind, we've all been there. Come every day for a month, though, and you'll have a new body and a new outlook on life."

Or I'll be dead. And what? Her body was bad? She thought she was looking all right these days. There was still too much of her in a bathing suit, of course, and she'd just make absolutely sure Will didn't see that, not that she'd planned anything different. But this thing wasn't going to work if she didn't look like anybody Will would really date. Not that she hadn't thought that from the beginning. Not that she wasn't feeling so gloomy right now, she wanted to lie down and cry.

"We'll get on, then," Miriama said. "Let Faith breathe. See you tomorrow."

Maybe *she* would. Faith wouldn't.

"A bit much?" Miriama asked chirpily when Faith had made it to the front door at last after swimming through the soup of water and sweat molecules that was the studio's air supply, and was taking in deep lungsful of the crisp autumn atmosphere outside.

"You could say that," Faith managed.

"Well, a lovely ride home and a shower will help," Miriama said, and Faith remembered with horror that she was supposed to ride a bicycle back to Will's house. Maybe she could call him to come get her instead. And maybe he'd laugh at her if she did. Maybe she should just suck it up and try to make it without falling off.

She did, in the end, though her legs felt so shaky, she could barely pedal, and once again, she was having difficulty keeping up with Miriama.

"Go take a shower," Miriama instructed when they got back to the house and were stowing the bicycles beside one of the garages. "Meet me in the spa pool afterwards. Best part."

Half an hour earlier, climbing into hot water would have been the last, the very last thing Faith would have wanted, but she was shivering a little now from cool air meeting sweat-soaked clothes, and she muttered agreement and staggered her way upstairs and into Will's bathroom. She was glad he wasn't here. She couldn't negotiate one more thing today, and she didn't even care anymore that she would be sharing a bed with him tonight. If he didn't make moves on unconscious girls, she was all good, because she was going to be unconscious for sure.

She twisted the taps of the shower, peeled her soaking-wet clothes from her abused body, climbed under the spray, and let it wash the sweat away. It worked, and in about five minutes, she felt a little better. And in about ten minutes, she was realizing that if she didn't get out now, she was going to stay in here until the water ran cold, and have to explain to everyone that Will's grandmother had kicked her butt so badly in yoga that she'd fallen asleep in the shower.

She turned the water off with reluctance, toweled dry, dug her swimsuit out of the drawer, and started to put it on, then realized that the bedroom door wasn't locked and ran hastily across the room to do it. She caught sight of herself dressed only in her black bikini bottom in the mirrored closet door and groaned a little. No question, Will wasn't seeing her in this, boot camp or no, flirting or no. He'd signed up for the photo shoot because of Gretchen, she knew, and there was about twice as much of her as there was of Gretchen. She fastened the top, pulled on her robe, and headed downstairs to the spa. She was going to fall asleep in there for sure, but right now, that sounded great.

in hot water

♡

Will lay back and let the heated water do its work. He opened his eyes when he heard the ranch slider moving in its track, and then he kept them open. Faith was standing there in her dressing gown, her hand still on the door, looking like she was about to turn around and go back upstairs.

"There you are," his grandmother said from her spot across the spa pool from him. "Don't just stand there getting cold again. Get in. We have company, you see. Isn't that lucky."

"Uh...yeh," Will managed to say. "Get in. Please."

He could see Faith swallowing hard, could sense her hesitation. Then she looked at him, took hold of the tie fastening her dressing gown, and tugged it loose. She shrugged out of its pale-blue folds and dropped it over a chair, and she was walking towards him, lowering herself to slide into the water, and coming to rest beside his grandmother.

She gasped. "Whoa. Hot."

That was the understatement of the year.

Will was looking. He shouldn't be, he knew, because that wasn't going to do him any good at all, but he was looking anyway,

151

because—because bloody hell. Her bikini was black, and it wasn't that it was so small, it was just that it had to cover so much luscious territory. He wished she'd get out again. He wanted to watch her climb out. Except that he wanted her to stay in. With him. He very nearly groaned. He was in so much trouble.

He got his voice back, said, "Bubbles," then twisted around, reached for the controls, and turned the jets on. He was going to need all the camouflage he could get. He turned the temperature down while he was at it. It was already too hot in here for him, and he wasn't going to be able to get out for a while.

It got worse, too. "What are you doing all the way over there?" Kuia asked Faith. "That's no way to greet your man after months apart from him. He doesn't want to sit with his granny when he could be sitting with you." She gave Faith a shove. "Go on."

"That's all right. I don't—" Will began, then shut his mouth. What was he saying? He wanted her over here. True, it might kill him, but what a way to go.

Faith looked at him, took a deep breath that did interesting things to the black bikini, and slid around the square spa pool until she came to rest ten cautious centimeters away. She bounced in the rush of the jetting water, her knee bumped his, her elbow brushed his side, and she jumped and blushed, which all made him harden that much more. He was downright aching by now, and every encounter only made it worse.

"Don't mind me," his grandmother said cheerily.

"Did you—" Now he was the one swallowing. "Have a good time?"

She laughed, seeming to lose a little of the tension. "Not exactly. I'd tell you the truth, but I'd have to kill myself out of sheer humiliation. How was the gym?"

"Oh, you know," he said. "It was the gym." And then he sat there like a fool and perved at her, trying not to look down her top and failing utterly, and she stared across the water as if something extremely fascinating were going on in the garden.

Kuia rose from the water. "That's enough for me. Enjoy

yourselves."

"I'll get out, too," Faith said, and all but levitated across the pool to scramble out.

"You were in there two minutes," Kuia said in surprise.

"That was enough. I'm still really tired. I think I'd better go upstairs and lie down. I mean, take a nap," Faith hurried on, wrapping herself in her dressing gown again. "I mean, I need a rest."

She fled into the house, and his grandmother watched her go, then turned back to Will.

"I'd say," she told him, "that you've got a bit of work to do there, in the girlfriend department." And then she went inside, too, and Will was left alone again.

$$\heartsuit\heartsuit\heartsuit$$

He sat down there for ten more long minutes, staying in the water until he could trust himself to get out again, then sitting on the side of the pool, keeping his feet in for warmth, giving Faith time to shower off and get dressed.

His mum came out to collect the washing. "You've been in there for ages," she had to comment. "You and Faith having trouble already? She went up the stairs fast."

"It's a bit of an adjustment, that's all," he said.

"What adjustment?" She turned to face him, the washing basket still on her hip and the clothes on the line forgotten. "Having a holiday with you? If it isn't working now, it isn't going to work any better later, when the bloom is off the rose and you're just another man. Drama isn't excitement, it isn't romance, and it isn't true love. It's just drama. I should know. Got five kids out of drama, out of breaking up and making up."

Will winced inside. He hated to hear this. He'd been trying to make it better for ten years, and he never could, because it wasn't something he could fix.

It had been a mistake not to tell the truth to his family, but he hadn't trusted Mals and Talia not to spread the word, and to be honest, he hadn't wanted to disappoint his mum again, either, have her look at him in that way that meant only one thing. That he was exactly like his dad.

It would have been all right if he and Faith could have kept their distance, the way he'd planned. The trouble was, Faith wasn't a good enough actress to be able to spend a week with his family and pretend to love him.

He should have done what his agent had suggested and hired somebody to play the part of his girlfriend. When Ian had suggested Gretchen, though, it hadn't just been her pregnancy that had had Will saying no. He'd seized on Faith from the beginning. If he were going to do it, he'd thought, he'd do it with somebody he liked. Somebody he actually wanted to be there. It had been—well, an excuse, maybe, to see her again. If it looked like it had been a mistake—well, this whole thing had been one giant mistake, and he just kept digging himself in deeper.

"Yeh, well," he said, and then didn't know how to go on. "Guess we'll see how we go." He stood up, collected his towel and wrapped it around his waist, then began to unclip clothes from the line. "I'll do this." He took the basket from her, set it on the wooden deck, and bent to kiss her cheek. "Go on in, Mum," he said gently.

She put her arm around him, held him close for a moment, then stood straight, blinking a bit. "I'll go finish dinner, then. Hope Faith will make it this time."

"I hope so, too. But jet lag's a bugger. And Mum," he added impulsively, "no worries. She'll be right. It's a week's suspension, that's all, and then it's all over." She was worried, he could tell, and he understood the worry, a bit. But he hadn't failed her yet, had he? At least not in that way. Not financially.

She opened her mouth to say something, probably that that was what his dad had always said too, and then closed it again. "Thanks," she said instead, and walked into the house.

He folded the clothes, took them in to her, and then went

upstairs. He didn't need to worry about forgetting himself with Faith again, at least. He wasn't feeling too cheerful just now.

He knocked softly at the bedroom door, glad nobody was around to see him do it. He hadn't thought out the details of this thing nearly well enough.

"Come in," he heard, and went inside. She was dressed, of course. Wearing the purple tunic and leggings, sitting on the bed, propped against the pillows with her laptop, although the lid was shut again, her hands held protectively over the cover.

"You can use the desk over there, if you like." He indicated the built-in area under the windows. "I'm quite happy to shift myself downstairs."

"Thanks. I will, but this is more comfortable right now." She hid a yawn behind her hand. "Your grandmother really did kick my butt," she confessed, and he smiled and felt better. He sat down on the edge of the bed beside her, and she shifted over, but not in an avoiding way, even though he was wearing nothing but a towel. In a companionable way.

"A bit harder than we thought, all this," he said.

"Yes. It is. I'm sorry that I'm not holding up my end of things better. I'm just not...used to, I mean, I haven't..." She stopped. "I'm not good at pretending."

"You didn't even have to tell me that." He smiled at her, and she smiled back. "I'm good at pretending," he confessed. "Always have been."

"And it doesn't feel a little..." She hesitated. "A little empty?"

"Yeh," he said, sobered again. "It does, at times." He shoved himself off the bed. "I'll go take a shower, eh, get dressed."

"Good idea. It's easier for me to pretend when you're dressed."

He wasn't sure what that meant. He wasn't sure he wanted to know. So he went in and took his shower instead.

♡♡♡

He was knocking on the door again an hour later, but didn't get an

155

answer this time, so he opened the door a crack and peered cautiously inside.

Her hands weren't busy over her laptop this time. They were still on the keys, but she was asleep.

"Faith," he said softly. "Dinner."

She didn't respond. He went to stand beside her, reached out to touch on the shoulder, then changed his mind and lifted his hand again. Instead, he slid the computer out from under her hands, and, when she still didn't stir, closed the lid and set it on the bedside table.

He considered her clothes, and decided to leave them. If she woke up to find him undressing her…that wasn't going to go over well. Instead, he went to the closet, found an extra duvet, and covered her with it. She sighed, murmured, rolled over, and snuggled in, and he smiled, gave in to temptation, and bent to kiss her cheek.

"Night, baby," he said softly, then was startled to hear himself say it. But he needed to practice, didn't he? He needed to pretend.

flying high
♡

Faith woke to another much-too-early morning after another much-too-early night, and how Will managed to fly from one continent, even one hemisphere to the next and play rugby, she couldn't imagine. She couldn't even stay awake past six o'clock.

At least this time she'd slept until five-thirty, so who knew? Maybe tonight she'd manage to have dinner with Will's family before she collapsed. As long as she didn't go to yoga.

She'd had her phone by the bed this morning, anyway, and had been able to use the flashlight to get out of the bedroom without waking Will up. Of course, that was because she hadn't had to get dressed. She'd fallen asleep in her clothes, and he'd covered her up, obviously, which was so...so sweet. But then, he *was* sweet. She'd always known that.

Another nagging splinter of guilt stabbed her as she propped herself at the end of yet another leather couch—brown this time, for a little variety—in the expanse of space that was the great room of this comfortable family home. He wouldn't like it if he knew what she was doing, she thought even as she was opening her laptop. He wouldn't like it at all.

157

But it wasn't up to him, and they weren't even involved, so what did she have to feel guilty about? Besides, he wouldn't find out, would he? Her relationship with him wasn't real, and anyway, she had to do this.

The decision to take her story beyond Calvin's site, to publish the episodes in serial form on all the online bookstores, had been the scariest one she'd ever made—and the best. For the first time in her life, she was loving her work, and to her astonishment, she was making more money doing it than at all her jobs combined. Her bank account was growing every month. She had to keep going, because this was her future. And anyway, she didn't have a choice. People wanted to hear the rest of her story. They were writing to her and telling her so. And she wanted to tell it. So she opened her document and started to type.

It was bad enough. And then, when I walked into the office that Monday morning, it got worse.

I was more than half an hour late, because Karen had been sick again. But surely, considering all the extra time I'd put in over the months I'd worked here, that wouldn't matter. Surely.

I could tell something was wrong as soon as I stepped through the door. The tension in the Publicity department hung in the air like an invisible gray cloud. What could have happened?

"Panic stations," Nathan muttered as he passed, ostentatiously studying a pile of papers. "It's you."

I made it to my cubicle, but had barely rid myself of my coat before Martine was gliding toward me on her stratospheric heels, the soles flashing Manolo Blahnik red, her entire sleek form radiating feminine power.

"I'd like to see you in my office, please," she said.

I grabbed my laptop case again in the hope that this might be work-related, but then, what else could it be? It couldn't be anything else. Nobody knew. Did they?

My heart beat out an apprehensive tattoo as I followed my boss's elegant back. Could I have done something wrong? More wrong than usual?

"Please. Sit," Martine said as soon as the door closed behind us, and I did my best to breathe—and sat.

"I'll be frank." Martine took a graceful seat behind her desk. *"I'm concerned about you. I hope that you aren't letting your personal life get...away from you."*

You have no idea. *"I know I was late today,"* I said. *"I'm sorry. It won't happen again."*

Martine waved a slim red-nailed hand. *"It's not so much the tardiness,"* she said, and I flushed a little. That made it sound like I'd been late constantly, instead of once. *"It's more the...the special arrangements."* Her glance was knowing, as if she were aware of exactly what I'd been doing this weekend, and exactly whom I'd been doing it with.

"Is there a problem with my work?" The special arrangements are over, I didn't say, because there was one way this situation could get worse. If I cried and told the truth—that would be so much worse.

I wished for the hundredth time that I hadn't taken this job. Quitting wasn't an option, though. Not when I so desperately needed the salary, and, even more than that, the health insurance.

Now, Martine frowned, and I fought to keep my breathing under control. I could tell something bad was coming. Please don't let me lose my job, I prayed. Please, no. Please don't make me have to crawl to Hemi and beg.

"I'm going to give you a piece of advice," Martine said, and my panic receded, at least for the moment. *"Just because you remind me of myself, not so long ago. Be careful. I know you feel...special, right now. But you're not."*

I tried to keep my face neutral, but knew I was failing utterly as she went on. *"You think that if you follow all his...all the rules, it will last. But it won't. Nothing you do, nothing you say will matter in the end, because you're just one in a line that stretches a long, long way back. And one that will stretch a long way into the future, too. So..."* She smiled. *"Don't quit your day job."*

She stood up, opened the door, and I scrambled to my feet. *"But for now,"* she said, *"I suppose you'll do what you have to do, because you don't really have a choice, do you? You'll go where you're taken, and you'll do what you're told. You'll take...advantage of the situation. Who could blame you?"*

Her gaze swept over me, lingered on my feet, on the new boots I'd worn today despite everything that had happened, and she didn't have to say anything else.

I did my best not to stumble over my heels on the way back to my cubicle, fought back the stupid tears that insisted on rising despite all my efforts, and began to go through my assignments all the same, to plan my day.

Everyone might think I was a fraud, but I didn't have to be one. I would know the truth, even if I were the only one who did. I would keep my self-respect, even if I couldn't keep anything else. Or anyone else.

♡♡♡

This time it wasn't Will who caught her at it. It was Talia.

"Oh. Hi," the girl said, hovering on the stairs as if she were about to run back up them.

"Hi." Faith closed her laptop with what she hoped wasn't undue haste and set it on the chunky square coffee table that provided a massive centerpiece to the leather couches and chairs around it. "I sure hope you're about to go into the kitchen for breakfast. And that you can point me to the coffee, because I'm starved and desperate, and I'm not sure what the rules are about what I can eat, or whether I'm supposed to wait."

Talia smiled, and Faith realized that it was almost the first time she'd seen that expression on her face. The girl came the rest of the way down the stairs in her checked skirt, blue blouse, navy cardigan, and matching knee socks, and Faith stood up and followed her into the modern kitchen. It was stone-floored like the rest of the common spaces, and her stocking-clad feet curled a little against the cold. Maybe she needed to get into the hot tub again. Or maybe not.

"Don't think we have coffee, actually," Talia said. "Sorry. We have tea, of course."

"Of course," Faith said glumly.

"You can go out for a coffee, though." Talia filled an electric kettle, set it on its base, and flipped the switch. "Easy as. That's what people usually do."

"Oh?" Faith filed that one away for book-reference. "Because back home, we make our own coffee. I mean, regular coffee. Drip coffee."

"Drip coffee? What's that?"

"It's...never mind." It was much too early in the morning to explain regular coffee, in a regular coffee machine. "Tea's good."

"Want eggs, too?" Talia bent to take them out of the fridge, the heavy braid that hung halfway to her hips barely moving. "That's what I'm doing."

"Sure. What can I do to help?"

"Toast, if you like." Talia pulled out the loaf and handed it to Faith.

"You're up early," Faith commented. Talia was already pouring boiling water into mugs, she saw with gratitude, because if she didn't get some caffeine in her fast, she was going to kill somebody, and tea was better than nothing. "I don't remember being an early riser when I was a teenager. Do you have an early class? And is that a school uniform?"

Talia laughed, which was another first, and shoved the mug across the counter at Faith. "I wouldn't be wearing it otherwise. Not exactly a fashion statement, is it."

Faith cast a glance at the skirt. She didn't miss that Talia hadn't answered her other question. "Can I ask? Do you roll up the waistband once you're out of the house? I always heard about girls doing that."

"Maybe," Talia admitted, peeping at Faith from under long dark lashes that Faith would have killed for. "Because it's so *long*, isn't it."

"I think they choose the most unflattering length possible," Faith agreed, "so girls won't look pretty. Too dangerous. They might forget themselves, or the boys might, as if they wouldn't anyway."

She got a little smile for that. "So girls don't have to wear uniforms in the States?" Talia asked. "Can you wear whatever you like?"

"You can. Of course, that's got a downside, too. It seems to me, if everybody wears the same uniform, it's less about who has how much money. If you're a girl who doesn't have the right clothes, a uniform could just be the answer to your prayers."

"I never thought of it like that. Just thought it was ugly, and wished we could wear mufti. I can't *wait* to get out of school." Talia's tone was almost savage as she poked with a spatula at the eggs she'd broken into a pan on the stove. "Go to Uni and get *out*. Like Mals."

Faith started to ask a question, then thought better of it. "Hmm," she said instead, focusing on buttering slices of toast as if it required all her concentration. "Maybe it's easier to be a boy."

She thought Talia was going to say something. But instead, like Hope in the conference room, she seemed to catch herself. She turned away, pulled plates out of the cupboard, and slid eggs onto them. Faith added the toast, and they pulled stools up to the kitchen counter and began to eat.

"So what is there to do after school around here?" Faith ventured after a minute. Talia hadn't been around the previous afternoon, she hadn't missed that. "Seems like it might be a little easier to get together with your friends than where I grew up."

"Where's that? Vegas? I always wanted to go there. Sounds so glamorous. Not boring like here."

Faith laughed. "And here I've been thinking how beautiful New Zealand is. How much there is to do. The ocean, the lake, the mountains? It seems like paradise to me."

That was met with a look of incredulity. "Ha. Dead bore. Everybody I know wants to emigrate to Aussie, or the UK, or even," Talia said with a sigh, "the States. When I told them you were from Vegas, all my friends were jealous as."

Jealous as what? Faith wondered. "Well, I guess everything looks different from the outside, because it's not glamorous at all. I work in a casino. I practically grew up in one, so I ought to know. It's people losing their money, and outside of that? It's suburbia, and your friends from school live miles away, and you don't have a car. I'd think it might be better here. What do you do after school?"

"Huh," Talia said. "We usually go down by the lake. You know, hang out. Have a chat."

"I haven't seen the lake yet." Faith concentrated on her toast. "I wonder—" She stopped. "No, probably not. I know, I'm kind of old. Never mind."

"What?" Talia asked. "You're not old. You're pretty cool, actually."

"Really? Well...do you think—would you be willing to show me the lake, maybe? Show me around a bit? Because I'll bet Will's going to go to the gym this afternoon again, and your grandmother said something about yoga again, so...please."

Talia laughed, for real this time, her perfect smooth oval of a face lighting up with it, her dark eyes showing a light Faith hadn't seen in them, and Faith laughed back.

"Yeah," Faith admitted, "I'm begging here. Please. Hide me."

♡♡♡

She did end up seeing the lake before the afternoon, though. She saw it on the way to her Canopy Tour with Will.

His mother had come into the kitchen while Faith and Talia were finishing up, and Talia's face had gone shuttered, their conversation at an end. Faith had sat at the breakfast table with the others once Talia had taken herself off, had offered to do the dishes, and had had her offer accepted, to her relief.

"You can do them with me," Miriama said. "Emere is off to work today."

"Oh, do you work?" Faith asked, and then could have kicked herself, because the woman had raised five children.

"Yeh," Will's mother said. "At the i-Site—the tourist information site—a few days a week. Keeps me busy. How do you stay busy, Faith?"

Her glance held not-so-veiled hostility, but Will just laughed. "You're offside there, Mum. Faith has three jobs." Well, four, but who was counting? "She's been working already since she's been

163

down here, haven't you noticed? She doesn't spend her time trolling the casinos for hot rugby boys with big bikkies, whatever you may be imagining."

"Big…" Faith uttered faintly. What had he just *said?*

"With money," he said. "Why, what did you think? Got to stop looking at those naughty pictures, eh. They're giving you a dirty mind."

Faith choked back a laugh, because Will's mother didn't look amused, and Miriama's sharp eyes were on the two of them again.

"Hoping to tear you away today, though," Will said. "I thought we could do a bit of sightseeing. In fact, I already booked, so no choice. As Kuia pointed out to me, here you are in En Zed, and I'm duty-bound to give you an adrenaline rush, aren't I."

His face was nothing but innocent, but Faith knew better. She looked right back at him and said, "An adrenaline rush? You think you could?"

This time, he was the one choking, to her satisfaction. He recovered himself fast, though, and said, "Well, maybe somebody else could. And I could watch."

She started to smile, caught the look on his mother's face, and got up hastily and began to collect plates instead. "I'll just start this, then. I'd like to help more instead of just falling asleep on you, since you all are being kind enough to let me visit." Yes, it might have been a blatant attempt to win a little favor with his mother, but she wasn't used to being hated, and it was wearing on her.

Will got up with her. "We'll do it together. And then go for my outing."

"Don't *do* that," she hissed at him under cover of the running water when she was scraping plates and filling the dishwasher.

"Who, me? Did I start that?"

"Your grandmother knows," she muttered. "I'm sure she does. And, what? Now I'm not just a gold-digging tramp, I'm a gold-digging *exhibitionist* tramp?"

His laugh rang out, and she had to laugh too. "Because you're bad," he said, the smile reaching all the way to his eyes as he looked

164

down at her. "I've always known it. It's all a front, that good-girl thing you do. See, there you are turning red again, bang on cue. Nothing better than a good girl succumbing to her dark side. Nothing sexier than thinking about helping her do it."

"Stop," she warned. "Stop right now. That's our deal."

He sighed. "Right. Washing-up, sightseeing, showing my innocent American girlfriend the beauties of my native land. The program as scheduled."

♡♡♡

It didn't turn out to be sightseeing. It turned out to be a heart-stopping journey through the treetops with two guides and five other guests, none of whom had recognized Will, because none of them had been Kiwis. The guides had known who he was, but they hadn't made a big deal of it. But then, Kiwis didn't make a big deal out of much, Faith was figuring that out. Well, nothing except rugby.

It all began frighteningly enough, with following their guide—or, in her case, following Will's tight, muscular, absolutely fantastic rear view, in a pair of shorts again—up an endless ladder set against a tree trunk that was a good six feet in diameter.

Higher and higher into the air she climbed, wanting to stop, wanting to climb down, but that wasn't an option, because there was somebody else behind her. Finally, she came gratefully to rest on a platform set high in the treetops, a canopy of green and birdsong all around her. She felt a little better when her feet were on solid wood again, despite the fact that the platform was completely open, and that there were nine people crowded around it, including one of them who would rather have been hugging the trunk. That would be Faith.

"Please tell me it's not possible to fall," a middle-aged woman, sharing the adventure with her husband and already looking dubious, said to some nervous laughter from the rest of the group.

"Haven't lost one yet. That's what the harness is for, eh,"

Roman, their male guide, said, exchanging a laughing glance with Will. "Want to show them what happens if they let go?"

Will grinned at the young man, and before Faith realized what he was doing, he'd leaned back from the edge of the platform and stepped off, was dangling in midair from the chest, twisting a little in the wind.

Faith gasped, cried out, and in the next two seconds, she'd reached for him, grabbed him around the waist, and pulled him back in, and everyone was laughing. Everyone but Will. His arms had come around her instantly, and he was holding her tight.

"Sorry, baby," he said. "No worries. It's all good. Nobody's falling today."

"Apologies for the moment of heart failure," Roman said cheerfully as Faith disengaged herself from Will, tried to calm her racing heart and pretend that the whole thing hadn't happened. "But, yeh, the harnesses are there for a reason. You're safe as houses, and we've just experimented with our million-dollar man to prove it to you."

That was it. Will's cover was blown, because all the guests were looking curious now.

"You'll hear," Caroline, the other guide, was piping up on the other side of the platform, "that nothing matters more to Kiwis than the All Blacks. That may be a bit of an exaggeration, but it's true that our rugby team is our most famous export. If we're willing to dangle our starting first-five from his harness thirty meters above the ground ten days before he's due to lead New Zealand to another hard-won victory against England? You know it's safe."

"Maybe we should drop him, then. I've got twenty pounds on that match," the British lady's husband said, and the group laughed again. Everybody but Faith. She was still too embarrassed.

"We'll start with something easy," Roman said. "Across the swing bridge you go. One at a time, please. Start us out again, Will."

"Nah," he said, his arm still around Faith. "We'll let somebody else go first, give Faith a minute."

"I'm all right," she hastened to say.

"Then why don't you lead us off?" Roman asked her, and if he wasn't a sadist, Faith didn't know who was.

"You don't have to," Will was murmuring. "Just say no. You know how to do that. I've heard you."

That did the trick. Faith took a breath and said, "Sure." Her new life was about taking chances, after all, about putting herself out there, not taking the easy route.

This wasn't the easy route, no matter what Roman had said. It was just walking, true. But it was walking across two narrow planks set on cables, with two more waist-high cables at either side to hold onto, desperately in her case, until she'd crossed to another platform, the whole thing swaying dizzyingly with every step and sending her heart galloping along with it. Finally, though, she came to rest on solid wood again, and this time, she really did have to force herself not to reach out and hug the tree trunk.

"What you're standing around is a totara," Caroline said when the group had reassembled. "One of our most beloved native trees. This one is about four hundred years old."

Faith's eyes flew to Will's again. That had been the tree in the Maori saying, she remembered, the one about his grandfather. He looked back at her, not smiling for once, and she knew he remembered, too.

After a while, when the message got through to her stiffened limbs that she really wasn't going to fall, she relaxed a little and began to enjoy her adventure. Moving from one platform to the next, surrounded by the murmuring canopy of green, with monstrous ferns sprouting directly from the bark and fern trees swaying in the breeze with all the grace of palms and none of the wicked sharp edges. The melodious song of tui and bellbird filled the air around them, and she was so high, so remote, it was as if she were a bird herself.

She relaxed, that is, until she had to fly, feeling exactly like a baby bird being pushed out of the nest. When she stepped off her first platform into thin air, clutching the handles of the zipline with desperate urgency, the canopy flashing past her with dizzying speed, she thought her heart would stop.

At least she hadn't been the first to do this one. Will had already done it, had bounced off a far-distant tree and landed on the platform with ease, so she knew it was possible. But it was all so…high. So fast. So scary. And, in the end, so exhilarating.

By the fifteenth or sixteenth time, she was grabbing the handles with eagerness, her blood rushing in her veins, her heart pounding with joyous adrenaline. When she took her final ride, the longest and most thrilling yet, she was laughing out loud, whooping with the fun of it, lifting her feet to bounce off the tree at the other end and releasing the handles of the zipline, moving to re-clip her line so the next person could go, as if this were something she did every day. As if she actually were an adventurous traveler instead of Faith Goodwin, conservative stay-at-home worker bee.

Will's arm had gone around her to cushion her landing as she bounced, and she laughed up at him, the adrenaline still surging. "Still think you need to hold me? I'm all brave now, see?"

"Or maybe I'm just looking for an excuse," he said. "But you're right. You are. Awesome, eh."

She was here, sharing the moment with him, and she also knew that she had to go back and write Hemi and Hope doing this. She had to let Hemi share this adventure with Hope. He had to be able to show Hope his other side, even if—especially if—he showed it to nobody else. Because a man who would do that for you, a man who wanted to have fun with you without making fun of you, who enjoyed making you smile, and laugh, and *live?* He was a keeper.

"Thanks," she told Will when they were safely at the bottom again, had bade their fellow adventurers goodbye. "I'm a little wobbly still," she admitted. "Glad to be on solid ground again. But that was super fun. Thank you."

"Thought it might be." He reached into his pocket and pulled out the car key. "Want to have another adventure, drive home on the left? We should get you practicing."

"You'd trust me with your car?"

He shrugged. "Why not? I've got insurance in case you have a smash. And how are you going to be the perfect houseguest, endear my mum to you with your helpful journeys to the supermarket, if you can't drive?"

She groaned. "Was it that obvious?"

"Well, yeh. Good try, but I think it's going to take more than that, if you keep tempting her baby boy. So...drive?"

She was about to say no, but the challenging light in his eyes, the keys dangling from his hand, made her change her mind. "Sure," she said. "Why not?"

"Why not. Famous last words, eh. I remember saying them myself a few months ago."

"If I start posing for naked pictures," she said, punching the key fob for the door and then promptly going around to the wrong side, "stop me. I think I'm all right with driving."

"They weren't naked." He waited until she'd gotten out of the way, then slid in on the passenger side. "As somebody told me over and over again, they were just suggestive. Very tasteful. Hardly even sexy, come to that."

"Yes." She shoved the key into the ignition and told herself that she could do this, that she knew how to drive. "But then, I was trying to talk you into it."

She peeped across at him, and he was smiling. "Think I know that," he said. "Why d'you imagine I did it?"

"Well, not because of me."

"No? Sure about that? Because I'm not. But today...I had fun today, suspension or no, because that's what you are. Fun. I'd forgotten how much I liked being with you. And, Faith..." He sighed. "You're so bloody pretty."

Surely there wasn't enough air in this car, not with him looking at her like that. "I've been jumping around in trees for three hours," she managed to say. Her heart had begun to knock against the wall of her chest as if it were trying to escape, because her heart was smarter than she was. It knew how much danger it was in. "I don't have any…any makeup on. I thought…" She swallowed. "It would smear." She was turning red now, she could tell, and she was babbling like a fool, and she needed to shut up.

"Yeh. You don't. And you're still pretty." His hand had come out to caress her cheek, his thumb brushing lightly over the mole above her lip that had been the bane of her teenaged existence. "Thanks for caring that I might fall," he said softly. "Thanks for pulling me back."

His thumb was tracing the curve of her upper lip now, her lips were parting under his touch in spite of herself, and in about ten seconds, he was going to be kissing her. She knew it, and she knew she should care.

"Want to change our deal?" he murmured. "Say the word."

She wanted to. She wanted to so badly. "I can't," she forced herself to say instead. Because she liked him too much. She wanted him too much, and if she had him, she'd want to keep him.

His smiled a little crookedly, and his hand caressed her cheek one last time, then fell. "Right." He shifted in his seat. "You can't. Got it."

He was back to his cheerful, teasing self again after that, as if the tender moment hadn't happened. He coached her as she drove around the lake and into town, somehow managing not to hit anything, and only once starting to turn into oncoming traffic, until a sharp word from Will and his quick hand on the wheel swung them out of danger.

"Sorry," she said shakily, her heart pounding for an entirely different reason now.

"No worries. Everybody does it once, usually just when they've started to relax a bit, have stopped paying quite so much attention. Same for me when I drive in the States. Pull over and park here, and I'll take you to lunch."

"You know what?" she said when she'd managed the nerve-wracking ordeal that was parallel-parking on the wrong side. She blew a tendril of hair out of her face, then kept exhaling, because she had so much tension stored up in her body by now, she was like an overfilled balloon.

"What? And keep breathing," he advised. "You did it. First time's always the worst. That's what I tell all the girls."

That surprised her so much, she laughed, and he was laughing, too. "What?" he asked again.

"You're nice," she said. "You are a nice man."

"Hmm. That sounds suspiciously like 'I value our friendship.' But come on. Rattle your dags, because I've got a date with the gym this afternoon, and unless I'm guessing wrong, Kuia's going to be dragging you off to yoga again. Need to get you fortified."

"Nope." She hopped out of the car. "She's not, because I'm one step ahead of her. Never underestimate the power of desperation."

close personal friends
♡

At three o'clock that afternoon, sure enough, Faith was on a bicycle following Talia's blue-cardiganed back. She was breathing cool outdoor air, too, however tinged with sulphur it was, instead of the Sweat Vapors of the Damned.

They rode through city streets, skirted the bowling green and the rose garden beside the flamboyant half-timbered expanse of the Rotorua Museum, then turned onto a paved path. The smell was stronger here, steam rising in plumes on either side. When they reached the lake, Talia hopped off her blue bicycle and began pushing it by the handlebars, and Faith followed suit. She followed the girl down a path edged with the ever-present ferns, the expanse of Lake Rotorua on one side, the green hills and the clouds overhead reflected in the water. Black swans floated, majestic and serene, in the shadow of weeping willows that draped their branches over the water's edge, while mallard ducks paddled nearby.

"So pretty," Faith said, feeling all the inadequacy of the word.

Talia didn't answer that, because, Faith supposed, this was nothing but her back yard. "There they are," she said instead, and

Faith had to hurry to keep up as the girl rushed the last few yards, left the path, and dumped her bicycle on a rocky shore where a group of five or six young people were gathered, some sitting on a log, a couple standing.

A young man in a hoodie and jeans turned his head at their approach. The only one of the group not in school uniform, he looked a little older, too, with a faint mustache and beard decorating his lean face. He was Maori, Faith thought, at least partly so. Not as tall or as well-built as Will, but with the thin build in skinny jeans that would appeal to a teenage girl.

"You're late today," he told Talia.

"Sorry," she said, sounding a little flustered. "I had to go home first and get my...Will's partner. This is Faith, everybody. And this is Chaz," she said, indicating the young man. She went around the group, naming the rest of them, and Faith did her best to smile and look young and fun, like somebody who wanted to kick back and share the moment.

Chaz pulled a pack of cigarettes from his pocket, shook one out and offered it to Talia. "I can't," she said, with another quick glance at Faith. "Will's here."

"Wouldn't want to get big brother's knickers in a twist," Chaz said. "So, Faith. Escaping the house? Talia's mum giving you a bit of a bad time, with Will in the naughty chair and all?"

The rest of the group laughed a little nervously, and Faith smiled coolly. "Oh, I don't know," she said. "I think mothers tend to be protective of their sons. Your mother's probably exactly the same."

"Yeh, Chazzer," a boy named Tom said. "Think I hear your mum calling you right now. Better run home."

"My mum knows better," Chaz said. "But then, I only like the kind of girls she likes. Nice, pretty Maori girls."

"Too bad for Will," Faith agreed. "But then, you know what love is. It can strike when you least expect it, even in Las Vegas of all places. So do all of you go to school with Talia?"

"For our sins," a girl sitting on the log beside Tom said. Sophia,

Faith thought. "All but Chaz. Least until we can leave, though Talia will stay all the way through Year Thirteen, because that's her family's thing. Stay there all alone, though."

"Speak for yourself," Tom said. "I'm going to Uni, myself."

"Yeh? With your marks?" Sophia jeered.

"I'm doing better," he said. "Got big plans, haven't I."

"Yeh. You and your big plans," she said, and he gave her a shove, and she shoved back, and they laughed, and Faith smiled. This was more like it.

Talia sank onto another log, looking a little more relaxed, and Faith sat with her.

"Are you really from Vegas?" Sophia asked, a bit shyly.

"I really am."

"What's it like? Glamorous and all?"

Faith laughed. "You and Talia saw the same movie, I think. No, it's pretty much like everywhere, except in the desert and with more casinos. And with a lot of traffic," she added. "In fact, I'd trade places with you. That's what I was telling Talia."

"Are you…" Sophia asked, then stopped herself.

"Am I what?" There was no better way to get to know a teenager than getting to know her friends, so Faith relaxed her posture, picked up a handful of pebbles from between her feet, and dribbled them through her hand, doing her best to project ease and approachability.

"Are you…trading places, then?" Sophia asked. "Because Will—he's fit, eh. I know he's your brother and all," she said hastily to Talia. "But he's bloody fit, and he's an All Black, and if he looked at me?" She sighed. "I'd look back, and that's the truth."

"Too old for you," Tom said, frowning a little. Faith couldn't blame him.

"Well, I know *that,*" Sophia said. "I'm just saying, if he did. I'm just asking Faith."

"Who knows?" Faith said cheerfully. "I'm visiting, that's all, and enjoying it. Will took me on that treetop walk this morning. I loved that."

"Tourist stuff," Chaz said.

"Probably," Faith said. "And I loved it anyway, but I guess that's because I *am* a tourist."

"What are you on about with 'tourist stuff?'" another boy, Andy, asked Chaz. "Make a pretty good living on that tourist stuff, don't you. Wish my whanau had a show. I'd be in like a flash."

"You?" Chaz scoffed. "Think the French chicks want to look at your fat arse?"

"Better than looking at your skinny chest," Andy shot back.

"That's what you think," Chaz said, then glanced at Talia and cut himself off, which Faith didn't miss either.

"So you do something for tourists, too?" Faith asked him.

"His whanau—his family," Talia explained. "They have one of the Maori cultural shows, do some songs, the greetings, the haka, explain a bit of the history. Like that. It's pretty awesome. A good job, if you can get it. But you have to have skills."

"What kind of skills?" Faith asked.

"Fighting," Chaz said. "Got to be good at fighting."

"Well, I'm shit at fighting," Tom said cheerfully, and Faith laughed. "Means it's Uni for me, eh, or I'm doing construction on the Gold Coast like my brothers."

"That's what I decided, too," Faith said. "Because I'm shit at fighting myself, and I hate doing construction." They grinned at each other, Sophia laughed, too, and Faith felt a little better about Talia's friends.

"So did you go to Uni, Faith?" Chaz asked, lighting another cigarette and sitting down beside Talia at last. "Not what Talia's mum thought, then, eh."

"Oh really?" Faith asked, keeping it light with an effort. "What was her guess?"

"Stripper, wasn't it?" Chaz asked Talia, his mouth curving beneath the stubble. "Bloody funny, we all thought, old Will going to Vegas and bringing back a stripper. Pity it isn't true."

"Nope." Faith saw the dusky color stain Talia's cheeks a deeper shade of bronze, and answered for her. "Not a stripper, alas.

Nothing so exciting. I'm a photographer's assistant, just like the newspaper said, and I'm a marketing writer, too. My mother was a stripper, though." She looked around Talia and straight at Chaz. "Feel free to share."

He laughed. "No shit? Maybe I will."

"Hey. Knock yourself out." She shouldn't have said it, any of it, but he was on her last nerve by now, and slapping him wasn't an option, unfortunately.

"Don't share," Talia said with a quick, wild glance at Faith. "Please. Will doesn't need—"

"Your big brother doesn't need your help," Chaz said. "Got himself into hot water, didn't he, and he'll get himself out of it, too." He put an arm around Talia and kissed her cheek. "No worries, babe."

Talia stood up, adjusted her skirt, and finally looked at Faith. "We should go," she said. "I've got homework."

"Got to do the homework." Chaz stood with her. "See you tomorrow, then?"

"Yeh."

He kissed her again, still on the cheek, but with a glance at Faith that let her know why. "Don't be late next time."

"Nice to meet you all," Faith said, picking up her bike with Talia. "See you again soon, I hope." And it was mostly true.

♡♡♡

"You have some nice friends," she told Talia once they had gone through town and were in the quieter residential streets again. "Thanks for taking me to meet them."

"Yeh?" Talia said cautiously. "You liked them?"

The direct approach might not be best here, Faith decided. "Chaz is out of school, huh?" she said casually. "How old do you have to be to do that here?"

"Sixteen. But he's nineteen, actually. Just had a birthday." Talia's casual was almost as good as Faith's. "I'm sorry he said that, about the...about the stripper thing. I didn't think that, I mean, I didn't think you were. I don't really think my mum did either. She was just angry at the time, you know. Because of Will." She was embarrassed, obviously, but points to her for actually acknowledging the issue instead of pretending it hadn't happened. Not easy, at fifteen.

"Mmm. And now he does some sort of fighting exhibition for work?" Faith could easily imagine how attractive and exciting that would seem.

"Not *fighting*. Not like you're thinking. It's just a demonstration. He's wicked good, though," Talia added proudly, as if she couldn't help herself. "Dead fast. He's won competitions and all."

They'd made it to the house again, so Faith put her bike away, then followed Talia upstairs.

"I do have homework," the girl said. "Or I'd hang out some more. You know, keep you company."

Faith smiled at her. "That's all right. I've got work to do, too. But thanks."

She went into the bedroom she shared with Will, which was empty. He probably wasn't back from the gym yet. She turned on her laptop and sat at her desk with her hands poised over the keyboard for a minute. She should work on the Roundup copy, and she should polish her latest episodes and post them, too. But she didn't do either. Instead, she called her mother.

They got through the preliminaries, and then her mother was asking, as Faith had known she would, "So. You sleeping with him yet?"

"You know what?" Faith said. "I'm actually not going to tell you. And before you say anything, I'm just about exactly as surprised to hear that as you are, so don't even start. But I was so careful last time, and I missed him anyway after he left, so what difference would it make?"

"Getting a man out of your system by going ahead and sleeping with him? It never works. Take it from me. Unless he's lousy in bed, and honey, I doubt it."

"Maybe there are worse things than having your heart broken, though," Faith found herself saying.

"You think so?"

"Like never having your heart be touched at all. Wouldn't that be worse? But that isn't actually what I called you about," Faith hurried on. "There's something I do need your advice on."

"Shoot," her mother said, even though Faith could tell that she wanted to talk more about Will. But Faith didn't want to, because she didn't know what she felt. Or rather, she was afraid she did, and her mind kept skittering away from it. It was more than a crush now, she was becoming increasingly and uncomfortably sure of it. She was afraid that she was falling in love. And in a little more than a week, she was leaving forever. Will had never pretended anything else. If it had been a bad idea to have a fling with him, how much worse would it be to fall in love, act on it, and have all those feelings crushed? To fly back across the ocean, knowing that she'd offered him her heart, and that he didn't want it?

No. That wasn't happening, because it would be more than she could take. Her vulnerable heart seemed to curl up into a tight little ball at the thought, and she had to force herself to breathe.

She'd be brave, she promised herself. She'd take a risk, would let her heart be touched. Later. When it made sense. With somebody else, when it would have a chance of working out.

She made herself go on. Maybe she could at least help Will with this while she was here. "It's Will's sister," she told her mother. "She's fifteen. And I think she's getting...call it entangled, with a boy who's nineteen. A boy I don't like much, and that I don't think her family knows about. He's not even in school anymore."

"Too big an age difference," her mother said. "Red flag. How entangled?"

"I don't know. But she's on her phone all the time, texting, and I don't have a good feeling. So what do I do about it? Do I tell Will? Do I tell his mother—who hates me, by the way, so she'd probably just hate me more if I did that. I could tell his grandmother, though."

"His mother hates you? Why?" Faith could hear the outrage in her mother's voice.

"Black widow?" she suggested. "Entrapping him?"

"You? Guess they don't grow them very wild in New Zealand, if you're a black widow."

"Right. But what do I do? Do I tell her mother?"

"No. Last thing you want to do. Then she gets even more rebellious, if she shared something with you and you ran away and tattled, got her mother coming down hard on her."

"Tell Will, then?"

"Mmm...still no. Not unless you think it's desperate. Same deal."

"Then what? Lecturing her on why it's a bad idea wouldn't work, I'm smart enough to know that. You were so good at being a mom to a teenager, but I'm not her mother, and I've got no power to do anything at all."

"What did I do when you were going out with that guy in college? That Trey?"

"I don't remember. Just that I was going out with him, and I thought he was really cool, and then I didn't, and I broke up with him. Did you do something?"

"See? You don't even remember. I invited him to dinner. Over and over again. Let you see him sitting there, hear how he talked to me, let you get a little embarrassed, while I killed him with kindness. I let you see him through my eyes, is what I did, and that was all it took. He wasn't a sexy bad boy then, he was just a jerk."

"Huh. That's exactly what I'd say about this guy. I can't invite him to dinner, though."

"Then some other way. See if you can spend time with the two of them. See what you can do. You're a black widow, after all," her mother said, sounding happy at the thought. "I'll bet you can figure it out."

179

cultural evening
♡

"Where's Faith?" Will asked the next day. He'd come back from the gym at five as usual, and hadn't seen her since. He'd assumed she was out with his grandmother again, or on a walk, maybe, but now his mum and grandmother were starting their dinner preparations, and there was still no sign of her.

"Talia took her to a concert," his grandmother said. "The Kupe one, I think."

"What? Without telling me?"

"Last-minute thing. They fixed it this afternoon."

"Could be she thought she'd taken enough of your time today," his mum said.

"That's why she's here," Will said. "To take my time. Happy to spend it with her."

It was even true. He'd loved doing the treetop adventure with her yesterday. When she'd shrieked and pulled him in, and he'd felt her tremble at the thought of him falling…that had been worth the price of admission all by itself. Today, he'd taken her to a geothermal area, had watched a geyser erupt and walked over boardwalks across steaming hot pools in vivid shades of turquoise, orange, and green, had stood over bubbling mud pots and seen her laugh in delight at the silly sounds they made. All so familiar to him, but seeing it through her eyes had made it new. Special.

Now, he wandered around the kitchen, leaned back against the bench, then had to move out of the way so his grandmother could get into the fridge. He thought about having a beer, then abandoned the idea. He was going to be ready for training on Tuesday, that was the one thing he was bloody sure of.

"Have a good day today, Mum?" he asked instead.

"Not too bad," she said without looking up from the board where she was preparing vegies to roast. "Pretty busy day at the i-Site, considering it's nearly winter."

"How did they get there?" he asked.

"Who?" His mother was still chopping, still not looking up, as his grandmother washed mussels in the sink.

"Faith and Talia." he said. "Did Faith drive?" She wasn't ready to drive at night yet, at least not without him in the car. If she turned out of the carpark onto the wrong side without thinking, still caught up in the show, and somebody else came around that corner…He was sweating at the thought.

"Whose car would she drive?" his mother asked. He had to move out of her way again as she headed from the island to the oven. "They were collected in the van, of course. A couple of lovely Irish boys in there, too, that I booked into the show today as well. They'll have a good crowd for it, I'm thinking."

His grandmother had filled a pot with water and was beginning to lift it from the sink, so Will took it from her and set it on the stove.

Kuia looked at him and sighed. "You have two choices. Get out of the way so your mum and I can get dinner on, or go on and join them for the hangi, if you're worried."

"I'm not worried. Just surprised, that's all, that she went without me."

His grandmother stood with her hand on her hip and scrutinized him, and Will fought the urge to shuffle his feet. "I

181

don't know what's going on between the two of you," she said, "but I know what your Koro would've said. You want that girl? Go and get her."

"I'm not—" he began, then broke off, because he didn't know how that sentence ended. "Right," he said instead. "I'm off."

It made sense anyway, he told himself as he drove the fifteen kilometers around the lake and took the turning to the Kupe Maori Village. If he were meant to be the besotted boyfriend, surely he wouldn't be sending his partner off on her own for the evening during their brief time together. Yeh, that was it. It made total sense.

He walked across the carpark, opened the door, and entered a broad hall thrown up in a hurry and meant to look the opposite, like it belonged on a marae. Its wooden beams were painted with Maori designs, and there was a fairly crude wooden carving of a god in each corner. There must have been 150 people seated at round tables holding ten diners apiece, all eating the meal their hosts had roasted for them in the earthen pit. Doing the Rotorua tourist thing.

Now that he was here, he was beginning to feel stupid, especially as he wandered around looking for her. How was he going to explain this? And then he found her, and didn't feel nearly so stupid.

She and Talia were sitting near the front of the room, at a table with two older couples who were talking to each other, because all the younger people were busy. Talia was focused on some bloke who was sitting between her and Faith, a bloke who had his arm over the back of Talia's chair and was leaning in farther than Will felt happy about. Faith should have been doing something about that, but she wasn't, because she was laughing and talking herself. To three men.

All of them looked to be hanging on her every word. The lovely Irish boys, Will assumed. Of course they were interested in what she had to say, because she was wearing the short, swingy gray skirt and red jersey she'd had on when he'd met her at the airport, which was more than a bit tight for the occasion, wasn't it? He could tell the lovely boys thought so.

There wasn't room at the table for Will, but he didn't let that stop him. He went to the back of the room again, grabbed a chair, and hauled it up to the table, which was when she noticed him at last, and looked nothing but surprised.

"Sorry I missed you, darling," he told her. "And the show, too, of course. Got here as quickly as I could. D'you mind?" he asked the fella next to her, who was sitting back now and looking startled, as well he might.

"Of course," he said, and the three fellas shoved over, and Will pushed his chair on in there and sat down. He gave Faith a kiss while he did it, just in case any of the lovely boys was still unclear on the state of things. And he enjoyed it.

"Why are you here?" she hissed at him the moment his mouth left hers.

"Wanted to see my girlfriend, didn't I. Who's that?" he asked with a nod towards Talia's companion, who had taken his arm off her chair now, at least.

"Tell you later," she said, but it wasn't necessary, because Will had caught the young man's eye.

"Evening, Will," the boy said as if he knew him, with a cocky edge that Will didn't care for one bit. "You missed our show."

"This is Chaz," Talia said. "He's one of the performers here."

"And a friend of Talia's," Faith said brightly. "A school friend, except not exactly, because you're out of school now, is that right, Chaz?"

"Yeh," he said. "I'm done with that. A man needs to be earning the dosh, eh, and I do all right."

"Was this the first time you'd seen him do his routine, Talia?" Faith asked.

"It's not a *routine*," Chaz said. "It's a performance."

"Oh, excuse me," Faith said. "Is there a difference?"

"What is it you do here, during your...routine?" Will asked, choosing the word deliberately.

"I use the taiaha," Chaz said, getting some of the swagger back. "Speak softly and carry a big stick." He laughed and exchanged a look with the Irish blokes. "Or don't speak softly and use my big stick. I like that one, too."

"He's good," Talia hastened to tell her brother. "You should have seen him."

"Course I'm good," Chaz said. "Wouldn't be here otherwise." He lunged forward suddenly, eyes staring, mouth stretched in a grimace, tongue reaching nearly to his chin. *"Hah!"*

You could call it a wee bit more performance, or you could call it a challenge. Will knew which one it was. Faith jumped, the Irish blokes laughed, and Will sat solid and stared Chaz down.

"Not saying I'm the best." Chaz sat back again and went for breezy unconcern. "But I'm not bad. It's not easy, the taiaha."

"Will knows that. He knows taiaha himself," Talia said, her eyes flying to Will's.

"Everybody knows it," Chaz said. "But doing it as a game when you're a kid, that isn't the same thing. That's not combat, eh. I just might be able to kick your arse," he told Will. "You never know."

"You might." Will kept his voice even. "And I might be able to kick yours."

No *maybe* about it. There'd been nobody better than Koro, and Koro had taught Will. Some of the deftness of Will's handling on the paddock wasn't just from growing up holding a rugby ball, it was from the practice he'd had with the ancient skills. Anyway, when you got down to it, it wasn't about poncing about and looking good for tourists. It was about the will to win. If this arrogant little prat had half as much of that as Will did, he'd be surprised. What was he doing with his sister, and why had Faith brought her here to see him? He was burning to find out both things.

"You about ready to go?" he asked Faith, because one thing was certain. She wasn't spending another minute with the Irish boys.

She looked startled, but she and Talia seemed to be done eating to him, and he wanted them both out of there.

"I guess," she said. "Talia?"

"I want to stay," Talia said. "It's not over yet, and I can get a ride home in the van." She glanced at Chaz. *Or you can drive me,* Will could almost hear her say, and that was happening over his dead body.

"Your big brother wants you to run along," Chaz said. "Thinks you can't handle yourself, maybe."

"Yeh," Will said. "I do. Want her to run along, that is." He stood up, took Faith's coat off the back of her chair, and held it for her. "You can tell their van driver," he told Chaz, "that I took them home."

Talia shot him a look like thunder, opened her mouth to say something, then shut it again. Too accustomed to respect for her elders to make a scene, to Will's relief, but on the other hand, she was still sitting down.

Faith stood up, though, to Will's deep satisfaction, and told the Irish blokes, "Very nice to have met you. Enjoy your stay."

"Yeh," the one who'd been sitting next to her, a big red-headed fella, said. "You too."

Talia gave Chaz one more look, leaned close to whisper something in his ear, then stood up and shoved her coat on, her movements jerky, and Will let out a breath. He wasn't sure what he'd have done if she'd refused. And now, Faith was going home with him. The way it should be.

conduct unbecoming
♡

"All right," Faith said to Will. "What was that all about?" Had it just been Talia? Or had it been something else, too?

They were finally alone again. Talia had gone straight up to her room the minute they'd gotten home, and all Faith's efforts to befriend the girl looked to have been in vain, because the atmosphere in the car had been thick with tension the entire way. Faith had done her best to draw Talia out about the evening's entertainment, to get her to describe it to her brother, but without much success.

"What?" Will had shed his jacket and was leaning into the refrigerator, pulling out containers.

"Are you telling me you didn't even eat? That you rushed over there to...what?"

"Could've told me you wanted to go to a concert." He dished shellfish and vegetables onto a plate and shoved it into the microwave without bothering to cover it. "I'd have taken you."

"That's nice, but maybe I thought I'd spare you one tourist activity, at least. I can't believe that you'd need to go see how the Maori welcome people to the marae, or how they fought.

186

Something tells me that you already know."

He shrugged. "We're meant to be together, aren't we. People may think we're having problems if you turn up without me."

"I was with your *sister*. I'd say that looks pretty convincing, girlfriend-wise. If anybody cares, that is, because I haven't exactly noticed any paparazzi lurking in trees to take my picture. Those few photos in the paper, a couple column inches, and that's been it. I hope it's going to be enough."

"Good job there weren't any journos about tonight," he said, sitting down at the counter and starting in on his dinner. "They'd have had a story then."

She eyed him suspiciously. "You're...Will. You weren't..." She'd wondered, but really? "You weren't *jealous,* were you?"

"Nah," he said, concentrating on his meal. "Course not. Why would I be jealous?"

"You were." She shouldn't be pleased. Jealousy wasn't actually a good thing. Except that it kind of felt like it. "You totally were. When you showed up...you looked scarier than any of those warriors. I thought it was because of Talia. What was I going to do, run away with some Irish guy?"

"Looked pretty friendly to me," he muttered.

"Oh," she said, feeling ridiculously cheerful, "it was. We were getting *very* friendly. I was asking them about their trip so far. It was some pretty sexy stuff. Good thing you showed up when you did, because we were about to take off in their campervan. Me and my three guys." She sighed. "Seems I get more adventurous every day. The craving...it burns."

He laughed, although it sounded fairly reluctant. "All right. Maybe it was a bit..."

"Stupid?" she suggested. "Unbecomingly possessive?"

"Aw, really?" he complained. "Unbecomingly?"

"Well," she admitted, "maybe not. Maybe it was the teeniest bit hot, having my big strong warrior show up and claim me."

She'd meant it as a joke, but she got a little shiver as she said it. That was exactly what he'd looked like, when she'd turned at the touch of his hand on her shoulder and seen him standing there looking so fierce, as if he'd wanted to pick her up, toss her over one broad shoulder, and carry her out. When he'd stood up and told her they were leaving...she'd been ready to go anywhere he took her. Except, of course, for Talia.

"I'm glad," he said. "Happy to claim you anytime." And that was hot, too, even if he was just doing his sexy, teasing Will-thing.

"For the record," she told him, "here is what we did. We rode in a van. We learned some history—well, I did, since Talia presumably knew all that already. We saw some weapons practice. We heard some songs. We watched some Maori guys looking really fierce. It was all very educational, and I enjoyed it. Oh, and we ate. So, much as I appreciate you protecting my honor, it probably wasn't necessary. I was probably going to be able to restrain myself, and beat them off, too."

"Good," he said, and that was surely satisfaction she was hearing. "But you should've beat that dickhead Chaz off while you were at it. What was that about? Taking my sister to meet some...some..."

"Yes. Exactly. I was thinking at first that it was bad that you'd come, that you'd made him seem even sexier, forbidden love and all that. But on the other hand, you got him being a jerk, which was the point. My mother was right, but then, she usually is."

He blinked at her. "Your mother? What?"

"An idea she had," Faith explained. "That's why I went there with Talia, to try to...bridge the gap. Make her see him differently, if what I thought was happening was really happening, and I think it is."

"I'd pretend to understand all that," he said, "but all I get is the forbidden love part. What is that bloke? Twenty-seven?"

She smiled a little despite her concern. "Nineteen. What age are your sisters when they're allowed to date? I mean, go out with a boy alone?"

"Dunno. I was gone, wasn't I. And I'll be gone again in a few days. Not sure what to do about it. Know what I'd like to do, but that'd probably be the forbidden love thing again."

"What, if you beat him up? Yeah, counterproductive, I'd say. Besides, she isn't the first girl to have a crush on an unsuitable older guy, and that's probably all it is."

"Hope so." He got up to put his dishes away. "But it's a problem for tomorrow, I guess. Talk to her then, d'you reckon?"

"Probably better. When she's calm, and you are, too, because calm's important. It would be good for her to talk to her family more in general, I think." She hesitated. "If you want my opinion."

"I want your opinion."

"Then here it is. I think maybe she's feeling a little…a little distant. A little alienated from her family, and that she's looking to her friends for what she isn't getting. To that guy, especially, and that's dangerous. I don't think she's very far down the road, but I think that's where she's going."

"Maybe talk to my mum, too, then, find out what the rules are, see what she thinks."

"Maybe. If you're careful not to just have them bring the hammer down."

"Huh. The hammer." He shook his head as if to clear it. "I'm rubbish at this. I'll think about it some more tomorrow, I guess." He leaned against the counter and looked at her. "For now, though…I think we should go to bed."

And just like that, with the way he said it, the way he was looking at her, the mood changed again.

He wasn't really her boyfriend, though. He hadn't really come to carry her away in a fit of possessiveness, and this was an arrangement. An arrangement she had every intention of continuing exactly the way it was, because anything else was impossible.

♡♡♡

He waited, his heart beating a little harder, and she stood up and actually dusted her palms together, then yawned behind her hand.

189

"Yep. Bedtime for me, too. Super tired."

Was it his imagination, or was she overdoing it? "So…" he said. "You want to go on up, have me give you fifteen minutes? We haven't gone to bed together before. So to speak."

"It's getting a little silly, isn't it?" she said, and he was definitely having some breathing issues now. "I mean, pretending like we can't resist each other," she hurried on. "Why shouldn't we be able to go up there together and get ready for bed? We're two adults."

That was the problem, as far as he was concerned. "Of course," he said, because there was no way he was saying anything else. "I can get ready for bed with you."

He walked upstairs behind her, turning off lights along the way. Nothing had changed, he reminded himself as he shut the bedroom door, went to the closet, and hung up his jacket. He got distracted all the same, though, when she took off her earrings and laid them on the bedside table, then began to unfasten her necklace. She was clearly struggling with it, and when she uttered a little exclamation of annoyance, he was obligated to help her, wasn't he?

"Here." He came to stand behind her, pushed the hair aside so he could reach the clasp, then took the delicate, fiddly silver thing in his hands and worked at it until it released. A shiver ran over her skin as he did it, the gooseflesh pebbling under his fingers, and he almost bent and kissed her nape, there where she was so soft and vulnerable. Almost.

He caught himself in time, handed her the necklace, then went back around to his side, where he pulled his shirt over his head, reached into the drawer of his nightstand for a muscle tee, and saw her watching him do it, because he was watching her, too. Pity that her jewelry was still the only thing she'd taken off.

"It's a bit like being married, isn't it?" he said. "Getting ready for bed together without any moves. I'm not used to it."

"I'll be unconscious again in about twenty minutes." She seemed to shake herself out of whatever thought she'd fallen into, grabbed her pajamas out of her own drawer, and went to the closet for her dressing gown. "No need to worry about those unaccustomed thoughts."

He opened his mouth to tell her that he wasn't worried, already kicking himself for making any reference to his past, but she was already gone. Almost as if she didn't trust herself to stay, whatever she'd said.

Sure enough, when he came out of the bathroom after getting ready for bed himself, she had her light off, the line of pillows marching down the bed like good little soldiers, and was turned away from his side with her eyes closed.

He slid into bed and switched off his light, shoved his hands behind his head, and stared into the darkness for a minute.

"You know," he said at last, because he could tell she wasn't asleep, "if we were really married, I could roll over and give you a kiss goodnight. We could do it now, take just the top pillow away, since we're working on pretending and all, need to keep ourselves motivated. What is it they call that in the States? First base?"

"Maybe in the 1950s they did. And I think we're all good, pretending-wise. But that would be all I'd get?" He heard the rustle as she rolled over to face his side. "As your non-wife, I have to say, that's pretty disappointing."

He had to smile. "What, that wouldn't be enough? I'd have to perform every night?" He gave a gusty sigh. "You're a cruel taskmaster."

"If you were going to be gone half the time, maybe I'd need it. Anyway, you'd leave me hanging like that, after all that talk? If you wouldn't be up to the challenge—now I'm *really* disappointed."

"Hmm," he said, grinning like a fool, "I might be able to manage that. Maybe. I'd have my away weeks to recover, after all. Yeh," he decided, "reckon I'd have to give it my best shot. Do my marital duty."

She laughed, and he was lying there on his back, smiling into the dark, separated from her by their wall. "So no kiss?" he prompted. "Not even one pillow's worth of a cuddle for your jealous non-husband?"

"You going to do that war dance thing while I'm here?"

"You mean the haka? Not a war dance," he felt duty-bound to point out. "It can be a challenge, it can be a tribute, but it's not a dance. And yeh, I am. With the All Blacks. You're going to see it."

"Then that's when I'll kiss you. I don't imagine I'll be able to help it, because it sure looked like a war dance to me."

"Could get up and do it right now," he suggested. "Take my shirt off again first, too."

"So tempting," she sighed. "But I am strong. No pillows. No haka. No kissing. Go to sleep."

foot-in-mouth disease
♡

He was lying in bed the next morning with his hands behind his head again and watching her put on her makeup in the mirror on the back of the door, which was nothing but a pure pleasure.

"I was thinking," he said, "that you might want to go for a walk today. Up on one of the forest tracks, maybe."

She finished filling those lush lips with pink, slicked on some gloss with a finger, then pressed them together in a kiss, and he rucked the duvet up a bit more around him. He didn't want to go for a walk.

"Do you think that's a good idea?" she asked. She'd come out of the bathroom in a white tank and tight black trousers that left absolutely nothing to the imagination. Now, she went over to the closet, took out a long pale-pink sweater, and tugged it over her head, where it fell off one shoulder, leaving just those two tiny straps showing, the tank and the darker pink bra underneath, and that was almost worse.

She turned to look at him inquiringly, and he realized she'd said something, and that once again, he'd lost the plot. "Pardon?"

"Maybe we should take a break." She came back to sit on the

side of the bed, picked up the delicate necklace she'd worn the night before, a mother-of-pearl wedge with a tiny pearl in the center, and fastened it around her neck. She didn't need his help this time, unfortunately.

"I mean," she said, "I've got a lot of work to do. I've been neglecting everything, just having fun with you. And maybe…maybe we should take a break," she said again. "It might be better, don't you think?"

"Uh…maybe." *No.* "I leave on Monday, though, for Dunedin." And he'd only have a couple days with her after the game before she left for the States again. So why shouldn't they make the most of the time they did have?

"With the All Blacks." Her hands were behind her head, twisting her hair up into that knot again, which was a pity, because he loved it falling around her face.

"Yeh. Finally."

"It's been really hard, huh?" she asked, her blue eyes full of nothing but sympathy. "I'm sorry, Will. I know I haven't said that, but I really am sorry it's been so hard."

He was sorry, too. In fact, he could fairly be said to be suffering. "No worries. Not your fault." He cleared his throat. "So…nothing today? Could I take you out tonight, maybe? We could go to the Lava Bar afterwards, do some dancing, a bit more pretending."

"Mmm." She was still working on her hair, all cozy on the bed with him, and he was dying. "The Lava Bar? That supposed to be hot?"

"That's the idea."

"I guess, since you've bought my services and all, I should give you your money's worth, you think?"

"Pretending-wise?" he managed to say. "Yeh. At least we could dance. And be out in public, of course," he hastened to add. "Someplace where heaps of people would see us."

She smiled. "Something to look forward to, get me motivated to get my work done. Sounds good. A real date. Well, a pretend date."

"Better than that fella in Vegas, let's hope."

"My failed interview? You still remember that? That was a long time ago. A few first dates ago."

The thought struck him in all its horror. "You don't have a...a partner back there, do you? That isn't why you've been saying no to me, is it?"

"Of course I don't." She looked nothing but offended. "What, I'd be dating somebody who'd say, sure, go off and pretend to be some other guy's girlfriend? Would I go out with a guy like that? No, I would not."

"Oh." He swallowed against the relief. "Nothing. Stupid idea. I'll tell you what. I'll take you to dinner, and then we'll go dancing, and I won't ask you where you went to Uni."

"You not going to be a back-door guy?"

He nearly choked. "You have to stop saying that. Not to a man. No."

"Oh." The red was creeping up past that low neckline, as always. "Right," she went on, trying for brisk. "Dinner and dancing. Sounds great. And I'll get some work done in the meantime. Were you planning to get up sometime soon? Should I wait for you?"

"Nah. You go on." It was going to take him a minute to be suitable for viewing. "See you downstairs."

♡♡♡

He picked up the pace as he pounded out one more kilometer around the lake. He'd chosen to run to the gym, then do a longer run afterwards, up into the hills, because match-fit was an entirely different animal than gym-fit, and he'd been out of it for ten days now. Besides, he'd needed to do something, since he wasn't spending the day with Faith, and he'd been restless waiting for their evening out. Their first real date, and he was looking forward to it. You could put it that way. Or you could say that he was dying for it.

He spotted the group of kids in their uniforms ahead, standing about on the beach, bikes flung to the ground around them, and smiled a bit.

It brought back some memories, even though he hadn't been here much himself. Too much rugby training, because even then, he'd taken it seriously. And once his dad had bunked off, of course, desire had become something much more urgent. He certainly hadn't been smoking, the way they were. Not cigarettes, and not anything else either. One would have cut into his wind, and the other would have turned up in a drug test and brought his rugby to a screeching halt.

He'd never envied the kids who had been able to hang about together, either. He'd had all the mateship a man could need. He'd loved the structure of rugby, had loved knowing exactly what he was meant to do, in this one area at least. And he'd definitely loved everything rugby had given him. The demands had been brutal, maybe, but the rewards had been worth it. Knowing that you were always giving your best, always being kept to the mark, and that you were providing for everything and everyone you needed to as well.

He recognized the bike before he saw her. A familiar white basket hanging from the front handlebars, with Talia's backpack stuck into it. She was standing on the beach, facing the water, with a tall figure Will recognized beside her. Somebody who had his arm draped around her shoulders, his head bent much too close to hers.

It wasn't even a thought. Will's feet had sped up, had left the track, were crunching over the stones at a pace that had the entire group turning in alarm. He didn't slow until he was nearly there, running a line that had him circling around and stopping bang in front of Chaz, who had jerked away from Talia and dropped his arm from around her.

"Will?" Talia said. "What are you doing here?"

"No," he said. "The question is, what are *you* doing here?"

"What d'you mean? I'm hanging out with my friends, aren't I."

Her voice was rising, already agitated, and he found his adrenaline spiking in response.

"And now you can keep me company on my run home," he said. "Go on and get your bike."

"Why?" she asked, her expression exactly the same as it had been when she'd been a little girl and their mum had told her it was time for bed.

He glanced at Chaz, who had one thumb hitched into the waistband of his jeans, his posture all calculated indifference. "Because I don't like the company you're in."

He knew it was wrong as soon as the words had left his lips, and sure enough, Talia was fairly spitting now. "What? Why?" she demanded. "If Mum doesn't care that I'm here, why should you? You can't tell me what to do! You don't even care!"

He moved instinctively towards her, she took a step back, and he realized with horror that she was scared he was going to hit her.

He bit the words back, the ones he wanted to say, because this wasn't the time, and it wasn't the place. "We'll talk about it at home," he said instead. He fought to get his temper under control, and nearly succeeded. He was always cool. Always. Except right now. "We're leaving. Come on."

"*Why?*" she asked again, nearly stomping her foot. "Why shouldn't I stay here and talk to my friends? You can do anything you want, and you get away with it, and nobody says anything? You have nasty pictures taken, you get suspended, you bring your girlfriend here and expect everybody to just say that's OK, that's fine, and I can't even stand with my friends in public, on the *beach?* I'm supposed to just stay home alone? What am I supposed to do? Who am I even supposed to *talk* to?"

"I didn't say that. And I'll talk to you. That's what I'm telling you, that I want to talk to you." He went for strong and stern and sure. It worked on the paddock, the only place he had to speak with authority. Surely it would work here as well. "I'm sure your friends are…fine." He looked around at them, at the veiled, uncomfortable expressions, the gazes dropped to study their feet.

They *did* look fine. They looked like teenagers. Most of them. "But now it's time to go home. So we can talk." About why a nineteen-year-old shouldn't be interested in her. *Wouldn't* be interested in her, except that he wanted a girl who'd be impressed. Who'd make it easy.

He should have talked to her the night before, no matter what, should have followed her into her bedroom and said...what?

Should have told her, that was what. Should have explained. Nobody better to do it, nobody who knew more about it.

"Yeh, right," she said, her voice shaking. "You'll talk to me like you always do? When you're even *here*? Which is *never*? Well, I'm not coming! I'm *not*! And you can tell Faith that I'm never, ever taking her anywhere again! Not if everybody's just going to spy on me!"

She'd whirled, and she was running, hurdling the log and heading up the path. He almost ran after her, then hesitated. And do what? He could run after her, of course he could. He could run her down, grab her, haul her home by force. Except that he couldn't. It was illegal, for one thing. And anyway, if he caught her, if he shouted, if he held her there to listen to him, all he'd be was a bully. It was all wrong, and it wouldn't work anyway.

He looked around at the downturned faces, the uniform shoes scuffling in the stones. And Chaz, standing there with an expression on his face that Will longed to wipe out in the old way, the best way.

He almost did it, except that he couldn't. The frustration was twisting inside him, and he didn't know what to do about it.

"When she comes back," he told the kids, not looking at Chaz, "tell her that I'll see her at home, and we'll be talking." It wasn't nearly good enough, but it was all he had. And then he took off.

going under
♡

I closed my eyes and let the water wash over my hair, down my back. I turned languidly, welcoming the gentle cascade on my breasts, the stream of water a warm caress as soothing as a lover's hand, as gentle as a kiss, trickling down my belly and pooling between my thighs.

I reached for the soap, slid it slowly over my shoulders, my arms, and then, delaying the moment, because I wanted to savor this, down my breasts. Over one rosy nipple, which pebbled at the contact, aching for more. Just that easily, just that quickly, because every inch of my body was sensitized these days, like I was nothing but throbbing need, nothing but anticipation, waiting and yearning for Hemi's touch.

So I obliged myself. I slid my hand up, down, around, played with the other nipple, and it felt so good, I got a little bolder. My soapy hand crept downward, slicked across my firm, smooth skin as I thought about Hemi, about the way he'd looked the week before. When he'd been holding me over him, driving himself into me, then pulling me down, rolling so he was on top of me. Murmuring in my ear, telling her that this was an easy night, but next time...next time, he had other plans.

I shivered at the memory, and the soap was slick between my fingers, and my fingers were slick, too, because next time was here.

The clear shower curtain was yanked back with a rasp of rings, and my eyes flew open.

"Aw, sweetheart," I heard. "You got started without me. But go on. Show me some more. I'd love to watch, and you need to warm me up, too. Because tonight…you're going to find out what happens to naughty girls who touch themselves in the shower."

♡♡♡

She got that far, and stopped. What *did* happen to naughty girls? She always seemed to balk at this point, her internal filter slamming down between her brain and her fingers, the little critic coming to perch on her shoulder, telling her not to go there, no matter how much she wanted to.

She made a few false starts, hit the backspace button and wiped them out, then sat back and sighed. Time to take a break. A shower of her own, maybe, because there was nothing like research. Research, and some thinking about—all right, about Will.

Fifteen minutes later, she was a whole lot more inspired. The faucet was the key. Hemi had some silk ropes in his well-equipped closet, she knew. Once he got Hope's wrists tied to that faucet and had the bar of soap in his hand—well, she'd just say that Hope was going to be one exceptionally clean girl. The rope and Hemi's strong arms might be the only things holding her up, though, because her knees were going to be shaking hard by the time he was done.

It was all there, and she needed to write it. She put the soap back into its dish, rinsed off as fast as she could, and shoved the faucet closed. It was a shame that its starring role was going to be limited to the page, but then, you couldn't have everything. She groped for a towel, added *heated towel rack* to the mental prop list, and took a couple swipes at herself. No time to dress, because she had to write it while it was in her head.

She flung the door open and headed into the bedroom to do it. And ran smack into Will, coming into the bedroom, moving fast.

She bounced off his chest, his hands came out automatically to grab her arms, and for one frozen second, she was staring at him, and he was staring back. Looking not one bit like her funny, relaxed Will, because he was sweating, and breathing hard.

"What's wrong?" she asked in alarm.

He didn't answer. He didn't even seem to hear her. Because, she realized with horror, she was naked. She stepped back and started to pull the towel around her, but his hand had shot out and grabbed hers just that fast, and the towel fell to the floor at her feet. Then one hand was behind her head, the other had slid down her back, and he was on her.

There was nothing soft, nothing sweet, nothing slow. Nothing but his lips claiming hers, his tongue deep inside her mouth, one hand fisting in her wet hair while the other slid down over the curve of a cheek and hauled her up onto her toes, pulled her more tightly against him.

She was making some sounds into his mouth now, smothered whimpers that she couldn't help one bit, and her hands were on his shoulders, trying to pull him even closer.

He stuck one hand out behind him and shoved the bedroom door closed, then seemed to catch himself. He looked at her, the question written in all its taut urgency on his face. She couldn't answer. She looked at him, and she shuddered.

It was enough. he'd taken hold of her again, his mouth was devouring hers, and he was backing her into the bathroom, all the way into the shower stall. She landed against the tiled wall, the shock of the cold a nearly unbearable contrast to the warmth of his mouth, his hard body. His hands were on her breasts, supporting their weight, his thumbs were moving over her aching, sensitized nipples, sending an urgent signal straight to her center, and she was burning for him.

"Please," she moaned, her back arching, everything in her body wanting to pull him into her. She needed him inside her. She needed him now.

He didn't answer. Instead, he pulled her out of the shower

again, leaned inside and twisted the faucet, and tested the water impatiently with a palm.

She didn't wait for it. She'd gotten hold of his T-shirt, was pulling him out of the shower, tugging the shirt over his head and tossing it, then running her hands greedily over his chest.

"Not waxed anymore," she managed to say. "I love it."

"But you are. And I love it, too."

She swallowed, feeling the warmth rising in her cheeks along with the steam that was filling the little room. "I'm so…I'm so…"

"I know you are. So am I. That's why we're going to do it." He yanked his shorts and underwear down his legs and kicked them loose. "Get in the shower," he told her, and then didn't wait for her to do it. Instead, he pulled her in with him and shoved her under the spray. She gasped at the warm water hitting her skin, and he was grabbing the soap and beginning to use it on her, and it was her fantasy, but it was so much better. Because it was Will.

♡♡♡

He could have had some finesse. He could have gone slowly, could have said all the things she probably wanted to hear. He could have made it last, drawn it out, done something special. But he didn't. He was behind her, pulling her into him, his soapy hands sliding over warm, soft flesh, and there was no time for finesse. His hands were on her breasts again, teasing and pulling and pinching at the deliciously erect nipples, so pretty and pink, so wonderfully responsive to his touch, and she was stretched out, her head back against his shoulder, her arms wrapping around his neck. She was moaning already, and there was even less time now.

His hand dove, and found her, and if the rest of her was wet…this was more. And it was his.

The water cascaded down, he had her hauled back against him with a hand on one white thigh, and his other hand was probing, circling, hard and slick and sure.

"Ah…Hah…" She wasn't managing words for once, just a

succession of keening moans, because he'd found the way she needed it. The perfect spot, the most wonderful pressure point, and it was like pushing a button. Like turning on a spigot and having the liquid flow, exactly the way the warm water was beating onto her breasts, down her belly. Her back was arching, she was rising onto her toes, and she was almost there, her cries growing louder.

"I'm going to fuck you hard." His mouth was next to her ear. "I'm going to make you scream. I'm going to do it now."

She hovered, trembling, at the brink, her entire body stiffening, and then she was convulsing, and he was driving her higher and higher, taking her over the top, her body jerking against him, the powerful orgasm taking her in its teeth and shaking her hard.

He kept his hand going until she'd finished, until the convulsions had turned to shudders, then yanked the tap closed, pulled her out of the shower again, grabbed a towel from the rack, and started rubbing her down as fast as he could.

"No," she said, and his heart very nearly stopped. "I don't care about being dry. Please. Will. Come on. Do what you said. Do it now."

She was the one tugging at him this time, taking him into the bedroom. She started to pull the duvet back, but he couldn't wait for that.

"Lie down," he said. "Now."

She shuddered, and she did it, and he made it to the bedside table in two strides, thanking every blessed providence that he still had some condoms in there, because stopping wasn't an option. He was ripping the packet open, and she was on the bed, shivering a little, her wet hair soaking the pillow.

He might have been cold, too, except that he wasn't. He was over her, kissing her again, devouring her mouth, his hand cupping one of those gorgeous breasts, until he finally lowered himself and took a luscious pink nipple into his mouth, bit down a little, sucked hard, and felt her respond as if it were wired straight to her core. Her hips were bucking under him, and she was crying out, telling him exactly what she wanted. Which was exactly what he wanted to give her.

He wanted to stay there and do it some more, but he couldn't. Not this time. That wasn't where he needed to be.

At last, he was getting what he'd craved since the first day he'd met her. He was sliding inside her, easing his way, because she was so deliciously tight, and his eyes were closing with the heat, the indescribable silk of it. He wasn't rushing now, because he wanted to feel all of this, and to watch it. To watch her eyes closing, her mouth opening, her hands flung out wide, fists curling around the sheets, grabbing, holding on. She was starting to pant now, and he was on his elbows, his hands in her hair, watching her beneath him, watching himself taking her, and seeing her wanting it. Needing it as badly as he needed to do it to her.

Long and slow, with her rising into every thrust, moaning out his name. And then, finally, increasing the tempo. Up on his hands, moving harder and faster, feeling what that did to her, and seeing it, too.

"More," she moaned, and he'd never heard anything better. "More. Please."

Her back was arching again, she was moaning louder, frustration twisting her face, and he'd paused, even though it was killing him, had a hand where she needed it, was stroking, teasing, driving her up again.

"Come on," he urged her. "Please, baby. Do it for me."

Her eyes opened, locked on his, her lips formed his name, and he said, "Yeh. Yeh. It's me. I'm here. Come on. Show me."

She did. She did it for him, because she'd have done anything for him, and he knew it. She was calling out, tightening around him, the contractions squeezing him, milking him, and that was it. It was tipping him over the edge, and he was on his hands again, riding her waves, surfing that exquisite knife-edge of pleasure, until he was tumbling, falling, groaning. Going deep. Going under.

Faith lay under him, still shaking, her eyes closed, because she didn't seem to be able to open them.

"Cold?" A gentle hand brushed a wisp of hair from her face.

"No," she sighed. "Just so...well done."

She heard the huff of laughter. "Yeh. Hope so. Hope that's what you are." He slid down and gave her a soft kiss on the mouth, his tongue brushing against the little gap between her front teeth, and then he shifted position to drop another kiss on her upper lip. "I love this. Been wanting to do this since the first day I saw you."

"What? Kiss my mole, or...?"

"Both. Absolutely. Both. Dreams come true, eh."

She opened her eyes and gave him a slow smile. "Told you I didn't need a vibrator."

He laughed out loud at that. "You kept me awake that night. Wondering if, somehow, you didn't touch yourself, or if it was just that you didn't need any extra help when you did. I was betting on didn't need it, so you know, but thinking about it cost me some sleep, no worries. When we were in that shop, the way you looked at me, when you had your hands behind your back..." He sighed. "I was betting on that."

"Hah. I *knew* it. I knew that whatever you said, you loved that ribbon. Or maybe I should say that you loved tying my hands." She smiled at him some more, and she could hear the hitch in his breath, could almost feel his heart pounding.

"Could be." His voice had come out a little strangled, and she felt a rush of purely feminine power.

"Mmm. I knew it. And that night, so *you* know? That night," she said, stretching against him, "I *really* didn't need any extra help, because the way you were looking at me when you did it—that worked. Oh, man. It worked so well. Besides, I'm fairly..." His hand was on her breast, stroking over it, playing there, the low tingle had started up again, just like that, and she was getting distracted. "I'm fairly responsive," she managed to say. "I can do it...oh, a lot. A *lot.*"

"Ah," he said on a long sigh of satisfaction. "Good times. Left you wanting just now, did I? But then, I was in a wee bit of a hurry." He rolled off her to the side of the bed and pulled the sheets back. "Come on, then. In you go. Give me a challenge like that? You know I need to answer it. Show you what else I can do, and see what you can. Some more of that boot camp, eh. Provided by your very own instructor."

"You may not be the hurtin' kind," she said as he pulled the covers over them both. "But you do a pretty fair line in dark and dangerous after all, don't you? You're not quite as easygoing as you pretend to be. You've got a little command in you there."

"Only if I really want it. And oh, yeh. I wanted it."

One big arm came around her to haul her close, and she had to shut her eyes for a moment at the rightness of being here, being held by him. And then she had to open them, because she hadn't seen nearly enough of him. All this time, she'd been avoiding looking too much for fear that he would catch her staring, and now it didn't matter. So she wriggled in closer, put a leg over his, and pillowed her head on his chest.

His hand cupped her head, and she turned her face to kiss the spot where his tattoo ended, a ribbon of deep blue against rich brown. She brushed a hand over acres of smooth, hard muscle with its light furring of hair, swirled a finger lightly over one flat nipple, and felt him respond instantly. His skin quivered at her touch, giving her a thrill that had nothing to do with her own desire, and everything to do with his. And made her want to do so much more.

"Does this mean I get to touch you anytime I want now?" she asked him, then had to kiss him again. Her hand, whatever his answer was going to be, was moving, stroking over his broad chest, across the heavy muscle of his shoulder, down the sculpted contours of his arm, tracing the whorls of the intricate tattoo. But then, what woman would have been able to resist?

"It does," he said. "Anytime you want. And it means I get to touch *you* anytime I want, too. I also get to kiss you anytime I want. And any *where* I want."

He had rolled them both, was over her again in one smooth, athletic move, one knee was parting her legs, and her hands had flown up by her head. "Starting right now," he told her. "You can stay exactly like that, because you're right, I've got a little command in me, and I'm going to use it. And oh, baby." He sighed. "I have so many places I need to kiss you."

man of the house
♡

Will woke to the predawn chorus of the tui in the back garden singing their delight in another new day, the answers to yesterday's questions staring him in the face so clearly, he couldn't believe he hadn't seen them before. Even though he hadn't got much sleep, not after taking Faith dancing, keeping her out late just to hold her, to watch her move under the flashing lights.

Dancing with her eyes closed, her body swaying to the pumping music. Running her hands down her sides, feeling exactly what he was, he could tell. So aware of her body, of every aching, tingling centimeter of it, and so aware of his, too. Opening her eyes again to smile at him, to move into his arms. The feeling when he'd wrapped her up in them, had held her, and had known he had the right to do it. That he wasn't pretending, and neither was she.

They had stayed until after midnight, then had stepped out of the doors of the club and walked the short kilometer home, and despite the fact that they had still been in the city, there'd been stars.

She'd tipped her head back to look at them. "A sky full of stars." And she'd sounded so happy.

"Not as good as it'll look when we're out in the bush," he'd told her. "On the coast, or out on a boat, maybe. Do a bit of a cruise, and I can really show you something. But still. Good, eh."

"Good." She'd snuggled a little closer, one hand tucked into the crook of his arm. "And you're right. The moon's upside down."

"Or right way up. I like to think of it like that."

They'd reached the house again, had climbed the stairs and got ready for bed together with no pretending, and no pillows.

They'd spent some time there, navigating in the dark. Sighs and murmurs, languid touches and slow, sweet kisses. Learning the curves and hollows of each others' bodies, eager explorers mapping their newfound terrain with hands and mouths, steering by sound and sigh. He'd slid his hand over the curve of her waist, down the swell of her hips, into that most wonderful indentation where her thighs began, feeling the shiver that ran over her skin at his touch. Over the slight curve of belly, then, and up over her sensitive midriff to the delicious roundness of her breasts. Over everything that had told him he was touching a woman. That he was touching Faith.

He'd kissed his way down her neck, had lingered again, had felt her hands on him, holding his shoulders, caressing the muscles of his back, his arms, and had known that she felt exactly the same way. That she wanted to touch him, because when she did, she knew he was a man, and she knew that it was him. And then, as he moved down her body, those eager hands were stroking over his nape, curling into his hair as if she couldn't stand not to. As if she couldn't bear to let him go.

So, no, he hadn't had much sleep. But then, sleep was overrated.

"Hmm?" Faith stirred now, rolled over, and opened her blue eyes, and he almost changed his mind about getting up.

"Go back to sleep." He tugged the duvet up a bit to cover her more snugly.

"Is it morning already?" she murmured, her eyes drifting shut again.

"Yeh." He smiled at her, because she was so pretty, all mussed and sleepy like that. "But early, eh. I'm going to the gym, and then the rest of the day, I'm all yours."

She didn't even hear that, because she was already asleep again. He'd worn her out, he guessed, and that was fine by him.

He headed downstairs, the house still Saturday-morning quiet. He didn't stop for breakfast, but he stopped in the kitchen all the same. His grandmother was in there having an early-morning cuppa, and that made his morning a lot less complicated, because she had the information he needed.

"Want me to fix you breakfast?" she asked after he'd got his intel from her and put his phone back in his pocket again.

"No, thanks. I'll get it at the café before the gym." He gave her a kiss on one soft, finely lined cheek and headed out the door, feeling as light as the birdsong all around him.

He reached his destination, a shabby house at the edge of town with grass that needed cutting. Not so different at all from the house he'd grown up in, except for the garden. Koro had cut the grass, or Will had. Their house might not have been flash, but it had always been tidy.

He got out of the car, walked up the concrete path, and a dog barked from behind a chain-link fence.

"No worries," Will told the animal. "Purely an exploratory journey."

He leaped up the steps to the porch and rang the bell, waited long seconds until he sensed movement inside, and then the front door was opening.

He smiled at the middle-aged Maori woman. Dressed in black leggings and a long T-shirt, her figure heavy from a bunch of kids, her hair in its knot, her face a bit careworn. She had a toddler on her hip, dressed only in a red shirt and nappy. A grandson, probably.

Not an easy life, and he knew it. He wasn't going to add to her cares, not if he could help it. He was here to make sure he wouldn't have to.

"Morning," he said. "I'm here for Chaz. He around?"

She blinked at him. "Will Tawera, isn't it?" The baby on her hip stared in fascination, fingers stuffed into his mouth, black ringlets springing up in wild profusion all over his head.

"Yeh." Will smiled again.

"He's not awake yet. He works nights."

"I know. I'll just nip in and have a chat all the same, if it's all right."

"Course," she said, because she was too polite to say anything else.

Will stepped into the little entryway with its worn lino flooring, and she waited while he bent to take off his shoes. "Down here," she said, leading him to a narrow passage. "Second on the right."

"Brilliant. Cheers."

She nodded and disappeared into the back of the house, and Will knocked on the wooden door.

"Bugger off," he heard. "It's Saturday."

Will opened the door and stepped inside, into musty air and a carpet made of dirty clothes strewn across the floor. A beer can lay on its side on the bedside table, another one sitting beside it. Chaz was a slob and no mistake.

"Nice way to talk to your mum," Will said, shutting the door behind him.

"What the hell—" Chaz was sitting up, blinking, groping on the floor for something to cover himself. "What are you doing here?"

"Came to talk to you. Get dressed and come outside."

"You think I'm bloody stupid?" Chaz gave up the search for the nonexistent shirt and crossed his arms across his pathetic excuse for a chest instead. "I'm not doing that."

"Then I'll open the door, get your mum in here, and say what I've got to say to her, too. That sound like a plan? Or better yet, I'll drag your skinny arse out there myself. Get dressed."

Chaz opened his mouth again, then apparently thought better and closed it. He shoved the rumpled bedclothes back, got out of bed, and shuffled around in his boxers until he picked up jeans and a T-shirt from the floor over near the dresser and shoved them on.

He could just bring Talia in here and have her see the place for herself, Will thought. That might do the business. But on second thought…no. She might think it was romantic.

Chaz still wasn't talking, though his eyes were shifting back and forth under the tousled hair, his cheeks looking a bit gray under the stubble. He'd done some partying after the show the night before, Will would've bet.

At last, Will was following him through the house, putting his shoes back on, although Chaz didn't bother. Chaz followed him out the door and down the steps, and the dog offered up a desultory bark or two from behind his fence.

Chaz stopped at the bottom of the steps. "I'm not going anywhere with you," he said, his expression sullen. "This is as far as I go."

Will smiled. Anyone who had ever played against him would have recognized that smile, when the easygoing mask dropped and the warrior emerged. Chaz's eyes widened, and he took a step backwards. Pussy.

"You'll go anywhere I take you," Will told him. "And if I have to come back here, I'll be taking you somewhere good. But I'm not going to have to do that, am I? Because I'm not going to know you. I'm going to be able to forget you ever existed."

"What are you…" The boy's Adam's apple bobbed in his scrawny throat. "What are you on about?" he tried again.

"You know exactly what I'm on about. Did you think, because she doesn't have a dad around, or a granddad either, that she didn't have anyone who would care?"

"I didn't—I haven't done anything."

"You've done enough." Will made sure his face and body were sending the message, just in case Chaz was too scared to hear. "You've done more than enough. It's time for you to get to know some girls your own age. Time for you to stay away from the lake after school. Time for you to find out, so sadly, that your taste doesn't run to fifteen-year-olds anymore. Or fourteen-year-olds," he decided to add, because Talia wasn't the only young girl in Rotorua without a dad in the house.

"You can't tell me what to do." Chaz was doing his best to bluster, but his eyes had darted towards the front door, and Will had seen it.

"Yeh. I can. And I am. This is my home, and that's my sister. Stay away from her. Because if I hear that you've touched her, that you're still hanging around her…" His voice had got quieter, not louder. "I know the taiaha, yeh. Know it better than you. But I won't even need it. I can kick your arse without it. I can beat you blind without any trouble at all. And I will. Do you understand me?"

He could read the thoughts chasing their way across Chaz's thin features. The defiance. The realization. And, finally, the angry defeat.

"Well?" Will prompted. "I've got a workout to do. I can start it with you, or I can start it at the gym. Your choice. Say yes and go inside. Or say no and stay out here with me. You might be able to crawl inside later. And you might not."

"Yes, then," Chaz muttered. "That what you want to hear? Going to stop threatening me then?"

"Oh, I'm not threatening. I'm telling. But, yeh. 'Yes' will do me. Go inside. And clean your room. It smells disgusting. Cut your mum's grass while you're at it. Time for you to step up and help out. Be a man instead of a bloody disgrace to your whanau."

Chaz shot him one last glare, then turned and headed up the stairs, thin shoulders hunched.

Will stood and watched him go, then stood planted on the path and counted to sixty. So the boy could look out the window, could sweat it, wondering if he'd changed his mind, if he would come after him after all. So he could imagine what would happen next. Then he turned, went back to the car, and started it up.

Breakfast, and the gym, and then the next thing. One down, one to go.

♡♡♡

He'd been ashamed, when he'd woken that morning, to realize that he'd forgotten all about Talia the day before. Faith had driven all thought of his sister completely out of his head. But being with her had also, somehow, showed him what to do. Had caused him to stand at the water's edge and, instead of his eyes going to his goal, that distant view, to look around him instead. And to see.

He'd had a bad moment this morning all the same when his grandmother had told him that Talia had spent the night with her friend.

"You sure?" he'd asked sharply.

"Course I'm sure. Called to tell me, didn't she."

"But are you sure that's where she actually is? That she isn't…with somebody else instead?"

"Talked to her mum myself, didn't I, to make sure she was really invited. Should I be thinking she could be with somebody else?"

"Maybe. She's gone a bit quiet, hasn't she. And I'm not sure about all her friends."

"Huh. This is new for you."

"Well, you know, sometimes new is better."

"Sometimes it is. But, yeh. She's at Sophia's, home around ten."

Which was why Will was here, his hair still wet from the showers, knocking on another door. A tidy little white house this time, not nearly as flash as his own, but kept in Kiwi style, the garden neatly tended, the paintwork fresh. And another woman coming to the door, a younger one this time.

"Morning," he said. "Will Tawera, here for Talia. The girls up yet?"

He waited outside until Talia came out, reluctance evident in every bit of her shuttered face and hesitant step.

"Why are you here?" she asked, halting on the threshold. "Can't I even spend the night with my friend now? Am I a prisoner?"

It wasn't the best start. "Course not," he said, and tried a smile.

"I thought you might go for a walk with me, have a chat, that's all. Please," he amended.

She wanted to say no, he could tell. But she didn't dare, because the old ways were too ingrained in her, and because maybe Faith was right. Maybe she wasn't too far down that road yet.

He thought about the lake, but that was a bit fraught, so instead, when she came out again with her shoes and jacket on, he turned his steps in the direction of Kuirau Park.

They walked in silence for a couple minutes while he tried to figure out how to begin. He finally decided on honesty, for lack of a better option.

"It was heaps easier," he told her, "when I didn't have to do this. When Koro was here to be the man. He was wise, eh."

"Yeh," she said, the word coming out pinched.

"Hard, having him gone."

"Yeh," she said again. "You'd know that if you'd been here."

"I was here. I know."

"No." She was walking faster now. "You weren't. You *weren't.* Everybody went home after the tangi, and you left. You went to the States."

"I wouldn't have been any use, though. And Mum and Kuia were here."

She shook her head, but didn't answer.

"What?" He tried to keep his voice gentle, to ask rather than demand. "What was wrong?"

She shrugged, hunched into her jacket, still not looking at him. "They were just…sad. It was all too…too sad."

"Too sad to notice how you felt, eh. Nobody paid any attention to you, maybe." It was what Faith had said, and it looked like she might have been right.

"My friends did. And now you don't even want me to have them."

He bit back the first retort that came to his lips, took a moment, and tried again. "Nah. That's not it. I do want you to have friends. And I'm sorry I got it so wrong yesterday, didn't talk to you in the way I meant to. Lost my temper, eh."

She cast him a quick, startled glance, but didn't say anything. They crossed the road, still quiet before ten on Saturday, and took the crushed-stone track through the trees.

"You learnt to ride your bike here, did you know that?" he asked her. "With me running behind you holding the seat. You probably don't remember that, but I do." He hadn't thought about that for a long time. "You were pretty determined. Did it over and over again until you could manage by yourself. And when you could do it, you were so happy. Missing a couple of front teeth, and you had this little lisp. You rode back to me and said, 'Will! It's just like flying!'" He smiled, remembering it. "That was a good day."

"I remember," she said. "I remember riding. I didn't remember it was you, though. Thought it was Dad."

"Nah. Dad had already left."

"I don't remember him much."

His mouth twisted a little at that. "Well, I don't remember him that much either. He came and went, you could say. And when he left that last time, he didn't come back."

"And then you left, too."

"Yeh. I did. For the rugby. Koro and Kuia and Mum were here, though, with all of you, and I needed to go. I needed to…" He stopped. This wasn't something he'd ever talked about with her, but maybe it was time. "Dad paid the maintenance for a bit. And then he didn't. So I had to go."

"I thought—I thought you just wanted to leave."

"Yeh, nah. I did, partly." Today, for once, he needed to be honest. "Whichever it was, though, I wasn't here, you're right about that. And with Koro gone, maybe I need to do more. I'm rubbish at doing more, though," he confessed, and was rewarded with a little quirk at the corner of her mouth that was the start of a smile, and he smiled back. "Yeh. We both know that, eh. I don't even know what doing more looks like. Except that maybe it's time to try. Can't get better unless you start. Spend more time here, maybe, when I can."

"You're not just saying that because of her, are you?" She had both hands stuck into her jacket pockets, was looking away again, into the trees. "Did she tell you to, the way she told you to come get me yesterday?"

"Who, Faith? She didn't tell me to talk to you today. Doesn't even know I'm here. And yesterday—no. She told me not to do anything like that, in fact. She told me to talk to you when you were by yourself. She said calm was good. I didn't do too well with any of that, did I? Trying to do it now, though. What d'you reckon?"

"Better than yesterday," she said, that hint of a smile there again.

"But, yeh," he said. "Maybe it's because of her at that. And maybe it's because of Koro. Because of being back here without him. It hit me yesterday when I was running home, after I tried to talk to you and stuffed up so badly. I was wishing I could talk to him, ask him what to do. And I realized..." He had to stop for a moment and take a breath. "I realized that you would be wishing that, too."

Her mouth was trembling now. He saw the unsteadiness in the hand that rose to swipe at her eyes, and his heart twisted with tenderness for the little sister who had been left so lonely, with nobody to even realize it.

"Yeh," he said gently, and stopped walking. "I miss him so much. But you miss him even more."

She was trying to answer, but she couldn't manage it, and Will did what he so rarely had, what she needed right this minute from a man who loved her, a man who only wanted to protect her and cherish her. He held her.

They stood like that for minutes, there in the center of the track, with Talia's face buried in his jacket, the sobs racking her shoulders. Will wondered who had held her since they'd put Koro in the ground. Since the unbreakable had broken, the totara had cracked and fallen. Since their family had lost its center.

"It's all right," he said, his hand stroking over her hair. His voice wasn't steady, but it didn't matter, because she needed to know that he cared, too, that it was all right to grieve. "Shh, now." The tears had risen in his own eyes, a few even making it down his cheeks, but for once, he wasn't feeling the pain for himself. He was feeling it for her, for the girl who'd been left alone.

"Better?" he asked when she'd quieted at last, when the racking sobs had eased into hiccups and her fingers had loosed their spasmodic grip on his jacket.

She nodded and raised an arm to scrub at her face, and the childishness of the gesture pulled at his heart. She was a young woman, and she was still a girl, too, who had lost her father and her grandfather, and couldn't afford to lose one more person.

"You're a beautiful girl." He bent to kiss the top of her head, that vulnerable spot where her part shone through the thick dark hair. "You have so much to offer." *Don't give it to somebody who doesn't deserve it,* he wanted to say, but he didn't, because he'd got a bit smarter, maybe, these past few days. "I want to see you more," he said instead. "I want to be your big brother again. I hope you'll give me another chance to do that."

She nodded, wiped at her eyes one more time, then headed up the path again, and he kept pace with her, shut his mouth, and waited. He might not have talked enough to her. But mostly, he hadn't listened.

"I knew you paid for things," she said at last. "But I didn't know—I didn't think about it. I've never said thanks."

"You don't have to say thanks."

"Yeh. I do. And so does Mum."

"You can't do anything about Mum. That's not your job."

"She thinks you're like Dad," she said with a sidelong look at him.

The dull kick to his gut was nothing but familiar. "Yeh. She does. Surprised you know that, though."

"I'm the youngest. They say things, because they don't notice me."

He put an arm over her shoulder, and they walked on for a minute in silence. "You're not like Dad, though," she said. "I don't think so."

"You don't know. You don't really know me."

"You're wrong. I do. Because I *don't* know him. He left, and he didn't come back. He didn't take care of us, and you did."

"Think you're giving me too much credit," he said over the lump in his throat.

"No," she said, sounding so much older than fifteen. "I don't think so."

He was the one looking into the trees now. "We need to stop talking," he told her.

She twisted in his grasp to stare at him. "What?"

He grinned crookedly at her. "Because you're about to make your big brother cry."

She laughed, and he did, too, and that was so much better. "Time to go back?" he suggested. "Give you a lift home?"

"No. I've got my bike."

He nodded, and they turned to retrace their steps. "Going to watch the ABs play tonight," he said after a minute. "Faith's going to need somebody to explain the game to her, since you know I'll be packing a sad about not being there, praying that Coops doesn't miss his kicks, and that wee nasty bit of me inside praying that he does. Think you could watch with us, give her a bit of a footy education?"

"Yeh." She sounded shy again. "I always watch."

He sighed. "It's definitely true. I haven't given you nearly enough credit."

She laughed, and he grinned, and he walked back up the track with his sister and felt like a brother. And maybe even like a friend.

maid service
♡

Faith bent, hefted the heavy mop bucket, and set it down at the edge of the carpet that marked the delineation between the house's living and dining areas. She gave a final few pushes of the mop across the last of the acreage of heavy stone flooring, then jumped and turned at the hand on her shoulder.

"Oh! Hi." She pulled the headphones out of her ears even as she felt the hot color rise.

Will grinned at her. "Can't believe you're blushing. All I'm doing is looking at you."

"I know," she said with chagrin. "So stupid. It's just...new, I guess."

He bent to kiss her, one hand resting beside hers on the mop handle, the other on her shoulder. "New's good," he said when he'd stood back again. "New's brilliant."

"Yeah. It kind of is, isn't it?"

She'd wondered, when she'd woken up to find him gone, what to expect. Whether it would be awkward when she saw him again, whether he would be sorry, or whether she should be.

She hadn't meant to do it. She'd had every intention of *not* doing it. She was pretty sure there was some major heartbreak ahead for her, but she couldn't bring herself to care. It might have been the wrong choice, but it hadn't felt like a choice at all. When he'd held her, when he'd kissed her, she'd been no more able to resist him than to deny the pull of gravity, and looking at him now, she knew it was still true.

"So..." He glanced at her bare feet, at the forgotten mop in her hand. "You've been busy yourself. Not quite how I was expecting to find you."

"Saturday morning's cleaning time, apparently." She brought herself back to earth with an effort. "And since Talia wasn't here, and I'm going for points with your mom anyway, it seemed like the thing for a houseguest to do." She wrung the mop out one last time, then hefted the bucket and headed for the garage.

"I've got it." He took it from her and carried it to the laundry sink. "So is that it? You done?" he asked hopefully after he'd dumped the dirty water and rinsed the bucket.

"Not hardly. This is one big house."

"Downside, eh. Never thought of it that way. I'd better help, then, because I've got plans for us today, and they're not mopping the floor."

"Well, my next job is cleaning a couple bathrooms. That sound any better?"

He laughed. "Not so much."

"It's what I'm doing, though. Want to join me, big shot?"

"Reckon I'd better," he said with a sigh. "If I were with the squad right now the way I'm meant to be, I'd be looking for something lovely and relaxing to do before the game. Be watching TV, walking by the sea, making the time pass until it was time to get taped up. I never thought of cleaning the bathroom."

"Live and learn," she said cheerfully. "How to behave yourself so you don't get yourself demoted to toilet duty."

"Oh, I don't know. It's had its compensations."

"Then let's go."

He followed her up the stairs and along to the big master suite and into the bathroom that his mother and grandmother shared between their bedrooms, and waited while she dug under the sink for supplies.

"Want to do the tub?" she asked.

"I don't mind," he said, then stood and looked at her expectantly.

"What?" she asked.

He shrugged a bit sheepishly. "You may have to tell me how."

"You're kidding. You've never cleaned a bathtub?"

"Well, not to say *cleaned.*"

"What, you just live in filth? I was in your house. I don't believe it."

"I've had cleaners for a good long time now, though. And before that, when I lived with mates—well, maybe we just…let it go. You're standing up anyway, aren't you. And there's water running."

"That is disgusting. Why even have a toilet? There's water running anyway."

He laughed. "Now who's disgusting? And that's why I don't live with my mates anymore. There's a reason I never sat in the tub, let's put it that way. So come on. If you don't want me to be disgusting anymore, show me how to clean it. In case I fall on hard times and have to rely on my own resources."

She gave him instructions and got him started, even though it made her want to laugh. "Put some of that muscle into it," she told him. "You have to scrub. Get all the walls and everything. Top to bottom."

"Why? They're not dirty."

"Because they got cleaned last week, that's why they're not dirty. You don't clean when you can see dirt. You clean so you *can't* see dirt."

"Right." He started in, and she had to smile. Her big tough rugby star, scrubbing his grandmother's bathtub.

"So how did you spend your morning?" she asked, starting on the toilet. To her, unlike Will, this was familiar territory. "That was a long gym visit."

"Wasn't, actually. It was a couple other things."

She set the brush back in its holder, flushed, and began to work on the sink. "Tell me," she said, because something in his voice told her it was important.

"Well, first I went by that bloke Chaz's house and told him he was done." Will was still scrubbing. "Can't believe I didn't do that yesterday."

"Yesterday? What?"

"I saw Talia with him, down at the lake. And I didn't do too well."

"You didn't tell me that. Was that why you—grabbed me?"

"Nah. I grabbed you because you were naked, and I snapped. And all right, maybe I was keyed up, and the naked part tipped me over the edge. And after that, you may have got me distracted enough that I forgot to mention about Talia."

"Well, I'm not sorry you grabbed me. But I'm sorry if things didn't go well."

"All good now, I hope. Or at least on the way, because this morning, when I woke up, it seemed pretty obvious that it was the thing to do."

"To tell him he was...done. And that was it?"

"It's all in how you say it. No worries. He's done."

"You didn't beat him up or anything, did you?" she asked in alarm. If he'd been suspended for some pictures, what would actual violence do?

"Nah. Didn't have to, did I. Pussy."

She had to laugh at that. "Really? That's great. Boy, sometimes I wish I was a guy."

"Well, if I get an opinion, I'm glad you're not." He'd finished scrubbing. Meticulously, she'd noticed, getting into all the corners. When Will decided to do something, he did it right. "What do I do now?" he asked.

"Spray it down," she said. "Wash all that cleanser off. I know you know how to do that. Just pretend I'm in there."

He grinned at her. "Yeh. I'd say you do know. Do we get to do our shower next? Because that could be an idea. Might work even better if we stripped down and attacked it from the inside. Much more efficient, eh. I'm thinking men might do more housework if women were willing to get naked doing it. Every fella loves a team sport. Specially if there's contact."

"Hmm," she said, fighting a smile. "We'd never get through the whole house, I have a feeling."

"Oh, I dunno. I think we could. The whole house? Yeh. Bet we could. If you were hoovering naked, especially. I'd watch every bit of that. Or scrubbing the floor." He sighed. "That one would be good. Course, then we'd have to take a break. You could be right at that."

"I notice I'm doing all the housework in this scenario, and you're watching."

"I could do the baths, now that I know how," he suggested, and she laughed. The terrible thing was, she wanted to do it. To scrub the floor naked, on her hands and knees, knowing Will was watching her, and then to have him take…a break.

"That sounds like a pretty good morning's work, though." She did her best to keep to the topic. "Of course, I wonder how Talia will take it."

"Well," he said over the sound of the spray, since he was wielding the shower nozzle with some gusto, "I had a wee chat with her too, actually."

"Oh, really?" He sounded much too casual. "How did that go? What did you say? You didn't threaten *her*, did you? Were you careful?"

"Not sure about careful. Maybe not so much. But we talked, about our Koro and all, and about our dad, too, and Mum. Didn't talk about that Chaz at all, come to think of it, but I think it was all right anyway. And then she cried. Sounds bad," he went on hastily, "but I don't think so. It was more…good. I hope."

"Sometimes crying's exactly what you need." Her heart was swelling a little now. She hadn't been wrong about him. She hadn't been wrong at all. "What did you do when she cried?"

"Just held her, I guess. Didn't know what else to do. She seemed to—it seemed all right. What, was I meant to do something else?"

"No." She smiled at him. "No, that was right. I'm betting that was right. You did all that today? You are such a good man," she went on impulsively, because the words were there, and they needed to get out.

"You really..." He stopped, cleared his throat, then made a business of putting the shower nozzle back into its holder and straightening the hose.

"And I'm wondering," she said. "This house. Exactly whose is it?"

"What d'you mean, whose? It's my family's, of course." He'd tossed the sponge onto the counter and was leaning against the wall by the tub, frowning at her.

"Is it yours?" It was the question that had been uppermost in her mind from the moment she'd seen it. It was none of her business, she knew it wasn't, but she needed to know. "You said your dad wasn't...in the picture. And your mom works at the i-Site, and your grandparents must have been too old, and your sisters are in Australia. Was it your dad, though, who bought it? Or your sisters, somehow? A group effort? Or was it you?"

"I bought it," he said, "if that's what you mean. Of course I did. Why?"

"Oh, nothing." The happiness was bubbling up inside her. "I just wondered why you wouldn't have mentioned that you'd bought a house for your family. One of Talia's friends said that going to university was your family's thing, too, and that made me wonder some more, because how does that happen?"

"Well...me. Of course me. Who else?"

"Uh-huh. And you started playing rugby when?"

"What, professionally, you mean? Nineteen. Soon as I left school. Soon as I could."

"Right. As soon as you could. You said you went to Australia for money, like you're some kind of playboy. And to the U.S., too, I remember that. For the money. But it wasn't really for that, was it? You went for your family. You went for this. For the house, and the university."

"Maybe," he said cautiously. "Maybe I did, partly. Why?"

"Don't you see?" She was still wearing her yellow rubber gloves, and he was standing there with his wet hands, but it didn't matter at all. "My mom told you that you were chocolate cheesecake, and you sat there and took it like you knew it, like you believed it. How could you believe it? Do you really not see how much more you are than that? Do you really not realize that you're the real deal?"

"Me?" he said, sounding nothing but surprised. "No. I'm no hero. The last thing from it, in fact. My Koro...yeh. Maybe. But not me. I didn't do anything anybody else wouldn't do. I just did what had to be done."

"Oh, Will," she said, the tears pricking behind her eyes. "Don't you get it? That's what heroes do."

change of venue
♡

He knew it wasn't true, and he didn't know what to say. So he decided to kiss her instead.

She squeaked a bit in surprise when he shoved off the wall and took hold of her, and knowing that he could do it—that was nothing but sweet satisfaction. His mouth closed over hers, he felt all that heat, all that softness as she opened for him, surrendered to him, and he lost it a little. There was nothing for it. He had to put his hands on her waist and lift her up to sit on the counter.

"Will," she said with an unsteady little laugh. "At least let me take off my gloves." She was stripping them from her hands, tossing them into the sink even as he was stepping between her legs. She wasn't saying no, not a bit of it, so he reached a hand around to unfasten her hair and sent the plastic clip after the gloves.

"Ah," he sighed, wrapping a hand through that soft mass, "I love this." He pulled her head back gently, exposing her throat, and set his mouth to her. When he grazed the skin beneath her ear with his teeth, she shifted against him and moaned, and just like that, he was gone. His hand was tightening in her hair, and he was pulling a

227

little harder, biting with a little more force, and she was wriggling under him, making some soft, urgent noises that were only making it worse.

He had to slide his other hand inside her neckline then, didn't he? Because there she was, all soft and round and sweet and needing to be touched. Her slim, vulnerable neck definitely needed his teeth, too. That hollow just above her collarbone, especially, where she was arching away from him. That needed him most of all. So he did it, and she was grabbing his shoulders and whimpering, and he was sliding right down that slippery slope, because this was only going to end one way.

"Ahem."

The cough came from the doorway, and Faith jumped beneath him. It took a moment for the message to get through the insistent drumbeat in his head, but he turned at last. And then he pulled his hand out from under her shirt.

"If you're all done here," his mum said, "I could use the loo."

"Oh. Sorry," Faith said. She scrambled down, stumbling a little in her haste, and he put a hand out to steady her. "We're all finished." She was shoving the cleaning supplies back under the sink, then reaching for her hair clip and gloves. "Sorry," she said again. "We'll just...go do our bathroom."

"Reckon I should be glad you did mine first," Will's mum said dryly.

Since that was about as close to a joke as she'd got since Faith had arrived, Will grinned at her and said, "Reckon you should. We may not get to ours for a bit, actually, but no worries, we'll do it tomorrow, now that Faith's taught me how to clean the bath and all."

"She has, has she?" His mum shot a glance at Faith, who was, of course, turning a delicious shade of pink. She was trying to smooth her hair while being inconspicuous about it, as if his mum wouldn't have known exactly what they were doing, and that made Will smile some more. Faith thought she was so naughty, when she was nothing but sweet.

"We've got a booking just now, though," he said. "We'll bring back a takeaway for the match," he thought to add. "Be back about seven."

"We will?" Faith asked. "You didn't say—"

"Saying now, aren't I. And we're late."

She was still talking when he got her through the door into their bedroom. "You didn't tell me we were going somewhere today. I'd have gotten this done sooner."

"Didn't know myself. Call it spontaneous."

"I need to change, then," she said, brushing at her jeans. "Outdoors or indoors? Dress up or down?"

He pulled out the drawer of his bedside table, took out a few packets, and shoved them into his pocket. "The dress code for this," he informed her, "is naked. Except that you can grab those undies with the bow on them. You're going to need those."

He could see her shudder, because that was just how easy she was. Exactly as easy as him.

"Are we going—" she began.

"Yeh. We are. We're going to a motel. Someplace where I can put you anywhere I want to, do anything I need to, and you can make as much noise as you have to, and nobody's going to be knocking at the door. I told Kuia we needed some privacy, remember? Turns out I meant it. Because there's so much more we need to do."

red ribbon

♡

He drove for less than ten minutes, but something had changed. His face was set, his expression intense, and he didn't say a word, other than a curt "Wait," before he left her in the car and went into a motel office.

He came out of it again a few minutes later, and was pulling around into a parking spot near a corner unit. "Let's go," he said, pulling the key from the ignition and opening the door.

"Will. Could you—"

"Could I what?"

'Could you *talk* to me? Please? I'm getting—" She stopped, then started again. "I'm getting really nervous." She tried to laugh, but couldn't. "You seem so...different. What are you planning to *do* here?"

"Aw, baby." He leaned across, cupped her cheek in his hand, and kissed her, long and deep, and she was melting against the seat, her hand going to the back of his strong neck, caressing him there.

He pulled back at last and smiled at her. "Sorry. I didn't mean to scare you. I'm going to make love to you, that's all. It may get a wee bit intense, because I've had some...fantasies, and I have to leave in a couple days, and—" He stroked his hand down her cheek, the gentlest of caresses. "It's feeling pretty strong just now. And I don't know what you've done before. I know what you put on that shot list of yours, and I've wondered a bit about that. About how much came from you. I'm guessing, but I don't know. So if I start anything that's too much for you, tell me so, and I'll stop. I can't promise I won't push, but we're not going to do anything you don't want. That I *do* promise."

She swallowed. "All right. But I don't want to…tell you so."

"Mm." He still had her face in his hand, and now he kissed her again, his mouth so sure against hers. "You like the command in me."

"Yes." She turned her cheek into his hand. "Yes."

"Then I'd better see what I can do about that. Let's get out of this car and get started, eh."

How could she still be nervous after he'd said all that? Anyway, this was *Will*, and she knew Will. So she grabbed her purse, got out of the car, and followed him into the room.

"Think we'd better get into the shower first, don't you?" he said, sounding exactly like Will again. "Wash all that cleaning stuff off us? Get clean, since we're going to get so dirty later? Tell you what. You go on in there, and I'll join you in a minute."

"Oh. All right." It was exactly like her scene. Except it wasn't. It was just a *shower*. She went into the bathroom and got undressed, trying to calm her racing heart. *It's just sex. Just good sex with Will, like you had yesterday. And last night.*

Fantasies, though. *What* fantasies?

Five minutes later, she was in the shower, a huge stone-tiled thing with showerheads at either end. She turned both of them on, and was being pelted from both sides, shivering and gasping at the sensation, hundreds of individual streams of warm water hitting her sensitized flesh.

The rattle of rings, the shower curtain flying back, and he was in there with her. "Our second shower together," he told her over the sound of the spray. "But this time, we're doing it slow. And we're doing it right."

"What do you mean, right?"

She expected him to kiss her again, but he didn't, just picked up a bottle of body wash and poured some into his hands. "Turn around," he said. "Put your hands against the wall."

Oh, God. It *was* her story. And she did it. She turned and pressed her palms against the tile, and Will was behind her, brushing her hair around so the nape of her neck was bare, and then his teeth were biting hard into the side of her neck. She gasped and lifted her hands from the wall in surprise, and he let go of her, just like that, and she moaned a little at the loss of him.

"Put them back," he told her.

She did it, even though they were trembling, because his teeth were there again, holding her, and his hands had come around to her breasts. Soap-slicked and strong, kneading and teasing, pinching and pulling at her nipples until she squirmed and moaned.

"That's right," he said. "Oh, yeh. That's it. Keep showing me that." He was pressed up close behind her, and she could feel how much he wanted her. Even so, he kept on, biting her neck again until her forehead was against the tile as well, her hips pushing back into him. Until she was liquid with need for him, burning to feel his hands on her. Where she needed him. Where she was melting for him.

"Touch me," she begged, because she couldn't stand it any more. "Please. Touch me."

"Oh, I don't think so. I think I'll make you work for it this time."

"Wh-what?"

He had a wrist in each hand, was pulling them down, and when she jerked back in surprise, he told her, "Hold still."

She did, even as she felt him pull her hands behind her back. And then something was wrapping around them, again and again.

"Ah," he said, the satisfaction dark and deep in his voice. "Oh, yeh. Turn around."

He supported her while she did, because her legs were a bit

shaky now, then reached over and turned off the faucet behind her. "It's time to get on your knees, sweetheart, because this next bit's yours."

She should be upset that her hands were tied behind her back. She knew she should. But he was breathing hard, too, standing there in front of her, big and naked and so strong, his broad back being pounded by the spray. He was looking at her, at the way her breasts were thrust out by her position, and he had his hands on them, was weighing them, playing with her nipples, then bending to take one into his mouth and sucking hard, and she was leaning back against the tile again with a gasp and letting him do it. Not that she had a choice, not with her hands pulled behind her back.

He stood up again, but kept his thumbs on her sensitized nipples, pinched them again, made her twist and moan in response. "A bit surprised about the ribbon, eh," he said.

"Uh...yeah," she managed to say. "I didn't know—where it had gone."

"Went into my pocket, and I've been waiting all this time to use it again the way I wanted to. And this time, I'm not going to waste it. So...if you want to do this, get on your knees for me."

She did want to do it. So dangerously close to the edge, exactly as dangerously thrilling. She wanted to do it all. Everything he said. Everything.

He had to hold her arms to help her, without her hands to support her on the slippery floor. The air was full of steam, the water pelted down against him and around her, and his hands were wrapping in her hair, pulling her into him, guiding her.

He still hadn't kissed her, she realized fuzzily. He'd just told her what to do, and she'd obeyed. Just like she was obeying him now. Letting him move her head, direct her, pushing just to the edge. Just this side of too far, and she loved it.

And then it all stopped. He shut off the water, sank down to his knees with her, and pulled her toward him, held her up, and kissed her, long and deep. His tongue where he had been, the taste of him still in her mouth.

233

"I'm not going to untie you," he told her when he pulled back at last, when her eyes had opened again to find him looking down at her, his expression so fierce, the warrior showing strong now. "Not unless you tell me to. But I'm going to tell you something. The whole day I had Gretchen like this? I wanted it to be you."

She shivered, and he saw it, had his hands around her upper arms, and was pulling her to her feet. "Come on. Let's get you dry."

Once again, he was toweling her off with heated towels from the rack, and this time, all she could do was stand passively and let him do it. He grabbed a glass from the sink, poured it full of water, put an arm around her, and lifted it to her mouth.

"Drink," he said, and she did, gratefully, leaning into his warm side. "You all right?"

She nodded. She could have talked, but something about having her wrists tied had changed something in her, too. She felt how much she was under his control, and she loved it.

He seemed to know it, because he smiled. "Yeh. Feels good, doesn't it?" He bent and kissed her again, his mouth so gentle this time, his hand cupping her cheek. "Feels just that good to me, too, baby," he whispered. "Just that good. Want to see what else we can do?"

"Yes." She managed to get that much out. "Please."

He kept his arm around her, led her out into the bedroom. Another king-sized bed with white linens. When they got there, he put a hand on her shoulder, turned her again, and untied the wet ribbon from around her wrists.

"Oh," she said.

"Don't worry." He lifted her face for another kiss, one big thumb stroking her cheek. "You're going to keep it on. But you can't be on your back with your hands behind you, can you? And I need you on your back. So get on the bed." He pushed her hair behind her ear with a gentle hand. "Corner to corner. Go on and do it, now."

She looked up at him, and then, slowly, she got onto the bed.

When she was on her back, positioned the way he wanted, he asked, "Remember when I tied your hands in that shop, and you asked me how it looked on you?"

She drank in the sight of him standing over her holding that red ribbon. Every fantasy she'd had for the past six months, and here he was, looking more than ready to fulfill them all.

"Yes," she said, and had to swallow against the desire that flooded her, just to say it. "I remember."

"I couldn't tell you then, so I'll tell you now. It looked so good. It made me so hot, and it still does. Put your arms above your head now, because I want to see it again."

She lifted her arms slowly overhead until they reached beyond the corner of the bed. "Like this?"

"Yeh. Brilliant." He was breathing heavily himself, and the desire was thrumming so hard in her, she was shaking with it. She'd have done anything to have him touch her.

But he didn't. Not in the way she needed. Instead, he was behind her, out of sight, tying her wrists together.

"Tug," he said, and she did, but she was held fast. She couldn't see him back there, and somehow, that made it even hotter. The hint of danger, the dark pleasure of control.

He leaned over from behind, tilted her face up to his, and kissed her, his tongue invading so deeply, his hand holding her head in place. "Oh, yeh," he breathed into her mouth. "Looks exactly as good as I thought. But if you want to be let loose—you tell me. Or you can do it yourself." He folded her fingers around the edge of the ribbon. "Got a bow here. You want to untie it, you pull. Or you tell me. All right?"

He'd come around to sit on the bed beside her, and she managed, somehow, to glare at him. "You do realize you're ruining it, right?"

A low laugh, and he was bending down to kiss her again. "I need you to know we're playing, and we'll stop anytime you say. But you want to play harder?"

Something in his face had changed again, and she was

235

responding to it like she was wired that way, because she was. Exactly that way. "Yes," she managed to say. "Yes."

And even though she knew he'd meant it, that he'd stop, that it was play...what he said next was still the hottest thing she'd ever heard.

"Then I'll tell you this," he said. "You're not going anywhere today. I'm going to keep you tied to my bed for exactly as long as I want you there. I'm going to kiss you, and touch you, and tease you until you can't stand it anymore. I'm going to make you come harder than you ever have in your life. So hard it almost hurts. And then I'm going to turn you over and..." He paused, stroked his hand over her cheek, then ran a thumb over her mouth, tracing the outline of her lips, and they were opening for him, just like that, so eager for his thumb. Closing around that thumb, sucking it, and she couldn't help it. She needed him so much.

He smiled, and it wasn't the Will-smile. It was something so much darker. "On second thought...I'm not going to tell you anything else. So much better if you don't know what's coming."

It was as if he could see through to the secret heart of her, to her most forbidden desires, and he was giving them all to her without her even having to ask. She didn't want him to talk anymore, though. She wanted him to do it.

He was over her at last, and she couldn't spread her legs for him fast enough.

"Oh, no," he said. "You're not getting away that easy."

She gasped as he put a hand behind each thigh, shoved them all the way up so her knees framed her head, and held her there. So open. So vulnerable.

"Will!" She made a halfhearted attempt to squirm away, but she couldn't escape that hard grip.

"So good," he said. "So good, and all mine. And I'm going to be using every bit of it."

He stopped talking then, because his mouth was at her breast, biting, sucking hard, and she was shaking again. He lingered there, making her moan, making her strain against her bonds, until, finally, when she couldn't stand it another second, his tongue was drawing a line all the way down. To her navel, and he was staying there, too, licking in and out, teasing and playing, his hands hard on the backs of her thighs, refusing to let her squirm.

And then, finally, he was moving again. Down, and down, across the sensitive flesh of her lower belly, and all she wanted was for him to keep going. She was aching for him, needing him not to stop, and she was telling him so, and he wasn't listening. Her hands were stretched tight above her head, her legs pinioned by his powerful hands, and he wasn't listening at all. The more she begged, the more he slowed down.

When his tongue flicked over the sensitized nub at last, she actually screamed a little. And then he did it all. On and on, tongue and lips and even, so lightly, so agonizingly, teeth. He made her pant, and then he made her moan, and finally, he made her cry out, and she couldn't stop.

And he refused to take her all the way there. Every time she got close, he shifted just a little, got himself barely, so frustratingly off target, while she tried to squirm and he wouldn't let her. Over and over again, while she begged him, pleaded with him.

"Let me…" She hardly knew what she was saying. "Will. Please. Oh, please. Let me."

"Almost. Almost." He let go of her legs, and she lowered them to the bed and shook, and then he had his hands under her, was turning her over, the ribbon crisscrossing over her wrists, and she was desperately gripping for the corner of the mattress.

"Up on your knees," he told her, and she scrambled to obey, her body nothing but a quivering mass of nerves, every bit of her screaming for release, for the satisfaction he was denying her.

He had her hips in his hands, was sliding inside her, and she backed into him and cried out as he filled her.

"Ah," he sighed behind her. "Ah." Her forehead was pressed into her hands, and she was gasping. And finally, his hand was there, and he was thrusting, rubbing, and she was almost…almost…

237

When he left her, she let out a cry of dismay.

"Will," she moaned, lifting her forehead from her hands, trying to turn to face him despite her bound hands, but his hand was there on her upper back, holding her down. "Please. Don't stop. *Please.*"

He didn't answer. Too many long seconds passed before he was inside her again, and his hand was back again, too, rubbing hard. The relief flooded her, the heady sensation filled her. Until he took his hand away, and she felt something else, and she was jumping.

His thumb, she realized with shock. Wet and warm. Circling, and diving, and thrusting where nobody had ever been before. Awakening every stimulated nerve ending, and her mouth was open, sucking on her own hand, biting down to try to bear it.

Pleasure. Dark and deep. So much. Too much.

It was so dirty. So good. He was filling her everywhere, overwhelming her, taking her over. Too intense, too much to take, and she was trying to get away, and backing into him at the same time. She needed it, no matter how much it was, how hard it was. She needed it *now*.

The orgasm came on her slowly. Faint ripples in the distance that intensified, gathered, built into a monstrous wave, loomed overhead and hovered for long, breathless moments, while she stiffened and trembled and shook.

"Please," she could hear herself moaning, as if her voice were coming from far away. "Please. Please." And then the wave broke over her, so strong, so intense, and she was wailing. *"Pleeease…"*

This time, he didn't stop. All the tension he'd built so agonizingly, torturously slowly was released in massive spasms that seized her, took her, shook her hard. She was still crying out, still rocking back and forth, the ribbon tightening around her wrists as he thrust into her again and again, taking her body over for what felt like minutes. Taking her higher, and higher still, all the way to the top and over the edge.

It was too hard. It was too rough. It was all the way to the limit. It was everything.

♡♡♡

When he'd untied her and she was lying under the duvet with him, curled against his chest, sated and sleepy, she managed to ask, "That's what you call 'just having a good time, and making sure she does, too?'"

She could feel the rumble in his chest as he laughed, and there was pure satisfaction in his voice. "Reckon you bring it out in me, eh."

"Mm. Or maybe you just weren't sharing."

"Could be."

"Next you're going to tell me that you actually *do* spank."

"Ah. Now that, I *haven't* done. I told you the truth about that. I knew I wouldn't hurt a woman, but I've always been afraid I'd scare her." Now, he ran a big hand over her bottom, and she shivered at the tingling pleasure of it. He gave her a hard slap there, and she jumped. "But I'm thinking," he said, and she could hear the smile in his voice, "that I may not have given you enough credit for courage. We'll wait until you're really, really naughty, eh. And then we'll see if you look as good bent over my knee as I was imagining that day."

"You really were?" She shivered. She couldn't help it.

"Oh, yeh. I really was. Couldn't cope too well with Gretchen in that spot where she had no place being, and I was pretty narked with you, so I put you there in my mind, and..." He sighed. "I gave you one hell of a spanking, got you all pink and warm for me, and then I put you on your hands and knees, and...well." She could hear the smile in his voice. "You know what else I did, because I just did it. But, yeh. We've got a fair few things we could work through before we got done with my list, let's just say. Now that I know you're open to it."

"I'm open to it." It was easier to say it against his chest, when she didn't have to look at him.

"Well, then." She could hear the satisfaction, the way he was all but humming with it. "We'll see what we can do."

consolation prize
♡

Faith was relaxed to the point of bonelessness by the time she was sitting on one of the big couches next to Talia that evening, eating Thai takeaway in front of the TV. She had no idea what she was watching, but who cared?

Will had paid about as much attention to her today as a man possibly could. Right up until they'd turned on the TV, because from then on, he'd been all focus. He wasn't even sitting with her. Clearly, this was work, not recreation, but of course it was. It was much more than a game for him. It was his job, and his entire family's livelihood.

He'd gotten distracted once, though. He'd even laughed. It had been before the game, of course, and he'd been laughing at her, but still.

Talia had been trying to explain the rules to her in one headlong ten-minute rush as the pre-match commentary had ticked down on the screen. The girl had talked about the breakdown and the ruck and the scrum and the lineout until Faith's head had been swimming.

"Wait, wait, wait," Faith said at last. "I'm completely confused.

Let's start over. The English guys are wearing white, and New Zealand's wearing black, right?"

"Yeh," Will said. "That would be why we're called the All Blacks."

"That's good. Means I can tell who's who," Faith said.

"Well, that and we're better-looking," Will said. "Because of all us brown boys."

"Obviously," she said solemnly. "That goes without saying. And they can only move the ball by passing it backwards."

"Or kicking it," Will said. "Or handing it off in the breakdown, of course."

Faith put up a hand. "No breakdown," she commanded. Will laughed, and she continued. "When our guys have the ball, they're trying to get across the line and fall down, and the other guys are trying to stop them, and then it switches around because…because reasons, and everybody goes the other way. We're ahead when there are more points for us in a little box that I devoutly hope will be on the screen. And that is all I need to know."

Will was grinning. "Got to get you up in the commentators' box. I'd pay money to hear that."

She needed to know a little more than that, though, when the anthems had been sung and the men in black were striding to the middle of the field, ferocious intent in every swinging arm, every hard line of jaw.

"This is how it starts?" she asked when they had lined up in several rows.

"Nah," Will said. "This is that thing you wanted to watch. This is the haka."

The camera zoomed in on a burly figure with a Maori tattoo even bigger than Will's decorating one massive arm. He stood solid for a moment, then began to pace on legs like tree trunks, shouting out what was clearly a Maori challenge at the top of his lungs.

His voice could have cleared a room, his battered face was twisted into a savage mask, and if he'd been coming at Faith like that, she'd have been running in the opposite direction. She barely

242

wanted to look at him, and as far as playing a game against him, where he'd be charging her at full speed like an enraged rhino, intent on bringing her to the ground, and probably killing her while he was at it...no.

A shouted instruction, an upraised arm, a clenched fist, and every man on the squad sank into a crouch, feet planted wide, bodies and faces signaling nothing but male aggression. The group began to slap bulky thighs and heavy biceps in unison, shouting out their own chant in the gaps between the leader's fierce exhortations. The stadium erupted in cheers and applause, and the hair was rising on Faith's arms.

The camera switched back and forth between the menacing men in black and the white-clad team who faced them, chests incongruously decorated with the red rose of England, their arms around each others' shoulders, expressions determinedly stoic as they waited it out.

It shouldn't have been so impressive, not from a group of men wearing tight, short-sleeved jerseys, little shorts, and knee socks. They could have looked ridiculous, but they didn't. They were too big, too strong, too fierce for that. They looked ready to go to war, and even with the distance of television, Faith's heart was beating faster, her breath coming more quickly.

She looked across at Will to see his reaction, and caught that same expression on his face. Hard. Set. Intent. She knew, as surely as if she were inside his head, how much he needed to be out there with his team, and how much it was hurting that he wasn't.

The men on the field stomped once more, slapped their biceps one last time, and shouted a final "Hei!" as gouts of flame flew skyward from the four corners of the field and a roar erupted from the capacity crowd. The Englishmen offered one final hard stare in response and turned their backs. The game hadn't even started, but the challenge had been flung down, and it had been accepted.

"Not an easy thing to face, the haka," Talia said proudly as the teams lined up for the kickoff and Faith tried to get her breath back. "Especially when you're facing the best team in the world, and you know they're about to come at you exactly like that."

"Be coming at them harder if our Will were kicking off, the way he should be," Miriama said from her chair. "Next week, eh."

Faith was starting to get it, and she didn't need to understand anything about the game to do it. This mattered. It mattered to Will's family. It mattered to the crowd. And it mattered to New Zealand.

But mostly, it mattered to Will. He was sitting forward in his chair, his elbows on his knees, his chin resting on his clasped hands, his eyes scanning the big screen.

The team in black kicked off, and Faith was immediately lost. Except that it was brutal. That part, she got immediately. The intensity of the collisions, the sheer physicality, the pace, the skill…it took her breath away. This couldn't be what she'd be seeing from her sweet, funny, relaxed Will, except that it had to be. These were the best of the best, and he was one of them.

But they weren't always the best in the world, maybe. Not every week. Not tonight, because the All Blacks were struggling, and even Faith could see it, if it hadn't been evident from the tension in the room, the rigidity of Will's posture. The little box in the corner of the screen was telling her so. The score was 13 to 13, and the clock was ticking down.

A blare from a horn that meant time had run out, and Faith sat back and exhaled.

"A tie," she said, but nobody was listening, and nobody onscreen had stopped. The All Blacks still held the ball and were battering down the field with it, going down in tackles from an equally determined English side, but getting the ball off again and going some more.

"Not over till the whistle," Talia managed to tell Faith, then caught her breath with a hiss, because the ball was on the ground, and the referee was blowing his whistle, his arm in the air, pointing towards the All Blacks.

"*Now* it's a tie," Faith said.

"Nah," Talia said. "Now it's a penalty. One of the Poms came in from the side."

Whatever that meant, but what it meant, apparently, was the All Black kicker lining up and putting the ball on the tee from what looked like the center of the field. A kick. It didn't matter how many points it was worth. One would be enough.

He stood back from the ball, braced himself, and Faith could see his chest heaving from the exertion of the previous eighty minutes. An excruciating pause while the crowd, and the group in Will's lounge, seemed to be holding its collective breath, and he took three steps forward, gave the ball a mighty boot...

And missed, barely. Wide to the right by what looked like inches. A groan from the crowd, the referee was blowing his whistle, and this time, it really was over.

"What happens now?" Faith dared to ask into the silence as the players on the field gathered themselves, began to form a line, to shake hands and slap the backs of the opposition, nobody on either side looking happy. A tie didn't seem so bad, except that it did. "There are three games, right?"

Will's grandmother was the one who answered. "Yeh. The All Blacks won the first one, and with a draw—we win next week, and we win the series."

And if we lose, she didn't have to say, *we don't.*

"Would a tie for the series be really...really bad?" Faith asked tentatively.

"Yeh," Emere said. "It would."

"Losing's part of sport," Will said. "Except for the All Blacks. There, it's not acceptable."

"Isn't that too much pressure?" she asked.

"Sometimes," he said. "Or it's exactly what it takes to earn that record, and to hold onto it, too. Depends how you look at it."

"And after that," she asked, "after this...this series, you go back to play the other games? The...regular games?"

"Yeh." He stood up and began to gather paper containers from the coffee table as if he needed to do something. "Got the rest of the Blues season."

"And then more of the All Blacks?"

"That's the idea, eh. If I'm selected. The Rugby Championship. Aussie, South Africa, Argentina. Depending how I go next week, of course," he said with a shadow of his usual grin.

"Depending how well you kick? If you make those long ones?"

"It's heaps more than that," his mother said. "It's how he manages the match, his decision-making on the pitch. The first-five drives the game."

"Lucky he's up to the challenge, then," his grandmother said briskly. "You'll be all right on the night," she told Will. "You would've been tonight, if the selectors had had any sense at all, and next week? No worries. When the pressure's on, that's when you show what you're made of. Come the hour, come the man."

"Thanks." He bent to kiss her cheek. "I'll be busting a gut, you can count on that."

She nodded, and Will smiled again and headed into the kitchen with the containers. Faith stood to gather plates herself, and realized, however much of a front he put on, that he wasn't always as confident as he appeared. That sometimes, he was pretending.

♡♡♡

"Here's that first time you wanted," she told him a half-hour later as she pulled her tunic over her head, then wriggled out of her leggings. "Our first time getting ready for bed together without any moves, when you can roll over and kiss me goodnight without a single pillow in the way."

She'd wanted to make him smile, and she'd succeeded. "No moves?" he asked. "Those the rules? Hope I get to take off your necklace, at least, because I loved doing that."

She turned her back on him, even though she didn't really want to, because he was standing there in only his boxer briefs, in all the glory of lustrous brown skin, hard muscle, and swirling tattoo. But sacrifices sometimes had to be made, so she pulled her hair away with one hand and looked back over her shoulder at him. "Well, since all I want to do right now is make you happy..." She sighed. "I guess you'd better come over here and do it."

He was there before she'd finished speaking, and there was nothing for her to do but lean back into him and enjoy it. His hands were at the back of her neck, unfastening the clasp, and he was handing it to her. She clutched it in one fist, then started at the brush of his lips over her nape. It wasn't long before she was pressed back against him again, though, because he was so solid, so strong behind her, and every bit of him felt so good.

"Wanted to do this so badly the other night." His voice was husky in her ear as he pulled her back into him with one big hand on her belly. He used the other hand to turn her head so he could kiss her mouth, and just being held by him like that, controlled by him only that much, was sending tendrils of excitement curling into every secret spot. And then she caught sight of their figures in the mirror, and felt the moment when Will did, too.

"Look at you," he said, turning her so she could see better. "And look at me. Look what I've got."

"Mm." It was all she could say, because she was breathing hard now. "I...Yes."

"And that necklace..." He sighed, his breath a warm caress against her skin. "That's so sexy, and so are you. I know you're trying to make me feel better, give me a consolation prize, and so you know...it's working."

"My necklace is *sexy?*" she managed to ask. "Uh...how?"

He stroked a thumb over her cheek, down her jaw, and she shivered. "Sweetheart. You've never noticed that it's a pussy?"

She actually jumped. *"What?"*

His voice was so deep and dark, his hands so sure. "That a bad word in the States? Not a bad word to me. One of my very favorite words, in fact, when I'm thinking about a girl. When I'm thinking about you."

The heat was flaming in her cheeks, and the thrum at her core had long since started up again. She wouldn't have thought he could possibly want anything else tonight, or that she would have, either, not after all the time they'd spent today, all the things they'd done. But the arousal was sending its tingling message to her breasts, so deliciously heavy and aching for him, up along inner thighs that were more than ready to part for him, to every last bit of her that needed him to cover it, to fill it, to let her know that she was his.

He put a hand over hers, took the pendant from her, and ran a big thumb over the little pearl nestled into the mother-of-pearl folds, over the delicate, ruffled edging of silver.

"Baby," he told her, "whoever made this had exactly one thought in mind. It works, too, because whenever I look at it, I have that same exact thought."

She closed her eyes, embarrassment warring with arousal. "I can't believe it. I've worn this so much. Don't tell me every guy who's seen it around my neck has imagined—"

"Maybe not," he said, although she could tell he didn't mean it. "Maybe it's just because I can't help but go there anyway when I look at you." He set the pendant onto the bedside table, and then his hands were on her again. Stroking over her breasts now, feather-light touches around the lacy edges of her satin bra, and then one hand was sliding slowly inside to tease and torment, and just like that, she was squirming, and watching herself do it. "But maybe better just to show it to me, eh," he whispered in her ear. "Just like the real thing. Just like all of this. Just like these pretty undies. I love that necklace, and I love these."

"You've mentioned that," she managed. "Or maybe you've just mentioned how much you like to take them off."

"Then lie down for me." His lips were brushing her ear, and her knees had begun to tremble. "I know you want to make me feel better, and I know exactly how you can do it. You can lie at the edge of that bed, let me take them off, let me kiss you and touch you everywhere until I find that little pearl. You can let me play with you, and you can watch in the mirror while I do it." His other hand had drifted down her belly, a whisper of sensation, and was tracing the wide edging of cream lace that sat low on her hips. She

248

held her breath as slow fingers found their stealthy way inside, stroked over sleek folds that parted for him, exactly the way her legs were parting now.

"Ah," he sighed. "Oh, yeh. That's it. That's mine." And she would have said exactly the same thing. If she could have talked.

♡♡♡

He lay beside her afterwards, one big arm wrapped around her, and toyed absently with a lock of her hair.

"I was wondering," he said, "if you'd like to come to the match on Saturday, and bring Talia with you. I can get a couple tickets, I'm pretty sure. Pity I didn't think about it sooner, or I'd have everybody down for it. Maybe even Mals, because I'm thinking I ought to see to Mals a bit more."

"Mmm," she agreed, so sleepy and satisfied she could barely speak. "A male influence might be good."

"Yeh. That's what I had in mind, too. Taken me a while to figure that out, I know, but I think so."

She turned on her side and ran a light hand over his chest, then snuggled into him more closely. "You're figuring it out now. I'd say you're doing a really good job."

He bent his head and kissed her on the top of hers. "You may be a wee bit prejudiced, but thanks. Anyway, it'd be good for Talia, I'm thinking, to know I want her there, and it'd give you a chance to see one more bit of En Zed while you're here. We could do better on that than we have. Quite nice, Dunedin, and you girls could fly down on Saturday morning, stay the night, fly on back to Auckland from here on the Sunday, when I'll be back as well. Dunedin's in the South Island, you know, or maybe you don't."

"I know."

"Let me guess. You did the research."

"Well, I was *traveling*." She smiled against his skin, and knew that he was smiling too, in the dark. "And of course I want to come. To see you play in person? Of course I do. And I'd love to go with

249

Talia. Not that she'll be much help explaining the game to me, because I have a feeling that she's mostly just going to be watching you, with her heart in her throat for you the whole time."

"Hope that's true. And I was thinking something else, too. That it might be better for you to stay in Rotorua this week, for Talia and all. I know we said you'd go back to Auckland with me, stay in my house, but maybe you wouldn't mind being here instead. You could work here just as well, couldn't you?"

Why didn't he want her in his house? Because he wanted her to stay with his family? Or because…because he didn't want her to get any ideas?

The thought was a shower of cold water dousing every warm feeling, a sickening jolt straight to her stomach. He must be wondering what she was thinking right now. He must have known that she'd be making more of this than it was, because she wouldn't be able to help it. But how he'd been with her earlier today… Which was the truth? What she so desperately wanted to believe, or what he'd always told her?

I don't stick. He'd said it the second day he'd known her, and he'd never said anything else. In fact, what had he said just now? *It'd give you a chance to see one more bit of En Zed while you're here.* He hadn't said *before you leave,* but he hadn't had to, because they both knew it.

"Sure," she managed to say. "If you think it's better. Sure, I'll stay here."

"Good." He sighed, turned his head, and gave her a soft kiss. "Night, baby. See you tomorrow."

He was out within a couple minutes, the regular rise and fall of the chest under her hand told her that. But she wasn't. She lay in the dark, eyes open, and faced facts.

See you tomorrow. Sunday. Sunday was all they had, because he'd be leaving on Monday to join the All Blacks in Dunedin, and he wouldn't be back in Auckland for nearly a week. Not until the following Sunday, and on Monday, she'd be gone, across the Pacific and back to work. And he'd be back to training again, back

just in time

into the long season that ran all the way through to December, with only one short October break.

A long-distance relationship like that would be unlikely to work with anybody, and it would be even more unlikely for the two of them, because Will wasn't anybody. He was a star. And she hadn't needed that newspaper article to know that he was a player. He wasn't going to make some kind of ridiculous commitment to her, not after knowing her for such a short time, after a few days of sex, however good they'd been. No, however *spectacular* they'd been. To her, anyway.

This had been their deal all along, and there was no other way for it to play out. He was looking at it realistically, that was all, and she'd allowed herself to forget.

Two weeks had seemed perfect when he'd first proposed it. Two weeks had seemed amazing. The longest vacation she'd ever had, because she was somebody with three jobs and bills to pay. So long, and not nearly long enough. Two weeks had become two days. Two days, and goodbye.

She'd been wondering again this morning, for the hundredth time since she'd arrived in the country, if she should tell him about her story. Four episodes of it, the fifth and sixth coming soon, uploaded to all those electronic stores. So visible, too, because they were selling so well. Every one of those episodes with his picture on the cover, looking dark and dangerous. Looking like Will.

No, looking like Hemi. Hemi, who didn't have anything to do with Will other than his body, the body of a man she'd barely known at the time she'd started writing. But Will might not understand that, and if he didn't, if he were upset, all she would do was spoil the little time they still had. If she didn't tell him, he'd never know, and he'd never have to worry about it. That was what a pen name was for.

She shouldn't have come here at all, she could see that now, and she definitely shouldn't have slept with him, but she had. The only thing to do was to embrace it, to take the darkness as well as the light, the pain along with the pleasure. To enjoy being with him,

251

even as she felt herself falling in love with him. Not just with his beautiful body, and not even because of the way he made love to her, the way he made her feel beautiful, and desired, and so very needed.

She would spend these final days with him, and she would love him. And then she would go home and remember him, and be glad, even in the midst of the pain, that she'd had the chance to know the man he was. The friend who'd put her palm fronds into her truck for her, had cared during every single shoot that Gretchen had been comfortable, had played miniature golf with a four-year-old. The sweet, demanding, breathtakingly unselfish lover. The generous, protective brother. The son, and the grandson.

The good man. The family man.

tribunal
♡

"Hang on a tick," Hugh Latimer told Will as the private dining room in the Dunedin hotel started emptying after breakfast on Tuesday morning. "We need a chat."

Will had stood up to leave as well, but he sat down again. It wasn't like he hadn't been expecting this. Just as it hadn't been a complete surprise when he'd arrived the day before to find that he'd been assigned to room with Hugh.

He would've expected to share a room with one of the younger boys and do the mentoring bit, the way he'd done with his Aussie squad and had continued with the Blues. Instead, he was in with the punishing flanker, his Blues skipper, a hard man amongst hard men. He was being sent a message and no mistake.

But that was the price you paid. The All Blacks' bus was driven from the back, by the group of senior players who not only set the tone for a team that meant more to them than almost anything else in the world, but enforced its rigorous code of conduct as well. The worst thing, when you'd crossed the line, wasn't facing the coaches. It was facing your teammates.

The most galling part was that Will was looking to be part of that senior leadership group himself. He wanted to be, he *needed* to be sitting on the other side of this tribunal. This was what happened when you took this kind of misstep, though, so he sat and waited while he and Hugh were joined by Koti James, his handsome face wearing an unusually serious expression. They weren't going to be doing any lighthearted arm-wrestling today, it was clear. Nic Wilkinson, the fullback, was here now as well, along with Kevin McNicholl, the wing, and Liam Mahaka, the ferocious hooker. And, of course, Nate Torrance, the captain, from whom intensity was nothing but normal.

The six of them didn't range themselves on the opposite side of the table from him, or anything like that. They didn't have to.

Nate spoke first, of course. "Can't say we're not disappointed," the skipper told Will. "You wear this jersey, you're expected to fill it up, on the field and off it. You don't want to do that, you're not fit to be in black. That's how it is, and I'd have thought you knew it. It wasn't like you didn't have a choice. It's just that you made the wrong one."

His pale-blue gaze held Will's, his face hard as stone, and Will remembered with a curling edge of shame that Toro and his partner Ally had faced something very much like this themselves. Photos online that she *hadn't* modeled for, a massive invasion of her privacy that had created a national scandal and sent her fleeing the country. It had all been raked up again after Will's own indiscretion, and that would've cut the skipper to the quick.

Not that Toro would've cared for his own sake, because there was nobody tougher-minded, nobody better able to disregard distractions and turn his focus to more important things. But he would've minded for Ally. Will knew, now, that seeing her hurt would've been worse than being hurt himself. And every man here would've minded for him, because that was how it worked.

"I let the team down." Will looked his skipper in the eye and let him know he meant it. "I let you down, and I know it. I knew it was a risk, and I took it anyway. I didn't think about the team, and I was wrong. Can't say more than that."

"Yeh. You can," Liam Mahaka said from beside Toro. "You can tell us why."

Mako's face, with its broken nose and cauliflower ears, all the scars earned in a lifetime of battling in the dark places, had a kind of formidable gravity in repose, like the fearsome sculpture of an ancestor, carved from the hardest wood. Just that much strength, and just that much mana. The liquid brown eyes were stern today, the incongruously sweet smile conspicuously absent. This wasn't the thoughtful, articulate ambassador for New Zealand rugby. This was the other Mako, the leader of the haka, calling Will to account exactly as if he'd been standing in front of the elders in the marae. Calling him to judgment, and to justice.

"No excuses," Will said, meeting the other man's gaze without flinching.

"No excuses, no," Mako said. "But reasons. There are always reasons, and you owe us those."

"Right." Will swallowed. This was the gauntlet he had to run, so he braced himself, took a breath, and did it. "It wasn't drink, or gambling, or Vegas. Wasn't anything like that. It was my grandfather dying, I guess, that did it. Knocked me for a loop, and I didn't even realize it until later."

"So you went to Vegas," Mako said. "For the tryout."

"Felt like I had to do something, didn't I," Will tried to explain. "Decided to follow the money. Told myself I'd be seeing to my family that way, even though that wasn't the way they needed me, in the end. I was thinking it might be easier in the States. Better money, easier on the body, and no pressure off the field, either. Nothing expected but a good boot, and not being held to a standard I didn't think I could meet. Sounds mad, I know. Sounds bad. But that was what it was."

He said all that, breathed again, and waited.

"Nothing to live up to," Mako said. "And this was part of that, somehow. Those photos, and that naff website. Putting yourself up there for all the girls to fantasize about, to write dirty stories about. Ego boost, maybe."

255

Will did his best not to wince. "Hope that wasn't it. Just…seemed like the sort of thing a footballer would do, I guess. Life on the edge. Taking a stupid chance because you could. Least that's the best reason I've got, because when I look back on it now, it doesn't make any sense at all."

Mako nodded slowly, as if he knew. "And there was a girl."

"Yeh. There was a girl. That one," Will found himself saying, "I can't be sorry about. If I hadn't done it, I would never have met her. And if everybody hadn't found out, I would never have brought her over here. And I can't be sorry about that, either."

Every gaze around the table had sharpened, and every eye was fixed on Will. "Think you'd better explain," Nate said.

Will's heart was thudding. He hadn't meant to say this. Why had he? Because he didn't want the responsibility falling on Faith anymore, that was why. He couldn't bear to keep casting her as the reason he'd done this, the seductress who'd lured him into it. There was no amount of money he could pay her that would make up for his mum looking at her like that, or having his teammates think of her like that, and there was no way out of it but the truth.

He should have told his family before he'd left, should have trusted them to keep the secret. Leaving her had been bad enough as it was. When he'd been driving to Auckland the day before, he hadn't been able to stop thinking about her face when he'd kissed her goodbye. About the way she'd smiled, her mouth trembling a little at the corners until she'd bitten her lip to stop it. About his last sight of her in the rear-view mirror, standing in front of the house, her arms across her chest, hugging herself. When he remembered that, his own chest ached. It wasn't the first time he'd driven away, because leaving was what he did. But it had felt like it.

He should never have left her with his family with his mum still believing so badly of her. He couldn't fix that, not now, because that wasn't a conversation he could have over the phone. But he could tell Faith that he planned to tell them. He'd do it when they were together in Auckland again, before she left, when they talked about what they were going to do about this thing between them.

If he could visit again, or she could. Or...what.

He didn't have a clue how that was going to turn out, but at least he could do the right thing here.

"Because I lied about her," he told his teammates. "It was all a lie."

He saw the startled expression pass over Mako's face, saw it change to something else as he went on. "She wasn't my girlfriend. She was a friend, least I thought so. I mean, I thought that was all she was. Having her come over here...that was a stupid idea my agent thought up, to make there be a reason for what I'd done, a reason beyond my own bad judgment. And..." He swallowed, then put it out there. "I paid her to do it. And I'm sorry about all that, sorry I didn't tell Ian where he could shove his idea. Sorry I didn't face up to what I'd done and take all the consequences, except that I can't be sorry. She wasn't just a friend, and maybe there was a reason I said yes, besides that I was afraid for my career. But I'm tired of lying about it, and I'm not going to do it to all of you. Not anymore."

Nate was exchanging a look with Mako, the seconds ticking by in silence. Five. Ten. And then Koti laughed.

"Bloody hell," he said. "That is the stupidest plan I've ever heard. Stupidest way to get a girl I've ever, *ever* heard."

There was some more laughter around the table. Disbelieving, maybe. Appalled, certainly. But laughter all the same.

"What?" Will asked. "Nobody here ever had to pay anyone to pretend to be his girlfriend?"

"Nah," Hugh said, a smile splitting the dark stubble on his hard face. "Don't ask us how many of us would've, though. Or how many of us have done some famously stupid things when it comes to women."

Mako brought them back to reality. "We've all done stupid things for one reason or another," he said. "And yours isn't the worst we've done, either. I know, because I'm still carrying that title. But this goes nowhere," he told Will. "It stays right here with us, because nobody else needs to hear it. Long as you're not lying now. Long as that's it."

"That's it," Will promised. He hadn't been planning to say it, not even close. But now that he had, he was so light with relief that he could have floated straight up to the ceiling. "That's all for me," he said again. "No more lying. No more pretending. No more secrets."

"One more thing." Koti was speaking up now. "Hope you've rung Hemi and talked to him about this, done some major apologizing. I don't know whose idea that name was, but if it was yours..."

"It was mine," Will said. Another secret revealed, that he'd been the one who'd named his dark, dangerous alter ego after his longtime predecessor in the All Blacks' No. 10 jersey. Hemi Ranapia, family man, team man, and about the furthest thing from Hemi Te Mana it was possible to imagine. "I thought it was funny, and that it would be my own private joke, and no, it didn't turn out that way, and that's on me, too. I rang him about it straight away, yeh, soon as the whole thing came out. Right after I rang my mum. Nowhere to go but up after that, eh."

"And?" Koti prompted.

"And..." Will laughed a little, ran his hand over his close-cropped hair. "That wasn't so bad, because actually, he thought it was a bit funny, too. Privately. But then Reka grabbed the phone from him, and..." He blew out a long breath. "If I don't have any hair left on this side, it would be because she scorched it straight off me. Haven't had an earbashing like that since I was a kid."

That one got some genuine laughter from everybody. "You got Reka backed into a corner, defending her man?" Koti said. "That wins some sort of bad-idea prize. Better you than me, cuz. I wouldn't accept an invite to dinner anytime soon, put it that way. Likely to find her standing behind you with a steak knife, eh."

Nate smiled, then stood up, bringing the rest of the men with him. "I'd say we're all done here. It's over, and time to move on. And if you plan to be directing us around the paddock on the night," he told Will, "we'd better get on the bus, get out there, and start getting ready. We've got a series to win."

waiting and hoping

♡

Faith sat down at the desk and opened her laptop. Seven o'clock Tuesday night, and Will had been gone nearly thirty-six hours. She'd had a text from him the day before saying he'd arrived in Auckland, that he'd had lunch with Mals before flying down to Dunedin.

Talked about his marks. Time to get serious.

Whether that meant Will getting serious with his brother, or telling his brother to get serious about school, she didn't know, but either way, the thought of him doing it, and telling her he'd done it, too, had warmed her heart. She'd texted him back, had had to erase and re-start a few times to get the tone right.

Good for you. Good luck this week. Looking forward to watching you.

Now he was getting serious in Dunedin, she was sure, which would be why he hadn't called her. Well, that and that he'd never said he'd call her. He'd never promised her anything.

She didn't need to think about that now, though. She could set it aside and go to a better place, where the problems were so much bigger, but were under her control. Where there would be a happy ending, because she could make things turn out the way they ought to be instead of the way they actually were. A better world, where true love was real, and men didn't leave. She opened her document and started to type.

The minutes ticked by, one eternal second after another. I sat in an armchair that should have been comfortable, except that nothing could possibly be comfortable now, and waited. Because that was what you did in a waiting room.

My mind tried to skitter down into panic, and I began to count the petals on the flowers in the huge framed watercolor opposite me in a desperate attempt to reverse it, or at least to stop it. That wasn't going to help. I needed to stay calm. For myself, and for Karen. When Karen opened her eyes again, she was going to see a sister who was smiling, who was telling her that everything was going to be all right, and who could make her believe it.

Surely it would be true.

I yanked my mind back to the flowers again. Nineteen. Twenty. Twenty-one.

"All right?"

I dragged my gaze to Hemi, and he must have seen what I was trying so hard to hide, because he was closing his laptop and setting it down beside him.

"It's going to be all right," he told me gently. One big hand smoothed over my hair, and his lips brushed my forehead, and that was almost worse. I was going to cry after all, if he kept doing that. I was going to lose it.

I pushed myself back from him. "I know," I said. "I know, because Dr. Feingold is the best. I'm all right. Really." My hands were cold. Shaking. I pressed them together for warmth, for stability, like a desperate prayer.

"I'll go get you a cup of coffee," he said, and I nodded. Not that I cared.

That was why he was in the little anteroom when Dr. Feingold came out at last, the green scrubs covering him from cap to toes. Not looking worried, and not smiling, either. Looking perfectly...neutral. But something in his face...

My legs trembled as I stood up and forced myself to walk to him. And if the minutes I'd waited had been long, this walk was a hundred miles.

"It went reasonably well," he said, and my legs began shaking so badly, my knees were actually knocking together. My arms had gone around myself, and even my lips were trembling, my teeth wanting to chatter, the cold fear grabbing at my heart and lungs. I couldn't get my breath. And still I waited.

"I'm still thinking we're probably all right," Dr. Feingold said. *"But I'm sorry, Hope. It's not quite as clear-cut as I could have wished. We'll have to wait for the results."*

Hemi *was there beside me. When had he arrived? I didn't even know.* *"How long?"* he asked.

"Tomorrow," the doctor said. *"If it's fast."* He exchanged a look with Hemi, *and I knew what that look meant. That* Hemi *would manage, somehow, for it to be fast. So I would know. So I could cope, and help Karen cope, too.*

But for now, all we could do was—

An electronic warble broke the thought, and she jerked her hands from the keyboard, sat back, and tried to gather herself.

Phone. Ringing. Where?

She scrabbled under the papers on the desk, then finally realized that it was hiding behind the screen of her laptop. By the time she pressed the button, it had gone to voicemail.

Another *ding* as she held it, and as she watched, a text came up from Will.

u srsly need 2 call faith

What? Another second, and a second text was appearing below it.

Here I am doing it. Call me back.

She was smiling as she pushed the button, and the phone rang only once on the other end before he was picking up.

"Right," he said, and she melted a little, just hearing that voice. She had it so bad, no matter what she told herself. "I know I want to call Faith," he said, "but why do I need to? Specially seriously. Oh, pardon. Srsly."

She laughed, wishing she didn't sound quite so breathless. "Was that Talia? Why?"

"Dunno. Waiting to hear, aren't I. Sorry I didn't ring you sooner. Finally got a chance, once my roomie left to go find a quiet spot himself to have a chat with his partner. Hard to talk dirty to your woman with your big ugly skipper sitting on the next bed, if you know what I mean."

"Um…skipper?" *Your woman.*

Stop it, she scolded herself. *Stop it now.*

"Yeh. Hugh Latimer. My skipper on the Blues. Captain. My roomie. Never mind. Srsly? What's wrong?"

"Nothing's wrong. Especially not srsly. Talia took me for that walk on the forest track after school, like you wanted to do, and it was fine. She seemed pretty good, to me."

"Hang on. I'm getting another one from her." She waited a moment, and he quoted, "*She's pining 4 you I think. So quiet.*"

"I am not pining. I do not pine." Well, maybe, but she wasn't telling him that. "She's being romantic, that's all. And all right, maybe I was thinking about some work stuff."

"Not going well?"

"No, it's going fine." She couldn't really explain about the story that, since he'd left, had filled her head and insisted that it be told, right now. About how impatiently she'd scribbled down her Roundup copy over the couple days since Will had left, had emailed back and forth with the webmaster on Calvin's site. She'd handled all those details she didn't care a bit about anymore, nearly having to hold herself in the chair to do it, aching to get back to the real thing. She'd wanted to go out with Talia, of course she had. But her mind had kept drifting back to her story during every quiet moment.

"How's that whole thing going?" he asked. "I've never asked you, I realize. Never wanted to look. The website and all. Must be doing all right, I guess, or I wouldn't have been found out."

"You don't really want to know that. It's got to be the last thing you want to hear about."

"Matters to you, though, doesn't it. I get that. And it's not your fault that I did a stupid thing in signing on for it."

"That's really…" She cleared her throat. "Really generous of you."

"Nah. Just realistic. And fair, maybe, I hope."

"Well, then, let's just say that Calvin's got a new shoot planned, and that he's ready to do it all again, because that's how well it's going. The subscription revenue is…wow. Beyond all our projections, which makes taking pictures for craft books, of little girls wearing the cute homemade barrettes they made, look a whole lot less lucrative. And you'd better tell your teammates to steer clear of Vegas, because I hate to tell you, but this time there are *two* guys. And a girl, of course."

"You're joking."

"Nope. Variety is the spice of life, I guess. And sharing is special. Going to be auditioning them next week, as soon as I get back." Which wasn't the best thing to remind herself of, even as it was exactly what she needed to remind herself of.

There was a little silence on the other end of the line, and then he said, "Yeh. You need to get back."

"Three jobs," she said, trying her best for brisk. "And only one of them with my mother. Career path and all that."

"Anyway," he said. "You get the hotel booking, the plane tickets, match tickets and all that I sent along for you and Talia?"

"I sure did. Not going to see you, though, I guess."

"Not till you get back to Auckland, when I collect you at the airport. But you'll see me on the paddock," he assured her. "One more New Zealand experience for you, and I'll do my best to make it a good one. And here's Hugh coming back in," he added in what sounded like resignation. "So all the dirty stuff will have to wait. I propose we skip the boring bits and get straight to the important part next time."

She laughed, even though she was a little hurt, maybe, to know that talking about sex was the important part. "I can read you the shot list I've worked up for Calvin. How's that?"

"Yeh, that'd work. You need a research partner? Help you think up something extra-good? Purely for the idea stage, of course," he hastened to say, "because that's research we're most definitely not testing out."

"Mmm. Because of your unbecomingly possessive tendencies."

"Those would be it. But we're getting a bit dodgy here, and Hugh's eyeing me suspiciously. Talk to you in a couple days, then.

Next time you srsly need me."

She smiled, said goodbye, and hung up. And tried not to think about how much she srsly needed him right now.

come the hour, come the man
♡

It was Saturday night at last, and it was going to be a good one.

From the moment the All Blacks had walked past the English to line up for the haka, Will had known they were in for a battle. The silence, the pride with which the other team carried themselves—that told the story. To beat the All Blacks, you had to believe you could do it. And to win a three-game series against them, you *really* had to believe. Which was why almost nobody ever managed it.

He lined up with the others, stood strong, flexed his fingers, breathed deeply, and let the aggression come. Let his own belief fill his lungs, as necessary as oxygen. By the time Mako started shouting out the challenge and he dropped into his crouch and began to slap his thighs, he didn't need any help at all, because the blood of warriors ran in his veins. The ferocious desire to prove himself in battle was right there in him waiting for the call, because the need to win was as deep as breath, as strong as life.

He let it take him over, let the power come, and released it. Eyes staring, mouth grimacing, everything in his body letting the Poms know that he was here to the death, that he wouldn't be

266

easing up until the final whistle sounded. That he would never quit.

After that, of course, he had to go sit on the bench with all that adrenaline coursing through his body and no way to release it. All he could do was let the shakes die down as he watched Coops kick off, then keep his body relaxed between bouts of jogging and warmups on the sideline during the ding-dong battle that resulted.

The line speed of the English was even greater than it had been the week before as they aimed to keep the All Blacks on the back foot, to keep them from playing the fluid, expansive game that was so hard to combat. And it was working. A too-hasty pass spilled here, a charged-down kick there. The English weren't dominating, but neither were the All Blacks. At twenty minutes in, the score was 0 to 3 in favor of England, a single penalty kick by the English the only points on the board, Coops having missed his kick on the All Blacks' one attempt.

And at halftime, the score was 3 to 10. Coops had nailed the second penalty kick, but the Poms had scored a try in the final two minutes, and the momentum and belief were with them.

Nothing but calm in the sheds, though, during the brief break. No panic, because that was why the All Blacks won. Patience, and belief. And this half, Will wasn't on the bench.

He ran out of the tunnel behind Nate and took the ball. A few deep breaths, and the strength and certainty were there. He needed a clear mind, a calm, still place from which he could see what was happening around him, could adjust, could keep a steady hand on the tiller. He had that, and he had this.

A drop-kick deep to the Poms, and it was on. After that, it was all action and reaction, furious pace and ferocious power.

The English were testing him, assessing his fitness and resolve after a week off and the cold start off the bench. He saw that quickly enough, and he gave them the answer just that fast. Ian Brown, the winger, took a pass and launched his 120 kilos straight at Will, and Will responded. No messing about; he wrapped the other man up in the low, jarring tackle that was the only way to bring a bull like Ian down, then rolled away fast, because the last thing they needed was another stupid penalty. Hugh was in there fighting for the ball with the blazing speed that was his trademark, Mako had joined him, and Will was straight into it, too, adding his weight to the battle until the referee blew his whistle. England had turned it over, and the ball belonged to New Zealand.

The All Blacks were moving down the field, and Will was running, shouting. The ball went through three sets of All Blacks hands like lightning, then Koti sent a tricky cutout pass behind his back, missing the next man in line and catching Will.

Too many white jerseys ahead, but a hole deep to the right. He went for the grubber, the short little kick that would put the ball into that vulnerable spot behind the front line that the English weren't defending, would allow All Black hands to touch it first, would break the line.

Always a risk, and this time, it didn't pay off. Robbie McCallister, the Poms' centre, got there first. Robbie, always fast and dangerous, took off like a streak down the left touchline, but Will was chasing, gaining ground, because he was even faster. The English centre was there, though, in support of his teammate, was taking the pass, and now Ian had caught up, his big frame moving with deceptive speed. Ian executed a tricky sidestep that Nic Wilkinson, the All Blacks' fullback, read perfectly. Nico, the last staunch line of defense, went for the tackle, and made it, but Ian's momentum was too much, and he was crashing over the tryline, there at the corner, and that made it 3 to 15.

A miss on the conversion, though, and 12 points were only 12, and there was no panic in the black jerseys. The crowd might be disheartened, but the players knew better. They had won too many times when they should have lost, because they held fast, and because there were eighty minutes in this game and you played to the end.

For the next thirty-five of them, the All Black defense tightened and held. The English got sloppy, got hasty. Two penalties, two tough kicks by Will, one from fifty meters out, the other from nearly forty and all the way from the side, and it was 9 to 15 with five minutes left on the clock.

Will didn't think about the series. His horizon stretched only five minutes. A long kick by the English, and Kevin McNicholl leaping high in the air to take it for the All Blacks, being hit while he was up there. The referee blew his whistle. Intentional or not, it didn't matter. You couldn't hit a man in the air. Will kicked the ball long again, safely into touch, and that was a lineout to the All Blacks near the English tryline, and a chance.

They won the lineout, Mako's throw-in as accurate as usual, and the ball was moving, bodies in black uniforms running hard, passing on the trot, relentlessly executing on one of those perfect sequences, and this was the moment. This was the time. They were down the field, well into England's territory, and it was in Will's hands.

He saw it. The spot. The opportunity. Another grubber, but this time, he got the bounce.

As soon as the ball left his foot, he was moving, sprinting for it. He, and he alone, knew where it was going to go, because he'd felt it. Which meant he was there first, that he'd caught his own kick while it was still bouncing, that he was behind the English line while they were still reacting. Over the chalk, diving for the try, the grin splitting his face. Koti ran up behind him, was already thumping him on the back as Will jumped to his feet.

The roar, then the chant. "All...Blacks. All...Blacks" from the crowd, back in it again. Believing again.

Will wasn't celebrating, though. The score was still 14 to 15, there was less than a minute on the board, and one opportunity to win the game.

He'd gone over the line in the corner. Of course he had, because that had been where the hole had been. Which meant he had to kick from the corner, too.

It didn't matter, though, how much he, or the team, or the country had riding on the kick. You did it exactly the same way every time. You focused on only this one moment in time, this one single kick. So he took the ball all the way to the 22, set it onto the tee, backed up, and focused.

His mouthguard tucked into his sock, the ritual as always. Three breaths in and out, looking at the ball, at the posts. Visualizing the curving trajectory the ball would take from the left side of the field to that perfect spot between the posts.

For this, too, he knew as soon as the kick had left his boot. He barely looked at the ball, or the officials beneath each post stepping forward, flags raised to signal the successful conversion. He barely heard the deafening roar of the crowd, their relief as great as their anxiety had been as the scoreboard ticked over.

Sixteen to fifteen, but the whistle hadn't blown yet, and until that happened, it was on. So he lined up with the rest to receive England's final kick. Kevin was jumping for it again as the men in white charged, desperate to get it back, hoping for that last-second miracle.

It didn't come. Kevin was safely on the ground, the hooter going even as he landed, the long, low blast signaling the end of eighty minutes, and Will had himself in position. A pass that was barely a handoff, and Will was sending it off his boot and safely into touch.

Now they could celebrate, because the whistle was blowing. The All Blacks had won, and Will was back with his team.

♡♡♡

Faith was standing, jumping, hugging an ecstatic Talia, who was hugging her right back. As a rugby education, it hadn't been very effective, because Talia had spent most of the match with her hands tucked beneath her, focused intently on the incomprehensible action below, especially once Will had taken the field. But as a bonding exercise, it hadn't been bad.

On the other hand, as an exercise in not falling in love with Will Tawera, the evening had been a complete failure. From the time that Talia had been stenciling a black "NZ" and fern onto Faith's cheeks, Faith had succumbed to the magic. Walking into the stadium, with its air of barely suppressed excitement even from the laconic South Islanders, seeing the black flags waving. Hearing the anthem sung, first in Maori and then in English, and seeing the players, their faces intent, their arms around each other, singing along to both.

And, of course, the haka. The spine-chilling sight of all that male purpose. Seeing relaxed, funny, cheerful Will transformed into a man she would barely have recognized. Finally seeing him run out onto the field and fulfill all that aggressive promise.

This, then, was the real Will, the one she'd only seen in bed. So calm, so sure, so powerful. Taking the ball again and again, handing it off in an impossibly skillful pass, without even having to look, as he was running. Or heading down the field with it, lowering his head and forcing the English to dispatch two defenders to bring him down, his feet still churning for those few more precious meters. Making the kicks that brought the score so close. So close, and not close enough, because close wasn't going to count.

Losing wasn't an option. She knew that much. Will hadn't been there the week before, and the team had lost on that final kick. He'd felt the responsibility for the loss on his shoulders, she was sure of it. That was how Will was. He took responsibility. He took it quietly, jokingly, without fanfare. But he took it all the same.

When he'd kicked the ball forward in those final minutes, she'd gasped aloud. They were so close, and he was giving it away?

"Oh, no," she'd groaned. And the next second, had been on her feet with Talia, with all the other tens of thousands, the roar all but shaking the domed stadium, as Will dove and slid across the grass, the ball held out in front of him like an offering.

She'd stayed on her feet along with everyone else, had held her breath for the kick, had willed him to success with everything she had. The crowd had gone nearly silent as he'd stood there, the big screen overhead showing the concentration on his handsome features, the steady purpose and the confidence, too. he'd run forward, had kicked, a beautiful, fluid motion, his leg following through after the ball had left his foot. He'd acknowledged neither

271

the applause nor the relief, had merely tossed the tee to the sideline, pulled his mouthguard from the top of his sock and shoved it back in, and trotted back out to finish it.

It was a game, and it was his job, and it was his passion. It mattered so much. It mattered more than anything.

Then he'd kicked it out again, but that was all right, because it had been the end. The end, and the players had hugged each other even as Faith had hugged Talia, as they'd laughed and cried a little. She'd pulled out a tissue to mop the smears of black paint from the girl's tear-streaked cheeks.

Because Will had proven himself. Because he was the man for the job. Because the All Blacks had won.

♡♡♡

When they were back in the hotel room again, when her pulse rate had settled down a bit from its rocketing gallop, she texted him.

Way to come back. What are a few sexy pictures when you can do that?

A minute more, and her phone was ringing.

"So what did you think?" she heard over the background noise of deep voices and laughter.

She laughed herself. There was nothing else to do, no other outlet for what she felt. "I think you were awesome. Of course I do. There can't be any other answer."

"I meant about your first match," he protested. "Pretty good atmosphere, eh."

"What atmosphere? What match? I was only watching one thing. But, yeah." She laughed again, the excitement and happiness fizzing over. "That thing was pretty good, that thing I was watching. That guy I saw out there. Thank goodness you already overcame my resistance, because otherwise, I'm afraid I'd be throwing myself at you, and what would that say about me?"

He was the one laughing now. "That's what it takes, eh."

"No. It just took you, and you know it. You're fairly irresistible all by yourself. But it was…what my mom called it. The cherry on top. But, really. I loved it, and so did Talia. Thanks for giving me the chance to see it for myself."

"She there? Can you put her on?"

"Sure." She handed the phone over, then sat on her bed and smiled some more at Talia's excited discussion of the match with her big brother. Faith didn't understand half of it, but she understood how much Talia cared, and how much it meant for her to let Will know it.

Then Talia handed the phone back to Faith. "Me again," she told Will. "So how sore are you, after all that?"

"Aw, baby," he said, "not sore a bit, not now. Sore is for Sunday. But you may have to be gentle with me tomorrow."

She melted a little bit more, just because he'd sat in the locker room, in the middle of his teammates, and called her "baby."

"I can be gentle," she promised. "I can kiss you everyplace you hurt." And if that was a little sexy for Talia, too bad. She hadn't said it for Talia.

"I'll be holding you to that. Literally," he said, and she shivered a little and smiled. "I'll ring off, though. The English boys are coming over in a bit to have a beer. Got to do my duty as a host."

"Really? You guys have a beer together afterwards? That really happens?"

"Fine old footy tradition. You bash the hell out of each other for eighty minutes, then you have a pint and a laugh and it's all over. I know it may look a little bit scary out there, but there's no point playing if you're not going to give it all you've got."

"Remind me never to actually do that boot camp with you, then. You'd kick my butt."

"Nah. I wouldn't *kick* it. I'll tell you some more about that tomorrow, though."

"See you then." She hung up the phone, still smiling, looked at Talia and sighed. "He's pretty great, isn't he?"

"Yeh," Talia said. "He is. He's the best. And I've never talked to him after a match before," she added impulsively. "Thanks for that."

"Really?"

"I'm the youngest. And he's the oldest, and he's the—well, he's Will." *The star,* she didn't have to say. "He talked to me heaps more last week than he ever has."

"Some of that didn't go all that well, I know," Faith said. "But if it helps—I know he cares."

"I know he does, too," Talia said. "Now."

rumors and revelations

♡

Will shoved the last of his things into his duffel, moving a little slowly as you always did on the day after the match. When the adrenaline of combat had long since drained away, and with the hurdle of the journey home still to overcome before you could climb into the spa pool or onto the massage table and start getting your strength back for Tuesday, when it would all start again.

Yeh, Sundays were a bugger, but today, he was happy to be sore. There was nothing like playing, and no anesthetic like a win. And this afternoon, he'd be seeing Faith. Another pretty good anesthetic.

The niggle tried to poke its nasty head through the surface at that. The reminder that tomorrow, she was leaving, because, as she'd reminded him over and over, she needed to get back. But they would deal with that. He could go back to the States for a week in October, maybe, during what he devoutly hoped would be his brief break between the Southern Hemisphere Rugby Championship and the Northern Tour to Europe, because he'd be busting a gut to be selected for the All Blacks for both of them. He'd have the offseason as well, all December and January. She could come out here again, maybe. And then they'd…see.

She'd wait for him, he was sure she would. Another niggle at that. Well, almost sure. He should've talked to her about it before, he knew that now. But it had all happened so fast. And anyway, they would talk about it today. They'd have this afternoon, and tomorrow as well. Heaps of time to hold her, and kiss her, and remind her why she wanted to wait for him. He hoped.

He heard the chime of his phone and dug into his pack to find it. Ian.

"That may have answered a few of the critics," he told his agent without waiting for a hello. "Back in business, I hope."

"I hope so." Something in Ian's tone had Will standing up a bit straighter. "But who knows, now. Can't believe you didn't tell me. Can't believe you still don't get it. I'm this close to dropping you, and that's the truth."

"What?" Will sank onto the bed. "What are you on about? I haven't done a bloody thing."

"Nothing but not tell me that your pretend-girlfriend is publishing porn about you. When that gets out, everything's going to hit the fan and no mistake. Not much we can do about this one, not at this point. Public breakup, sure. That may help. Maybe. But if you'd set out to do the most avoidable thing possible to torpedo your career, something there was no way in hell you had to do, I'm not sure you could have managed any better. Addiction, all right, I've had that. Anger management issues? All that. But *this?* Why? There's no twelve-step program for stupid."

"Wait." Will finally got a word in edgewise. "*What?* What porn?"

He heard the sigh down the phone. "Bloody hell. She didn't even tell you. You know how to pick them, don't you?"

"Tell me." He was up, pacing, because he couldn't help it. "Shut up about the rest and tell me."

"She's got a pen name. Olivia Jayne. And five episodes out of *Fierce,* with the exciting conclusion coming soon. You'll recognize them. They'll be the ones with your photo on the cover, looking dirty as hell. She wasn't content just to publish on that website, I guess. She had to sell the story—what everybody is going to think is *your* story, I can guarantee you that—to the whole bloody world. She had to make money off you."

Will had his phone shoved between ear and shoulder and was pulling his laptop out of his backpack, his breakfast turning sour in his stomach. He chose an online bookstore at random and hit the search button. "What was the name?"

"Olivia Jayne." Ian spelled it. "Go on, look it up."

Will did. And sure enough, up came five titles. He clicked on one at random. Its cover showed him, his face in shadow, his white shirt open all the way. He was staring down at Gretchen, on her knees in front of him in a pale bra and undies. All black, gray, and white, except for one splash of color. The red ribbon tying her hands behind her back.

"That's not...you're saying those are *Faith's?*" he said. "I don't believe it. She'd have told me. They're stock photos. For sale everywhere, to anybody. And of course people are writing stories. That was the point, wasn't it? Somebody told you this Olivia Jayne is her? They're lying. Trying to make more trouble for me, maybe, or just stirring the pot."

"Oh, really? What if I told you that the person who told me that got it from the model?"

"Right," Will managed to say. "Tell me the whole thing. Now."

Ian's sigh came down the phone. "Simple chain of events. A reporter calls the photographer to get more of the story. Human interest. Photographer gives him the name of the girl. Reporter calls the girl. Girl tells reporter all about how lovely you were, what a gentleman, what a 'sweetheart.' All very heartwarming, all very helpful, and if it had stopped with that, we'd be nothing but good. But it didn't, did it?"

"I don't know." Will was having a hard time getting his breath. "You tell *me.*"

"No, it didn't, because then the reporter asks about Faith. About the two of you falling in love and all. And up the girl pops and tells him all about Faith's wonderful stories, and he calls me for your reaction, and I tell him I'll get back to him. There we are, and that noise you hear? That's the sad sound of your image deflating. I doubt this one will keep you from playing, not if we throw her under the bus, which I sincerely hope you're willing to do. If she really didn't tell you about this, you'd bloody well be willing to do it. But it isn't going to do you any good at all, and you can forget about any product endorsements for the next year or two. I don't think the All Blacks are going to be rapt about you doing condom adverts, and that's about the only industry that's going to touch you now."

Will had heard enough. "I need to talk to her," he said, "and I need to think. I'll ring you again when I'm in Auckland."

"Not soon enough. I need to start damage control now."

"Well, you're not going to. You'll wait until I tell you what to say."

"That's not how this works," Ian said. "I tell *you.*"

"Not this time. Not anymore. I need to get on the bus in—" Will held the phone away from his ear to check the time. "Twenty minutes. And I need to talk to Faith. If the world's going to blow up in the next few hours because somebody wrote naughty stories about me, it's going to have to blow up, because I'm not doing anything else without thinking about it first, and talking to her. Could be this whole thing was a misunderstanding, or even a lie. I'll ring you when I'm in Auckland, when I've got a bit of privacy. I'll tell you then what I want to do."

"Mistake," Ian warned.

"Then it's my mistake. Because that's what's happening."

He rang off, then thumbed through for Faith's number. His fingers, he noticed in a detached sort of way, were shaking. He took a couple deep breaths, the same kind he took to steady himself for a tough kick. And then he pushed the button.

attitude adjustment
♡

Faith climbed the stairs to the bedroom. Not "her" bedroom, she reminded herself. Will's bedroom, that she would be leaving today for the last time, because their time together—her job, which was all this was—was over.

She needed an attitude adjustment. She'd been so excited last night, had let herself feel, for just a little while, that Will was really hers, and she was really his. But it wasn't true, he'd never pretended it was, and if she were going to see him today, if she were going to stay with him tonight, and most of all, if she were going to be able to leave tomorrow without doing or saying something she'd regret, she needed to get her head on straight.

A run around the lake, that was the ticket. A *long* run, because she didn't have to leave for the airport for more than two hours, and hanging around here, waiting to go—that was just going to make her feel worse.

She pulled her workout clothes out of the drawer. She'd gotten into her capris and bra, had her shirt in her hand when the phone rang. She tossed the shirt onto the bed and dug her phone out of her bag. It had to be Will. Or her mother. She looked at the screen and couldn't help a happy little sigh. Will.

"Hey," she said, feeling unreasonably better just because he'd called, and that he didn't want to wait until this afternoon to talk to her. That was exactly how foolish her demanding, undisciplined, irresponsible heart was. "I was just thinking about you, big guy. How are you feeling today?"

"I was feeling better before I heard the news."

Something in his voice sent a chill straight down her back, and she sank onto the bed without even realizing what she was doing. "What? What's wrong? Did something happen? The team? Your family—"

He cut her off with none of his normal courtesy. "Are you Olivia Jayne?"

No. How could he know? The blood was draining from her head, and she felt a little sick. "Wha—what?"

"You heard me. Have you been writing books about me?"

"Not—not about you. But I've been—" She had to stop and get her breath. "Yes. Yes, I have. I've written a serial. I wrote episodes for the website, and they were received really well, so I published them. And I'm selling them." If she were going to have to tell him, it was better to say it all at once.

Silence, for a long moment. "Will?" she asked tentatively. She wanted to explain, wanted to say something to make it better. But she couldn't think what it would be. And there was still nothing but silence on the other end.

"Right," he said at last, the word an exhalation. "Right. And you didn't think this was something you should tell me about." He wasn't shouting. It was so much worse than that. He was...defeated. "That you were writing porn about me, and publishing it. When you knew what my life was. You knew what those pictures did to me, and you did this anyway, something that's going to make it all so much worse, and you didn't even have the grace to tell me you were doing it so I could protect myself."

"It isn't—it isn't porn," she tried to explain. "It's erotic romance. And it's *not* about you. It's about my character. It's about

Hemi. Remember? Hemi."

"Who looks exactly like me. And who was written by *you*. By my girlfriend, the woman I'm sleeping with. Do you think anybody is going to believe for a second that that isn't me, doing...whatever you have him doing to her? That it isn't some kind of memoir?"

"What?" She actually laughed, she was so startled. "How could anybody think that? He's a tortured multimillionaire CEO. Nobody who knows you could think you're him."

"But the people I'm talking about, they *don't* know me. That's the point. All they see is an image. Haven't you realized that by now? And do you really not get that my image matters?"

"But I haven't hurt your image. I *haven't*." She didn't know how he'd found out, but she needed to make him understand. "Because nobody's ever going to have a chance to make the connection. Because I'm *not* your girlfriend, and I'm leaving tomorrow, and anyway, I have a pen name. That's why I didn't tell you."

"Really." His voice was soft now. Deadly. "Then how do I know?"

"I...I don't know." The hand holding the phone was trembling a little, because it was getting the message before her brain did. "How?"

"Gretchen. You told bloody Gretchen. And she told a reporter, and any minute now, he's going to be telling the rest of New Zealand."

"Oh, no." It was a breath, about the last breath she had.

"Oh, yes. And what I want to know is," he said, his voice finally rising, "was all this just part of a...part of a plan? Were you planning to leak it once you'd got safely back home? Was Gretchen going to do it all along, just maybe sprang it a bit early, or was it going to be you? Was that the real reason for the new hair, the new clothes, the...the new body, so you could go on some chat show and talk about it? And being with me. Was that all just a way to sell more books, too?"

"No!" She pressed her knees together to keep them from shaking. *Oh, no.* "No. Will, no. You have to believe me. I don't know why I even told her. I didn't tell anybody else. I never dreamed—I never imagined it would get out. It was just—" She closed her eyes and rubbed her forehead with a couple of fingers, trying to think. "It was when I first...when the stories were first going up on the site, after the first couple weeks. When I was getting votes, and I logged on and saw I was number one, and I kept looking, all day. I was so excited that somebody was reading what I wrote, that they *liked* me. And I was having lunch with Gretchen, catching up, and...and I told her. It just...slipped out. She was the one person I could tell, because I was still a little...a little embarrassed, but I knew she wouldn't judge. And I had to tell *somebody*. I just...I *had* to."

"And you didn't think," he said, "that the person you should tell was me?"

"Well, no." Suddenly, she didn't feel quite so horrible. Not about this part. "How would I even have done that? You were *gone*. It's not like you'd kept in touch. It's not like we had some kind of relationship. You were just some guy I'd known for a little while, once upon a time. I started the story before I'd said more than twenty words to you, when all I knew about you was that you had muscles and a tattoo. We both did this, and we both made some money at it. And then you called me, out of the blue, and offered to pay me to come over here and pretend to be your girlfriend, and you said that was all it would be. Pretending."

"Except it wasn't, was it?" he asked, taking the wind right back out of her sails again. "Or was it? Was it all just pretending after all?"

"No! No. Of course it wasn't. How could you think that? And I should have told you, but then I thought, no, don't, because it's only for a few days." She was pleading now, she could hear it, but she couldn't help it. "I thought you might feel this way, that you wouldn't understand, and I didn't want to wreck it. It was so good, and I didn't want to ruin the little bit of time we had together, don't you see?"

"Except that something can't really be good if it's not real. If one person's still pretending after all."

She sat there, the guilt a leaden lump in her stomach, because she didn't have an answer for that.

"You should have told me, Faith," he went on after a minute, sounding so...sad. So final. "You should have given me the choice. I gave you the choice to get involved. You should have given it to me."

Her chest was aching, the tears trying to come. Because he was right. And it hurt so much.

"I'm sorry," she said, feeling all the inadequacy of the word. She wanted to crawl into a corner and hide. She'd done so much damage. She hadn't meant to, but that didn't matter. "I'm sorry if it's going to hurt your image. If it helps, I'll..." She fought to keep her voice under control while she cast around for something. Anything. "I'll...tell people I wasn't writing about you. I'll tell them you didn't know. That will help, won't it? Maybe?"

"I don't know. Maybe. I need to go. I need to get on the bus. When you come, we'll plan a story, I guess. Figure out how to pretend some more. One last time."

"All right." Her voice was so small, because that was how she felt. Small. "I'm sorry," she said again.

"Yeh," he said. "I'm sorry, too."

they always leave
♡

He had gone through the motions of getting on the bus, riding to the airport, going through check-in, just following the back of the fella in front of him. Not that anybody else was too chatty, either. It was always quiet the day after a match.

He needed to think, but he couldn't think. Too much anger. Too much disbelief, still. And too much...too much something else that he didn't want to examine too closely, because it might look like pain.

When he was in the Koru Lounge waiting for the flight to be called, the men around him thumbing over their phones, reading, or listening to music, he started to think that he should know. If he were going to talk to Ian about it, if he had to decide what to do, he needed to see for himself what was in those books, and exactly how bad it was. Because if she'd written anything too far out there, if she had Hemi hurting Hope...that could be very bad indeed. Ian could call it fiction all he wanted, and still, people would wonder how much of it was true. If she could really have made all that up.

Anyway, he had a choice. He could sit here packing a sad, or he could do something about it. At least he could read what she'd written. At least he could face the truth.

So he pulled out his laptop, went online, and bought all five stories, hating that he was giving Faith yet more money, paying her once again for the privilege of ruining his reputation, and began to read.

At first, he rolled his eyes in disbelief. Of course Hemi was a CEO. The only acceptable profession, apparently. And a multimillionaire. Not a billionaire? Wasn't Faith selling him a little short?

A designer, too—that was nothing but ridiculous. At least she could have let the bloke do software, or own a construction firm. Something remotely manly. He didn't see how this underwear magnate could maintain the physique she was describing, either. Building a body like that took time, and Hemi seemed to spend all of his sitting at the head of conference tables, jetting around the world in his company plane, and scheming to seduce his staff. But at least it wasn't too horrible. It was just...ridiculous. And it wasn't him. It so very clearly wasn't him.

By the time they got to Paris, though, he was...all right, he was interested. In fact, he'd almost forgotten that Faith had written it, and why he was reading it. And when Hemi pulled out his red ribbon...

Unfortunately, that was when they got the call to board. He wished he'd thought to download the story onto his phone, but too late now. He waited impatiently as the aircraft climbed, leaving Dunedin behind and heading over the Pacific.

The announcement came at last, and he was opening his laptop again. And an hour and a half later, he wasn't rolling his eyes anymore.

For the first few episodes, the story had been steamy enough that his eyes couldn't have rolled, because they'd been glued to the screen. This was *Faith*? They said men never read the instruction manual, but they were wrong, because he was pretty sure he was reading it, and he suddenly knew why everything they'd done in that motel room had worked for her. He was still furious with her, of course he was, but he was turned on as hell, too, and he couldn't help being impressed.

After that, though, he may have had to dab at his eyes a time or two. When Hope had been sitting at Karen's bedside as she regained consciousness, trying to be strong for her sister—well, you could hardly blame him, because he had a few sisters of his own, didn't he?

Now, his cup of tea was sitting cold and forgotten on the tray table, and he was still reading.

I opened the door to find Martine on the other side. "Nice place," she said. "Lucky you." She looked as polished as always, in a knit suit today that emphasized her willowy proportions. "Your sister's doing better, I take it?"

"Yes," I said. "Thank you," I hastened to add.

Martine didn't mention anything further, to my relief, while we sat at the round table in the suite's dining area and went through what looked like far more than a week's worth of work, but that I was somehow going to have to accomplish anyway.

"And that's it," Martine said crisply, shoving her laptop back into its Kate Spade bag. "Shouldn't be a problem, not with all your other needs taken care of so…thoroughly."

Her gaze traveled around the room, from the huge arrangement of roses and calla lilies on the marble coffee table to the windows overlooking the city, not to mention the two closed doors leading to the bedrooms.

Her eyes met mine again, and I realized I hadn't answered. "No," I hurried to say. "Of course it won't be a problem."

Martine hesitated, tapping an elegant fingernail against the clasp of her bag. "Can I make one more suggestion? A little word in your ear?"

"Of course." I managed to get the words out, hoping that my galloping pulse wasn't obvious. My emotions were so volatile these days, rocketing from the giddiest heights to the darkest depths. My brain and body seemed determined to force me to acknowledge the extent of my terror, now that it was over.

The lesser but still powerful anxiety about my job, my apartment, Karen's school, both of our futures still loomed. And always, underlying everything, the overwhelming need for Hemi, undeniable and irresistible as the tides, and just as dangerous.

There was desire there, of course there was, but that was the easy part. It was remembering his tenderness that was so devastating. The sweet rightness when I'd been in his arms after we'd made love, when his hand had been stroking down my back to soothe me. The leaping pleasure I'd felt at every text, every phone call. The thrill I'd received every time I'd opened my apartment door, had seen him standing outside, and had known that he was there for me.

I'd long ago been forced to admit, to myself if nobody else, that I loved him with an intensity, an understanding, and a connection that was all the more powerful for being unspoken. I loved him for his strength, yes, but I loved him more for his weaknesses. For how hard he worked to be the best, and how deeply he feared that he wasn't enough. And I missed him. I missed him so much.

Now, Martine smiled at me, and I had the uncomfortable feeling that all those thoughts were there to read in my transparent face.

"I know it's so tempting," she told me, "to think it will last. It's a beautiful dream, isn't it? But you know," she sighed, running two fingers lightly over the diamond pendant at her throat, "that's all it is. A dream. One brief shining moment. And the thing about dreams? You wake up."

I swallowed, but didn't trust myself to speak.

It's not a dream, *I wanted to say.* It's real. Because Hemi was *real. He might be handsome, he might be rich, he might be powerful, and Heaven knew he was the most desirable man I'd ever met. But he was so much more than that. He was a living, breathing, caring man whose emotions were as deep and strong as they were hidden.*

It wasn't the myth I loved. It was the man, in all his shining, glorious light and all his dark, disturbing shadows. The man who thought he had to hide both those sides from everybody, but who couldn't hide them from me, because I saw him, and I knew him, and I loved him.

"And then you wake up," Martine continued, and I forced myself to focus. "And you get a lovely present. A nice farewell gift. That's when you know it's over, when you get that token that you can keep to remember him by. Or that you can sell, of course, if you need the money more. If you've been picked up from the gutter, and you can't stand to go back there again."

I barely heard her, because Martine's fingers were still at her throat, stroking the huge diamond solitaire on its chain that she wore every day.

No. Surely not. It couldn't be true.

"Well." Martine stood to go. "You'll want to get to that work. You don't want to go back to the gutter, I know you don't, and for that? Work is the only solution. That's what's left after men leave. Because the thing about men?" She put a hand over mine for just a moment, the lightest of caresses. "They always leave."

♡♡♡

He didn't hear the announcement the first time, didn't realize they were landing until the flight attendant stopped by his seat, whisked his teacup into her rubbish bag, put a light hand on his laptop cover and said, "Time to shut it down."

He closed the lid hastily before she could see what he'd been reading, stowed his computer away in his backpack even as his fingers itched to open it again, to learn what was going to happen next.

Faith hadn't written porn. She hadn't even written erotica. She'd written a romance. She'd written a *story*.

Then his thoughts took another turn, and that was worse, because he was having to entertain an entirely new idea.

He's not you, she'd said. *He's my character.* And all the same…maybe it was more complicated than that.

Could she really have made all that up? Or was it possible, somehow, that some of that was…him? And her? He thought it could be. He thought it might be, and the idea was shaking him to the core. After everything that had happened, after everything he'd said to her, everything he'd thought…

The idea that she knew him. That she saw him, in all his light and all his shadow. And that despite all of that, despite everything she knew…that she loved him all the same.

forgiveness
♡

Faith was still sitting on the bed, still holding the phone in a nerveless hand, when the knock on the door came.

"Come in," she called.

Talia opened it, then made as if to shut it again. "Oh! Sorry."

"What?" Faith looked at her in surprise, then down at herself, realized she was still sitting in her bra and capris. "Oh. That's OK." She pulled the T-shirt over her head and tugged it into place.

"Um…" Talia said. "Mum says, can you come to the kitchen. Please," she added.

"Sure." Faith followed the girl downstairs, trying to force her mind back from the black hole it kept trying to fall into. From thinking about Will, and how he'd sounded. About how something that had seemed like the best thing that had ever happened in her life, being able to write a book, and having other people want to read it enough to pay money for it, had become—this. Was costing her—well, not Will, because she'd never had Will, and she never would. But was going to cost him so much, and that was just as bad. Or worse, because that was what it was. It was worse.

She tried to put on some kind of face for his mother. This

would be about the lift to the airport, maybe. Emere had finally thawed a bit, but soon, it would all be worse than ever. Faith entertained the craven hope that Will's family wouldn't find out about the books until after she'd left. Facing them would be so hard, if they heard the news while she was still here, if Will called back and told them.

Emere was standing in the middle of the kitchen, though, her body stiff, her face like iron. And it looked like it was all going to be happening now.

"I just got a call from a newspaper reporter," Emere said without preamble as soon as Faith and Talia walked in. "Telling me that you're writing books about your sex life with my son. Asking me if I have a comment."

Talia's shocked gaze flew to Faith's face. "No," she said. "Faith wouldn't."

"No," Faith said. All of a sudden, she couldn't feel her legs, was having to reach out to the counter for support, and was stumbling over the words. "I didn't. That is, I did, but it wasn't that."

Emere crossed her arms. "If you did, you did. I've had you in my house. I've fed you. And you've been doing that. And what I want to know is, did he know? Is this all some...joke, between the two of you? Bringing you here to be with us?"

Talia was backing away, but her mother put out an arm out for her. "No. You stay. You want to be grown up? Be grown up. Stay and face the truth. There's nothing to be gained by lying to yourself, or by not seeing what's in front of you. *Exactly* what's in front of you." Her hard stare let Faith know exactly what that was.

And then it got worse, because Miriama came into the room. "What's going on?" Will's grandmother asked. "Something's not good, eh."

"No," Emere said. "Something's not good."

Faith took a breath. Nothing to do but face this. Nothing left to do but tell the truth. As much of the truth as she could tell without hurting Will more, because she wasn't doing that. "Emere has found out," she told Miriama, "that I've been writing romance books, and publishing them."

Miriama cocked her head to one side. "And? Nothing wrong with romance."

"They're...steamy," Faith said. "They have sex in them."

Will's grandmother laughed, the sound incongruous in the midst of the tension that held the room in its grip. "And that's got your knickers in a twist?" she asked her daughter. "Seems to me, when you were Talia's age, I had all I could do to keep you from taking your knickers *off* for her dad. Have you forgotten that much? You need a man and no mistake. Nothing wrong with romance, and nothing in the world wrong with sex. And sex in a book? What could possibly be wrong with that?"

"It's not just sex in a book," Emere said. "It's sex about Will."

"No." Faith found her courage, because this was just wrong. She might as well practice saying it. She was going to be saying it again. "No, it isn't. It has nothing to do with Will, except that he's the cover model. The story is about an entirely different person. A fictional character."

"Except," Emere said, and there was that damning, inescapable truth, "that Will's photo is on the cover."

"Well," Miriama admitted, "that *is* a bit worse, maybe."

"A bit worse?" Emere demanded. "A *bit* worse?"

"Yes," Faith said. "His picture is on the cover. Of all five books," she added. That wasn't going to take them two minutes to find out. "Because Will posed for those pictures, and they're available on stock photo sites. The photographer's sold a lot of them, and I suspect that if you look around, you'll find that they're on quite a few other book covers, too. They're good shots, and Will is a very good-looking man."

"But none of those other books," his mother said, "was written by his girlfriend."

"That's true," Faith said. "At the time I started writing them, though, we weren't dating."

"Which excuses just about nothing," Emere said. "You could have taken them off the market. You could have changed their covers, I'm guessing. You could have done heaps of things. But I don't care about that, because I don't care about you. What I care about is Will. And what I want to know is, did he know?"

"No. He didn't." Faith looked around at the three women, Emere's face accusing, Miriama's thoughtful, and Talia's miserable. "He does now, because I just spoke to him. He's not any happier about it than you are. For the record, I didn't know it would get out. I have a pen name for exactly that purpose, to keep it private. But apparently it *has* gotten out, and that's my fault, too. I only told one person, but that was one too many. Except that I should have told one more. I should have told Will."

"Yes, you should have," Miriama said. "If he mattered to you. If you care." Her gaze was sharp, and all too knowing. "Which I think you do. Now."

The implication was clear. "You're right," Faith said. Time for honesty, as much as she could manage without making things worse for Will. "Things were a little...different at the beginning between us." That was all she was going to say about that. "But they changed. I do care now. I care a...a lot. I was wrong, and I'm sorry, and I know that's not enough. But I'll do whatever I can to make this easier on him."

Miriama nodded. "That's all you can do. It's a mistake. No," she corrected herself, "it's a wrong choice. A weak choice."

Faith winced, but it was true, and she had to face it.

"But we've all made wrong, weak choices," Miriama continued, and looked at her daughter. "Every single one of us. Especially when it comes to men."

"Don't you dare be comparing me to her," Emere's voice was rising. "Don't you *dare*. She did what she did for herself, and herself only. Every mistake I made, I made out of love for my kids, and for Anthony. Everything I've done since has come from trying to protect my kids."

"Maybe so," Miriama said. "And maybe a few things have come from trying to protect yourself. You'll know which are which, if you take a good hard look inside, the way Faith's doing now. But

Faith's just told us she's going to be trying to protect Will. That she knows she's hurt him, and that she's sorry for what she's done. And I'm guessing that some of her mistakes may have come from her feelings for him as well. Things are never quite that simple, because we're all human, eh."

"Human," Emere scoffed. "You always say that, like it excuses everything. Like everything is forgivable."

"Nah," Miriama said. "Some things aren't. Your man running out on you and your kids? That's not forgivable. But loving him so much that you kept taking him back when you shouldn't have? Loving him enough to get those kids? That's forgivable. Even if the person you have to forgive is yourself."

Emere was shaking, leaning back against the kitchen counter. "I'm not—I'm not talking about myself."

"Oh, darling," her mother said, the sharp planes of her face softening. "We're all talking about ourselves. Always, because the only way we see the world is through our own eyes. The way you've always seen Anthony in Will, and you're so scared that he's his dad all over again. That he's weak at the core after all, and that he'll disgrace you in the end, and desert you, too. This is all just one more way you're afraid he's done it. But he hasn't, and he won't, because he's not his dad. He's got you in him, too. He's got the mum who stayed, and stuck. That's why he'll never do a runner on the people he loves, no matter how heavy the burden gets. He'll take care of you until you're in your grave, and he'll take care of his brother and sisters as well. Because he's strong to the core, and solid to the bone. Because he's a good man."

Faith was frozen. She saw Talia standing just that still, too, but not Emere. Will's mother was trembling, the tears coming, and her own mother came to her, wrapped her slim, strong arms around her, and held her close.

"It's going to be all right in the end," Miriama told her daughter. "Will's going to cope. Just like you did. He always has, because he's got so much of you in him. He's got his Koro, too. That blood runs strong and deep, no matter how flash he may be on the surface. That's mana. And it sticks."

Faith felt the tears spilling over her lids, down her cheeks, brushed them away with a shaking hand, and saw Talia doing the same. She couldn't move. She was seeing something…something so private. Something so powerful.

Miriama looked at both of them from where she stood, still holding her weeping daughter. "All of us have made mistakes," she said. "Including me. Will told me—he was careful, but he told me all the same—that we hadn't paid enough attention to Talia since her Koro died, and he was right. Wrapped up in ourselves, weren't we. In our own grief, our own ways to cope. All you can do, though, when you make a mistake, when you make a wrong choice, is do your best to put it right. You've told Will you were wrong. Now, you'll make the choices you have to make so you don't hurt him more. That's putting it right, and it's all you can do."

♡♡♡

Faith slipped out of the kitchen. No point in staying here, because that was exactly the opposite of what she had to do, the choice she had to make so she wouldn't hurt Will more.

She had to leave. So she sat on the bed again, called the airline, and arranged for it to happen. The last thing he needed was to have her in his life anymore. So much better if it were over. If it came out, and she was gone, because she'd used him, and she'd left him. Exactly the way they'd planned in the beginning, and so much more necessary now.

So she made her arrangements, then hung up the phone, went to the closet, and pulled her suitcase down from the high shelf with an effort. She flung it onto the bed, began to pull clothes off hangers and fold them hastily into it, and tried not to think.

It took a different kind of effort not to look at Will's clothes hanging there beside hers. Looking like they belonged together, when they didn't. When that, like everything else, was an illusion that was over.

When a bubble popped, there was no magic and no power in the world that could put it back together again. That was why a bubble was so beautiful. Because it was so fragile, and because it was temporary.

She heard the knock at the door, and brushed a hasty hand across eyes that still insisted on leaking. "Come in," she called, and braced herself. If this was Will's mother coming up to tell her something else she'd forgotten to say, well, she had the right, and Faith was just going to have to endure it.

It was Talia.

"Hi," the girl said. She looked at the suitcase on the bed. "Um, I just wanted to…"

Faith sighed. "Sit down. And you can say it. Whatever it is." She tried to smile. "He's a pretty good brother, I know. You're allowed to defend him." She kept on packing, though, because it helped. She had no choice but to listen, but she couldn't stand to look at Talia while she did it.

"I didn't come to say anything bad," Talia said. "I came to say…I don't get it. So you wrote a story that has sex in it. Is that so bad? I mean," she hurried on, "I know Mum thinks so. But people do it, don't they, and if they like to read books about it, well…" She looked down and picked at the comforter a little. "I don't think it's so wrong. You can't help…thoughts. And," she said, looking at Faith again, "I think it's kind of cool that you wrote a book, actually."

"Well, that's how it felt to me." Faith was unable to resist the cowardly relief. At least *somebody* didn't think she was the devil personified. "It was about the coolest thing I've ever done, and I loved it, and it wasn't," she couldn't help saying, "It really *wasn't* about Will, so you know. I know people will think so, but it wasn't. It was my story, and my characters. I shouldn't have used him on the cover, and then it would have been better, but that was how the site started off, so…" She was running out of steam a little. "And he's so handsome," she admitted. "The book covers—he was the best."

"Yeh. He is. All my friends think so." Talia smiled at Faith a little proudly. "If you're going to write a sexy book, you have to use a sexy fella."

"But it was wrong not to tell Will about it," Faith went on hastily. "Don't let me off the hook that easily. Too many secrets, and the secret coming out to bite him, hurting him like that, well, of course he's upset, and of course your mother's upset for him."

"Mum's always upset," Talia said simply. "She worries something will happen, and then when it happens, she thinks she was right. So what are you going to do?"

"I'm going to leave." No point in not saying it. It was obvious.

"Well, I knew that."

"No, I mean I'm going to leave sooner. Tonight. Maybe it'll help. It's all I can do, so I'll do it. I've got to be at the airport in an hour, in fact. I guess I'd better call a taxi, because I don't think anybody's driving me." Faith hesitated for a moment. "You could do a favor for me, though, if you wouldn't mind. It would mean going as far as the bank with me, and mailing something to Will. Would you be willing?"

"Course. I could ride to the airport with you, too, see you off."

Faith choked up a little at that. "Thank you," she managed to say. "But I don't want to upset your mother and grandmother any more. But...the bank. That would be good."

die trying
♡

Will shuffled off the plane with the others and headed down the steep, narrow steps to the tarmac, following Koti's back. Just one of thirty-three blue dress shirts straggling in a queue across to the terminal, everybody moving a bit stiffly, three hours of sitting having tightened abused muscles once again.

He waited until the cameras had had their moment, and then he was pulling out his phone and ringing Faith, not even sure what to say.

No answer. Of course there would be no answer. She'd be on the plane to join him already, or waiting to board. And being Faith, she'd have turned off her phone, because that was the kind of good girl she was. He'd just have to wait until he saw her, would have to trust that feelings that strong couldn't have been destroyed by his anger, by the mess that was their situation just now, by the fact that he couldn't see exactly how they were going to get out of it.

If he'd been right, that is. If her feelings really *were* that strong. If it were real.

He couldn't wait for one thing, anyway. He needed to find out whether Hope could believe in Hemi.

297

Of course she could. It was a romance. It could only end one way. But all the same, he needed to read it for himself. Maybe what he needed to see most of all was whether Faith could believe. If he read it, he would know, because Faith couldn't tell anything less than the truth.

He was standing with the other fellas at the carousel, waiting for his bag, but he had his laptop out again, held in one arm, and was waiting impatiently for Book Five to appear on his screen.

"Cuz," Koti said beside him. "All right?"

"Huh?" Will looked up, blinking.

"You look … a bit odd," Koti said cautiously. "Something the matter? Bad news?"

"Nah," Will said. "I'm all good."

He wasn't. But he needed to read. So he went on and did it, all the way to the end. He was reading Hemi's thoughts, Hemi's reactions. But the answer still wasn't there.

I paced from the living room to the bedroom once again, not taking in one bit of my surroundings, unable to concentrate on the emails and calls I should have been answering. The suite at the Four Seasons Milano could have been the Holiday Inn, for all I was aware of it.

I should have heard from her by now. Had she hated it? Had she thought it was over the top? Or had she…I turned on a heel again on the thought as if walking faster could allow me to outrun it.

Had she decided, after all, that what I was offering wasn't enough? Now that Karen was out of danger, was she looking at her situation clearly for the first time, deciding that she didn't want a man who could never be there for her the way she needed him, could never say the words she needed to hear? Whose silences and absences were more than she could bear? All Hope's warmth, the shining force of her spirit—had it hit the wall of my reserve one too many times?

I should have called her more. I should have gone back sooner, no matter what. Or not have gone at all.

But this was who I was. This was all I had. My drive, my ambition, my success. What if it wasn't enough?

The phone vibrated in my hand, and I glanced at the caller ID. The leaping hope was there for a second, then gone in an instant.

"Te Mana."

"Mr. Te Mana, this is Charles Farquar at Tiffany," I heard. And then, damningly, the hesitation, and even before the man spoke again, I knew. I knew. *"I'm sorry, sir, but the necklace…came back."*

"Came…back." My blood was ice. "How?"

"The messenger said…" More hesitation.

"Just tell me," I snapped.

"Yes, sir. He said that he was still in the lobby when she came…flying out of the elevator. Agitated, he said. That she shoved it at him and said, 'Take it back.' I'm sorry, sir," he said again. "We'll credit your account of course."

I didn't answer. I was already hitting the End *button, getting my pilot on the phone.*

"Warm it up," I said. "We're going home."

Maybe I couldn't do it. Maybe it was going to be the thing that defeated me. The thing that crushed me.

But I was going to do it anyway, or I was going to die trying.

♡♡♡

Will looked up again, blinking. Koti was setting his duffel next to his feet.

"One too many knocks last night?" his teammate asked. "Need a ding-dong test? When the bags come along on the wee roundabout, we pick them up."

"Oh. Thanks."

"Need a lift? Kate will be out there."

"Nah." Will brought himself back to earth with an effort. "Hanging about here for a bit, meeting Faith's plane in an hour or so."

And then he'd be saying…something. He wasn't sure what. But surely he could think of something by then. He had an hour to do it.

Except that he didn't. An hour later, he was standing outside Security, and the flight had landed twenty minutes ago, and Faith wasn't here.

He couldn't have missed her. He'd scanned every face, had tensed with every new group that had come through, had rehearsed what he planned to say again and again. But she'd never come out. He'd rung her twice, and his phone had gone straight to voicemail both times.

Finally, he walked to the Air New Zealand counter, stepped up behind the single person in the queue at Premier Check-in, and waited some more, until the woman behind the counter was looking up and beckoning to him.

"Hi," he told her. "My partner was meant to be on Flight 2354 from Rotorua, and she didn't come out. Can you check for me?"

He gave her Faith's name, and she looked at her monitor. "She's not listed on the flight," she told him.

"What?" Cold fingers of dread were creeping up his spine. "I know she was. I saw her make the booking, and she sent me a copy of the itinerary."

"I'm sorry." She knew who he was, he could tell. "But she's not on it."

"Then...what? Another flight?"

"I can't check that. Against the rules. Sorry."

"Please. I've rung her, got no answer, and I'm worried."

"Sorry," she said again. "I can't. I would if I could."

He wasn't going to get anywhere, and anyway, he didn't have to, because, he realized, he could just ring his mum. He didn't know why he hadn't thought of that.

He did it, and that was when the fun didn't start. It took ten minutes of listening, of trying to explain, to get her past it.

"So she left early," he finally said. "Why? And to go where?"

"I don't know," his mum said. "We weren't exactly having a cozy chat, were we."

He finally rang off in frustration, thought a moment longer, and rang Talia.

"D'you know where Faith is?" he asked her. "She left early, eh. So where did she go? Did she come here? I can't get her to answer, and I'm worried."

A long silence on the other end.

"Talia?" he prompted. "You there?"

"Yeh," she said slowly. "But I'm not sure if I should tell you."

"Tell me. Tell me what she said."

"Well...she's going back to the States."

"I know that," he said impatiently. "Of course she is."

"I mean, she's going today. She got an earlier flight, so she could. Flying to LA. I saw the boarding pass, when she...when we were in the taxi."

"What?"

"She gave me an envelope. To post to you."

"And? Did you post it?"

"No. Not yet."

"Then get it. Please," he thought to add. "Open it. Read it to me."

"I guess if she gave it to me, it doesn't matter if I post it or open it now. I mean, if it's for you anyway."

"Of course it doesn't." He did his best to soften his tone. "Please, Tal. Please read it to me. I need to know what it says."

She exhaled. "Right, then. Hang on."

He waited, pacing in front of the windows near the ticket counter, oblivious to the occasional curious glance of recognition.

"OK," he heard at last. "I'm back. I'm opening it."

A rustle, and he was pacing again.

"Money," she said.

"Money? Why money?"

"Dunno. Looks like...six hundred dollars. That's a *lot* of money. And a note. D'you want me to read it?"

"Yes."

"OK. Here you go." She cleared her throat and began.

"Will—

This is all I could take out of the ATM. I'll get you the rest when I'm home. I shouldn't have taken it. I shouldn't have come at all. I know it, and I'm sorry.

301

I'm flying home tonight. I hope that'll make it easier for you to do what you have to do.

Faith."

"Something else," Talia said. "Written at the bottom. Can hardly read it. It's a bit—scrawly."

"Read it," Will commanded. "Much as you can."

"Being with you wasn't about the money, or the books," his sister read slowly. *"It was about you."*

"What money?" she asked him when she'd finished. "I don't understand. Did she steal from you? I can't believe Faith would do that."

"No. I've got to..." He was having trouble with his voice. "Got to go."

"I think you should find her," Talia said. "I think she loves you. When she gave me this...she was crying."

♡♡♡

He rang off, tried to ring Faith again in the hope that she might have turned on her phone. Voicemail again, but he knew where she was now. She was here.

Back to the Air New Zealand counter again, back in the queue, behind two other passengers this time. A middle-aged couple who fumbled for passports, then seemed to be buying a cruise, based on the amount of time the agent was spending tapping details into her computer, and Will was bouncing the phone in his hand, seething.

At last, though, it was his turn.

"I still can't tell you," the agent said, eyeing him suspiciously.

"I don't need you to tell me," Will said. "I need you to get me on tonight's flight to LA."

More tapping from long red-varnished fingernails, while he shifted from foot to foot and waited.

"Sorry," she finally said. "Sold out."

"What? No."

"Sold out," she repeated. And then, as if he might be too dim to get that, "No seats left."

"I know what sold out means. Sell me one anyway. Somebody can volunteer to be bumped, right? Get a lovely voucher for a free journey. Happens all the time. I'll pay for it myself, but I need to get on there."

She stared at him. "No."

"Look," he said. "My girlfriend's on that flight. She's leaving me. I need to get on there and get her back."

"You think that's making it better," the woman said, "but you're wrong, because you just escalated from Potentially Scary to Security Risk, and I'm about two seconds away from getting them over here. If I didn't know who you were, I'd have done it already, but that blue shirt's only going to take you so far, and you've just reached it. I can't sell you a ticket I don't have. No."

"Right," he said. "Plan B." There was always a Plan B, and a Plan C, and on down the list. "Sell me a ticket to Las Vegas however you can do it, the one that gets in at the closest time to the flight that connects from LA."

More endless clicking. "Have to connect through San Francisco," she said. "And a three-hour layover."

"Fine. Good. Do it." He pulled out his credit card and shoved it across the counter together with his passport. "Go." He glanced at the monitor above the woman's head that listed the departing flights. San Francisco in two hours. And LA in one. He hefted his duffel onto the platform. Sacrificed to the cause.

"You know," she said as she began the insanely tedious process of booking him in, "if she doesn't want you, there's no point."

"That's helpful. Cheers."

"Sometimes a man has to take no for an answer," she said, "no matter who he is."

And sometimes, Will didn't say, because that would have brought Security running for sure, *he has to die trying.*

After that, it was passport control, and security, and all the rest of it. And then he was running, because the flight for LA left in forty-five minutes, and they'd be boarding any minute. Up the stairs, taking them three at a time, past the wine bar, all the way to the end of the corridor.

Where he stopped. Because he'd forgotten this. Completely forgotten.

Another security gate, a cobbled-together one just beyond the seating area where the passengers waited to board. Two little tables, each manned by an agent. One last scanner to walk through. One final inspection before boarding a flight to the States.

Maybe, though…He pulled out his passport and boarding pass, chose the table with a woman at it, and handed them over. He gave her his best smile in hopes that it would distract her, keep her from looking too closely at what was on that boarding pass. Who knew, maybe she liked big, wild-eyed, sweating Maori blokes.

Or maybe not, because she was handing his documents straight back to him. "Wrong gate, love," she said. "You want 13 for San Fran."

"Actually," he said, trying, this time, for something that sounded more confiding and less like a mad, scary ex, "I was hoping to nip in for just a moment. My partner and I got separated. Flight's sold out, eh. She's on this one, and I need a quick word."

"Can't do it, sorry. Why don't you call her, have her come out? They haven't started boarding them yet."

"See, that's the silly thing. Her phone's off. If I could—just for a minute."

"Can't," she said again. "It'd be my job." She glanced at the fella at the other table, and he nodded.

"Can't," he told Will, as if he wouldn't have heard it the first time. "Will Tawera, aren't you?" he asked. "Well done last night, by the way."

"Cheers," Will said. "So you see, not a security risk. Tell you what, you can hold my passport and boarding pass," he thought to add. "I won't be going anywhere without them. Five minutes. That's all."

"Nah, mate," the man said. "Sorry. Can't."

Will could hear the announcement coming over the

loudspeaker. They were about to start boarding, and it was now or never.

Die trying.

He filled his lungs with the training of years spent shouting to his backline over the voices of sixty thousand rabid fans.

"Faith!"

Both agents jumped, and he heaved in another breath and did it again.

"FAITH!"

"What are you doing?" the woman exclaimed as the man began to rise, his radio in his hand.

"What you said," Will said. "I'm calling her."

stay

♡

Faith sat with her forehead pressed against the little oval window and watched the ground fall away beneath her. The ribbons of rain that streaked horizontally across the glass were a perfect match for the tears that ran down her cheeks. She'd tried so hard not to give into them, but it wasn't possible anymore, not now that she was here. Not now that she was leaving.

She had one last brief glimpse of silver lake, the green folds of the hills. The emerald of fern trees, and the darker color of the mighty giants through whose tops she and Will had walked, on a carefree day that felt like a lifetime ago.

Just one glimpse, and then it was all gone, lost beneath a layer of gray cloud that lay between her and her last moments in Rotorua.

Kua hinga te totara i te wao nui a Tane. A totara had fallen in the forest of Tane. When it fell, it left a hole in your life. In your heart.

A mercifully short flight, this one, and they were through the cloud cover again, descending over the western suburbs of Auckland, and touching down. Passport control, security, one last polite Kiwi smiling at her and telling her to have a pleasant flight, and that was goodbye. She was at the gate for Flight NZ6 to Los Angeles, almost the only passenger here this early, sitting for two hours as the seats gradually filled around her. Sitting looking out at the big white jets lined up on the tarmac, *Air New Zealand* emblazoned on their sides, the stylized swirl of the koru on their tails.

The symbol of life, of hope, of new beginnings. Of everything that was New Zealand, but not for her. Not anymore. Not ever, no matter how it had felt, because she'd never really belonged here. Because it had all just been pretending after all.

There was a dad beside her now, big and brown, holding a curly-haired toddler in one broad arm to look at the jets, a stroller at his feet. She saw the flash of white teeth as he talked to his little boy, his big hand at the end of a tattoo-bedecked arm pointing to a baggage cart trundling out to load suitcases onto a jumbo jet.

That was nothing to do with her, either. That was the worst kind of wishful thinking. She could put it into a book, and that was all.

Those who can, do. Those who can't, teach. She'd always hated that saying. But she knew one that worked, at least for her. *Those who can't, write.*

And all the same, she would sit here and look at all of it until she couldn't see it anymore. Until she was in a darkened cabin, flying through the night back to her real life, her lonely life, drinking one too many glasses of wine and watching a movie she wouldn't really see, just so she could finally find the comfort of sleep.

She would go back to her life, she would live it as best she could, and she would try to be grateful for what New Zealand had given her. Even if that was only book material.

She didn't realize the shout was for her at first, so lost in her thoughts was she. But as the second one came, she was rising in disbelief.

"FAITH!"

It was a bellow, and other passengers had turned to check out the disturbance, but Faith barely noticed them. She was hurrying through the gate area, her laptop bag swinging from her shoulder, banging against her side. And then she was screeching to a stop at one side of the security post.

Because, of course, the bellower had been Will.

Will, standing smack-dab in the center of two beleaguered security agents who were on their feet now, his legs planted as if it would take an army to move him. Showing, for once, how much of the easygoing manner was a disguise for the steel beneath.

"Will," she said weakly. "Why?"

"We were going to talk," he said. "Remember that?"

Her heart, which had begun to beat so hard at the sight of him, settled right back down again. Sank, if the truth were known. Of course that was why he was here. He thought she was running away so she didn't have to face him. And it was true, but not in the way he thought.

"If you came here to yell at me some more," she said, "I guess you've got the right. I'm here, and so are you. So go ahead." She wrapped her arms around herself to bear it. "I thought this would make it easier for you. That you could say whatever you needed to say about me that would make things better, without worrying about hurting me. Because I knew you'd worry about that, no matter how angry you were. I thought that this way, I could be gone. I could have run, have used you and dumped you. I could just be the bad guy."

"And you think that's all I care about. You think that's all that matters." His own arms were folded across his broad chest, and he looked nothing but fierce. Nothing but furious.

"I know it is," she said sadly. "I know how much it matters. You care so much about rugby, and you care about taking care of your family. Which is nothing but good, and which is what makes you so..." She swallowed. "So special. But what I did, what I am...it's in the way of both things, and I don't want to get in your way. I'm trying to do the right thing, and it's so..." She took a breath and tried to still the trembling that was taking over now.

"It's so hard. But I'm trying to do it anyway. So say what you need to say to me, and I'll listen, and then I'll leave."

"That would be brilliant," he said, "if that was what I wanted. But I care about more than that. This thing coming out right now—it isn't good. I'd be lying if I said it was. But it isn't the end."

"But it *is* the end, whether I leave today or tomorrow. It was always the end." It hurt so much to say it. Even more than it hurt to know it.

His arms weren't folded now, and he was leaning forward a little. Looking like he wanted to walk straight through the barrier, and her heart had begun to beat out a wild tattoo of wishing. Of longing. If only…if only…

"Only if you want to go," he said, and her heart was galloping so fast now, it was about to leap from her chest. "Only if we make that true. But we have a choice. We can choose to ride it out instead, and there's no reason in the world we can't do that. All right, you wrote some sexy books, and there'll be a bit of excitement about that. And so what?"

"So…plenty." She fought to pull herself back under control. He *wanted* her? He did? How could that even be possible? "Plenty, because they've got your picture on them. And because I wrote them, and because my hero looks exactly like you. Because everybody's going to think he *is* you, and if I'd known everything that would happen, I'd never have done it, but I did, and it's out there, and it can't be undone. Because I can't put the genie back in the bottle. It's too late."

The two security agents, who had sat down again, were twisted in their chairs now, looking between the two of them with some fascination. "Really?" the woman said.

"Yeh," Will told her. "This is Faith Goodwin. My girlfriend, who's written some sexy books with my photo on the covers. You can read all about it tomorrow. And you can read the books, too. You should, because they're good. Even though, sorry to say, they're not about me."

"You didn't…" Faith tried to say. "You didn't read them."

"Yeh. I did. And you're right, and you're wrong. Hemi isn't me. Nothing like me. And Hope isn't you. But you haven't just written sexy books. You've written a story, and it's a bloody good one. You've written something real. You made me choke up, and you may even have made me cry. You made me care."

"I...I did?" She couldn't believe it. She'd made him *cry?*

"Yeh," he said, and his face was so—so sweet. "You made me need to read the end, to know that Hemi's going to be able to convince Hope that she can trust him. I need to know that he's going to be there for her and Karen. And I wouldn't say that I'm your target audience. So if you want to write stories, I think you should go on and write them. We all need to do the thing we're best at. I need to play rugby, and you need to write books. And I think we need to do those things together."

She made a little gesture, just a rise and fall of her hand. Helpless. Hopeless. "But it's...we can't. Not now, not with all this happening. It's too late."

"No. No. I'm not going to believe it's too late. It's never too late. Meeting you, knowing you, all of this? It happened at the right time. The only time I could hear it. The only time I could know it. It happened just in time."

"I need to..." She was having trouble breathing. "I need to go back. I have a ticket. I have...jobs."

"I know you do. But it seems to me—" Now he was the one hesitating. "That you could have a new job. Just one this time. That you could stay here and write books. That you could stay with me."

"With you?" She still had her arms wrapped around herself, and she was still shaking, but for a different reason now.

"Yeh. With me. You could stay here, and we could see. I know it's mad. I know it's too soon, and I don't care. Because I also know it's right, and I think you do, too. And I can't stand to let you get away without trying to hold you. I don't know many things for sure, but I know this. When you put yourself to the test, when you put everything you have on the line—that's a risk, because you could find out that you're not good enough. You can play your guts out, and it still may not be enough. But if you don't play, you'll have no chance at all."

"Calling your flight," the male security agent told Faith helpfully. She looked back behind her and hesitated.

"No," Will said, and she looked back at him. "Stay. Please, Faith. Stay. Walk to me. Just take the walk."

"And then what?"

He closed his eyes, then opened them again. "I don't know," he admitted. "I don't have a clue, because this isn't a book, and I'm not a billionaire, and I don't have all the answers. I'm just a...bloke. I don't own a company, I don't have a jet, and I don't have a limousine, and I never will. I'm just a bloke who makes a pretty good wage that could end the day I get one too many concussions or bugger my knee one too many times. I'm a bloke who's got two mortgages, and a mum, and a grandmother, and a brother and sister to put through Uni. I didn't send you a necklace while I was gone. I barely sent you a text. But for better or worse, this is me. No more pretending. This is everything I am. Just a man, standing here in front of you and telling you that I want you, and I need you, and I...I think I love you."

She stared at him, and tried to think of something to say, and failed completely.

"You don't think I mean it," he said. "Or you don't think I can do it. And the truth is, I don't know either. I don't know the first thing about being in love, and I'm sure I'll stuff up all over the shop. But I know it's there, I know it's real, and I don't want to let it go. I can't let you go without a fight, because we're worth taking a chance on, if you think...if you think you might be able to love me, too."

"I don't..." she said. "My suitcase is on the plane. I don't have any clothes. And your mother hates me."

He laughed a little at that. "Oh, baby. We can go shopping. And your mother hates me just as much. It doesn't matter. We've got all the time in the world to change their minds. Just...stay. Please. Stay. Even though I'm not a billionaire, and I've never been the

311

hero of anybody's story. I'm nowhere close to perfect, and I know it. But I need you to believe in me all the same."

She couldn't help it, the tears had spilled over again, and she was crying. Because maybe, just maybe...it was true.

"Of course you're a hero," she told him. "You're your family's hero, and you're mine. You're such a good man, and you don't even know it. And I love you, too. Of course I do. I think I've loved you since that night on the roof, when you opened your heart that little bit to me, because your heart is...it's beautiful. There's so much more in you than you show, and it's so special. I don't know why you don't know that, but if you need me to believe in you, you don't have to wish for that, because I already do. And why would I want a billionaire if I could have you? Why would I want a tortured soul? If I didn't write you, it's only because some things are too precious to share. Some things are just...mine. Some things are only for my heart to hold. I don't want Hemi any more than I hope you want Hope. I want you."

"Well, that's good." He was smiling a little now, even though his smile didn't look very steady. "Because I don't want Hope. Not that she isn't awesome. But she's not funny enough for me, and not curvy enough, and not saucy enough, either. I don't want Hope. I want Faith. Because hope is...hope is wishing. But faith is believing."

She was *really* crying now. Standing there on the other side of the barrier and completely losing it, and behind her, they were calling her name.

"Please, baby." His face was so sweet, and so urgent. Like this was all he wanted. Like it was everything. "Walk to me. Stay. I need you. Please. Stay."

It was a choice, and it was no choice at all. She took the walk. Right through the barrier, and straight into his arms.

"Closing the door," the female agent said.

"Yeh," Will told her, his arms around Faith, holding her so close. Holding her so tight, her face buried in the damp cotton of his shirt. "You tell them to go on and close it. Faith's suitcase can go all the way to Vegas. But she's staying right here."

epilogue

♡

Two months later

"What do you think?" Faith burst out as if she couldn't help herself.

"Shh," Will said. "Let me finish."

He could feel the tense expectancy vibrating in her where she lay stretched out beside him on the deck of the sailboat. It made him smile a little, and touched him, too, that she cared so much about his opinion.

She'd refused to publish the final installment of her novel until the fuss had died down over what she called "my dirty stories," and until she'd known that he was securely back in the New Zealand rugby fold. Today, though, two weeks into the Rugby Championship and with his starting position on the All Blacks secure, she'd pushed the button, and Hope and Hemi's final episode was live.

There'd been a few rocky weeks in there, it was true, but nothing the two of them hadn't been able to ride out together. And the delay, the publicity, the anticipation hadn't hurt her sales one bit. Faith had become, in fact, almost the only person he loved who didn't need his money, and wasn't that something?

And yet, despite nearly two months of delay, she hadn't allowed him to read this final episode until she'd published it.

"I can't stand to," she'd tried to explain when he'd asked. "If you don't like it, what do I do?"

"I'll like it, though. I know I would. I've liked it so far, haven't I?"

"You *said* you did. But if you thought it was cheesy..." She'd hid her face in her hand. "Oh," she'd groaned. "What if it *is* cheesy?"

"Well," he'd said reasonably, "that could be why you'd want me to read it."

"No. Not until it's up."

So he'd waited. Now, he held the tablet up against a backdrop of stars and read. And when he finished, he set the tablet down, barely knowing what he was doing, put a finger and thumb to his eyes, and sighed.

"What?" Faith asked, her voice anxious. "What? Bad?"

"Sweetheart." He laughed a little. "No. You've made me..." He did a bit more repair work. "You've made me cry."

"Really?"

"You don't need to sound so pleased about it," he said a little crossly. "Bloody hell." He sniffed. "They'd better not make a film, or I'm going to lose it."

She sighed gustily with relief. "Oh, good."

"Yeh," he said. "Just that good. How did you think of all that? All those...feelings?"

She turned her head to look at him. "How? From loving you, of course. From knowing how I felt about you. How scared I was that you could never feel the same way, and how hard I fought it, because I was so sure there was nothing but pain there for me. From thinking about what would make my own heart swell to hear, and what would make me cry."

He swallowed at that. "Well, so you know—If you said those

things to me, they'd make my heart swell, too. And you already made me cry."

"Mmm." She snuggled closer, put an arm across his chest, and he got an arm under her so he could hold her. "So it was good, huh?" she asked again, as if she couldn't help it.

"Yeh," he said. "It was bloody good, and I'm so proud of you. My brilliant partner. But maybe what I'm offering this weekend isn't quite enough. Should I have brought you a necklace instead?"

She levered herself up to kiss his cheek, then settled down again. "No," she said tenderly. "That's fiction. I love what you're offering. Because mostly, what I want is you."

It wasn't her story, now, that was making him choke up, and he pulled her a little closer and bent to kiss her himself, because unlike Hemi, he didn't have words for this.

He had the right place, though. They were anchored off Tiritiri Matangi in the outer reaches of the Hauraki Gulf, the gentle slap of the waves against the hull the only sound breaking the winter silence. A bit chilly, of course, but they were cozy all the same in their sleeping bag, and if she got too cold, all he had to do was take her to the berth in the cabin below. There was nobody else around, not even another boat, on this early-September Sunday. Nobody to keep them company but the handful of visitors bedded down in the bird sanctuary's bunkhouse, the little blue penguins, and the kiwis, and that was fine by him. That was perfect.

"I promised you a sky full of stars once," he said at last. "Took me a while, but I got there in the end. I may not have brought you diamonds, but I brought you these. Or at least I brought you to them."

"You did." Her satisfied sigh came to rest somewhere deep in his soul. "And they're exactly what I wanted."

They lay a minute more in silence, the black night around them broken by a million tiny pinpricks of stars, and best of all, the broad swath of creamy light that was the Milky Way. He heard her intake of breath, and a split-second later, saw the reason for it. A meteor arcing its way across the vastness of space, trailing a cloud of white behind it.

"What is it to the Maori, do you know?" she asked, sounding dreamy. "A shooting star. Does it mean something?"

"It's a Raririki. A little shining one. One of the children of Rangi, the Sky Father, playing across his father's robe, tripping and falling."

"A good thing, or a bad thing?"

"A bright one like that? Good thing. Good omen."

"Good." She snuggled closer, and he held her just a little bit tighter.

"What does it mean to you?" he asked.

"Well, when I was a little girl, I read that it meant you got one wish. But I've never seen one before, because I haven't seen the stars enough. This is my first."

"So what's your one wish?"

Silence, and then a sigh. "If I tell," she said, "it doesn't come true."

"Ah. Scared to trust it, are you, even after everything we've been through. Scared to think it could last. Or that's wishful thinking of my own, maybe."

"Not—no. Not wishful thinking." Her voice was so tentative. As if she didn't dare believe it. As if she hardly dared even wish for it. He knew exactly how she felt, because he felt the same way. But it was time to go ahead and speak the wish aloud. There was a point when you had to put it out there, and it was now.

He waited a moment, trying to think how to say it, and then decided there was no perfect way. There was only doing his best, and hoping it was enough. So he took a breath and did it.

"It's hard, isn't it, to take that leap," he said. "To close your eyes and step out into space, and trust that I'll be there to catch you. Even that you can say it, that you can tell me what you wish for. But you can, you know. I'm standing right here with my hands out to pull you in, and I'm going to stay here. And I'll be counting on you the same way, because it's exactly the same leap for me. Nothing to hold onto but you, nobody but you to catch me if I fall.

317

It's a leap of faith, is what it is, and the only way to take it is together."

"Oh. That's..." She'd turned onto her side, not looking at the stars anymore. She was looking at him instead.

"Solomon rang me the other day to tell me he's got that spot at last," he told her. "That he'll be on the squad for the Outlaws, and not the practice squad. He may be a starter and he may not, but he'll be digging deep for it. If he doesn't make it, it won't be because he didn't try."

"That's...that's great news."

"And you're wondering why I told you that at this particular moment. It's because of this. Because that last day, when I was leaving Las Vegas, he and I were talking about this mad life we've got, about how much he's had to move, all the teams. About all the travel you do when you're a sportsman. And he said something to me, talking about Lelei. He said, 'Home is where she is.' I wondered how that would feel, and I knew I didn't have a clue. And now I do. I know that these past couple months, when I've been gone, when I'm flying home...I'm coming back to New Zealand, yeh, and that's home, and that matters. But I'm also coming home to you. I know it's home, because you're there."

He thought she might be crying a little. He put a hand out and found he was right, wiped the tears from her cheek with a gentle thumb. "Dunno if crying's a good thing right now, or a bad one," he said, trying to laugh and failing. "I've got my heart in my throat here. Or maybe I should say I've got it in your hands. Maybe you could give me a hint."

"It's—it's a good thing," she said. "Because this isn't my home, but it...it is. Because you're here. Because when you come home, it's the day I've waited for."

No woman whose eyes are lighting up because you're home, and this is the day she's had circled on her calendar.

He heard Koro saying it, and he looked out beyond Faith to the stars overhead, and knew that he was up there, and that somehow, he knew. That his wayward grandson had found it at last, and that, most of all, he'd been able to recognize it. Because of everything his Koro had taught him about living his life like it mattered.

You can stay. You can stick. Your choice. Your life. You can run away from it. Or you can run towards it.

He was going to run towards it. Starting right now.

"Your tourist visa's almost up," he told her.

"Uh...I know."

"Another thing you're wondering why I'm saying. I'm saying there's another kind of visa you could get, so I can keep coming home to you. If this is a life you think you can live, and if you want to live it with me. And it's a..." He breathed deep, felt all those old shackles falling away, and said it. "It's a fiancée visa. And if it's too soon," he hurried to add when she didn't answer right away, "we can wait as long as you like for the wedding. We can wait a year, if that's how long it takes you to be sure. But I can't let you go home, not without trying to keep you. I've got to try. I've got to take the leap. I've got to hope that you'll be there to catch me."

"Oh, Will." She was crying for real now. "Of course I'll catch you. I'll always catch you. And how can I go home?" She laughed a little, and it wasn't steady at all. He could feel her shaking, and he needed to hold her so badly.

"I'm already here," she told him, her voice so tender, "because that's what love is, isn't it? I'm already home. Because I'm with you."

♡♡♡

the end

319

a kiwi glossary

A few notes about Maori pronunciation:

- The accent is normally on the first syllable.
- All vowels are pronounced separately.
- All vowels except u have a short vowel sound.
- "wh" is pronounced "f."
- "ng" is pronounced as in "singer," not as in "anger."

ABs: All Blacks
across the Ditch: in Australia (across the Tasman Sea). Or, if you're in Australia, in New Zealand!
advert: commercial
agro: aggravation
air con: air conditioning
All Blacks: National rugby team. Members are selected for every series from amongst the five NZ Super 15 teams. The All Blacks play similarly selected teams from other nations.
ambo: paramedic
Aotearoa: New Zealand (the other official name, meaning "The Land of the Long White Cloud" in Maori)
arvo, this arvo: afternoon
Aussie, Oz: Australia. (An Australian is also an Aussie. Pronounced "Ozzie.")
bach: holiday home (pronounced like "bachelor")
backs: rugby players who aren't in the scrum and do more running, kicking, and ball-carrying—though all players do all jobs and play both offense and defense. Backs tend to be faster and leaner than forwards.
bangers and mash: sausages and potatoes
barrack for: cheer for
bench: counter (kitchen bench)
berko: berserk
Big Smoke: the big city (usually Auckland)
bikkies: cookies
billy-o, like billy-o: like crazy. "I paddled like billy-o and just barely made it through that rapid."

320

bin, rubbish bin: trash can

bit of a dag: a comedian, a funny guy

bits and bobs: stuff ("be sure you get all your bits and bobs")

blood bin: players leaving field for injury

Blues: Auckland's Super 15 team

bollocks: rubbish, nonsense

boofhead: fool, jerk

booking: reservation

boots and all: full tilt, no holding back

bot, the bot: flu, a bug

Boxing Day: December 26—a holiday

brekkie: breakfast

brilliant: fantastic

bub: baby, small child

buggered: messed up, exhausted

bull's roar: close. "They never came within a bull's roar of winning."

bunk off: duck out, skip (bunk off school)

bust a gut: do your utmost, make a supreme effort

Cake Tin: Wellington's rugby stadium (not the official name, but it looks exactly like a springform pan)

caravan: travel trailer

cardie: a cardigan sweater

chat up: flirt with

chilly bin: ice chest

chips: French fries. (potato chips are "crisps")

chocolate bits: chocolate chips

chocolate fish: pink or white marshmallow coated with milk chocolate, in the shape of a fish. A common treat/reward for kids (and for adults. You often get a chocolate fish on the saucer when you order a mochaccino—a mocha).

choice: fantastic

chokka: full

chooks: chickens

Chrissy: Christmas

chuck out: throw away

chuffed: pleased

collywobbles: nervous tummy, upset stomach

come a greaser: take a bad fall

costume, cossie: swimsuit (female only)

cot: crib (for a baby)
crook: ill
cuddle: hug (give a cuddle)
cuppa: a cup of tea (the universal remedy)
CV: resumé
cyclone: hurricane (Southern Hemisphere)
dairy: corner shop (not just for milk!)
dead: very; e.g., "dead sexy."
dill: fool
do your block: lose your temper
dob in: turn in; report to authorities. Frowned upon.
doco: documentary
doddle: easy. "That'll be a doddle."
dodgy: suspect, low-quality
dogbox: The doghouse—in trouble
dole: unemployment.
dole bludger: somebody who doesn't try to get work and lives off unemployment (which doesn't have a time limit in NZ)
Domain: a good-sized park; often the "official" park of the town.
dressing gown: bathrobe
drongo: fool (Australian, but used sometimes in NZ as well)
drop your gear: take off your clothes
duvet: comforter
earbashing: talking-to, one-sided chat
electric jug: electric teakettle to heat water. Every Kiwi kitchen has one.
En Zed: Pronunciation of NZ. ("Z" is pronounced "Zed.")
ensuite: master bath (a bath in the bedroom).
eye fillet: premium steak (filet mignon)
fair go: a fair chance. Kiwi ideology: everyone deserves a fair go.
fair wound me up: Got me very upset
fantail: small, friendly native bird
farewelled, he'll be farewelled: funeral; he'll have his funeral.
feed, have a feed: meal
first five, first five-eighth: rugby back—does most of the big kicking jobs and is the main director of the backs. Also called the No. 10.
fixtures: playing schedule
fizz, fizzie: soft drink
fizzing: fired up

flaked out: tired
flash: fancy
flat to the boards: at top speed
flat white: most popular NZ coffee. An espresso with milk but no foam.
flattie: roommate
flicks: movies
flying fox: zipline
footpath: sidewalk
footy, football: rugby
forwards: rugby players who make up the scrum and do the most physical battling for position. Tend to be bigger and more heavily muscled than backs.
fossick about: hunt around for something
front up: face the music, show your mettle
garden: yard
get on the piss: get drunk
get stuck in: commit to something
give way: yield
giving him stick, give him some stick about it: teasing, needling
glowworms: larvae of a fly found only in NZ. They shine a light to attract insects. Found in caves or other dark, moist places.
go crook, be crook: go wrong, be ill
go on the turps: get drunk
gobsmacked: astounded
good hiding: beating ("They gave us a good hiding in Dunedin.")
grotty: grungy, badly done up
ground floor: what we call the first floor. The "first floor" is one floor up.
gumboots, gummies: knee-high rubber boots. It rains a lot in New Zealand.
gutted: thoroughly upset
Haast's Eagle: (extinct). Huge native NZ eagle. Ate moa.
haere mai: Maori greeting
haka: ceremonial Maori challenge—done before every All Blacks game
hang on a tick: wait a minute
hard man: the tough guy, the enforcer
hard yakka: hard work (from Australian)

harden up: toughen up. Standard NZ (male) response to (male) complaints: "Harden the f*** up!"

have a bit on: I have placed a bet on [whatever]. Sports gambling and prostitution are both legal in New Zealand.

have a go: try

Have a nosy for… : look around for

head: principal (headmaster)

head down: or head down, bum up. Put your head down. Work hard.

heaps: lots. "Give it heaps."

hei toki: pendant (Maori)

holiday: vacation

honesty box: a small stand put up just off the road with bags of fruit and vegetables and a cash box. Very common in New Zealand.

hooker: rugby position (forward)

hooning around: driving fast, wannabe tough-guy behavior (typically young men)

hoovering: vacuuming (after the brand of vacuum cleaner)

ice block: popsicle

I'll see you right: I'll help you out

in form: performing well (athletically)

it's not on: It's not all right

iwi: tribe (Maori)

jabs: immunizations, shots

jandals: flip-flops. (This word is only used in New Zealand. Jandals and gumboots are the iconic Kiwi footwear.)

jersey: a rugby shirt, or a pullover sweater

joker: a guy. "A good Kiwi joker": a regular guy; a good guy.

journo: journalist

jumper: a heavy pullover sweater

ka pai: going smoothly (Maori).

kapa haka: school singing group (Maori songs/performances. Any student can join, not just Maori.)

karanga: Maori song of welcome (done by a woman)

keeping his/your head down: working hard

kia ora: welcome (Maori, but used commonly)

kilojoules: like calories—measure of food energy

kindy: kindergarten (this is 3- and 4-year-olds)

kit, get your kit off: clothes, take off your clothes

Kiwi: New Zealander OR the bird. If the person, it's capitalized. Not the fruit.

kiwifruit: the fruit. (Never called simply a "kiwi.")

knackered: exhausted

knockout rounds: playoff rounds (quarterfinals, semifinals, final)

koru: ubiquitous spiral Maori symbol of new beginnings, hope

kumara: Maori sweet potato.

ladder: standings (rugby)

littlies: young kids

lock: rugby position (forward)

lollies: candy

lolly: candy or money

lounge: living room

mad as a meat axe: crazy

maintenance: child support

major: "a major." A big deal, a big event

mana: prestige, earned respect, spiritual power

Maori: native people of NZ—though even they arrived relatively recently from elsewhere in Polynesia

marae: Maori meeting house

Marmite: Savory Kiwi yeast-based spread for toast. An acquired taste. (Kiwis swear it tastes different from Vegemite, the Aussie version.)

mate: friend. And yes, fathers call their sons "mate."

metal road: gravel road

Milo: cocoa substitute; hot drink mix

mince: ground beef

mind: take care of, babysit

moa: (extinct) Any of several species of huge flightless NZ birds. All eaten by the Maori before Europeans arrived.

moko: Maori tattoo

mokopuna: grandchildren

motorway: freeway

mozzie: mosquito; OR a Maori Australian (Maori + Aussie = Mozzie)

muesli: like granola, but unbaked

munted: broken

naff: stupid, unsuitable. "Did you get any naff Chrissy pressies this year?"

nappy: diaper

narked, narky: annoyed

netball: Down-Under version of basketball for women. Played like basketball, but the hoop is a bit narrower, the players wear skirts, and they don't dribble and can't contact each other. It can look fairly tame to an American eye. There are professional netball teams, and it's televised and taken quite seriously.

new caps: new All Blacks—those named to the side for the first time

New World: One of the two major NZ supermarket chains

nibbles: snacks

nick, in good nick: doing well

niggle, niggly: small injury, ache or soreness

no worries: no problem. The Kiwi mantra.

No. 8: rugby position. A forward

not very flash: not feeling well

Nurofen: brand of ibuprofen

nutted out: worked out

OE: Overseas Experience—young people taking a year or two overseas, before or after University.

offload: pass (rugby)

oldies: older people. (or for the elderly, "wrinklies!")

on the front foot: Having the advantage. Vs. on the back foot—at a disadvantage. From rugby.

Op Shop: charity shop, secondhand shop

out on the razzle: out drinking too much, getting crazy

paddock: field (often used for rugby—"out on the paddock")

Pakeha: European-ancestry people (as opposed to Polynesians)

Panadol: over-the-counter painkiller

partner: romantic partner, married or not

patu: Maori club

paua, paua shell: NZ abalone

pavlova (pav): Classic Kiwi Christmas (summer) dessert. Meringue, fresh fruit (often kiwifruit and strawberries) and whipped cream.

pavement: sidewalk (generally on wider city streets)

pear-shaped, going pear-shaped: messed up, when it all goes to Hell

penny dropped: light dawned (figured it out)

people mover: minivan

perve: stare sexually

phone's engaged: phone's busy
piece of piss: easy
pike out: give up, wimp out
piss awful: very bad
piss up: drinking (noun) a piss-up
pissed: drunk
pissed as a fart: very drunk. And yes, this is an actual expression.
play up: act up
playing out of his skin: playing very well
plunger: French Press coffeemaker
PMT: PMS
pohutukawa: native tree; called the "New Zealand Christmas Tree" for its beautiful red blossoms at Christmastime (high summer)
poi: balls of flax on strings that are swung around the head, often to the accompaniment of singing and/or dancing by women. They make rhythmic patterns in the air, and it's very beautiful.
Pom, Pommie: English person
pop: pop over, pop back, pop into the oven, pop out, pop in
possie: position (rugby)
postie: mail carrier
pot plants: potted plants (not what you thought, huh?)
poumanu: greenstone (jade)
prang: accident (with the car)
pressie: present
puckaroo: broken (from Maori)
pudding: dessert
pull your head in: calm down, quit being rowdy
Pumas: Argentina's national rugby team
pushchair: baby stroller
put your hand up: volunteer
put your head down: work hard
rapt: thrilled
rattle your dags: hurry up. From the sound that dried excrement on a sheep's backside makes, when the sheep is running!
red card: penalty for highly dangerous play. The player is sent off for the rest of the game, and the team plays with 14 men.
rellies: relatives
riding the pine: sitting on the bench (as a substitute in a match)

rimu: a New Zealand tree. The wood used to be used for building and flooring, but like all native NZ trees, it was over-logged. Older houses, though, often have rimu floors, and they're beautiful.

Rippa: junior rugby

root: have sex (you DON'T root for a team!)

ropeable: very angry

ropey: off, damaged ("a bit ropey")

rort: ripoff

rough as guts: uncouth

rubbish bin: garbage can

rugby boots: rugby shoes with spikes (sprigs)

Rugby Championship: Contest played each year in the Southern Hemisphere by the national teams of NZ, Australia, South Africa, and Argentina

Rugby World Cup, RWC: World championship, played every four years amongst the top 20 teams in the world

rugged up: dressed warmly

ruru: native owl

Safa: South Africa. Abbreviation only used in NZ.

sammie: sandwich

scoff, scoffing: eating, like "snarfing"

second-five, second five-eighth: rugby back (No. 9). With the first-five, directs the game. Also feeds the scrum and generally collects the ball from the ball carrier at the breakdown and distributes it.

selectors: team of 3 (the head coach is one) who choose players for the All Blacks squad, for every series

serviette: napkin

shag: have sex with. A little rude, but not too bad.

shattered: exhausted

sheds: locker room (rugby)

she'll be right: See "no worries." Everything will work out. The other Kiwi mantra.

shift house: move (house)

shonky: shady (person). "a bit shonky"

shout, your shout, my shout, shout somebody a coffee: buy a round, treat somebody

sickie, throw a sickie: call in sick

sin bin: players sitting out 10-minute penalty in rugby (or, in the case of a red card, the rest of the game)

sink the boot in: kick you when you're down
skint: broke (poor)
skipper: (team) captain. Also called "the Skip."
slag off: speak disparagingly of; disrespect
smack: spank. Smacking kids is illegal in NZ.
smoko: coffee break
snog: kiss; make out with
sorted: taken care of
spa, spa pool: hot tub
sparrow fart: the crack of dawn
speedo: Not the swimsuit! Speedometer. (the swimsuit is called a budgie smuggler—a budgie is a parakeet, LOL.)
spew: vomit
spit the dummy: have a tantrum. (A dummy is a pacifier)
sportsman: athlete
sporty: liking sports
spot on: absolutely correct. "That's spot on. You're spot on."
Springboks, Boks: South African national rugby team
squiz: look. "I was just having a squiz round." "Giz a squiz": Give me a look at that.
stickybeak: nosy person, busybody
stonkered: drunk—a bit stonkered—or exhausted
stoush: bar fight, fight
straight away: right away
strength of it: the truth, the facts. "What's the strength of that?" = "What's the true story on that?"
stroppy: prickly, taking offense easily
stuffed up: messed up
Super 15: Top rugby competition: five teams each from NZ, Australia, South Africa. The New Zealand Super 15 teams are, from north to south: Blues (Auckland), Chiefs (Waikato/Hamilton), Hurricanes (Wellington), Crusaders (Canterbury/Christchurch), Highlanders (Otago/Dunedin).
supporter: fan (Do NOT say "root for." "To root" is to have (rude) sex!)
suss out: figure out
sweet: dessert
sweet as: great. (also: choice as, angry as, lame as ... Meaning "very" whatever. "Mum was angry as that we ate up all the pudding before tea with Nana.")

takahe: ground-dwelling native bird. Like a giant parrot.

takeaway: takeout (food)

tall poppy: arrogant person who puts himself forward or sets himself above others. It is every Kiwi's duty to cut down tall poppies, a job they undertake enthusiastically.

Tangata Whenua: Maori (people of the land)

tapu: sacred (Maori)

Te Papa: the National Museum, in Wellington

tea: dinner (casual meal at home)

tea towel: dishtowel

test match: international rugby match (e.g., an All Blacks game)

throw a wobbly: have a tantrum

tick off: cross off (tick off a list)

ticker: heart. "The boys showed a lot of ticker out there today."

togs: swimsuit (male or female)

torch: flashlight

touch wood: knock on wood (for luck)

track: trail

trainers: athletic shoes

tramping: hiking

transtasman: Australia/New Zealand (the Bledisloe Cup is a transtasman rivalry)

trolley: shopping cart

tucker: food

tui: Native bird

turn to custard: go south, deteriorate

turps, go on the turps: get drunk

Uni: University—or school uniform

up the duff: pregnant. A bit vulgar (like "knocked up")

ute: pickup or SUV

vet: check out

waiata: Maori song

wairua: spirit, soul (Maori). Very important concept.

waka: canoe (Maori)

Wallabies: Australian national rugby team

Warrant of Fitness: certificate of a car's fitness to drive

wedding tackle: the family jewels; a man's genitals

Weet-Bix: ubiquitous breakfast cereal

whaddarya?: I am dubious about your masculinity (meaning "Whaddarya … pussy?")

whakapapa: genealogy (Maori). A critical concept.

whanau: family (Maori). Big whanau: extended family. Small whanau: nuclear family.

wheelie bin: rubbish bin (garbage can) with wheels.

whinge: whine. Contemptuous! Kiwis dislike whingeing. Harden up!

White Ribbon: campaign against domestic violence

wind up: upset (perhaps purposefully). "Their comments were bound to wind him up."

wing: rugby position (back)

Yank: American. Not pejorative.

yellow card: A penalty for dangerous play that sends a player off for 10 minutes to the sin bin. The team plays with 14 men during that time—or even 13, if two are sinbinned.

yonks: ages. "It's been going on for yonks."

Sign up for my mailing list at:
http://www.rosalindjames.com/mail-list
and receive a free book!

Find out what's new at http://www.rosalindjames.com
"Like" my Facebook page or follow me on Twitter
(RosalindJames5) to learn about giveaways, events, and more.

Want to tell me what you liked, or what I got wrong? I'd love to
hear! You can email me at Rosalind@rosalindjames.com.

other books from rosalind james

The Escape to New Zealand series

Reka and Hemi's story: JUST FOR YOU
Hannah and Drew's story: JUST THIS ONCE
Kate and Koti's story: JUST GOOD FRIENDS
Jenna and Finn's story: JUST FOR NOW
Emma and Nic's story: JUST FOR FUN
Ally and Nate's/Kristen and Liam's stories: JUST MY LUCK
Josie and Hugh's story: JUST NOT MINE
Hannah & Drew's story again/Reunion: JUST ONCE MORE
Faith & Will's story: JUST IN TIME

The Not Quite a Billionaire series

Hope and Hemi's story: FIERCE

The Paradise, Idaho series (Montlake Romance)

Zoe & Cal's story: CARRY ME HOME
Kayla & Luke's story: HOLD ME CLOSE (December 2015)

The Kincaids series

Mira and Gabe's story: WELCOME TO PARADISE
Desiree and Alec's story: NOTHING PERSONAL
Alyssa and Joe's story: ASKING FOR TROUBLE

Cover design by Robin Ludwig Design
Inc., http://www.gobookcoverdesign.com

Read on for an excerpt of FIERCE!

shaken and stirred
♡

Have you ever noticed how, when you're around certain people, you seem to grow an extra thumb, and not in a good way? That you say the wrong thing and trip over your feet, and the more you realize you're doing it, the worse it gets? That's what that day was like.

"You're late," Vincent snapped at me the second I hustled through the door of the photography studio.

I handed him his coffee. "Sorry," I said automatically. Even though I wasn't. Sorry *or* late. I just wasn't as early as usual, because I'd woken to find the double bed I shared with my sister Karen empty, and to the sound of her moaning behind the flimsy partition of the bathroom. She only just made it out the door to school on time, insisting she was "fine."

"Have you managed to forget since yesterday," Vincent said caustically, "that this is, oh, only maybe the most important day of my *life?* Something else matter more? Your girls' softball team win the championship and stay out late having pizza? One too many wine spritzers during St. Theresa's annual quilting bee?"

"I'm here now. Put me to work." I managed to get the words

out around the tongue I was biting for the 2,763rd time, and stuck another mental pin in my Vincent-doll. The things I put up with for the twenty-two bucks an hour that, with the Social Security check Karen had been getting since our mother's death, was all that was keeping us clothed and housed. Well, you did what you had to do.

Vincent shook his handsome head of jet-black hair and snapped his manicured fingers at the studio space beyond. "Get set up. White seamless. Go."

You might think that working for a New York fashion photographer was glamorous. You might, until you took a closer look and saw that I was a gofer. It was my job to make sure everyone was comfortable; that coffees and bottled waters and exotic teas were available on demand for everybody from the photographer to the stylist to the models; to keep track of the shot list and move the lights and, in general, do whatever anybody said. There was no room for ego. But then, another ego wouldn't have fit in the studio anyway. Between Vincent, the clients, and the models, there was always more than enough ego to go around.

Especially today. The first day of a shoot for Te Mana's menswear line, the first time Vincent had landed this most coveted of contracts. As he'd told me again and again in the past weeks, this was his ticket. If I didn't screw it up.

Like the assistant was the linchpin. Yeah, right.

I was hustling like always, keeping track of the models, half a dozen ridiculously handsome, sculpted men who were getting their hair and makeup done now. Checking that everyone had everything they needed, obeying Vincent's hissed, frantic instructions, all while I kept an anxious eye on the clock as it ticked ever closer to ten.

Business as usual, until I set the shot list down for Vincent, and he reached for it and knocked over his coffee.

"Clumsy *bitch,*" he hissed, whirling, and I really thought for a second that he was going to slap me. Too late, because I was already moving.

I grabbed the roll of paper towels and dropped to my knees to mop up, and he shoved his chair back, caught my hip a painful blow, and sent me sprawling. My arm landed in the pool of coffee, the brown liquid instantly soaking the sleeve of my white long-sleeved T-shirt.

That was when *he* walked in. To the sight of my butt in its tight jeans sticking straight up into the air, my hair in my face, and my arm in the coffee.

"Good morning, Mr. Te Mana," I heard Vincent say.

I took a couple final hasty swipes, clambered to my feet with my hands, full of sopping paper towel, tucked well behind me, and smiled. My hair was still in my face, and I reached a quick hand up to dash it away even as I was stepping back, staying out of the way. Staying invisible. And trying not to stare.

In this business, you get used to hype. Everything's the most. No, the *utmost.* Everybody's drop-dead gorgeous, and everything is fabulous. Except he actually *was.*

Hemi Te Mana. Wunderkind designer and, some said, ruthless investor, the man who'd assimilated lesser enterprises as fast as they'd run into trouble. The man with the golden touch.

And the golden skin. Or bronze, because that was the word. The *perfect* word. For a statue.

Maori, I reminded myself. From New Zealand. Tall and big and so clearly strong. His great-great-grandfather had been a warrior chief, they said, and it wasn't one bit hard to believe.

He was shaking hands with Vincent now, a frown on his face. His *amazing* face, which seemed to have been made out of some different material than other people's. Deep, liquid brown eyes carved by an expert hand; eyes that would surely reveal his soul if they ever softened. A straight nose; a square jaw and chin; high, strong cheekbones. It was a warrior's face, proud and firm. And the finishing touch—those full, firm, chiseled lips that any woman with a trace of estrogen would have to imagine kissing. Or, rather, lips she would have to imagine kissing *her,* because if ever a man screamed, "I'm in charge" without saying a word, that man was Hemi Te Mana.

336

It was the way he stood, maybe. The controlled way he moved, or maybe *stalked* would be a better word, one that would go with his predator's gaze. The way he took up every inch of space he inhabited. The voice he didn't raise, because he didn't have to. As soon as he'd walked in the door, the room had gone still, and I had the feeling that it would be true of any room he entered, anywhere on the planet.

His head swiveled, those liquid eyes widened a fraction, and he was looking at me.

I forgot to smile. I very nearly forgot to breathe as he stepped forward and said, "I don't think we've been introduced."

"Hope," I said, wishing I didn't sound so breathless. "Hope Sinclair. Vincent's assistant. If you need anything."

The eyes had softened the tiniest bit. He put out his hand, and I reached for his. Which was when I realized mine was still full of wet paper towels. I could feel myself blushing as I held up the dripping wad with a rueful smile. "A little accident."

He wasn't smiling. He was just staring. Burning me. My eyes were locked on his as he put that strong brown hand up to my face and brushed my hair back, and I'd stopped breathing. He rubbed his fingers over my cheek. And then he *licked* them.

"You have coffee on your face." His gaze flicked down my body, over the brown stain decorating my arm, and he smiled for just a moment. Only a moment, but I saw it. "It's a good look on you."

He turned away again, and Vincent hissed furiously at me, "Go clean up. You look disgusting," and I ran, and kept running all the rest of the day. While Vincent barked and swore, and I got clumsier and clumsier, and Hemi stood and watched. Until I looked up from my knees to find him gone.

So, yes, you could say I was at a low point that day I met Hemi Te Mana. But it wasn't as low as I'd go.

337

about the author

Rosalind James, a publishing industry veteran and former marketing executive, is an author of Contemporary Romance and Romantic Suspense novels published both independently and through Montlake Romance. She and her husband live in Berkeley, California with a Labrador Retriever named Charlie. Rosalind attributes her surprising success to the fact that "lots of people would like to escape to New Zealand! I know I did!"

22768895R00221

Made in the USA
Middletown, DE
08 August 2015